Don't Lo

Don't Look Back

GREGG HURWITZ

PENGUIN BOOKS

PENGUIN BOOKS

Published by the Penguin Group
Penguin Books Ltd, 80 Strand, London WC2R ORL, England
Penguin Group (USA) Inc., 375 Hudson Street, New York, New York 10014, USA
Penguin Group (Canada), 90 Eglinton Avenue East, Suite 700, Toronto, Ontario, Canada M4P 2Y3
(a division of Pearson Penguin Canada Inc.)
Penguin Ireland, 25 St Stephen's Green, Dublin 2, Ireland (a division of Penguin Books Ltd)
Penguin Group (Australia), 707 Collins Street, Melbourne, Victoria 3008, Australia
(a division of Pearson Australia Group Pty Ltd)
Penguin Books India Pvt Ltd, 11 Community Centre, Panchsheel Park, New Delhi – 110 017, India
Penguin Group (NZ), 67 Apollo Drive, Rosedale, Auckland 0632, New Zealand
(a division of Pearson New Zealand Ltd)
Penguin Books (South Africa) (Pty) Ltd, Block D, Rosebank Office Park,
181 Jan Smuts Avenue, Parktown North, Gauteng 2193, South Africa

Penguin Books Ltd, Registered Offices: 80 Strand, London WC2R ORL, England

www.penguin.com

First published in the United States of America by St Martin's Press 2014
First published in Great Britain in Penguin Books 2014
001

Set in 12.5/14.75 pt Garamond MT Std
Typeset by Jouve (UK), Milton Keynes
Printed in Great Britain by Clays Ltd, St Ives plc

A CIP catalogue record for this book is available from the British Library

ISBN: 978-1-405-91067-5

www.greenpenguin.co.uk

MIX
Paper from
responsible sources
FSC® C018179
www.fsc.org

Penguin Books is committed to a sustainable
future for our business, our readers and our planet.
This book is made from Forest Stewardship
Council™ certified paper.

For Delinah Raya,
'Little Hercules'

Who proves year after year to be the
best choice I ever made

Use *all* your voices. When I bellow, bellow back.

— James Goldman, *The Lion in Winter*

Life is so fucked-up now, and so complicated, that I wouldn't mind if it came down, right quick, to the bare survival of who was ready to survive.

— James Dickey, *Deliverance*

. . . he must not turn his eyes behind him, until he emerged from the vale of Avernus, or the gift would be null and void.

— Ovid, *Metamorphoses*

Don't Look Back

Prologue

Terror came as a vibration, a plucked-wire note more felt than heard, primary to the deadening heat, to the flick of unseen insects against her face, to the oppressive night humidity that pressed into her pores. There was excitement, too, the familiar stomach-flipping rush of the 'get' and the piano-trill naughtiness of being where she knew she shouldn't be. But terror was paramount.

As Theresa stole along the trail leading upslope from the river into the jungle, mud caked the soles of her sneakers, making her legs wobbly with a sensation like floating. It wasn't surreal so much as *un*real. Dewy orchids wet-kissed her legs, calves, and arms as she brushed through, her silver digital camera in hand, set to night-vision mode.

Appropriate, since she was on a night hunt of sorts.

She broke into the clearing. At the far edge, a fallen tree trunk lay like a parapet. Beyond, the earth dipped sharply into a canyon.

Breathing hard, she dropped to her stomach and army-crawled across the clearing, coarse stalks tickling her chin, insects stirring, dampness pressing through the knees of her hiking pants. But she couldn't take any chances.

She reached the log and rested for a moment, hiding behind it. She thought of Grady as she most often did – laughing the belly laugh he'd had even as a baby, the one that could spread through a room, contagious. She knew that her being here had something to do with him – not just here in Mexico but here in this clearing well past dark, away from the safety of the lodge.

Readying her camera, she rose inch by inch and peered over the top of the log.

Down below at the base of the canyon, a squat concrete house sat backed into the far rise, earth spilling across its slab roof. Through the night-vision filter of her little camera, the world appeared green-tinted, an alien landscape.

One window was shoved open, a winking eye. Leaves bobbed around the frame's edge. Blackness beyond.

He was inside.

Theresa's head buzzed. For a moment all she heard was the thrumming of her heartbeat and the whine of flying bugs. She took a picture of the black square of the window. Zoomed in. Took another. And then several more.

One clear image. That's all she hoped for.

It came as quick as the strike of a snake, a face morphing abruptly from the darkness, shadowed eyes oriented upslope, locked on her precise location.

Staring back up at her.

For an instant his dead gaze nailed her to the spot. And then she unclenched, a gasp escaping her lips, the camera slipping down from her panic-sweaty face. Lurching away from the log, she fumbled the silver case, feeling it fall through her slick fingers. As she scrambled to find her feet in the moist vegetation, she knew she couldn't afford to search for the camera. The time for hunting was over.

Now she was prey.

I

'How many . . . ?' Her mouth was dry. 'How many times?'

Rick looked up at her from his perch on the faux-leather chair, elbow resting on the desk they'd crammed into the master bedroom. The computer monitor at his shoulder gave his face a jaundiced pall. 'Five, six. Maybe seven.'

Eve wet her lips, fought her breathing into some semblance of a rhythm. 'Where?'

'Her place, usually.'

'Usually?'

'A car. Once.'

'A car,' Eve said. 'Jesus. A car.' Her hand had made a fist in the bedspread, pulling the fabric into a swirl.

That strangled Inner Voice piped up: *Don't ask. Don't –*

'What's she look like?' Eve asked.

She could feel the sweat beading above the neckline of the worn nursing scrub top she slept in – Los Angeles hadn't gotten the memo that it was supposed to be winter.

Rick rested the points of his fingers on his kneecap, as if to extract the bone. He cleared his throat. 'She's . . . elegant. Does Pilates. Blond. An accountant. From Amsterdam.'

Elegant. Blond. Pilates. Each specific, an arrow punching through flesh.

Eve looked down at her stretched-out scrub top. She

had the kind of plain good looks that aunts called pretty, but never had she been described as 'elegant.'

That's enough now. Trust me, you don't *want to know anything else.*

'How . . . how old is she?'

He waved a hand. 'I don't know what that has to do with it.' It was a halfhearted attempt, she could tell, and he relented under her skeptical glare. 'Twenty-six.'

Her mouth made a few attempts before she got the words out. 'So she was eight when we were eighteen.'

'Why is that . . . ?'

'We could legally *vote*, Rick. And she was having a My Pretty Pony-themed birthday party.'

An image swept in unannounced, her and Rick's third date, them in the car, driving up PCH to Malibu for a lazy beach day. He'd guessed her favorite Beatles song on the first try – 'Let It Be.' Two hundred and thirteen songs, and he'd known.

How far from there to here. And no bread-crumb trail leading back.

'Remember Malibu?' she asked. Their shorthand.

He gave a woeful nod.

'I wish you still looked at me like that. Like I was . . . special.' Her vision was blurry – she'd held out until now, but then she'd heard the words, even from her own mouth, and that had done it. She hated herself for being such a goddamned open book.

He spread his hands, laced them again. 'What am I supposed to say?'

You're supposed to say, You're still *special.*

She wiped her cheeks. 'I don't know.'

A burst of animation rocked him forward in the chair. 'I feel like our lives have turned into this soulless, scheduled bullshit. E-mails and PowerPoint presentations and e-mails *about* PowerPoint presentations, and none of it matters. None of it. Matters.' He was talking fast, which he did when he was upset, words and sentences tumbling out. 'It's like we never stopped and looked at each other and said, "We don't want to live like this."'

Her gaze found the airplane tickets in their optimistic yellow sleeves on the bookshelf. Their ten-year anniversary was nine months off, and just last week she'd cashed in miles for a vacation package – a full week in the jungles of Oaxaca. Rick thought the trip ambitious, but she'd studied biology with a minor in Spanish, so why not? Plus, the state was the safest in Mexico, none of the narco violence that had people going missing and decapitated corpses washing up even in Acapulco. Just a chance to escape all the petty distractions, the tentacles of modern communication, the tiny violations that chipped away at them minute after minute. A chance to clear their heads, breathe fresh air, get out of range. A chance to remember who they were.

Seven times. Seven. Times.

Rick's cell phone chirped a text alert, and she couldn't help wondering. Past his sallow face, the computer glowed, his Gmail open, four unread e-mails. The screen refreshed, another bold message ticking into the in-box. The life of a public defender, always on call for crises most likely to occur at night, on weekends, in the middle of marital catastrophes.

'– job I hate, can barely keep us in the house,' he was

7

saying. 'I'm grinding out hours, get home, no energy, you're there with HGTV on –'

'I watch TV at night,' she said, 'because I'm lonely.'

'I'm not a mind reader, Eve.'

A metallic scrape of latch against strike plate announced the door's opening. Nicolas stood in the narrow gap, door and jamb pressing either shoulder, his seven-year-old face taut with concern.

In his droopy pajamas, he brought to mind John Darling from *Peter Pan*, with his tall, dignified forehead, the glasses framing oversize Disney eyes. His tufts of blond hair were tinged faintly green from chlorine. Despite the avalanche of emotions currently threatening to submerge her, she had to be up in six hours to get him to swim practice.

'Why are you yelling?' Nicolas asked.

She forced a smile out of the black inner swamp, fought it onto her face. 'I'm sorry we woke you, Little,' she said. 'We're having a . . . disagreement.'

'No,' Nicolas said. '*Daddy* was yelling.'

'I wasn't yelling,' Rick said.

'I think we could both stand to keep our voices down,' she said.

Rick dipped his head remorsefully, and Nicolas withdrew. The air conditioner labored ineffectively.

'I didn't know you felt alone when you watched TV,' Rick said. 'I thought you didn't want to talk to me.'

His expression of vulnerability choked off her reply. Fourteen years in, and still the sight of his suffering gave her an ache beneath the ribs, no matter – evidently – the circumstances.

'I thought you were sick of me,' he said. 'Last month . . .' His lips trembled, and he pressed his knuckles to his mouth. 'Last month you purse-dialed me. You and Nicolas were singing in the car – "Hey, soul sister, I don't wanna miss a single thing ya do . . ." It was magical.' He took a jerky breath. 'I wished I was with you.'

She wondered when they stopped telling each other things like that. Pulling a thread in the hem of her scrub top, she watched it neatly unravel the seam.

'Then I thought,' he continued, 'if I *was* with you, maybe you wouldn't be singing.'

She didn't say anything, because he was probably right.

'We never found our way back to each other after Nick was born,' he said, with a slightly practiced air that made her wonder if he'd made this case before, to friends, his shrink, maybe even to *her*. After *Pilates*. 'All the craziness of a newborn, the adjustments. And when he got sick, those sleepless nights ruling out the scary stuff. Then the diet, which grains are okay, where to find gluten-free pasta, all that *attention*. I wonder sometimes what we'd have to talk about if it wasn't that.'

She'd wondered the same but had never voiced it. She marveled at how Rick *did* that. Just stated what he was feeling, bold and direct, hitting the nails on the heads, one after another, no matter what they pierced. And her, lost in a haze, groping for bearings.

A car? Really? In a *car?*

'I feel like I always let you down, Evie.'

His cell phone sounded again. She looked away, her eye again catching on the anniversary-trip tickets resting hopefully on the bookshelf. Behind them *Moby-Dick* sat

9

dusty and unread, glaring out from beneath the price sticker it still bore from the UCLA bookstore, inducing guilt with all 1,011 pages. She was always going to read it next month. When she looked back, she saw that three more e-mails had arrived in Rick's in-box. She wondered how many waited in her own, from the nurse manager, the swim coach, the orthodontist. Life cranking mercilessly onward.

She tried to pull words from the molasses of her thoughts, to piece them together. 'We fail each other,' she said. 'That's part of being human. No one can be perfect. But we try to figure it out *together*. Not with . . .' She swallowed back the bitterness. 'That's the deal, right? We keep fighting and fixing and trying. Which is the best anyone can ask for. So many couples just . . . give up or give in.'

'I'm tired, Evie.'

His blond hair was shaggy, his face unshaven, the messy good looks on display that had drawn her to him their senior year at UCLA. College sweethearts. They'd been warned, but no. It was gonna be all candlelit meals and late-night assignations in the Jacuzzi. And now he'd found someone *elegant*.

'We were gonna be different,' she said.

'Something's just not there,' he said. 'I can't find it anymore. In you.'

The words blew a fist-size hole right through her chest. Her voice, barely audible: 'It's there.'

'You never show it to me anymore.' He saw her expression and started to cry. 'I'm sorry, Evie. I'm so goddamned sorry.'

She wanted to tell him to go fuck his elegant Dutch

Pilates accountant, but she thought of Nicolas beyond the thin wall and bit her lip, hard.

She lowered her head, picked at the sheet, waiting for her throat to open back up. She couldn't push out the words, but her Inner Voice was there, clear as day.

It said, *When did I stop being something worth fighting for?*

2

Eve was driving home from work when she ran herself over in her Prius.

It had been eight months since The Conversation, and her whole life had grown not unrecognizable but *too* recognizable. After a cynically brief interval of 'trying,' Rick had moved to Amsterdam with his elegant girlfriend to live in an elegant apartment where they hoped to spawn elegant children. Eve had assumed the role of over-taxed single mom always driving car pool or working her hateful better-paying new job. After a training seminar – five days in Appleton, Wisconsin, during which Rick had returned to resume parenting duties – she'd left nursing to take a managerial position with Banner-Care Health Insurance, elucidating the small print for angry and despairing policy-holders. This morning she'd been reduced to tears with empathy and self-loathing after explaining to an elderly former schoolteacher that he held no rider for in-home hospice.

It had been that kind of day, a day that had never gotten bright enough to keep the existential questions at bay. The nagging sense that somewhere along the way, she had misplaced herself. That she was plodding along like a draft animal, pulling her load, managing three gym sessions a week, hating herself for caring so goddamned much about firming up her body, about wanting men to want her whom she had no interest in wanting back. Where did it lead? She didn't want to become one of *those women* – strategically applied makeup, Trader Joe's Syrah perennially open in the fridge, happy-hour tequila on Thursdays. Trying to get back a glimpse of her former self, a taste of the marrow, the squish of mud between her toes. Desperate to recapture that lighting-bolt shudder that had gone through her when Timmy Carpenter felt her up through her sweater behind the gym during the eighth-grade Sadie Hawkins dance, when the better part of her life still stretched out in front of her, undiscovered and full of promise.

The night was moonless, overcast, the freeway a dark river glimmering with brake lights. Fifteen more minutes to the new town house outside Calabasas, closer to her new job. Every home looked the same; more than once she found herself pulling in to her neighbor's driveway, puzzled that the garage door wouldn't lift when she pressed the remote.

She checked the clock, then spoke to her car: 'Dial One.'

Hands-free Bluetooth recognized 'one' more readily than 'home,' and so she'd changed it for convenience. *Home. One.* When had efficiency become a priority above all else? It never seemed to yield more time; the contrary, in fact, seemed true. With all the screen tapping and speedy downloading, her attention span had shrunk to a meager increment, a tweet. She missed putting on a tape, a CD even, anything other than virtual clicking and instant gratification. She missed waiting for a favorite song to come on the radio. She missed not just having patience but *requiring* it. In college she was the girl who'd sneak away to read *The Great Gatsby* in the stacks, who showed up barefoot to outdoor seminars – a bit affected, sure, but still. Where had that girl gone? How had her entire life gotten reduced to two exits on the 101?

Convenience had been the death of her.

Lanie, the sitter, picked up. 'Hey, Mrs H. Sorry, I mean *Mizzzzz* H.'

Eve heard her shift heavily, pictured her reclining on the couch in a shapeless sweater, purple streak in her bangs, bare feet propped on the coffee table next to that stack of pre-med textbooks she dutifully lugged to the house each night.

Eve said, 'Home in fifteen.'

'Bated breath.'

'All good?'

'No fires.'

'He there?'

A rustling, then Nicolas said, 'Mommy? Mom, so Zach? He got the David Finch Batman figurine, you know the one with the new Batsuit?'

His voice made her smile – her first of the day, it seemed. 'You're *such* a nerd.'

'Thanks, Mom. That's a lifetime of video games and being smart.'

'You're right. Nerds shall inherit the earth.'

'Can I go spend the night? At Zach's? Can I please?'

The old fight.

'Honey, we've talked about this. A sleepover's tough. Other parents don't get your diet.'

Wounded silence.

'Look, I'm sorry. I just don't want you getting a rash again. Or cramps. I know it doesn't seem fair.'

It sure didn't. Nicolas had been a great fat, calm baby – his *elbows* had chins – before he'd leaned out overnight in his second year, save a perpetually distended abdomen. After a few go-rounds with various pediatricians, Eve had finally diagnosed him herself. Celiac disease, a huge relief and a lifetime pain in the ass. For the past three years, he'd been largely thriving – in fact, she'd gotten home yesterday to discover that, in a single lurch, he'd outgrown *all* his clothes – and she didn't want to risk a setback.

'*When* then?' he asked.

'I'm not sure, honey. But not tonight.'

A longer silence. She screwed up her face, awaiting his reply. After the call with the elderly schoolteacher, she wasn't sure she could withstand administering another disappointment today, no matter how small.

'Okay, Mommy,' he said.

She eased out a breath. 'Tuck you in soon, Little.'

'Okay, Big.'

She clicked off. As the Prius bounced onto the exit, she ran through the list of what she needed to take care of before morning: review homework, pack lunch, do laundry. God, she needed a vacation. She pictured those plane tickets, still waiting there in front of *Moby-Dick* on the bookshelf in their cheery yellow sleeves, another promise she and Rick had failed to keep. For months she'd been meaning to cancel the trip, and now it was three weeks off. Well – *enough*. She'd do it now, pay the fee, and reclaim her miles for another vacation someday. One less thing to do tomorrow, one more chore to cross off the list.

These things were so easy now: You asked your phone to do something and it did it. It took a few commands to navigate Aero-Mexico's menu, and she got a customer-service rep on the line in short order. Eve's explanation came out bumbling, and she felt a flush in her cheeks and realized why she'd actually been putting off the cancellation all these months.

'Oh,' the rep said, still misunderstanding. 'Happy anniversary.'

'No.' Eve fumbled to bring up her frequent-flier number on her iPhone. 'It's not – We're not –'

She didn't see herself until it was too late. At first a dark streak off the corner of the front bumper and then a single flash of clarity. It *wasn't* her, of course, but the biker looked just like her. More precisely: a *better* version of herself. Same build, slightly more fit. A sleeker model of her Diamondback mountain bike. Same hair – same hair*cut* even, if more stylish, that straight fringe across the back of the neck.

Eve hit the brakes, hard, and the Prius started to skid. The iPhone flew from her grasp into the passenger seat. Rubber screamed. She choked on a breath, waiting for the sickening crunch of metal grinding, for the thud of flesh against shatterproof glass. But, miraculously, the hood swept through the space the biker seemed to occupy and the car lurched to a stop, piling Eve against the door.

She fought the handle and tumbled out, ground scraping her palms. She stood, night air scouring her throat, sweat trickling cool-hot down her back. The wide residential road had no streetlamps, just flares from her headlights and various porches and windows.

Up ahead, the biker continued on, tires purring, chain clicking, spokes winking in the high beams.

'Hey,' Eve called out. *'Hey!'*

The helmet didn't rotate. The biker didn't slow. Was she spooked and eager to get away? Or blaring an iPod, oblivious?

'Wait!' Eve shouted after her. 'I'm sorry! I just want to make sure you're okay!'

But the woman kept on, fading into darkness.

Eve leaned heavily, hands on thighs, panting, her gorge rearing. She thought she might throw up from the adrenaline. A muted squawk broke the nighttime stillness.

'Ma'am? Ma'am?'

The phone. On the passenger seat.

'Ma'am? Mrs Hardaway? Are you all right?'

Eve crawled across, lifted the phone in a trembling hand, pressed it to her hot cheek.

The silky-smooth voice, now in her ear. 'Are you there?'

Eve's breaths came in shallow puffs. A bitter taste suffused the back of her mouth. She couldn't find her voice. Bridging the console, one hand shoved into the bisque cloth of the passenger seat to support her weight, she stared disbelievingly through the windshield at the spot of inky blackness into which she had just vanished on a better model of her bike.

'Mrs Hardaway? Are you still there?'

She thought of herself up ahead somewhere in the night, spared. She thought of the cheery yellow sleeves of the airline tickets, the miles she'd planned to reclaim for

17

another trip someday if she ever found the time. She thought of Oaxaca, the safest state in Mexico, wild and new and set like a jewel against the Pacific, a cosmic distance from the hamster-wheel cage she'd created for herself.

She slid back behind the wheel of the stalled-out Prius, angled toward the curb, going nowhere.

'I don't know,' she said.

Friday

3

Through dust-dappled windows, Eve marveled at the endless walls of green on either side of the winding dirt road. She and five fellow tourists sat crammed in the back of the Chevy Express passenger van. It carved through the foliage, rising toward the azure sky at an alarming rate. In fact, this stretch of the Sierra Madre del Sur range represented the quickest altitude climb in all of Mexico. It ran at a north-south tilt, throwing winds into unpredictable swirls that crushed humidity from the Pacific down unevenly onto folds and barrancas, ridges and canyons. She'd picked this up over the past week, latent geek that she was, from various travel and nature books.

Their destination, the indulgently named Días Felices Ecolodge™, was nestled in the transition zone bridging the gap between low-growth jungle, which ended at five hundred meters, and the cloud forest, which began at eight. Never was the jungle more vibrant and chaotic than now in August, smack in the middle of the wet season. This made Eve uncomfortable and excited her darkly. *Bugs and slugs and rains! Oh, my!* The whole trip, after all, was a statement to herself. It was about taking risks, pushing beyond her comfort zone.

The van crossed the Río Zimatán and forged east into increasingly wild terrain. Asphalt gave way to dirt and dirt to mud. A few tiny hamlets flashed by, and then there was nothing for hours but the unbroken corridor of vegetation and a single-lane bridge across an offshoot of the river. Eve closed her eyes, telling herself to leave everything behind. Her two freeway exits connecting cubicle to gym to home. Mexico City Airport, with its missing-person flyers and machine-gun-toting guards. The flight to Huatulco, jammed with surfers and photographers and families of every stripe and shade. Thoughts of Nicolas flashed – he'd be finishing morning swim practice right about now – and her hand twitched in an instinctive reach for her cell phone, which was long out of range.

That's the whole point, her Inner Voice said. *Out of range. You wanted this, remember?*

Ernesto – who went by 'Neto' – straightened up behind the wheel, flicking back his lush black curls and turning slightly, bringing a doughy nose into profile. '*Listen!* One acre of this jungle here has *more species* of trees and insects than exist in *all of Canada.*'

Though Neto spoke very good English, he maintained his native intonation, hitting all the wrong syllables, the cadence forceful and impassioned. He and his wife, the proud proprietors of Días Felices Ecolodge™, hailed from Mexico City. Eve liked him instantly. And disliked his wife in equal time. Lulu – from 'Lourdes' – commandeered the passenger seat. With blue eyes and flaxen fairy-tale locks that required constant readjusting in the visor mirror, Lulu seemed as contrary to the surroundings as did the Americans bouncing behind her on the serape blankets covering the bench seats.

The Baby Boomer couple two rows up oohed and aahed at Neto's bit of trivia, and Eve did her best to retrieve names from the cursory introductions made at the airport. Harry – retired businessman in a guayabera, who stood too easily corrected by his wife. And the wife was . . . *Sue*. Sue from Omaha with the khaki travel getup.

Behind them, two men traveling together. Will, a sportswear designer from Portland, was of the why-are-all-attractive-men-gay? variety, with the intense jawline and emerald eyes and exemplary stubble. And his partner, a muscley Abercrombie type who'd introduced himself wryly as Gay Jay. They'd come directly from a tour group in Oaxaca City that had included two other Jasons, so droll adjectives had been assigned.

Beside Eve in the back sat a sullen woman in her thirties who'd staked out her seat before the others had arrived. Claire. Ruler-straight dirty-blond hair and focused, intelligent features. The newish dive watch strapped to her wrist signaled her intentions: She'd come accessorized to tackle the jungle. She noticed Eve looking and shot back a look of her own. Eve's smile went unreciprocated.

Up front, Baby Boomer Sue chattered on. So far she'd done most of the talking, her stories invariably featuring her as a crusader of common sense triumphing over bureaucratic inanities. 'So I told him,' she was concluding, ' "Why are you gonna fax something when you can walk it – I don't know – *down the hall*?" ' She rotated, pointing her perky round face at Eve. 'And what did you say *you* do?'

I'm a sellout who explains arcane contract exemptions to policy-holders.

'I work for a health-insurance company,' Eve said.

This was met, appropriately, with bored silence.

Charitably, Will spoke up. 'You said you have a seven-year-old boy? That's gotta keep you busy, too.'

She heard herself say, 'Never a dull moment,' and cringed. It had been her experience that people who said 'Never a dull moment' experienced plenty of them. She flicked her thumbnail nervously against her wedding band, which she now wore on her right hand. She liked knowing it was there, that when she was out at the gym or a restaurant and wanted privacy, she could pop it onto her left ring finger and voilà – she disappeared.

'*Bueno.*' Neto veered onto a dirt apron between mossy trunks and slammed the van into park. 'We have arrived, my friends.'

They clambered out, tugging luggage from the back. Aside from a raised bamboo walkway vanishing into the undergrowth, there was nothing man-made in sight. Just lush Sierra foothills. And the air. Eve's lungs ached from the freshness.

Back in the van, Claire slid across and paused by the open side door, adjusting something through the loose cotton of her pants. A metallic clank sounded over one knee, then the other, and then she used her hands to hoist herself up. Her legs stayed locked now, and Eve saw where orthotics bowed the sides of her sneakers. Claire took a few short, stiff-legged steps forward, her torso swaying.

'Oh,' Sue said. 'I didn't realize you were . . .'

Claire smiled brightly. 'A cripple?'

Sue flushed.

Lulu came around from the rear of the van, hoisting a pack of supplies onto her back. 'Welcome to the paradise.' She grinned cosmetically and headed for the walkway.

As the others started after her, Sue's whisper to her husband rose to audibility. '– just gonna slow us down.'

But Claire moved with surprising proficiency. Her disease – *cerebral palsy? multiple sclerosis?* – must have been at an early stage. Even so, she fell behind, and Eve hung back to keep pace with her as the others pulled ahead.

'You don't need to walk with me,' Claire said.

'I know.'

'I'm fine on my own.'

'Okay,' Eve said, and quickened her stride.

Around the first bend, the jungle opened up where patches had been cleared between copses of trees to allow for upscale *palapa*-style huts and a central cantina. A stable/garage at the periphery housed a Jeep Wrangler, some mud-spattered ATV-quads, and a few weary burros. Lengths of bamboo walkway, complete with tiki torches and vine-wrapped wooden posts, connected each structure, forming a tree-fort-like atmosphere. If Nicolas were here, he'd have certainly drawn an Ewok parallel. The thought of him opened up an array of concerns, and Eve wondered for the umpteenth time since stepping onto the plane if he missed her, if he was okay, if Lanie would precisely follow the gluten-free menu painstakingly charted out and magnetized to the refrigerator.

At Neto's command several silent *indígenos* appeared, smiling as they distributed coconuts with protruding straws. With nut-brown skin and Picasso eyes, the workers were shorter and squarer than their Mexico City counterparts. Neither Neto nor Lulu introduced them to the tourists.

'What do you think?' Lulu asked proudly.

'It's like we're *in* the postcard,' Will said.

Gay Jay toasted him, knocking shells. 'What happens in the Oaxacan jungle *stays* in the Oaxacan jungle.'

A burst of laughter contorted Neto. '*See?* There you go, *amigo!*'

Eve plucked at her sticky shirt and stepped back into the shade, taking another sip. The coconut water tasted divine. 'Your Web site said you have some way for us to make calls? I have a son –'

'Here in our office we have Skype.' Lulu gestured past the cantina to an adobe shack that sported a satellite dish. 'But we prefer it is used sparingly.'

'So you've got Internet,' Harry said.

'It is really intended for us to confirm reservations,' Lulu said. 'Not for checking e-mails.'

Sue directed a strained smile at her husband. 'We're not here to e-mail anyway, right?'

Neto ushered them to their respective huts, Claire waving off help and lugging her suitcase herself. His attention fixed on Eve, the other solo female.

'Come,' he said, all but ripping her bag out of her hand. 'I show you your accommodation.'

The huts were all more or less the same, aside from the fancier double-story number that Harry and Sue were settling into. Neto barreled up the brief walkway ahead of Eve. A rhino beetle the size of a fist inched across the threshold to her hut; Neto swept it aside with a sandaled foot. Beyond, a peaceful, airy space awaited. The palm-thatched roof tented pleasingly over a white double bed. What she first mistook for a canopy proved to be a framework for mosquito netting. A gas lantern pinned down a small nightstand, and the facing wardrobe stood closed. Past the headboard a bamboo pony wall hid a humble yet clean toilet and shower.

'We tell age by roofs here.' A broad smile stretched his mustache. 'This hut, it is three roofs old. We have this hut only for single travelers. I put Claire in a couples one because for the space to maneuver.' He gestured around. 'It is okay?'

Eve took out *Moby-Dick*, set it down next to the lantern. 'It's perfect.'

A length of duct tape had peeled away from a split in the ticking on the side of the mattress. Neto firmed the tape again to the fabric, giving a self-conscious smile. 'Make sure no bugs crawl in there.'

'It's okay,' Eve said. 'I'm not queasy.'

Neto snatched fresh, glistening spiderwebs from the edges of the room. 'No one has used your hut in *months*. We get mostly couples. And we have not been as busy as before the economic troubles. Tourism has been slow.' His heavy-lidded Buster Keaton eyes grew wistful. 'The times, they are not what they were.'

She was about to express her sympathy when the screen door banged open and Will leaned through, distractingly shirtless. '*There* you guys are. Lulu already had us load the raft onto the Jeep.'

'Raft?' Eve said.

'White-water time.' Will's smile was equally distracting, and she had to remind herself that yes, he *was* gay. 'Come on,' he said, grabbing her hand. 'Let's get out there and see what's waiting in the jungle.'

4

He led with his machete, slashing through foliage. Heading home. String of fish over his shoulder. Stiff scales pressing wetly through his sleeveless undershirt. The air tasted of leaves. Lush. They said it rained green paint in the Oaxacan Sierra. Here in the foothills, it seemed so.

He sensed a vibration. Footsteps.

He paused. Cocked his head. Read the ground.

Human. Female.

Despite his big, broad frame, he moved gracefully, like a dancer. Controlled, fluid motions, fading into the jungle. Then he stopped. Blended in. Watched the game trail ahead. He could smell himself. The exertion of the morning. An animal musk, like a horse in lather.

A vibrant sarong appeared at twenty paces, glowing through the leaves. Bright stripes. Purple dye from sea snails plucked out of the crevices of the rocky shoreline. And blood-red from pulverized scale insects found in the nopal cactus.

She came into latticed view through the branches. Young. Firm legs. A dagger of ankle showed through a slit in the wraparound skirt. Her dark skin, one shade from home.

He waited. Chewed a twig, sweetening his breath.

She neared. In her hand an *ojo de venado* – a doe-eyed seedpod. Good-luck charm. She worked it with a thumb.

Painted nail. Her blouse unbuttoned. Hair done up in ribbon-laced braids. Against her hip a laundry basket. Carrying it back from the river. An *indígena*. He watched her hips sway. This way. That.

Ten paces now. Five. He breathed.

A bird exploded out of the brush before her, honking. A *chachalaca*. The name, like its noise.

The basket tumbled to the mud. White blouses. Undergarments. She clutched her heart, perspiring. Looked for the fallen seedpod. There. Crouched to pick it up.

His huarache eased from the brush and set down atop the seedpod, smashing it into the moist earth. She froze in her crouch. Her reaching hand trembled inches from the cuff of his pants, which was cut carefully so it did not hang beneath the ankle – a small way he could show respect and obedience, even here.

'*Stand, sister,*' he said. His voice, tranquil as always. His Spanish, serviceable.

'*You startled me.*' Her Spanish, too, was accented. She was accustomed to speaking *dialecto*. She rose.

He was careful not to look above her chin, though he could sense her stare picking over his face. His olive complexion. The raised freckles across his cheeks. Rings like smudged charcoal around dark eyes. His dense hair, flecked with gray. His beard was wispy, tufts of brown and white wire. Cut tighter to the chin than he would've preferred. It was mottled on the left side, a pitted snarl like a handprint on his jaw and upper neck. He was in his late fifties now and thick, mass packed over strong bones. But still he moved like a whisper.

'*You should be more modest. In your dress.*' He turned the

29

machete in his hands. His right pinkie no more than a nub. The string of fish dangled, now looped through his belt. He wanted his hands free.

She hesitated. Then picked up a blouse and covered her arms. The slash of thigh still peeked out from the garish cloth. Tempting. She was astray. So far astray.

'*Your leg,*' he said.

She pinched the sarong closed. Taking shallow sips of air now. Fear. He could smell it on her breath.

'*Lower your eyes, sister.*'

She did. He lifted the machete. Her head tracked its movement. He slipped it into the soft sheath across his back. She was trembling. Perspiration shone on the strokes of her collarbone. Her hair uncovered. Teasing him.

'*Pick up your private clothes,*' he said.

He remained still, crossed arms like bars across his barrel chest. She labored beneath him, mud weighing down her sarong at the knees. Picking the fallen clothes from the wet ground. Soiled. She made little noises with her breaths. Straws of light filtered through the canopy. The jungle crackled and buzzed and hummed. Finally she stood, dirty hands gripping the dirty basket, head lowered.

'*Walk away from me modestly.*' His words so calm, like a purr. '*Do not look back, or I will be obligated to teach you a lesson. Not with malice. But to calm you down in compliance with my duty. Do you understand my words?*'

Rapid nods, like a child's. She was shuddering now. Her nipples showed through her thin blouse. She clutched her basket with mud-streaked hands and walked away.

He waited. He chewed his twig. He watched her

shoulder blades ripple beneath the fabric. Hanging vines brushed her cheeks. Her head stayed bowed, her eyes trained ahead.

Then, stepping over a moss-soggy length of deadwood, she glanced back. A flash of the whites of her eyes.

He started after her. Not running but gliding across rocks and dirt, his feet cupping each step, propelling him. She yelped. The basket fell. She ran, but the sarong constrained her legs. He trod a pair of white panties underfoot. She stumbled.

He kept on. His breathing did not quicken. He did not exert.

He enfolded her arm. Like a chicken bone in his grasp. He could clench and it would turn to powder. Her scream lifted hidden birds from the boughs.

'You will learn respect,' he told her.

The ground yielded beneath his palms. A bird-size butterfly danced jaggedly in a patch of nearby light. One of the dead fish came free from the string as it dragged back and forth in the dirt.

' *"Please will you teach me a lesson?"* ' he said for her.

'. . . *Please* . . . *teach me* . . . *lesson* . . .'

'*Good.*'

After, he crouched and adjusted the sarong to cover her caked knees. He helped her to her feet. She drew a knuckle beneath each eye, leaving smears of dirt. Her elbows were bloody.

He rolled the twig from one side of his mouth to the other. *'Let this guide you.'*

She bent robotically and began gathering her fallen clothes. Her shoulders trembled. She breathed wetly.

He put his back to her, threaded the loose fish onto the line with the others. The game trail made for easier going. He hastened his step.

With any luck he'd be home for evening prayers.

5

The raft shot through two boulders, Neto screaming, *'Down! Down!'* from the bow. Eve tucked her paddle and slid off her perch on the side tube, dropping into the center with the others as stone scraped the tough vinyl and froth arced overhead. The raft undulated, then fell away, and they all caught a few seconds of suspended air before the self-bailing floor rushed up and caught them again. They pulled themselves back up to their spots, laughing and high-fiving with their paddles. The raft slipped between the foundations of the narrow bridge she remembered being driven across just this morning. How different to see it now from *this* perspective, not as a tenderfoot tourist peering through the window of a tour van but as a jungle adventurer drifting along, part of the river itself. They coasted sideways, easing into a stretch of wide, lazy water.

There was no mystery why this finger of river was called Sangre del Sol; with its winks of gold and copper, the gleaming stream seemed bled from the sun itself. Leaning on the stern, Eve looked across as Claire freed her foot from its wedge beneath one of the thwarts and adjusted her life jacket. Though she'd left her braces back in the Jeep, she seemed to manage without them.

Claire clicked the side of her dive watch, freezing a timer. 'How 'bout you let us take a turn up front?' she called out.

'It takes *more muscle* to steer up here,' Neto said. 'Gives us better control of the boat.'

'How do you know *we* don't have more muscle?' Claire asked.

In the section in front of them, Gay Jay popped a bicep, and Will shook his head. 'You're *such* a fag.'

'Ya *think*?' Jay pulled off his Mariners cap, dipped it overboard, and clamped it back atop the blue bandanna fastened over his scalp. He swiped the oar through the water a few times, propelling them in lurches.

'We can steer,' Claire persisted. She glanced at Eve for solidarity. It *did* look more fun up there. 'Don't you want to ride closer to the bow?'

Eve felt all seven sets of eyes settle on her and focused more than necessary on wiping drops from her Ray-Bans. 'I'm okay.'

'That's not what I asked,' Claire said.

But the others had already moved on, rowing and chatting, and Eve felt a burn in her face, the shame of having failed some test she hadn't signed up to take. *You're a grown woman. You can't ask for a damn seat you want?*

Claire held a contemptuous stare on Eve. 'Why don't you speak up?'

I'm trying.

'I do,' Eve said.

Her face still hot, she considered herself with frustration. When had her voice – her *real* voice – maddeningly faded? She remembered it when she was a girl, braying laughter and sitting side by side with her father at the listing upright Yamaha, his callused hands raspy over hers, guiding her to the right keys, making her fingers sing. And when she was a teenager, sticky with sweat on the soccer field, stretching or running bleachers with her teammates, chatty and uncensored, sharing wisps of gossip, half-formed theories on boys, lurid rock-song lyrics, her mouth barely pausing to catch a breath. Where had it gone? Into the void her father left when she came home from junior finals to find the mint green Tercel hatchback gone for good and her mother sitting on the porch in her bathrobe, smoking one of her hidden cigarettes in the flagrant open? Or had it gone underground later, after she'd tucked safely into her life with Rick? No, she'd still had it then, and then. Or at least *some* of it; she could still hear her own music, give it expression. It had never vanished, but the volume knob had been adjusted down ever so slightly, by indiscernible degrees, the invisible drift of twilight into darkness.

Will stood, wobbly in the raft, bringing Eve back to the present and the Great Seating Debate. 'I'll switch with you, Claire,' he said. 'Who'll give up their spot for Eve?'

An awkward silence. Finally Sue said, 'I don't care *where* I sit.'

'The only thing worse than a controlling person,' Claire said, just loud enough to be overheard, 'is a controlling person pretending to be flexible.'

Harry gave a wobbly look to his wife and then rose in her place, relinquishing his seat instead, and Eve and Claire moved up toward the bow. Lulu rode in the very front with Neto, displaying skill controlling the raft. Her hair was taken up in a ponytail, revealing a CARPE DIEM tattoo across the base of her neck. Clearly she was more than the princess Eve had first pegged her for.

The shoreline scrolled by, buttress roots that would dwarf a human, elephant ear fronds nodding, white ceiba trees thrusting above the dense canopy, spreading fans of branches. A great blue heron *whoomped* overhead, its wingspan so vast it looked aeronautical. The sweet smell of organic rot crept beneath the fragranced air.

Eve raised a hand against the glare, and Jay said, 'The Mexican sun's gonna have its way with that milky-white skin, girlfriend.' He pulled off his baseball cap and flipped it to her. 'Take this. I got my do-rag.'

She pulled on the hat. 'My milky-white skin thanks you.'

They drifted around a bend, and a cluster of *indígenos* came into view. Women with plastic laundry baskets on their heads. Others bent to the river, cracking ear-shaped pods from the guanacaste tree and raking the pulpy flesh over wet clothes, releasing suds to the current. A sinewy older man wearing nothing but his *chones* stood thigh-deep, eyeing the water and readying a sharpened car antenna as a harpoon. He paused to offer a single-toothed smile. Sue gasped with delight and fumbled for her waterproof camera. She had shapeless arms, bones loose in wattles of flesh, and a horseshoe of perspiration darkened the back of her shirt. It took steel for a woman of her shape and age to ride the river, and yet she manned her paddle without complaint.

'These people here are Zapotecas,' Neto said, waving. 'He is spearing *chacales* – freshwater . . . um, like the lobster?'

'Crayfish,' Lulu said.

They paddled over, and Neto negotiated with the man, trading pesos for a basket brimming with life.

As they pushed off, Will said, 'I could get used to that. Living by the rhythm of the day. Wake up, spear some *chacales*, wash out my underwear in the process.'

The raft coasted around the next turn, and it was again as if they were the last seven people on earth. The river carried them on. Eve trailed her fingertips through the glassy surface, leaving tiny wakes. Five or fifteen feet below, black tadpoles sat on mossy brown rocks, tails oscillating in the invisible current.

'I wish I'd done more of that when I was younger,' Harry said.

'Spear *chacales* in my underwear?' Will said.

Harry waved him off. 'You know what I mean. To not be busy being busy. I remember putting my tax files up in the attic this April, realizing that another year had whipped by.' Sue reached across, took his hand, and Eve felt a twinge at the sweet, instinctive gesture. Harry smiled dryly. 'It just goes faster, you know.'

'Stupid march of time,' Jay said.

'It's good to get out here,' Sue said. 'Try to find . . . I don't know, *focus*.'

The passing shore showed a dense rise of jaw-dropping lushness. Strangler figs wormed through tree trunks, weaving them together. Lilac-crowned parrots sparred, flitting among branches, purple heads pronounced against vibrant green feathers. The sunlight pulsed, redolent of orchids.

'I know what you mean,' Will said. 'I took a trip to Prague last year, and I was going through the pictures on iPhoto. Turns into a chore, right? I realized I barely remember the trip itself 'cuz I was so busy recording it. It's like

37

we're more interested in documenting our lives than *living* them. We run around archiving everything. For what?'

'How 'bout in theaters now?' Sue said. 'The instant a movie ends, you see everyone lighting up their smartphones. Have to be reachable *every second*.'

'I tried to fast-forward a live TV show last week,' Eve confessed.

Will laughed. 'I saw a commercial the other day, some guy invented a brush that sticks to the shower floor so you don't have to bend over to wash your feet. Are we really *that* busy? That we can't bend over to wash our own feet?'

'It's important to remember what matters,' Harry said. 'To do what you want to do and not waste any time about it. You'll be sitting here at my age in the blink of an eye.'

'What I really want to do,' Jay said, 'is *dance*.'

Will knocked him with the handle of a paddle, and Jay had to grab it to keep from going overboard. Everyone laughed except for Claire, who'd withdrawn into herself.

'It's good advice,' Will said. 'Taking stock like that. Think back to when you were a kid. What were you gonna do when you grew up?'

'Astronaut,' Jay said.

'Big-league pitcher,' Harry said.

Sue blushed. 'Fashion designer.'

Eve said, 'Surgeon.'

There was a moment of silence, and then Neto smiled over at them, dipped his paddle into the water, and swung them for shore. 'I'm doing it,' he said.

They sloshed onto a beachy shoal where a hand-dug fire pit indented the scorched sand. Lulu unearthed a cooler from beneath frond cover at the base of a tree and removed pots and cooking utensils. Paper plates and cups came out of a nylon compression dry bag that had been wedged under one of the raft tubes.

'Our famous zip line.' Neto pointed to a taut cable stretching from bank to bank, disappearing into the tree line on either side. 'Not for the faint of heart.'

As the others prepped the fire for lunch, Gay Jay ran off toward the line, and seconds later he exploded out of the foliage ten feet above the river, hanging from a hand trolley. He backflipped into the water and reared up, eight-pack flexed, arms spread in Rocky victory. He called them over, and Will and Claire came and gave it a go while the others skewered fish on branches and roasted them over the fire like hot dogs. Lulu put on a pot of river water and boiled the giant brown crayfish until they turned red. Eve noticed Neto kneeling in the moist sand at the river's edge, watching for bubbles and digging up translucent shrimp. She helped, dropping squirming fistfuls into the pot. Sand chafed her fingers and knees, scales coated her hands, sweat matted her bangs beneath Jay's cap – she was a comprehensive mess, and yet she couldn't remember the last time she'd had this much fun. It struck her that for the past few hours she had thought about nothing except precisely what she was doing. She'd been – as the yoga types at her gym called it – *present*. And she felt a stab of gratitude that she'd pushed herself to come here to this hidden place.

They finished prepping and gathered to eat.

'Where should I go to the bathroom?' she asked Neto.

'If you're a *guy*?' He gestured to the river, the bank, all around, and the men laughed. 'For *women* there's some privacy up there. And a camping toilet. Look for ticks under the lid. This is not your Four Seasons.'

A trail led from the shoal through a rise of orchids with white flowers the size of Frisbees. Eve stepped through into the jungle itself, which breathed around her. Philodendrons climbed toward the canopy. Bromeliads sprayed spikes. Giant tree ferns rose Jurassically. The trail twisted upslope. She ducked beneath a witchy dangle of hanging moss.

A fallen tree had left a hole in the canopy, the resultant halo of sunlight giving rise to a contained world of color. Petite purple daisies and morning glories described a near-perfect circle on the jungle floor in which, centered like a holy relic, sat a stained plastic toilet. She almost laughed at the beatific presentation.

As she moved into the light, a swarm of zebra butterflies stirred from the carpet of blossoms and whirled around her. Enchanted, she lifted her arms, half expecting them to perch as in a cartoon. They seemed to carry her across the clearing. She was captivated, lost to the beauty. She followed them or they her through the fall of warmth to the dark edge where the ground sloped precipitously away.

That was when she heard the thud.

Crunching footsteps.

Another thud.

Man-made sounds.

Tentatively, she drew to where the fallen trunk rimmed the lip before the sharp drop. Through a web of branches and leaves, she could see a dwelling at the base of the small canyon beyond. Truck tires formed a retaining wall, buttressing the humble house against the rise. Vines devoured the slab concrete roof and walls, hacked off over the windows, which seemed to peer out of the hill itself.

Something streaked into sight through the branches, and the thud echoed again through the canyon. A burly, bearded man followed patiently in the hurled object's wake, his footsteps packing down dead leaves. Eve shifted along the log, straining to see what he was doing as he flickered behind tree trunks. The spot provided an excellent spying vantage down on him and the house. Tracking him, she picked out a rusted Jeep Wrangler languishing beneath a carport rigged up from interwoven fronds inside a copse of close-packed trees. Like the house, the vehicle blended into the jungle.

He stopped. His broad back wiggled as he seemed to pry something loose. Then he shifted, a machete swinging at his side. The piece of plywood propped against the tree behind him came into sudden focus and, on it, the spray-painted silhouette of a human. Splintered impact marks from the thrown machete hacked the face and chest.

Target practice.

Sweat filmed Eve's body – her arms, her neck, beneath the baseball cap – the humidity, condensing as if in a single burst, leaving her skin tingling. And yet her breath had gone cold.

The man pivoted and started back to his mark. Even from this distance through the trees, she made out a stab of color high on the left side of his neck, a burned snarl of hair and angry pink flesh.

Then he paused.

Somehow Eve sensed that his head was going to lift even before it did. Just before his dark eyes reached her, some instinct made her drop behind the fallen log. Her jagged breaths fluttered a green sprig by her face.

No sound from the canyon below.

She flattened to the earth, coming eye to eye with a praying mantis the size of her thumb, clinging to the sodden deadwood and twitching its raptorial legs. Beneath the log a thin silver edge winked at her. Metal? Her hand quaked as she reached into a nest of leaves to unearth it.

Not a piece of trash but a slender digital camera. Someone had dropped it here, probably another rafter – a woman like her who'd hiked up to the royally displayed toilet. Eve swiped her thumb across the dirt-caked backing, and sure enough a neat sticker from a label maker was revealed: THERESA HAMILTON.

Eve still heard nothing from the canyon. She tried to slow her breathing, to calm her pulse. Nothing but silence below.

And then the crunch of a footstep.

Eve tensed. The mantid watched her. She realized she was holding her breath, clutching the camera to her chest. Listening.

Another footstep.

Then another.

Though the canyon played games with the sound, it seemed the man was coming toward her. The time between steps shortened. Was he climbing the rise? Speeding up?

Gasping, she shoved the camera into a pocket and slid

away from the log, backing up on all fours to remain unseen. A safe distance from the edge, she rose, scaring up flurries of butterflies, and ran across the wildflower clearing that moments ago had been charming. A panicky sprint down the muddy trail and she stumbled back out into the unforgiving sunlight of the shoal.

As she hurried across the sand toward the group clustered around the fire pit, she shot a nervous glance at the trail. No one behind her. Already feeling sheepish, she neared the others.

Gay Jay was standing back, shading his eyes to gaze up the incline. 'Before I go home, I'm gonna take the mountain.'

'It's even denser than it looks,' Lulu said. 'You wouldn't make it all the way up there.'

'I've hiked Whitney and Shasta.'

'This is *jungle*,' Lulu said.

Neto saw Eve coming and moved to greet her with a full plate. 'Wait till you taste *this*.' His brow furrowed as she drew close. 'What's wrong?'

Eve glanced again over her shoulder. Her Inner Voice piped up, *What is wrong, Eve? You saw a guy practicing knife throws?*

'What?' Neto said.

Don't tell him. He'll think you're being hysterical.

She kept her voice low. 'I saw someone back there. A man with a burn – here. He was throwing a machete at . . . at a drawn human target.'

Neto gave a faint chuckle and foisted the plate on her, though she'd lost her appetite. 'People do all sorts of things in privacy. Now, hurry and eat. We need to clean up.'

43

With a hint of self-loathing, she asked herself how Rick would handle this. He would be direct, stubborn, persuasive. She cleared her throat. Toed the sand. 'It freaked me out a little.'

Starting back for the fire, Neto looked at her across his shoulder. 'It is safe here.'

She stood apart for a moment before helping tidy up, shooting occasional glances at the trail. When they finally pushed off in the raft, the sun was no longer at its peak but still klieg-light intense. Her shirt clung to her. The breeze did little to cool her; she was still overheated from the adrenaline rush. She tugged off the Mariners cap, set it on her knee, wiped her forehead. Jay held up his hand as a target, and she flipped him his hat, which he dipped overboard and pulled on.

The others chatted and joked, but she didn't feel like joining in. The jungle scrolled by, and she drew a deep breath, held it, trying to dissipate the knot in her chest. As they neared the broad bend, she cast a final backward look at the shoal.

Barely visible in the shadows, floating a step back from where the trail buried itself in a tangle of vines, a seam of cheek caught an edge of ambient light. A frayed curve of beard disintegrated into the scrambled flesh of a jawline. Eyes glinted like dimes.

She blinked, and the face was gone.

6

Beneath the thatched veranda of the cantina, the light of the tiki torches flickered over picnic tables. As Eve approached, a faint breeze blew through her long, sleeveless dress, making her skin feel bare. The blunt edge of her wet hair lay cool across her neck. She was the last to heed the dinner bell, taking extra time to shower off the fear that had gripped her as she'd crouched behind that fallen log in the jungle. Any threat – imagined or otherwise – seemed distant now in the happy glow of the group.

Baby Boomer Sue was finishing another story: '. . . so I told her, I don't care how important you *think* you are – not on *my* shift you don't. Well, my girlfriend from my women's group just about *died*.'

Sue's tales referencing various clubs and societies and leagues painted her as a woman interwoven seamlessly into her community. Eve felt a pang of yearning for the social contentedness that this implied, the sense of belonging that somehow always seemed to evade her. It occurred to her just how out of her element she felt here, crowbarred from her protective shell and plopped onto a new backdrop that seemed to highlight her contrasts and insecurities.

As Eve neared, Sue's husband looked up, his eyes

flashing immediately to her chest. He caught her catching him and colored slightly, his gaze darting away.

How refreshingly simple it must be to look at one readily visible feature and decide whether someone turned you on. When it came to men, Eve found there were so many other things. Their hands. The way their eyes crinkled when they laughed. One boyfriend in college could trickle his fingers along her ribs and it would put a charge through her whole damn spinal cord. But no: *Harry of Omaha, Looking at Boobs*. A still life.

She reached the group, and Will stood up too quickly, knocking his thighs against the table. His T-shirt fitted, his hair mussed just so. He offered her the seat next to him, holding eye contact for an extra beat as she moved past him, and she wondered if her gaydar was broken or just momentarily jammed by his unreasonable good looks. Claire observed them, her own eyes gleaming with dark interest.

Sue kept on, undeterred: 'Can we serve?' A loving hand on her husband's back. 'He gets low blood sugar. I have to carry snacks in my purse. I'm married to the Cookie Monster. Who wants to be married to the Cookie Monster?'

Harry laughed and kissed her neck.

The table overflowed with exotic dishes. Halved pineapples stuffed with shrimp and melted gouda. Squid cooked in its own ink. Chicken slathered in red mole sauce. Montejo beer bottles rose from an ice-filled cooler, as well as a plastic two-liter of Mountain Dew. Breathing in the rich scents, Eve sat, setting down by her plate the book she hoped to read in a hammock after dessert.

Gay Jay zeroed in on it right away. 'You brought *Moby-Dick* as a vacation read?'

She glanced down at the brick-size paperback, the spine unbroken. 'Been meaning to read it since college, but I never get to it.'

Will said, '*Moby-Dick* is your Moby-Dick.'

Up close, she noticed that his nose was a touch off center, his smile slightly crooked, and understood that her attraction to him came less from his actual features and more from the way he carried them off. He had an easy charm, a gift for paying attention while stopping short of unctuousness.

As they all dug in, *indígenos* hustled and plated and cleared in the background. Eve took a pull of *cerveza clara*, which tasted divine against the night heat and the lavishness of a dozen new spices. Will plucked another small fried husk from a bowl. 'What am I eating?'

'*Chapulines*,' Neto said.

'What's that mean?' he asked, chewing.

Eve stifled a laugh. 'Grasshoppers.'

Will's jaw stilled. 'You're joking.' Then, to Neto, 'She's joking.'

At the other end of the table, Sue distributed eyedrops of iodine into her and Harry's iceless water, drawing a tight smile from Lulu, who said, 'The water is all filtered here.'

'Just making sure,' Sue said. 'The diet change can be upsetting. At home I make us a power shake every morning with acidophilus. I add lots of berries, kale –'

'*Kale?*' Claire asked, packing into the syllable more derision than seemed possible.

'You'd be amazed at the nutritional benefits of kale,' Sue said. 'Detoxifying, cholesterol-lowering, antioxidants –'

'I've heard there's a ceremony around here,' Gay Jay said, slicing in mercifully with a topic change, 'where the men of a village marry a crocodile. I shit you not. There's a whole ceremony, something about reaffirming their relationship with nature.'

'*Yes*, it is *true*,' Neto said. 'It is to signal a *fresh start*. And the crocodile, she is the mother of the land. She is *fearless*. And so they embrace her.'

'There's another culture in Oaxaca,' Claire said, 'that's a true matriarchy. The women run *everything*.'

'The village of Juchitán,' Lulu said. 'When a male is born, they say, "Better luck next time." Many boys become transvestites as the next-best thing' – she ran her fingers through Neto's loose black curls – 'to being a woman.'

'I don't know,' Jay said. 'I like my men to be . . . *men*.'

A wickedly segmented wasp landed on the congealing gouda, and Harry reared back. Neto reached across, pinched it by the head, and tossed it aside. He grinned at Lulu. 'Next time I let the matriarch get the wasp.'

'Sorry,' Harry said. 'I'm allergic.'

'You're allergic to bee stings and you came to the *jungle*?' Claire asked.

Sue said, a touch defensively, 'We're armed with Benadryl and EpiPens.'

Harry exhaled. 'And undaunted courage.'

'We *all* have conditions we struggle with,' Sue said, still focused on Claire. 'Do they know what caused yours?'

Claire offered a dry smile. 'Not enough kale,' she said.

A breathless moment ensued in which no one seemed sure whether to laugh. Before anyone could decide, two of the workers burst out from behind the curtain, the younger one bearing a little cake with a candle in it, the other knocking on a pan with a wooden spoon. Eve assumed it was someone's birthday until they veered toward her and she read, misspelled in icing, HAPY ANIVERSARI. Neto was waving off the workers, but they didn't notice until the cake was displayed before the group. The makeshift kettledrum silenced, Lulu barked something in Spanish, and, confused, the workers whisked the cake out of sight. All focus turned to Eve.

'I'm sorry,' Lulu said. 'There was a note in the reservation. We didn't update it, so the kitchen workers –'

'No problem,' Eve said. 'Totally understandable.' She found herself avoiding Will's stare. 'It *was* supposed to be an anniversary trip . . .'

'Oh,' Sue said, still a beat behind. 'Where's your husband?'

In Holland screwing his new girlfriend.

'He had other plans,' Eve said.

'Yeah?' Claire said. 'What's her name?'

7

Reading *Moby-Dick* in the hammock after dinner proved an unmitigated failure. The hammock was too sway-y, which in fairness was the whole point, but every time Eve shifted to sip her beer, the thing threatened to deposit her in the dirt. Then there were the elusive tiki-torch flames, their light challenging to catch on the page. And the *bugs*. Tiny flies – no-see-ums – that didn't siphon your blood like mosquitoes but actually bit out small pinches of flesh. Tackling a 1,011-page novel about nineteenth-century whaling seemed onerous enough without a small-scale Inquisition of irritations, so Eve retreated to her hut to finish unpacking.

She lugged her suitcase from the bed to the wardrobe. Within it, the hangers were raked to one side. From the last in the row, a thin white ribbon dangled. Eve reached out, lifted it off. It was a hanger loop, torn from a sleeveless blouse or dress, as if the article of clothing had been ripped free. She dropped the ribbon in the trash basket and then hoisted her suitcase onto a sturdy ledge inside the wardrobe. She set her shirts in the top drawer and moved on. Her pants, neatly folded, went in the middle drawer. She opened the bottom drawer and halted. Wadded in the rear was a single pair of panties.

Someone had packed hastily.

Eve's eyes tracked back up to those hangers. One of

them was distorted, the wire bent out of shape. Those clothes had been pulled off *hard*.

A trickle of discomfort moved feather-light between her shoulder blades.

She dumped the left-behind panties into the trash basket as well, then stared down at them. She caught herself fussing with her wedding band unconsciously, a nervous habit she'd made efforts to extinguish.

Move on.

In the bathroom she started to collect her toiletries from where she'd strewn them around the sink. Cradling an armful against her belly, she swung open the medicine cabinet's door. The plastic shelves were bare.

She moved to put her toothpaste inside when her gaze snagged on a spot of white in the corner, wedged into the gap where the middle shelf met the bracket. She stared at it a moment, her jaw tensing. Her stare didn't waver as she dumped her stuff back on the sink.

With a fingernail she teased up a white, round pill. She set it on her palm to read the imprint code: F L on one side, 10 on the other. Ten milligrams, a low dose. Her nurse's brain was out of practice, so it took a moment for her to retrieve the drug name from the imprint code – Lexapro, a selective serotonin reuptake inhibitor, used to treat all orders of anxiety, mostly prescribed to women for moderate depression.

A pair of panties was one thing, but you'd think if you spilled your antidepressants, you'd make sure you reclaimed every last one.

The last guest had cleared out of here in a hurry.

Why did that make Eve uncomfortable? Perhaps her

nerves were still on edge from the near run-in in the jungle. Or maybe being this far from home made everything seem a touch more alien and threatening.

The pill slipped from her trembling hand. Annoyed, she crouched to retrieve it, but just as she was about to rise, a small orange tube against the back wall caught her eye.

A pill bottle.

A single dropped pill *might* be overlooked, but the bottle?

She strained to reach it, her face pushing against the cool metal of the U-pipe. Her fingertips rolled it in the seam a few times, and then it caught traction and came into her palm.

The lid was missing. Stamped across the label in bold type: LEXAPRO 10MG.

Her breath caught when she saw the name. THERESA HAMILTON.

Her gaze rose from the pill bottle, crept slowly across the boards to where she'd kicked off her breathable nylon pants before hopping into the shower. She reached for a cuff, pulled them across to where she sat on the floor. In the front pocket, forgotten until now, was that little digital camera she'd found by the log. She turned it over, checked the label on the back.

THERESA HAMILTON.

Eve bit her lip. Examined the camera. Fancier than she'd thought, with night vision, high-speed action, and multiple flash options on the dial. She pushed down the top button. The camera gave a faint whir, and the screen flickered to life. She caught a glimpse of a handsome woman in her thirties with loose dishwater-blond curls, holding the camera at arm's length to take a picture of herself before the Mexico City Airport sign. Then the camera died.

Eve stared at the black screen, chewing her bottom lip. Then she got up, walking with purpose into the main room. She scooted the nightstand out a few inches from the wall and checked behind.

Just as she'd hoped, a black power cord lay coiled in the dust. Tense with anticipation, she picked it up, plugged it into the back of the digital camera.

It fit.

She sat on the bed, turned on the now-charging camera, and began clicking through the photos, a neat chronological journey through Theresa Hamilton's vacation. The first time stamps showed May 7, just about four months ago. From the airport to a fancy restaurant. Several tourist shots of Mexico City followed, six lanes of traffic crammed into three lanes, the Museo Nacional de Antropología, the zoo. Then a photo of a smaller airplane, maybe even the one Eve herself had taken to the coast. Flight pictures through the fogged glass down at the glorious bays of Huatulco. Next came Neto and Lulu, the Ewok paradise of Días Felices Ecolodge™, a different smiling group around the same tiki-torch-lit picnic table, same dishes on the table. Then a series of pictures of the group on a hike in the dark, everything bathed in a green, night-vision glow. One shot captured a great cat — maybe a black jaguar? — in the distance, so far away it was little more than a dark smudge with glowing eyes. Eve smiled a bit at that, imagining the excitement at getting even a *bad* picture of such a rare creature.

The next photos flashed up daytime-bright again. The white-water raft. Theresa's group, high-fiving with paddles. Aside from Lulu, all the rafters were men.

Eve clicked to the next picture and felt a pulse start up in her temple. A view down at a familiar little house embedded in a canyon slope. Slab concrete roof. Truck tires buttressing a wall. Windows all but devoured by vines. The log in the foreground looked newly fallen, less moss along the rotting bark, but it was clearly the same one Eve herself had crouched behind just hours ago at the edge of the butterfly-rich clearing by the camping toilet.

It occurred to Eve that she was inadvertently following in Theresa's footsteps – staying in the scarcely used hut for solo travelers, using the less trafficked women's rest stop on the rafting trip, drawn to the same canyon to spot the same house. Well, then. What next?

A held breath hissed through her teeth.

Her thumb hesitated over the button that would bring her to the next photo. Then clicked.

There was the bearded man, stepping into view between tree trunks, his face drawn, the snarl of color pronounced at his neck and jaw. A local woman trailed behind him, her bright dress flaring in her wake. He was guiding her by the arm.

Eve's mouth had gone dry. She realized by degrees what she didn't like about the picture. Not just the man's rough bearing. But his biceps was tensed and his fingers looked pale, bloodless, indenting the soft flesh of the woman's arm.

He was steering her into his house by force.

A few pictures followed. The house façade. Nothing more.

A single-file trail of ants threaded across the floor beneath Eve's bed, and outside, the jungle hooted and chirped. Her arms glistened with sweat.

She took a deep breath, unsure if she wanted to continue. But of course she had to. Pictures of breakfast, smiling group members, huevos rancheros and some Pan Bimbo packaged cinnamon rolls. A shot of Lulu with her arm around Theresa, Theresa clutching a thin sheaf of papers to her chest, looking distracted, her smile flat, her strong jaw tensed.

Eve moistened her lips. Clicked again.

A picture taken with the night-vision setting. That little canyon house, same angle down from the clearing.

Theresa Hamilton had gone back there at *night*? *Alone?*

Eve wiped the sweat off her neck. Brought up the next shot.

The house, closer. Theresa zooming in.

Then zeroing in further on the maw of a shoved-open window, vines and leaves crowding the aperture, blackness beyond.

Same image, time-stamped a few seconds later.

Same image, time-stamped a few seconds later yet.

The next picture came up, and Eve inhaled sharply.

A blurred photo – obviously, Theresa had been startled, as well.

In the window now, looking up, a ghostly face. The movement of the tumbling lens had pulled the features into a streaked oval, the mottled jaw stretched as in a fun-house mirror, the eye sockets elongated like holes in a Halloween mask.

Eve tried to swallow, with little success.

The man had spotted Theresa Hamilton up in the clearing.

Had he spotted Eve too?

8

Bamboo planks creaking underfoot, Eve crept toward the adobe shack behind the cantina. The torches had been extinguished for the night, and jungle sounds reigned. Theresa Hamilton's camera, zipped safely into a cargo pocket, tapped reassuringly against Eve's thigh. She came around a bend, confronting a bullfrog the size of a coconut, and she stepped off the path, ceding right-of-way.

Continuing on, she glided into the dark embrace of the shack, which housed the admin office. File cabinet, wooden desk, computer and battered printer, credit-card scanner. For the fifteenth time in the last two minutes, she wondered what the hell she was doing.

Looking into Theresa Hamilton.

Why?

Because something's wrong.

At this late hour, wouldn't logic make a better ally than instinct? After all, there was a simple explanation to be had. Theresa's concern had been aroused on the rafting trip when she'd spotted an *indígena* being manhandled into the little house. She'd gone on a spy mission to the canyon at night. When she'd seen the man looking up at her, she'd spooked, dropped the camera, rushed back to the lodge, packed hastily, and left. Any dark fantasies or nightmare scenarios beyond that should be sliced away by Occam's razor.

And yet now Eve watched her hand curl around the handle of the file drawer, watched her fingers walk across the alphabetized folder tabs. Bills and licenses, brochures and supply invoices. Nothing about guests. She closed the last drawer in the cabinet, glanced over her shoulder like a low-rent cat burglar.

She fired up the computer, which took an ungodly long time. As she waited, she clicked her nails against Theresa's camera through the thin fabric of her pants. The home screen loaded, and she snooped around until she unearthed a reservations file, only to find it code-protected. Frustrated, she moused over and tapped an Internet icon. Little xylophone bars filled in one after another, and then an error message read INTERNET INACTIVE.

'What are you doing here?'

Eve jerked back in the chair, grabbing at her chest. The dark form in the doorway reached over, clicked a light switch. Leaning against the jamb, Neto glowered at her. He held a cup of tea, the string curled around his forefinger.

'God, you scared the *hell* out of me,' Eve said. She shot a glance at the monitor. 'I thought I'd Skype my son.' She twitched the mouse, closed the window showing the locked reservations folder. 'It's an hour earlier in L. A.'

'Why are you in the dark?'

'Didn't want to disturb anyone. And to be honest, I didn't look for a light switch, this being the jungle and all.' She pretend-frowned at the screen. 'Internet's out.'

'It is the HughesNet dish. It relies on . . . atmospheric conditions, yes? Strong wind drops service. Weeds in front of the dish drops service. *Breathing too hard* drops service.'

Eve rose. 'Guess I'll try tomorrow.' She stood, pausing behind the desk, trying for casual. 'Hey, what do you know about Theresa Hamilton?'

Neto's eyes drilled into her as he took a sip of tea. 'Theresa . . . ?'

'A guest here.'

'Ah, yes. Blond-hair lady. Why do you ask?'

'She left some things in my room,' Eve said. 'I found a prescription pill bottle with her name on it.'

'The other items? They are valuable?'

'Nah. Nothing important. It was curious, that's all. Why she left so much stuff behind . . .'

Neto's finger flicked, and the tea bag rose and dunked. 'She was a nervous woman. *Loca.* She got impatient, ran off early back to Mexico.'

'Mexico?'

'That's what we call Mexico City here.'

'Why was she crazy?'

'She was on the medications.'

Eve felt an instinctive defensiveness for Theresa. Ten milligrams of Lexapro hardly qualified someone for the asylum. The average Calabasas housewife probably downed twice that in her Escalade before morning car pool.

'Any idea *why* she ran off?' she asked.

'Like I said.' Neto gave a dry smile. 'She was crazy.'

9

Eve crawled into bed, lowering the mosquito netting around the frame until she felt encased, a zoo animal awaiting display. Reaching through a gap, she turned up the gas lantern on the nightstand and grabbed *Moby-Dick*. After a ceremonious recracking of the spine, she thumbed through the front matter. *List of Plates and Acknowledgements, Biographical Notes, Introduction*. Christ, no wonder she'd put this off so long. She had to wade through a PhD just to get to the first chapter.

Her attention wandered back to the odd standoff she'd just had with Neto in the admin shack, questions leading to more questions. Realizing she was making little literary headway, she thunked the book back onto the nightstand and cranked the old-timey lantern knob down until the wick alone faintly glowed.

She looked across the expanse of the bed, realizing that she'd kept neatly to her side – the *left* side – as she did at home. Months since Rick's departure and still she stayed in her marital lane. She slid a hand across to the unexplored terrain. A strand of hair beneath the pillow caught between her fingers.

She raised it to the faint light. Long and curly and blond.

Theresa Hamilton's.

She stretched it straight before her face, let it corkscrew

back. Then she slipped her hand through the mosquito netting and dropped it onto the floor.

After a moment's consideration, she scooted to the center of the bed, reluctant at first, as though she were doing something wrong. Relaxing, she unfurled her limbs. Sprawled. Then thrashed around, mussing the sheets.

She fell asleep with a contented half grin.

A faint cry awakened her.

Eve froze in the middle of the bed, unsure if she'd dreamed it.

But no, there it was again, a feminine whimper.

As her eyes adjusted, she noticed that the mosquito netting seemed to have turned opaque. But then a large moth lifted off with a leathery brush of its wings, letting through a mosaic tile of less pronounced darkness.

The other tiles, they were squirming.

Slowly, Eve pushed her fingers through the slit in the netting, feeling the screenlike fabric whisper along her wrist, her forearm. She reached the lantern and cranked it up.

Clinging to the netting, a living film. Stick bugs and moths and mosquitoes, a few spindly spiders for good measure.

Another high-pitched moan carried in from outside – a woman crying?

Eve took a deep breath, lowered the lantern to the floor, and heard the carpet scurry away, hard shells rasping against floorboards.

She slithered from the embrace of the netting, shook bugs from her sneakers, pulled them on. Her sweat bottoms and T-shirt would suffice in the humid night. Carefully picking her steps, she forced herself across the threshold and onto the bamboo walkway before allowing a convulsive shudder to move through her.

She sourced the sound of wet breathing to the neighboring hut – Claire's hut. The thatched palm roof was painted with lantern light, and through the slats of the wall Eve detected movement. She progressed carefully along the walkway, dodging slugs, and knocked.

The door swung in against her knuckles.

Claire stood contorted, her foot brace locking out her knee, forcing her to double over uncomfortably. It took Eve a moment to see that the metal band running beneath Claire's bare foot had wedged between the floorboards where an eroded knot had widened the gap.

Claire's face was flushed with frustration, her hair pasted to one sweaty cheek, and her eyes smoldered; she'd been stuck for some time.

'Don't you do it,' she said. 'Don't you fucking pity me.'

'Okay,' Eve said.

Claire tried to lunge forward to unlock the brace, the metal digging into the raw skin of her ankle. She bit back another yelp.

Eve remained in the doorway until Claire looked up again, breathing hard, nostrils flaring. 'Fine,' she said. 'I need your help, okay?'

Eve entered and knelt before her, shifting Claire's weight and freeing the catch. The metal gave, squeaking around the hinge, Claire's knee sagging into a relieved bend. Eve gripped the orthotic at either ankle, working it back and forth until Claire's leg lifted free. Claire staggered back two steps and sat heavily on her bed. The women regarded each other.

'Okay,' Claire said. 'We don't need to have a big sadpocalypse over this.'

'Got it,' Eve said. 'No sadpocalypse.'

Claire blew the hair out of her eyes. 'I bet you feel all Florence Nightingale, sweeping in here saving the day.'

Eve watched the bugs flutter around the lantern. A moth touched the glass, crumpled, dropped to the floor.

'Anika,' she said.

'What?'

'Her name is Anika,' Eve said. 'And – stop me if you've heard this one – she's younger. *And* elegant, I'm told.'

Claire's face shifted, the squint softening, angry lips unpursing until they grew fuller, prettier.

Eve had never been one of those *Sex and the City* women who struck up instant friendships in line at a grocery store, bonding over Kate Spade, bitching about men. Truth be told, she envied those women, their ease and here-I-am confidence. Her relationships tended to be fewer and older, the kind that could go months without a phone call and then resume midsentence. Quick intimacy was not second nature. And yet if she'd learned anything this past year, it was that her instincts required improvement.

She cleared her throat though it was not in need of clearing. 'We got married a few years out of college,' she continued. 'I wasn't . . . *formed* yet. Relationships like that, they're like bad horses. You're never sure how to get free because you're too busy trying to hold on.'

'Men can wear you down,' Claire said. 'But not unless you let them.'

Eve allowed the sentiment to sit for a moment, sensing there might be something beneath the rebuff. Claire pulled her ankle into her lap, rubbed at it angrily. After a moment she looked up, her eyes loosely focused on the wall above Eve's head.

'I was seeing someone,' she said. 'Good enough guy, left the toilet seat down. Moved in together, all that. We were right there, on the verge. Then I got diagnosed. I told him he could leave, that I'd understand.' A one-shoulder shrug. 'So.'

Eve nodded once, slowly. 'That sucks.'

'This is gonna be no picnic,' Claire said. '*I* wouldn't stick around.'

'Really?'

Claire picked lint from the sheets. 'I'm your age. Too old to take a wedding seriously. But still. You figure maybe there could be something, a white sundress, view of the water, someone . . . I don't know . . . *kind.*'

'You don't think there can be?'

Claire gestured to the walls of the hut. 'I'm taking this trip while I still can,' she said. 'I got a ticking clock. You don't.'

'We all do.'

'A little easier to say when you're *you*.' Claire released the catches on her brace, snapping them with aggressive twists. 'You have everything going for you. Attractive, smart –'

Eve laughed. 'Come *on*. You're tough. Fearless. You speak your mind.'

'And every day that matters a little less.' Claire tugged off her orthotic and threw it onto the mattress beside her.

'You can do anything you want. And you don't even have a fucking clue you can.' She shook her head. 'If *I* had what you had –'

'You'd *what*? Be cheery?'

Claire leaned back, turned down her lantern. 'Thanks for the help, Florence.'

Saturday

10

Eve came awake with a dull throb between the temples, a stress-and-jet-lag hangover. After pulling on clothes, she stepped out of her hut to see the camp already bustling with movement, *indígenos* scrambling around shifting crates of supplies, leading burros by their noses, hauling linens, sprinkling pesticide around the cantina's perimeter. No sign of Neto, Lulu, or the group, but voices and the hum of machinery carried from several roomy canvas tents erected by the outskirts – 'activity centers' if she remembered correctly from the Días Felices Ecolodge™ Web site.

Eager to hear Nicolas's voice, Eve ducked into the admin shack to check the Internet connection. Still not working. She closed the screen and headed back out.

Grabbing a cup of coffee at the cantina, she wandered toward the tents, passing through shafts of intense sunlight breaking through the canopy. Given her pre-caffeinated state, the play of brightness and shadow had a dreamy, strobe-light effect, and she slipped into the first activity center slightly disoriented.

The confusion of scents inside didn't help. Rose, mandarin, and mint, freshly chopped into bowls, perfumed the air. Claire, Sue, and Harry stood over various pots, boiling glycerin, stirring dye, pouring waxy liquid into molds. The cooling products, laid out on a table beneath

Lulu's imperious eye, were colorful hand soaps in the shapes of turtles and crocodiles.

Lulu paused from tying bamboo ribbons around cutesy bottles of massage oil. 'Morning, sleepy.'

'What time is it?' Eve asked.

'Isn't it nice not to know?'

Claire glanced up from her witch's cauldron behind Lulu and rolled her eyes – the first gesture of public bonding she'd offered up.

Eve manufactured a smile for Lulu. 'Where's everyone else?'

'At the artisanal mezcal station next door.'

'The other men opted for alcohol over soap,' Harry said. 'I know – *shocking*. But me? I'm in touch with my feminine side.'

A clanking carried to them through the canvas walls, followed by animal braying.

Eve lifted her eyebrows. 'This I must see.'

The second activity center was a study in focused chaos. Neto leapt back and forth, stoking burning stones, juggling agave *piñas*, pouring juices into vats. Airplane-miniature spirit bottles, arrayed on the shelves in rows like missiles, bore rugged Días Felices Ecolodge™ labels. Gay Jay chopped fermented agave with a cartoonishly large knife. Beyond the vented canvas rear wall, a burro yoked to a millstone had halted stubbornly, and Will pushed at it from behind, trying to get it to continue along its pre-scribed circle. He set his back against the burro's flanks and shoved, shoes slipping in the crushed pulp. He spotted Eve and paused. The burro brayed again, displeased.

'I swear,' Will said, 'this *isn't* what it looks like.'

Eve laughed.

But Neto kept on, a commander pacing the deck, throwing out orders and bits of knowledge. 'Come *on*, amigo. Move that burro. You see these beautiful piñas? We have to wait *eight years* to harvest them. There, no *there*. We burn them in the buried fire, see? For *three days* we'll wait. No – use the *hardwood*. We want *good* charcoal, *sí*?' He leaned over a copper still, adjusting a connection, his mouth never slowing. 'We don't need no yeast, we will pull bacteria *from the air* to ferment. Is why mezcal is *más puro*.'

A tinny melody shattered the atmosphere, filling the canvas tent. A familiar diva voice sang, *At first I was afraid, I was* petrified!

A musical hiccup and then again: *At first I was afraid, I was* petrified!

Neto finally stopped, as frozen as the burro: 'Is that . . . ?'

Eve said, 'Gloria Gaynor?'

Jay sheepishly removed from his pocket a sleek phone with a fat folding antenna.

Will pointed. 'Contraband!'

Neto frowned disapprovingly at the phone.

Jay said, 'Sorry. I day-trade, and I told my broker to text me if we hit any limit orders.'

'Any way I can borrow it to make a quick call home?' Eve asked. 'I haven't connected with my son, and Skype's out.'

Neto redirected his look of disappointment at Eve. Then he said, 'I will have the dish looked at for you by one of the peons.'

The term, Eve gleaned, was not derogatory here.

'Feel free to pass on the number in case he needs to reach you.' Jay flipped her the satellite phone, then shot Neto a wry glance. 'Not that I'll ever have it on me.'

Eve retreated to the cantina, choosing a picnic table in the shade. To her side, two so-called peons scrubbed at oxidized patches on the cladding that protected the stove, the shushing of wire brushes against aluminum oddly soothing. Despite the phone's impressive antenna, the reception bars flickered in and out as she dialed.

A few rings and then a cheerful feminine voice: 'Hardaway residence, substitute matriarch speaking.'

'Lanie.'

'Mizz Hardaway.'

'See the number on caller ID?'

'Registered and recorded.'

'How is he?'

'Aside from the F he's gonna get on his summer-reading book report?'

'An *F*? Why?'

'He did a report on the *book*,' Lanie said.

'Isn't that what he's supposed to do?'

'Oh, no. Permit me to read.' Rustling pages. 'Here we go.' Lanie cleared her throat theatrically. ' "This book is forty-three pages long. It costed three dollars and ninety-nine cents plus tax. It is filled with chapters and words, except for inside the front and back covers. Those parts are blank. It is a half inch thick and weighs –" '

'Put him on,' Eve said.

'Hold, please.' Then: 'Brainiac! It's your mom.'

Scampering footsteps. 'Mom? Hi, Mom!'

His exuberance softened her instantly. She had been warned that in a few years her son would be pathologically unappreciative, that he'd prefer hard labor to spending time with her, but he was still such a baby at times, and she missed the crackle of his voice, the dimples of his knuckles, the way his head smelled when she lay next to him at night.

'Are you in the jungle?' Nicolas asked. 'Is it fun? Are there velociraptors?'

'No velociraptors. What's with this book report?'

The line fuzzed, and for a moment she thought the call had dropped.

Then he said, 'I thought it'd be funny.'

'But Lanie didn't think it was funny.'

'. . . No.'

'Do it over.'

'It's *Saturday*. And it's *summer*.'

'I'm aware of that.'

'If I do it, can I *please* –' His last words dropped out.

'What? Nicolas? You there?'

The connection came back on, picking him up – of course – mid-request: '– I *please* sleep over at Zach's?'

'You want a reward for *undoing* F work?'

'No.' A beat. 'For working on a Saturday.'

'I told you, Little. Not with me gone. I can't risk –'

'The food. *Fine*, Big.' Pouty silence.

'What are you doing today?' Eve asked.

'Besides *not* sleeping over at Zach's?'

'Besides not sleeping over at Zach's.'

'Drawing,' he said.

'What are you drawing?'

A beat of pride found its way into his voice. 'The outer reaches of the universe.'

Eve grinned, amused. 'Some people say they don't know what that looks like.'

'Well,' Nicolas said, '*now* they will.'

She rotated the mouthpiece to her neck, stifled a laugh.

They said their good-byes, and she signed off. The sun had encroached on the shade, and she tilted her face to the warmth, closed her eyes, and breathed in the smells. The workers – a man and a woman – bantered in a dialect not unlike Spanish. Eve let the patter wash over her, deciphering every fifth word. She took in the soporific rasp of the brushes at work, the whine of a winged insect, the rustling of fronds.

And then a phrase sailed out of the conversation and smacked her.

'– *la desaparecida.*'

Eve rose abruptly and walked over to the workers. They paused in their task, at nervous attention. She recognized the young man as the bearer of the anniversary cake.

'Hi, I'm Eve.'

They nodded at her.

'You are?'

'I am Fortunato,' the man said. 'This is Concepción.'

The woman smiled shyly, hooked her hair back over her ear.

'What were you saying?' Eve asked.

'I am sorry.'

'No, it's okay. You didn't do anything wrong. I was just curious.'

74

Fortunato cleared his throat. 'She say you remind her of another tourist who come here months past. She sit by herself also. And be thoughtful.'

'*La desaparecida?*' Eve asked. 'The disappeared woman? What do you mean, "disappeared"?'

Fortunato shifted from one bare foot to the other. 'She leave here early.'

'Theresa Hamilton? A blond woman?'

'I do not know her name.' Fortunato cast his gaze everywhere but at Eve. He was even younger than she thought, maybe seventeen. 'We have many reservations.'

'*Why* did she leave the lodge early?'

'I don't know.'

'Did it have to do with a man with a scar here?' Eve circled her neck and jaw with her hand. 'Lives in the canyon by the zip line? You've seen him?'

Fortunato shook his head rapidly, picked up his bucket, and walked away.

Concepción gathered the brushes. She turned to leave as well but paused before Eve, her head lowered, straining to find words. 'Do not go . . . there.'

'Why not?' Eve asked.

'*Hombre malo,*' she said.

Eve watched her scurry off. The air tasted of dust, tinged with the bitter mist of the cleaning agent.

Hombre malo.

Bad man.

Steering crazily, Neto cried out, 'Look! Mexican zebras!'

In the back of the van, Eve and Jay strained to gaze ahead, only to see a few burros blocking the road. Neto erupted in laughter.

Jay looked at Eve, tapped an imaginary microphone. 'Is this thing on?' He rolled his eyes and went back to working the lid of his baseball cap into a better U, his softball biceps lifting and falling.

The van bounced across a series of hand-grenade-worthy potholes, Sue letting out a gasp from the front bench seat, Will almost smacking his head on the roof beside her. The ruins, their afternoon destination, were still a few hard miles out, and impatience was on the rise. Lulu had ceded the passenger seat to Harry after he'd complained of back tightness; she shared the middle bench with Claire, who remained as sullen as ever, gazing out the window, fidgeting with her dive watch. The roaring engine and branches rattling against the van's sides meant it took effort to communicate with anyone beyond those sitting adjacent, ensuring a measure of privacy for each row.

'Sorry!' Neto shouted back to them, proving he was equal to the task.

'Why don't you get a four-wheel drive?' Harry shouted.

'Four-wheel drive just means you get stuck *farther out*.'

Neto laughed, his fists fighting the wheel. 'The roads, the jungle is hard on them. You leave one alone for *six months*, you can come back and it is *gone*.'

As if to prove the point, the asphalt turned to mud. And then, at once, the ground past Eve's window fell away. She peered down the steep slope. A cargo truck had skidded off the road and rolled partway down the wooded decline before smashing into a tree trunk. The cracked trailer had led to a free-for-all, villagers crowding the fissure, carrying off the abandoned grain in sacks and buckets they had brought. The scene whipped by, and then the ground rose again back to where it belonged. Pressing her face to the glass, Eve peered ahead, spotting a cluster of half-built shacks among the trees. Several of the workers were on break, napping on the dirt road, using bricks as pillows. Eve tensed as the van bore down on them. The tires passed within feet of them, but they didn't so much as stir.

Same hemisphere, different world.

Neto jerked the wheel, and they bumped across a scalloped ditch, arms bracing, legs sprawling.

'So much for napping on the way there!' Will called out.

'Thank *God*,' Jay muttered to Eve. 'He snores.'

'That must get annoying in a . . .' Here she always struggled. *Boyfriend? Lover? Spouse?* '. . . a partner.'

Jay swiveled to her. 'Partner? *Partner?* Wait a minute. *Will?* He looked like he might heave. *'Gross.'*

'But I thought –'

'Will is *straight*. Like *rebuilds-engine-blocks* straight. Like *drinks-milk-from-the-carton* straight. He's such a *guy*.' This last with mild disgust. 'It's Gay *Jay*. Not Gay *Will*.'

77

Eve checked ahead, but thankfully the others were too busy riding the turbulence to overhear anything from the rear. 'I just figured –'

'Straight people think any guy who's friends with a gay dude must be a fag.' Jay thought about it, amused. 'Actually, *we* think that, too. But no, Will's my oldest friend. *Friend*. From elementary school. I just had a bad breakup – hel-*lo*? my *ringtone*? – and he said he'd go on a trip with me to keep me company.'

The van crowded up behind a *colectivo*, a bus-truck combination with a curtain in place of a tailgate, all order of *indígenos* crammed inside and hanging off the sides like human saddlebags. Neto hit the brakes, and Jay reached out one massive arm to catch Eve before she pile-drived into the seat in front of them.

'You haven't *noticed*?' Jay said.

'What?' Eve said.

'Man, you are *clueless*. The way he's been looking at you.'

'Okay, I –'

'You sure *you're* straight?'

'Fairly.'

They veered around the *colectivo*, Neto ticking a thank-you on the horn as they passed. With the movement Eve glided across the bench into Jay. He deposited her back on her side.

'Look, I *wondered* if he was straight,' Eve said. 'But, I mean, you guys are sharing a hut –'

Feigned indignation seized Jay's face. 'Oh, so straight people and gay people can't sleep in the same room?'

'Yes,' Eve said, already starting to smile. 'That's *exactly* what I'm saying. Straight people and gay people can't sleep

78

in the same room. Actually, they *can*, they just *shouldn't*. You never know what could happen.'

They rounded another bend, and Eve slid across again, this time turning and tucking in her knees to cannonball into him. They were laughing loudly enough now for Claire to shoot them a sour glance.

The jungle crowded in on the road, the van slowing gradually until it was creeping along, boughs scraping the roof. At last Neto stopped at a seemingly random spot. They spilled out, stretching their necks, testing sore limbs.

'Walk where I walk,' Neto commanded, shoving his way through a break in the foliage.

They followed blindly, struggling through thick underbrush that had covered the remnants of a trail. Despite being the oldest, Harry and Sue made good time, staying up with Neto to soak in every last bit of tour-guide knowledge. Claire struggled to keep pace, Lulu waiting back with her. The jungle grew denser. Will offered his hand, helping Eve over a gnarled root. Jay slowed to give her a told-you-so look over Will's shoulder.

Ducking under a branch, Neto scared up a swirl of tiny bees from a hive. Everyone froze, and Sue stepped protectively in front of her allergic husband. The swarm swept past them and off into the shadows, their buzz fading like the sound of a passing car. Harry exhaled a pent-up breath, and they continued on, winding deeper into the jungle.

Eve mopped her forehead with the collar of her shirt. Overhead, a black vulture coasted in lazy circles, its silver-tipped wings like a fringed cape. The trail dipped, and the sky vanished behind solid canopy, the bright day turning to false dusk. A trio of brilliant blue dragonflies urged them onward, porpoises at the bow of a ship.

Neto gestured to the darting insects. 'We call them *caballitos del diablo*. Little horses of the devil. So it is appropriate they are leading us . . . *here.*'

He parted a wall of fronds and stepped into a vast chamber within the jungle. The others slipped through, one after another, gazing up in awe. The clearing stretched the breadth of several football fields, broken by two pyramidal ruins with an ancient, sunken courtyard between them. To take in each structure, Eve had to tilt her head back, a tourist ogling high-rises. The closer one was more eroded, a rubble-topped heap, but the other thrust proudly thirty or so meters toward the canopy, its shape largely intact. The stone looked mossy and sleek, worn down by centuries of harsh weather. The whole area had the feel of a grand civic plaza, which is what Eve supposed it once was. Giant trunks scattered throughout the space propped up a dense ceiling of foliage, dripping with vines. The air was choked with humidity. It felt like stumbling into the insides of some great beast.

'El Templo de las Serpientes,' Lulu announced grandly, gesturing at the more intact of the two structures.

'There are a lot of snakes here?' Eve asked.

Neto removed a balloon from his pocket. 'We will call them.' He inflated it a few puffs, then squeezed the neck so it gave off a prolonged, breathy squeal. 'They think it's a wounded mouse or bunny.'

Sue toyed nervously with a turquoise bauble around

her neck. She said, 'Are we sure that's such a good idea?' and the others laughed.

'There's no way that works,' Jay said.

'Behind you?' Neto said. 'That's not a vine.'

They turned to see, swaying stiffly from the canopy far above, four feet of visible boa constrictor. Jay bellowed, and Sue nearly left her sandals. The snake bobbed curiously in their direction a few times, all dead eyes and flicking tongue, and then, with a tightening of scales, hoisted up and away, weaving itself back into the leaves. It could have been six feet long or twenty.

Eve's skin had been set tingling, less with fear than excitement.

'Come.' Neto slid the balloon back into his pocket. 'Stay close.'

'Gladly,' Will said.

They headed into the plaza, descending a run of reconstructed steps so eroded they seemed part of the ruins themselves, and stood at the brink of the courtyard with the temple looming over them.

'Archaeologists worked here last summer before the funding ran out,' Lulu said. 'We hope they will return when the economy improves.'

That explained the look of the ruins, half excavated, half lost to the jungle. Despite the high foliage ceiling, the chamber felt claustrophobic, as if it could close up on them at any moment, swallow them alive.

Lulu gestured to the temple at their backs, then to the other structure at the far end of the courtyard. 'These date to the seventh century, probably Zapotec judging from the *talud-tablero* style. See how the sides go up and in? Slope, then panel. Like that. And there –' She pointed to the sunken courtyard below them. 'That's a ball court. This all became an Aztec colony in the 1300s.'

'What happened in between?' Harry asked.

'Many cities were destroyed by floods,' Lulu said. 'Or abandoned for reasons no one knows.'

'*Lotta* things can go wrong out here, *amigo*,' Neto said. 'But the jungle comes back. The jungle *always* comes back.'

They passed the mouth of a narrow archaeologist tunnel at the temple's base, and a chorus of rattles came to life, underlining his point.

Jay said, 'Those are . . . ?'

Lulu nodded.

Sue, still on the prior point: 'Didn't Aztecs sacrifice humans like in that Mel Gibson movie?'

'*The Passion of the Christ*?' Will whispered to Eve, and she stifled a laugh.

'Mostly they made blood sacrifices without killing,' Lulu said. 'Literally giving their blood. They used the sharp tips of agave plants to poke their lips, fingers, even their penises.'

Jay signaled an invisible waiter. 'Check, please?'

'So they *didn't* sacrifice people?' Sue asked.

'I didn't say that,' Lulu said. They approached an eroded stone sculpture that Eve mistook at first for a table. But no, it was an enormous jaguar, its features smoothed by time, a bowl hollowed in its spine. Lulu placed her palm in the contour and smiled darkly. 'For *hearts*.'

A thin beam of sun filtered through a break in the canopy, catching the side of the temple. It refracted blindingly across the ball court, illuminating a wide passageway in the side of the far structure.

'The Zapotecs stuccoed the sides of the temple with crushed oyster shells,' Lulu said. 'To catch the light. The scientists recreated some there.'

'What's that passageway?' Will asked, already starting down into the courtyard toward it.

'A burial chamber,' Lulu said. 'These buildings became cemeteries for the invading cultures.'

Keeping an awed silence, the group crossed the sunken court to the tunnel. It bored through the base of the crumbling structure, ending in a tiny square of light on the far side. They stood at the entrance for a moment, Eve wondering if they were actually going to go in.

Neto turned on a flashlight, and they shuffled into the embrace of darkness. Spiderwebs brushed Eve's cheeks. A musky scent filled her nostrils. She took short, careful steps, letting her night vision adjust.

Neto's beam picked across the moist stone walls, finally illuminating a femur resting on an inset ledge. A slow pan revealed a shattered hip bone, a nest of ribs, and a jawless skull. Rats scurried among the shards. Where the neck had eroded lay a spill of horseshoe-shaped necklace links.

The air had grown cold here, locked in the chill of the stones.

Neto switched the flashlight to the walls ahead, revealing set after set of burial ledges, stacked like bunk beds, running the length of the catacomb. Most were empty, but a few housed fragmentary skeletons, this one missing a rib cage, that a skull. Rising from one slab was what looked like a bulbous growth, the bones fossilizing into the rock over the centuries.

Insect legs tapped across Eve's neck, and she brushed them away. Her senses soaked in the damp air, all but vibrating with the Indiana Jones thrill. If Nicolas were here, he'd explode in delight.

As they turned to reverse out, she rested a hand on Will's shoulder ahead of her. Without looking back, he tapped her fingers once, a quick, flirtatious gesture that made her smile to herself in the darkness.

Near the mouth of the passage, she slowed, seeing if there was enough ambient light for her crappy disposable camera to take a picture for Nicolas. The others kept on as she fumbled it out, turned it on.

She held the camera to her eye. Nothing but blackness. She lowered it again. The fall of light from outside ended literally a hand span away from the first skeleton, a viable photo just out of reach. Picturing her son's face, she exhaled with disappointment.

Jay's booming voice came audible, even from across the courtyard: 'Let's do that balloon thing again.'

Eve turned the cardboard box of the camera in her hands, squinting to make out the button for the flash. That would probably yield no more than a starburst of bleached-out stone. She needed something fancier, with night vision.

Of course.

She slid her hand down her thigh, finding the hard edge of Theresa Hamilton's camera, still zipped into her cargo pocket. Working it free, she thumbed it on.

It powered up to show Theresa's self-portrait at the

Mexico City airport. The glow of the screen illuminated a faint sphere around Eve's hands, and she noticed to her side a change in the consistency of the darkness.

A bulky form.

It shifted.

Eve's breath tangled in her throat.

A hand became visible, closing over the screen, drawing the camera and the sphere of light to a broad chest. The upthrown light caught a strip of mottled throat and jaw.

'Hello, sister.'

The words came on a puff of sweet breath. Square teeth glinted around a chewed twig.

Eve swiveled toward the mouth of the passage but he swept around her, impossibly fast, impossibly light-footed. A bulky arm leaned against the wall, eye level, blocking her.

They stood in the last band of full shadow.

Beyond the man she could see the group way across the courtyard, now at the temple, pointing and taking pictures and spreading out to explore. His free arm swayed at his side, meaty fist encasing the camera, though he paid it no regard. He hadn't so much as glanced at the screen, or he would have seen Theresa Hamilton's face, and something inside Eve told her that that would be very, very bad.

The man flicked his head to indicate the group over his shoulder. 'You are here. On a trip.'

His English was good, the accent not obvious enough to place.

She nodded, not yet trusting her voice.

'And those are your friends?'

He studied her, waiting. His lips pursed, shifted to one side. He held up the camera by its strap, letting it spin between their faces. Theresa Hamilton, rotating round and round. His steady gaze was not on the little screen but on Eve. A flick of the eyes and he'd see Theresa's photograph; he'd note the connection. Pinching the strap, he lowered the camera. Eve reached for it, but he tugged it up.

A game.

'The big man,' he said. 'With the hat. What is his name?'

She fought to keep her voice from wavering. 'Why do you want to know his name?'

'Sister, do not question me this way. Lower your eyes.'

She stared at him, too shocked to comply. Keeping the bar of his arm in place, he shifted his feet and leaned in slowly as if to kiss her, bringing his brown-black eyes inches from hers. Even over the musk of the tunnel, she could smell the sweat on him.

A hiss of breath. *'Lower your eyes.'*

She obeyed. Her lips jerked with emotion. 'Get out of my way.' Though she tried to put her full force behind the words, they came out sounding strangled. 'Let me go.'

She kept her gaze level with his chin, but still she could see the teeth appear around the twig. His body remained in place, his nose nearly touching hers. Past his locked elbow, she watched the others vanish around the side of the temple, and she choked down an incipient sob.

'What do you want?' she said.

'I want to be left alone.'

'Me, too.'

'You say that. Americans. But you *impose* yourselves.' He'd not so much as raised his voice.

She had no idea what was going to come next, but the drumbeat of terror in her gut warned that it would not be good.

'Eve!'

Across the courtyard by the temple, Lulu had stepped into sight, facing away at the jungle, cupping her hands around her mouth.

The man's head snapped around, and his body slackened, only for an instant. Eve snatched the camera from his grasp and ducked past his still-braced arm, her shoulder skimming the stone. Breathing hard, she shot free of the catacomb and ran across the plain of the ball court, ruins looming overhead. She heard no footsteps behind her.

But she didn't look back.

13

'Yes, the same guy. With the burned face. The one I *asked* you about.' Standing at the rubbled base of the temple, Eve did her best not to yell. She kept a nervous eye on the sunken courtyard and the catacomb across it.

Lulu and Neto regarded her with concern. The others were still off exploring. Warmth tingled beneath the surface of Eve's skin. The man had angered and terrified her in the tunnel, sure, but worse, he'd made clear her helplessness before him, and that felt like the biggest violation of all.

'Did he threaten you?' Neto asked.

'He *blocked* me.'

'Did he touch you?'

'I didn't feel safe, okay?' Her words seemed to vanish into the white noise of the jungle.

'So he *said* something dangerous?' Lulu asked.

'No, but his body language and manner –'

'Some people are not comfortable with locals,' Neto broke in helpfully.

'He's not a local,' Eve said. 'And it wasn't that. I'm a woman. I know when I'm being threatened.'

A pause, punctuated by the distant shriek of a laughing falcon.

Lulu shot her husband a glance. 'We need to take this seriously.'

'I *am*.' Neto mopped at his forehead. 'I just searched the

tunnel. No one is there.' He turned back to Eve. 'From now on, keep with the group. Do not wander off anymore.' His mustache glistened with sweat. 'I understand you were made uncomfortable. But let's not tell the others yet.'

'Why not?' Eve said.

'We don't want to frighten everyone if we don't have to,' Neto said.

'Then tell me who he is.' Eve tried to put force behind her voice, but to her ears it still sounded reedy. 'You don't expect me to believe you've never come across him.'

Neto blew out a breath, a dark corkscrew of hair floating up, then drifting back down over his forehead. 'He is just some guy, okay? Who lives in the jungle. No, he is not local, and no, he is not friendly. But he is not *un*friendly either.'

She caught Lulu looking at Neto and read in her face that some of this was news to her as well.

'Then why are the *indígenos* afraid of him?' Eve asked.

'The *indígenos* pray to snakes and marry crocodiles! Who knows what scares them and why! We all leave this man alone, and he leaves us alone. There's never been a problem.'

The strange man's words returned, an echo in Eve's head: *I want to be left alone.*

Lulu put a reassuring hand on Eve's arm. 'Let's make sure you feel *safe*,' she said. 'That's what's important.'

Eve could hear the others approaching now, rustling through fallen leaves, their words a low murmur. Sue came into sight at the clearing's periphery, birding binoculars pressed to her ruddy face. Harry trailed her, swigging from a canteen, halting to test the strength of a vine. Vacation fun.

Eve returned her focus to Neto. 'He asked about Jay.' Instinctively, she had lowered her voice, already – she realized – assenting to Neto's directive.

'What did he ask?' Neto asked.

'Just . . . who he was.'

'Please, Eve.' Concerned, he rested a hand gently on her arm. 'This is nothing. Why ruin everyone's vacation with worry?'

Because it might not be safe for them.

Because they have a right to know.

Because I'm fucking scared.

Jay and Will appeared from behind a crumbling mound of stone, Jay cracking a joke, Will giving him a healthy shove in response. In seconds they'd be within earshot.

Eve opened her mouth to reply. Closed it.

The dilemma drove home her *singleness*. She missed having Rick to rely on, missed making decisions in tandem. Being the sole authority wasn't just tough, it was at times frightening. She had certainly proved – in parenting and in other matters – that she was equal to the task. But then something unforeseen would smash her sense of competence to pieces. Like a man breathing down on her in a dark tunnel.

Drawing near, Will noted Eve. His smile faded. 'Everything okay?'

'Yes,' Lulu said, pivoting with a high-wattage smile. 'Everything's *fine.*'

Will held Theresa Hamilton's camera, scrolling through the pictures. Jay loomed behind him, peering over his shoulder at the screen. Eve, too, kept her feet, facing them in the cool of their hut. It was the kind of news best faced standing.

She watched their expressions darken by degrees until they must have reached the end, because Will lowered the camera and the three of them regarded one another heavily. As soon as they'd returned from the excursion to the ruins, she'd made the decision to bring them into her confidence despite the pressure from Neto and Lulu. She'd recounted her run-ins with the strange man, Theresa's rapid departure, and the various reactions elicited from the Días Felices Ecolodge™ staff.

'I had the camera *out* when the guy stopped me in the catacombs,' she said. 'Right in my hand. If he'd just lowered his eyes, he'd have seen it.' She took back the camera, shook it for emphasis. 'These pictures show that he probably did something bad to that *indígena* lady – and that Theresa Hamilton was onto him. And if he saw that *I* saw the pictures, then . . .' She faded off, the chill of the near miss tightening her skin.

Will whistled, paced a circle, running his fingers through his hair. His shirt was still drenched from the excursion to the ruins, pasted to his body, showing ridges of muscle. Jay drew himself to his full height, cracking his neck like a boxer, seeming to fill the space beneath the thatched roof. They were two able-bodied men, and Eve was glad for that.

'The man with the hat,' Will said. 'That's who he asked about.'

Jay pulled off his Seattle Mariners cap and regarded it as if it had something to say.

'I think he caught a glimpse of me from the bottom of the canyon,' Eve said, 'just before I ducked behind the log.'

'You were wearing Jay's hat,' Will said, putting it together. 'That's all the guy saw. The hat.'

'So he thought *I* was spying on him,' Jay said. 'Well, that's good.'

'Why's that good?' Eve asked.

'He doesn't think you were spying on him, so you're okay. He's worried about *me*.'

'Okay, great,' Eve said. 'But so am I.'

Jay offered a dark grin. 'I grew up gay in Yakima, Washington. I can take care of myself.'

'What do you think he wants?'

'Like you said, he probably thought he was being watched,' Jay said. 'If someone was watching *me*, I'd want to know why. Especially if I was up to sketchy shit, hurting people, whatever, and someone else had already found out about it. I'd be paranoid, too.'

'The guy followed us to the ruins, Jay,' Will said. 'You'd better keep your head on a swivel.' He turned to Eve. 'And we'll keep an eye on you, too. Just in case.'

She nodded a few times, quickly. Needing them made her feel weak, but she couldn't deny that having their support was comforting. 'Why do you think Neto and Lulu are being so defensive?'

'Their business runs on people staying happy,' Jay said. 'The last thing they need is a bunch of freaked-out people going home and posting warnings on TripAdvisor.'

'Right,' Will said. 'I'm sure Sue wouldn't exactly take this news in stride. She writes an online review about a psycho near the lodge? Who would ever come here again?'

'Neto'll be pissed if he finds out I talked to you about it,' Eve said.

'Let him be,' Will said.

But Jay nodded. 'We'll keep it between us.'

A knock on the door surprised them, and Jay lifted Theresa's camera from Eve's grasp. He leaned toward her, spoke in her ear. 'This is the smoking gun, so better it stays outta your hands. I'll keep it on me until we can get back to civilization, find Theresa Hamilton, and see what she has to say about all this.' Sliding the phone into his pocket, he turned to the door. 'Come *in*.'

Fortunato poked his head into the room tentatively. 'I sorry. I looking for you, Señora Hardaway. I fix dish for you. You can to make Internet now.'

Eve checked her watch – six o'clock in Los Angeles, Lanie cooking dinner, Nicolas practicing trumpet. '*Gracias*, Fortunato.'

He withdrew silently. Eve heard no footfall, but then again she'd heard none coming either.

Eve regarded the two men. 'I'm gonna Skype my son,' she said. 'But thank you both. I mean it.'

Jay caught her arm gently as she passed. She looked up into his face and saw he was doing his best to hold in a laugh. 'Sure you wouldn't rather stay and listen to Will's Barbra Streisand albums?'

Smiling despite herself, she stepped out onto the bamboo walkway. Through the closing door, Will's voice floated, in sotto: 'If you weren't twice as strong as me, I would *so* gay-bash you right now.'

Eve made her way to the admin shack. Fortunato had left the computer on, waiting, and she had to brush a few insects off the glowing screen. As promised, the Internet connection showed full bars, so she logged into Skype and dialed home.

Nicolas's face suddenly loomed large on the screen, the camera angled up his nose. 'See! I told you it was her.'

Lanie, off camera: 'So you did.'

A palm wiped out the view momentarily, and then the laptop lid rocked back and forth violently, finally settling on his face. 'Mom? Hi, Mom. I can see you.'

'I see you, too. How'd the book report go the second time around?'

'Good. It was about a astronaut. Guess what? Did you know? Did you know there's a planet' – a peal of laughter – 'a planet called Ur*anus*?'

'Indeed I did.'

'Oh.' This deflated him a little. Then: 'I miss you, Big.'

'I miss you too, Little. Just five more days.'

His face softened, his shoulders curling in, and for an instant he was a toddler again. She pictured his bow-backed waddle, all pot-belly and sagging diaper, and that big round face that combined her demure chin with Rick's knock-you-over green eyes.

'Mom?'

'What, Little?'

'Why isn't Daddy here? I mean, if you're gone?'

A charcoal-colored gecko inched across the ceiling. A cicada perched like a giant fly on the screen, and she flicked it away. It fluttered around, tapping walls, and settled invisibly. She was reeling, still, from the question, her answer overdue.

Because he's selfish.

'He's . . . he's far away, Little. I'm sure he wants to be with you, but it's a long flight. And he did come back when I had that job training.'

95

'That was like *five months* ago.'

His expression tugged at her. She moistened her lips. 'Yes, it was.'

'He hasn't even called.'

'I'm sorry, honey.'

'Since I finished my book report, can I spend the night at Zach's?'

Just like that. A seven-year-old's haphazard transition or a deliberation manipulation?

'Uh, *no*.'

'But you said!'

'I never said you could.'

'Fine. Okay, fine. I won't spend the night. I'll just stay here with you gone and Daddy not calling.'

Mercifully, Lanie leaned into the frame. 'What am I, chopped liver?' She mussed his hair roughly. 'Go set the table. Soon we feast on chicken dinosaurs.'

'There was no such thing as chicken dinosaurs.' Nicolas rolled his eyes. 'See ya, Big.'

'See ya, Little.'

He padded off-screen, and Lanie fell back into the couch, letting her legs rock up after impact. 'No such thing as chicken dinosaurs. Who'll he target next? The Easter Bunny?'

'Lanie? Am I one of those awful helicopter parents?'

'No?'

'With a question mark?'

'I don't know what a helicopter parent is.'

'Why'd you answer?'

'I was trying for polite.'

'Your technique is lacking.'

'Uh, hel-*lo* – out of practice.'

'Helicopter parents, always hovering, worrying.'

'No! Look, Mizz H. If my parents were half as cool as you are, I'd be out there having a life instead of studying molecular biology. I don't think you're uptight at all. I'm no parent, but I've seen him when there's been a gluten slip, and it's SFB.'

'SFB?'

Lanie lowered her voice, tilted her face forward so she could gaze with gravitas through her purple-streaked hair. 'Serious fucking business. What with the bloating and the cramping and the rashes. So no – you're normal. At least as normal as anyone is. So enjoy yourself. Have fun. Meet a guy named Enrique with swivelly hips.'

'Thanks, Lanie.'

Lanie clicked off, and Eve sat a moment, staring at the blank screen. Behind her the cicada screeched, the sound piercing off the close walls. She rose, took a step toward the door, then hesitated, seized by an impulse.

Reversing, she sat again, brought up Google, and typed in

Theresa Hamilton.

Waiting for the search results to load, she nibbled a fingernail.

The first link froze her in the cheap office chair.

May 16, Mexico City–Thirty-nine-year-old Chicago journalist Theresa Hamilton has been reported missing.

14

Eve scanned the article, grabbing the story in chunks, the unseen cicada shrilling like the string accompaniment to Janet Leigh's shower stabbing.

After earning a master's in journalism at Columbia, Theresa Hamilton had scored a job for her hometown paper, the *Chicago Tribune*. She'd worked her way up to the political beat, covering K Street before taking a personal leave of absence about a year ago. The explanation, in the next paragraph, stopped the breath in Eve's throat.

> Theresa's son, Grady, was killed last April by the building manager in her apartment complex, a registered sex offender. She was a single mother. 'The trip to Mexico was supposed to be a fresh start for her,' said friend and fellow reporter Maureen Sugden. 'It makes this even more tragic. I keep praying that she'll turn up and it'll all just be some big misunderstanding.'

The last eyewitness reports had Theresa Hamilton boarding a small plane for Mexico City, where she'd presumably disappeared. A few additional links, mostly from the *Tribune*, gave brief updates. 'Dearth of fresh leads in Hamilton disappearance ... No ransom demands ... Authorities fear worst.'

A tribute picture of Theresa from a Facebook memorial page showed her at a lake somewhere, laughing, wearing a black fitted tank top and cut-off jeans. One arm was slung across her young son, who leaned against her legs, squinting through a scattering of freckles. She looked younger, fresher, her face not yet lined with grief and stress. Whereas her son peered at the lens, Theresa gazed out toward the water, her straight, beautiful teeth even whiter against the slate-colored lake. Her smile, effortless — a joke had caught her off guard.

Theresa had come to Oaxaca, like Eve, to reclaim herself. She'd lost her child a year ago and had journeyed to the jungle, combating depression, determined to find a way back from the edge. By chance she'd come upon a man in the canyon menacing a local woman. Perhaps she'd gone to Neto with her concerns and he'd dismissed her the way he'd dismissed Eve. But that hadn't stopped Theresa. She'd stolen back under cover of darkness to . . . *what*? Gather evidence? Build a case? Check that the *indígena* was no longer captive? It had been brave, but foolish, too, and it might have cost her her life. Lying restlessly in the same bed Eve slept in, under the same tented roof of the same hut, Theresa Hamilton had made a choice. She'd decided that she wasn't going to stand idly by while an abuser roamed free. Maybe her will was fired by her son's death at the hands of a pedophile. Maybe her intrepid-reporter skills had kicked into overdrive. Or maybe she was simply a woman of conviction and courage.

Eve looked again at the candid snapshot of Theresa, that spontaneous laugh, the curve of her biceps across her son's chest. She stared until the photo grew blurry.

She realized that she wished she were a bit more like Theresa Hamilton.

So then: What would Theresa do?

Investigate?

Eve stared at the screen for a long time. Closed her eyes, picturing those time stamps on the photographs in Theresa's digital camera. The first had been May 7.

A simple click brought up the Web browser's History tab. A panel appeared, showing the URL for every Web site visited, organized by date and time, in reverse chronological order. Entries seemed sparse, probably due to the fact that Lulu and Neto discouraged Internet activity, but there were at least a few for every day. Eve scrolled through the dates, rewinding the calendar, until she reached the month of Theresa's trip.

May 7 through 14 had been deleted.

Nothing showed for those dates, not even the ecolodge's Gmail or reservation site, which came up every other day at a minimum.

Eve felt the grind of her teeth in her skull. The cicada shrilled and shrilled.

She rose and moved swiftly outside. Neto and Lulu bustled among the workers next door in the cantina, overseeing dinner preparation. Skillets of queso fundido. Pork cecina, thin slices doused in garlic sauce. Arrachera – skirt steak – sizzling on the grill. Lulu drizzled red guajillo sauce over thin strips of tortillas while Neto ladled frijoles charros into white bowls.

Eve knifed through the commotion, stopping before Neto. 'Why didn't you tell me Theresa Hamilton vanished?'

Neto paused, his brow twisting. 'Vanished?'

'When she got to Mexico City. She disappeared.'

Lulu came over, wiping her hands on a dish towel stuffed into her waistband. 'What's this?'

'Theresa Hamilton never made it back to America,' Eve said.

'I didn't know. Last we saw her, she was rushing off to a plane.' Neto's eyes ticked over to the admin shack, back to Eve. 'I don't run Google searches on people once they leave here.'

'Wait a minute,' Lulu said, concerned. 'She *disappeared*?'

'Yes,' Eve said. 'She was never found.'

Eve kept her gaze on Neto, his normally affable features furrowed, focused. A bead of sweat tracked down from his left sideburn. And Eve understood – he was lying, sure, but he wasn't dangerous. He was *scared*.

This gave her the extra blip of courage to press. 'And the history on the Web browser has been deleted for the days Theresa was here,' Eve said.

'We don't always use –'

'Seven days. Not a single entry.

Lulu was looking at Neto with concern. 'Why would that be?'

Neto half turned, now talking to them both. 'Why would I have any idea? You think I go there *deleting* things? You think I'm lying?'

Yes. Yes.

Lulu kept a cool stare on the side of her husband's face, a look of marital distrust that Eve recognized all too well. By the grill, Fortunato struck the dinner bell, two brisk clangs that rang through the lodge, but Lulu didn't so much as blink. It was clear she wasn't buying her husband's story either.

'Why are you doing all this?' Neto said to Eve. 'Why don't you relax and have fun? That's what you're here for, isn't it?'

Lulu regained her composure and took Eve's hand. 'Come, it's dinnertime.'

The others appeared on the paths, heading for the laden picnic tables.

'Thanks,' Eve said, pulling away, 'but I lost my appetite.'

Jay laced his fingers, flipped his palms outward, and cracked his knuckles as a set. 'I hate to say it, but people go missing in Mexico City a *lot*.'

They sat in a circle in Jay and Will's hut around a bottle of gold-colored mezcal, various shot glasses, and a plate holding sliced oranges and a tiny mound of sal de gusano that Will had liberated from the kitchen. The worm salt was made not in fact from worm but from ground-up caterpillar, seasoned with salt crystals and dried chili flakes.

Claire was there, too. She'd tagged along for the liquor and through the course of conversation had been looped in on the intrigue of Theresa Hamilton. Eve realized with some relief that she was building a mini-contingent, enlisting allies.

'You think Scarface followed her to Mexico City and killed her there?' Claire asked.

'I don't know,' Eve said. 'Sounds unlikely, I know, but *something* happened.'

Jay tossed back another shot, touched his pinkie to an orange slice, then his tongue, then pressed his wet print into the mound of worm salt and popped the finger into his mouth again. A variation on the tequila salt-and-lime routine.

'Look,' Claire said, 'your girl Theresa was pretty messed up and freaked out, had a lot of shit going on. Maybe she got into some other trouble in Mexico City.'

'Maybe she went *looking* for trouble there,' Jay added, aiming a shot glass at Eve to accentuate the point.

Eve felt a pull to defend Theresa Hamilton, an instinct she didn't entirely understand. A strange-looking beetle scuttled beneath the bed, and it occurred to her that somewhere along the way she'd stopped paying insects any mind.

Will sipped his mezcal, closed his eyes with pleasure. 'You can really taste the flame.'

'I'll take your word for it,' Eve said.

'It tastes like diesel,' Claire said. 'And the worm salt tastes like dirt.' She wet her thumb, pressed it to the plate, and brought more grains to her mouth. '*Good* dirt.'

'Okay,' Eve said. 'So what's up with Neto? He's lying. *I* know he's lying. *Lulu* knows he's lying. I can see it in her face.'

'Not sure,' Will said. 'But the guy's a goofball. No way he's a threat.'

'How do you know?' Claire asked, her words slightly slurred.

'I just do. I can tell.'

Eve prided herself on reading people, and the vibe she got from Neto matched Will's take on him. Neto wasn't menacing. He seemed more like a boy nervous about getting caught. But caught at what?

'Come on, Carry Nation,' Will thrust a shot of mezcal in Eve's face. 'One taste.'

'There is *no* way I'm drinking that,' she said.

Eve tossed back her fourth shot, felt the alcoholic flush lighting her cheeks, reddening her neck. 'And we were barely even having sex anymore. Whoops, sorry – TMI.' The words felt loose in her mouth, and the others were watching, cracking up. It was the most she could remember talking at one time, and yet the sentences kept coming, tumbling out one after another. She reached for the bottle, noticed it was almost empty.

Will started to speak, but she waved her shot glass, silencing him. 'And then *she* came along.' She mimed a European hair flip. '"I weel ensnare you with my magical vageen."'

'*Vageen!*' Claire doubled over with laughter.

Jay's broad shoulders shook. 'What accent is *that*?'

'I thought she was Dutch,' Will said. 'When did she become *French*?'

'Sorry, boys, dunno how to do a Dutch accent.' Eve popped a sal de gusano-dusted finger into her mouth. The taste, she'd found, was rapidly acquired over the course of a few shots. Or maybe she was too buzzed to tell that she still didn't like it.

'What is it with men?' Claire asked, grabbing the bottle and accidentally sloshing a bit onto her wrist. 'Like you're some rare bird that all womenfolk want to ensnare. Someone gave you a dick and you think everyone's panting to tend house for you. And you sit back, always looking for the next in line, the next one off the conveyer belt who'll take another five years to catch up to what a useless little boy you are.'

'Don't look at me,' Jay said. 'I'm a 'mo. And this month? I agree with you.'

Claire swiveled her gaze to Will, the token straight male, who held up his hands in surrender. 'I come in peace. Besides, just because we *look* at other women doesn't mean we want to *sleep* with them. It's like crashing open houses on weekends. You want to peruse the merchandise, admire the architecture. But at the end of the day, if you've got a good house, you still want to go home to it.'

'Merchandise,' Jay said. 'So romantic.'

'I liked you better,' Eve said to Will, 'before you started talking.'

'I think it goes downhill once that initial thrill is over,' Jay said. 'And you're committed. Together. Once you own someone, you start to despise them.'

'The trick is,' Will said, 'not to own them.'

'Thanks, breeder. I read that fortune cookie, too.'

'You learned to read?'

'Gay people are generally literate. It comes packaged with the superior fashion sense.'

'That's *another* thing,' Eve said, losing traction on some of her consonants. 'When did we get so fucking *glib*? I'm sick of irony, of flip, of snark. When did everyone get so desperate not to be not jaded?'

The others took a beat, either to unpack the double negative or because her rant was even more of a non sequitur than she'd thought.

'Are you referring to me?' Jay said. 'I thought I was being clever.'

'Everyone just chill,' Will said, laughing.

'No, no. This is good.' Claire pointed the empty bottle at Eve. 'You wanna be earnest? You first, then. Be earnest.'

Oops.

Eve wet her lips. 'About what?'

'You know.' Claire's eyes held that wicked gleam they got. 'Your deepest darkest.'

A challenge.

Eve searched for words but felt her insides churning, the room going slightly on tilt. She'd gotten drunk and opened her mouth and now couldn't back it up. The silence stretched out.

Talk. Just fucking talk.

'Look,' Will said. 'We don't have to do this.'

'It's fine,' Claire said. 'You don't have to rescue her. I'll go. You can ask me anything.' She held up a cautionary finger, then pointed to her leg braces. 'But not about this. And here's why. I'm here on this trip because *I'm* not a disease. People want to know so they can label me neatly, slot me into place beneath some heading.' She glared out from under a fringe of dirty-blond hair. 'I'm not gonna let you. So ask something else.'

There was a beat, and then Jay said, 'Okay. What's with the heavy-duty dive watch? I assume you don't dive given your not-to-be-asked-about medical condition.'

'This?' Claire held up her wrist, regarded the watch face like an adversary. Then she smirked at it. 'This is still-alive time. My-legs-mostly-work time. I-can-take-care-of-myself time. That's the only kind of time I keep now.' She looked at their faces, then cracked up. '*Man*, you guys look sober all of a sudden. Don't worry. I won't croak on *this* trip.'

Eve tried to loosen her face but was having trouble.

'C'mon,' Claire said. 'Who's next? I'm assuming one of you boys, since Eve lost her capacity for –'

'My dad,' Eve said, 'was a musician. He could play the trumpet with a cigarette sticking up out of his knuckles like a rooster comb.'

Will drew his head back, seemingly surprised by her rush of words.

Jay gave a nod. 'Great little flair,' he said.

'It wasn't flair. It was *magic*.' She smiled at the memory. 'He wasn't around much when I was growing up. Out on tour a lot, and then one tour, he just . . . didn't come home. So I married safe, or so I thought. Stable.' She laughed at herself, laughed hard and true.

'Dads are swell,' Claire said. 'Mine used to make me get up from dinner every time he wanted something. Glass of water. Fetch the paper. I had brothers, but no. And if I spoke up? "Sorry to step on your toes, Gloria Steinem." I learned young to do what I wanted on my own.'

'I guess I learned the opposite,' Eve said. 'As pathetic as that sounds.'

Her nails were clicking her shot glass, playing it like a flute. She stopped. They were still looking at her.

'I saw a picture,' she said. 'She's beautiful. With the hair, the accent. She's got this . . . *freshness* in her smile. And me, I let myself get lost. *Buried*. He didn't do that to me. Ms Pilates Accountant didn't do that to me. *I* did.' A stick bug crept across the floor, summited Eve's shoe, then ambled on its way. 'That's why I came here, I guess. Same reason Theresa Hamilton did. To find myself. If I'm honest . . .' A deep breath. 'If I'm honest, I would've left me, too.'

There was a silence, long enough to be uncomfortable.

Claire held up the empty bottle, gazed at her reflection, made a noise in the back of her throat. 'He found someone better.'

Will kept his gaze steady on Eve. 'I doubt that.'

Eve looked away so he couldn't see how pleased she was at the remark.

'My confession?' Jay said. 'I don't like Lady Gaga.'

Their laughter was interrupted by a brisk tapping on the door.

Sue entered, an odd contraption strapped to her head, tugging up her chin. It resembled a jock strap. 'Could you keep it down a little? We're trying to sleep.'

Jay covered his mouth with his hand. '*What* is on your face?'

Sue's own hand rose in chagrin, hovering near her cheek. 'It's a face bra,' she said, a touch haughtily. 'It's intended to reverse aging.'

'What's wrong with aging?' Claire asked.

But Sue had already retreated. They waited for the footsteps to fade, then burst out laughing.

'Okay,' Will said. 'Remember what Aristotle said: "When someone busts out a face bra, it's time to call it a night."'

Claire thunked down the empty bottle. Jay hoisted her to her feet, held her steady as she locked her leg braces. For once she accepted the help. Jay stooped so she could sling her arm across his broad shoulders. 'Come on, lady. I'll drag you to your hut.'

He paused in the doorway, looked back. 'Will, why don't you go back to Eve's hut and critique the window dressings?'

'Cute,' Will said.

'Or we could work on your jazz hands,' Eve said.

Will shook his head, fought a grin. 'This is how it's gonna go now, isn't it?'

'Yes,' Jay and Eve said at the same time.

Jay stepped out into the night, all but carrying Claire.

Will and Eve, alone. He shifted his weight, kicked at the floor. She scratched her neck.

Tell him. Tell him what you want.

Right now. Just go ahead.

'Look,' Eve said. 'I'm not old, but I'm old enough that my body feels . . . *lived in*. I have this knot in my shoulder that gets better and worse, but I know now it's never gonna go away.'

Will blinked a few times. 'O*kay*.'

'I have a kid and a mortgage, and I drive swim practice four times a week. I don't want games.'

'What *do* you want?'

You know. You know what you want. For once in your life, do it.

She was just drunk enough to listen.

She hooked his neck and stepped forward into him, her mouth finding his, tasting again the flame of the mezcal. He was the perfect height, taller but not too tall, so she could tilt her face to his but keep her feet flat on the ground. She sucked his bottom lip, pulled away, felt something wild and dangerous dancing in her stomach, flicking at her insides.

'Okay,' he said. 'Right.'

She led him by the hand down the bamboo path to her hut, and they kissed again in the doorway and then a few steps into the room. Hard-shelled insects pinged off the walls, and outside a hunting bird gave a series of triumphant hoots. They shed their clothes, slipped through the mosquito netting, fell into the enclosed safety of the bed. And then they were intertwined, their bodies slick with humidity, all mouths and hands and hips until they lay spent, panting.

Will rested his cheek on the slope of her stomach, his head rising with her breaths. 'You're quite an athlete.'

She made a soft noise of amusement. 'Not since high-school soccer.'

'Mmm.' He yawned, curled his back, his cheek damp where it met her flesh. His words, little more than an exhausted mumble. 'Were you any good?'

The room grew hazy at the dark periphery, whether from the afterglow, the late hour, or the tail end of the mezcal.

'Decent. I was fast, so I got slide-tackled a lot.' Her blinks grew longer and longer. 'I wasn't the best, but I kept getting up. Kept . . . getting up.'

Before she drifted off, a final thought caught the last ray of consciousness.

Maybe that girl's still in there.

15

He stood outside the window of the jungle hut. Peering in. His face inches from the mesh. His feet shoulder width apart. Solid. Prepared. As still as a carving of stone. He breathed the hot air. He stared at the sight inside, just beyond the sill. Through the box of netting, bare flesh lay spread across the mattress. Limbs tangled.

The woman from the ruins. A man as well. Her partner.

Breathing heavily. Asleep.

Turning the machete in his hands, he considered. They wore no rings. Unmarried. Like animals, these Americans were. The woman's flank was exposed, a firm rise, still ruddy from exertion.

The cicadas chirped and the wind blew, and he watched.

Moths fluttered and a mosquito whined, and he watched.

Leaves whispered and bullfrogs sang, and he watched.

The woman stirred, draping a porcelain-white arm across her face. Her bangs sweat-pasted to her forehead.

He flicked the machete's tip beneath his fingernails to clear the dirt.

Flick. Flick.

A hot coal glowed in his stomach. Not desire, no, but a higher love. He would love to educate them, to let his hand be guided by what was true.

Flick. Flick.

But no. This was the wrong hut and the wrong time, and his mission did not allow for such distractions.

He drifted silently up the bamboo walkway, catching shadows even in the darkness. His sandaled feet chose their spots carefully. Not a creak. Not a crackle of twig underfoot.

He entered the adjacent hut.

There the large man slept. The one who had come to spy on him in the canyon.

He was shirtless, with gym-honed muscles. The most significant physical threat of the group, certainly. A man best caught off guard.

Or asleep.

The door of the tall wardrobe hung open. Inside on a shelf rested the hat. An embroidered *S* decorated with a compass star. He eased silently across the hut, reached up, lifted the cap. Beneath it, folded pants. A pocket bulged. He pulled the pants from the shelf, unsnapped the tab.

The big man murmured something in his sleep and rolled over, hugging his pillow.

Stop. Freeze. Transform again to a carving of stone. His chest neither rose nor fell. He didn't blink.

Once the big man's breathing grew regular again, he tilted the fabric, and something square and hard slid into his palm.

A camera.

Even in the darkness, he read the white label easily: THERESA HAMILTON.

The camera gave a slight whir as it turned on. He clicked swiftly through the pictures until he reached the ones of him in his canyon. Gripping the woman's arm. And then at night.

His fear confirmed. The man, like Theresa Hamilton, had seen.

So be it.

He lifted the machete, tested the edge with the pad of his thumb. His breathing neither quickened nor slowed. He firmed his grip, used the tempered steel blade to part the mosquito netting.

The man was sprawled out, his neck bared. The angle direct.

His feet picked up a tremble in the floating floorboards. Someone approaching. He took three swift steps backward, vanishing into the dark space between wardrobe and door.

The other man entered. The sexual partner of the woman. Passing through the doorway so close that his shirtsleeve nearly brushed against the intruder's own shoulder. The man trudged forward, fell through the netting onto the other bed.

The big man shifted, groaned, rubbed at an eye. 'Have fun, Will?'

'A gentleman never tells. And *yes*.'

Within seconds they were asleep.

But he waited still. He watched them and he breathed and he studied the space between the beds and rehearsed. Backswings. Trajectories. Pivots. Like a dance.

But they were two able-bodied men, and the timing would be better.

A sideways slide and he was gone from the little hut.

As though he had never been there at all.

Sunday

16

As they parked their mud-dripping quads and stepped into the sloped village of Santa Marta Atlixca, the riot of colors seemed hurled down by a divine hand to brighten the mountainside. The humble houses ranged from sunshine yellow to Mexican pink. Green, blue, and orange flags were strung across the sole road, decorations for an upcoming feast in honor of a patron saint whose name Eve could neither recognize nor pronounce. A constant buzz of movement hummed all around the *zócalo*, the public square connecting a ramshackle school, an out-of-place-looking kiosk, and an open-air market shaded erratically by tarps.

Neto swung off his burro – they'd been one ATV short, and the bombastically named Ruffian had trotted gamely along the trails, failing to keep pace. The tour members remained in a self-conscious huddle, squinting and gawking. Eve took off her sunglasses, marred with the smudges left by splattered bugs from the ride, and wiped the lenses on her shirt. She glanced across at Will, caught him staring at her. He dipped his head and grinned shyly, the usual confidence giving way to schoolboy bashfulness. She liked him all the more for it.

'You are lucky,' Neto announced to the group, resting a hand on the wide horn of Ruffian's cowboy saddle, 'to see the pueblo so busy.' He gestured at the creamy gray clouds crowding the horizon. 'When the wet season gets going, everyone will clear out and head off to their *milpas* – the little cleared fields of their families – in safer parts of the mountain range to weather the storms.'

The village was so bustling, so vibrant, it was nearly impossible to imagine it abandoned. Kids ran and bounced across a dirt soccer field. A girl who couldn't have been older than four toddled by, carrying a naked baby with mind-blowing ease. Perched on the edge of a bench, two mustached men wrangled a grand bamboo framework of spinning wheels and crudely shaped religious images, tapping firework flash powder into the tubes, readying it for the celebration to come. Beside them a man with beef-jerky skin cautiously deposited fighting cocks into individual crates, packing them onto his pickup truck, probably for a tournament. As the birds pranced and preened, sharp metal spurs attached to their spindly legs glinted through the slats in the crates.

'Well,' Neto said, 'don't just *stand* there.'

Lulu, wearing a woven hemp backpack that sprawled across her shoulders, led the way toward the *zócalo*. The others followed her lead, dispersing.

Will touched his hand to the small of Eve's back. 'Jay wants to check out the fighting cocks. I know – insert joke here. Catch up to you in a bit?'

'I'd like that.'

She watched the others depart and took a moment to breathe in the scene. If she let it, her concern over the strange man would override everything, and she didn't want to waste her time here, didn't want to return home with regrets. In this moment there was no threat. In this moment she had no obligations, no schedule, no agenda. Just a mountainside pueblo and wherever her feet wanted to carry her. She made a deal with herself – explore a bit but keep the others within sight.

She was drawn first to the market, with its barrels of glossy chilies and dried grasshoppers, its produce trays showcasing more varieties of banana than she'd ever encountered. A hefty old woman who seemed part of the crate on which she sat was preparing hibiscus tea leaves, pulling the branches through a Y of split bamboo to separate the brilliant magenta flowers from the stems. Another woman made corn-coconut tortillas on a clay disk, her wizened hands dancing across buckets of ingredients, adding dashes of cinnamon, dabs of molasses. Captivated, Eve returned their gentle smiles.

She bought a tamale and ate it on her feet, peeling back the banana leaf to get to the rich paste of almonds, cacao, chili, and sesame. Ungodly fresh, flavors cascading after each bite like the finish on a good wine.

A stand to her left served thin slices of meat next to a do-it-yourself grill. Schoolgirls lined up with cardboard trays for their lunch servings, glancing at Eve, whispering, and tittering. They wore uniforms – lavender dresses paired with conservative white blouses, knee socks sporting oddly suggestive bands of lace at the tops.

As Eve turned to throw away the banana leaves, she came face-to-face with a young girl with smooth caramel skin. She wore a tattered princess dress – Belle from *Beauty and the Beast* – and a big dress-up ring with an oversize blue stone.

'*That's a beautiful ring,*' Eve said, the Spanish coming easier than she'd expected.

The girl smiled broadly and said, in proficient English, 'I will trade for one hundred dollars US.'

Eve laughed. 'I think it looks better on you.'

'My *mamá*, she has the bad hip. The money is for her medicines.'

But Eve was carrying much less than that. Rather than barter for a ring she didn't want, she smiled apologetically and wandered back toward the square. She realized that with the exception of last night with Will, this was the first stretch of time the man from the canyon had fully left her thoughts.

Distant thunder rolled across the mountaintops, an animal growl. So odd to hear the sound of a storm while standing beneath a blue sky and a sweltering sun. The others were bellied up to a row of stalls, perusing all order of trinkets – little wooden animals with bobbing heads, figurines carved from coconut shells, tiny ceramic busts of women with pronounced earth-goddess breasts. Even Neto seemed taken in, weighing a tiny carving of the three monkeys in his palm.

'Hey, priddy lady. Look at these beautiful *rebozos*.' The beckoning man had his shirt unbuttoned to his waist, the billowy fabric evoking a cape.

She reached across the counter and fingered the scarves, which were indeed beautiful. Her hand dropped to the price tag, and she saw the tourist markup in full effect. She glanced across at the others, shelling out wads of pesos, and realized she was the only one of the group checking prices. A wave of embarrassment washed through her as she backed up, shaking off the man's entreaties. Walking away, she felt a renewed appreciation for the all-inclusive nature of the lodge, which was, aside from Harry and Sue's HutMansion, an egalitarian setup.

She crossed the square, passing coffee beans roasting on a concrete patch of sidewalk. She asked a pregnant woman where the coffee fields were, and the woman smiled, showing chipped front teeth, and pointed to the surrounding jungle. Sure enough, there were the dark-leaved coffee bushes, sprouting in the shade of larger trees, wreathed with a flutter of metallic blue spots that resolved as morpho butterflies. No crop fields, just bushes spread at random through the jungle. The woman gestured at a crumbling brick compound that resembled a prison. *'The coffee workers used to stay there during the season, but since the economic troubles they do not come anymore.'*

Eve shaded her eyes, checking out the houses wedged into the hillside beyond. Many were literally coming apart, corrugated metal walls rusted through, wood eroding. In others rebar had been stubbed up through concrete-slab roofs in expectation that another story would be tacked on one day, but the metal had long gone to rust, a fine metaphor for abandoned optimism.

A half block off the main square and all color seemed to have drained from the pueblo. Eve turned back, but the pregnant woman had shuffled on, drawing Eve's eye to a dilapidated church. Soft pastels tinted the crumbling walls, yellow-hued volcanic stone composing the broken-up floor. Half of the roof was missing, likely torn away by a storm, revealing an Easter-egg curve of gilded flowery ceiling that ended in jagged nothingness. The dented church bells had been preserved and resurrected outside the building, where they hung side by side from makeshift scaffolding built of thick branches.

Eve gave a slow turn, eyeing her surroundings, ensuring she wouldn't be caught off guard again by the scarred man. But there was no one suspicious in sight, and the others remained at the tchotchke stalls, a shout away.

Drifting across, she entered the shell of the venerable church, marveling at the intricate ceiling design. The pews had been smashed by a fallen tree, its gnarled roots rearing up like an enraged squid.

The creak of a footstep near a side entrance tensed her, and she turned to run, her retreat path clear. But it was just the little girl in the Disney dress, peering around a shattered pillar.

'Your sunglasses, then.'

'What?'

The girl picked her way across the wreckage. 'I will trade you my ring for your sunglasses. My *mamá*, she has the bad eyes. Look, it is very shiny.'

Eve couldn't help but smile. 'Let me see.'

The girl held up her fist proudly, the faux sapphire winking in the light filtering through the ruptured roof. Eve's smile froze on her face.

The ring was from Columbia University's School of Journalism.

17

The ATV lurched and spit game-trail mud, skidding sideways between two trunks. Eve squeezed the throttle, Theresa Hamilton's ring and her old wedding band pinching into the knuckles of her right hand. The convoy stopped at a clearing beneath an open patch of canopy, and Eve hopped off, wiped dried tears from her temples, already missing her Ray-Bans. At least the sun was less intense, a puffy blanket of clouds unfurling overhead.

As Harry arched his back and Sue massaged out cramps from her forearm, Neto lurched into sight on Ruffian, who chewed his bit with apparent boredom, rippling the star of white fur on his muzzle. Neto looped the reins around one of the ATVs and clapped his hands together, a solicitous waiter eager to announce tonight's specials. 'All right, my friends. Wait till you see *this*!'

'Hope you remembered your swimsuits,' Lulu said, then grabbed a machete from Neto's pack and hacked at a rise of near-solid underbrush. The wooden handle came apart in her hand, and she frowned down at the bare curve of steel, then tossed it aside. '*This* is why we have a backup.' She lifted another machete from the pack and pushed through the wall of green, vanishing completely.

Harry shrugged, took Sue's hand, and made the plunge after her. As the others started to follow, Eve grabbed Neto's arm, holding him back in the clearing.

She drew close, picking up the conversation where they'd left off back in the village. 'We should go back now and let someone know about this.'

'*Who?* And over what? A *ring?*'

'Theresa Hamilton went missing *here*. Not in Mexico City.'

Neto's irritation was evident. 'How do you know she didn't give her ring away?'

'Her *class* ring? From Columbia?'

'It's just a *thing.*'

No. You and I know she didn't give that ring away.

An image floated to her: Rick, stating his case, cross-examining, making the argument. She cleared her throat, stood her ground nervously. 'Someone should look into this. Someone should know.'

'This isn't America. They don't send in SWAT teams and CSI groups to look at clues.' Neto blew out his cheeks, let his hands slap to his sides. 'Look at the sky. See those clouds? Soon it will storm. This may be the last chance to see the cascade. I have five other people who signed up for this trip, who paid good money to see this. I should cancel *all this* because you found a ring?'

'I don't care about the cascade right now. I'd like to go back to camp.'

He hoisted a bulging pack onto his shoulders. 'Well, I have the supplies. I *must* go to the cascade. You are welcome to go back to camp alone.'

How the hell would I do that? I'd get lost in minutes, and you know it.

She set her teeth. 'Where is it?'

'Five kilometers northeast.'

'I thought it was south.' The jungle was like that for Eve, a hall of mirrors, every scene a slight variation on every other.

'This is why you should just wait,' Neto said. 'And for your sense of safety, as we discussed at the ruins yesterday.'

I don't want to wait.

'Well?' he said. 'Do you want to see the cascade?'

No.

She glanced nervously at the dense trees all around. 'Fine,' she said, and followed him through the wall of foliage.

The path was so overgrown it hardly deserved to be called a trail. Will and Jay brought up the rear with Claire. Neto sauntered past, whistling, but Eve slowed to match their pace.

'Any headway?' Will asked.

Leaves and shoots brushed Eve's cheeks. 'Nothing.'

Lulu was out of view ahead, but the swish and chop of the machete drifted back to them.

Claire paused, grabbed a trunk, and bent over, adjusting her braces. 'I don't know what you expected *him* to do about it.'

'Contact the authorities. There would've had to be an investigation.' Eve looked across at Jay. 'Do you have your satphone on you?'

'Yeah,' Jay said. 'But what should we do? I mean, we can't just call 911. With so much lawless shit going on in Mexico, the local cops won't care about a class ring. So do we go all the way back to Huatulco, file a report in person?

Or do we have to fly back to Mexico City to find anyone who'll take it seriously? You know how this Third World crap works –'

'Technically, Mexico is a *developing* country,' Will said.

'Thanks, PC douche. But seriously. There's no move but a *big* move.'

'Look,' Claire said. 'Let's even say Theresa Hamilton *was* killed here four months ago because she chose to night-commando over and tangle with this guy. Like they say on *Law & Order*, that's pretty victim-specific.' She gritted her teeth and started up again, pulling her legs forward with visible effort. 'What are we gonna do? Cancel our trip? Go home? Because – *news flash* – there's someone dangerous in Mexico?'

Eve glared at her, feeling her face redden. *Maybe*.

'We should watch our asses, is what we should do,' Will said, speeding up to take the lead. 'There's someone dangerous within hiking distance of our camp. Who is focused on Jay.'

'A *two-hour* hike away,' Jay said. 'And unlike Theresa Hamilton, I'm not a defenseless woman. No offense. The guy's half my size.'

'More like *three-quarters* your size,' Eve said.

'But can he squat five hundred?'

'What are you gonna do if he comes after you?' Will called over his shoulder. '*Squat* him to death?' He bent a branch forward and let it snap back into Jay's chest. It staggered Jay a quarter step, and Claire laughed and high-fived Will.

'We can figure out some way to get in touch with someone without canceling the entire trip,' Eve said.

'You're right.' Jay paused to brush off his shirt. 'As soon as we get back to the lodge, we'll get online, do some research, figure out who to contact about the case – either here or in the US. Someone who (a) cares and (b) can do something about it.'

'It'll have to be the *federales* or the FBI or something,' Claire said. 'Not Los Keystone Kops Locales.' Through the trees they heard Sue gasp with delight, and Claire gazed wearily at the trail ahead. 'Maybe she found a kale farm.'

But Eve understood Sue's reaction when they stepped around the turn. Set against a natural stone amphitheater beneath an awning of trees, a waterfall tumbled two hundred yards to an emerald pool. Even Eve's fears seemed small in the presence of such breathtaking beauty. On a broad flat stone overlooking the water, Neto and Lulu were unpacking, laying out a picnic.

Jay stripped off his shirt and leapt off the stone, cannonballing fifteen feet into the natural pool. He came up with a whoop. 'This is incredible.' Treading, he pointed up the rock face. 'If we hiked around the mountain, we could come out up there and cliff-dive right down the front of the waterfall.'

'Not without a guide,' Lulu said. 'It's a long way around.'

'Not if I climb up the face.'

'You want a challenge?' Neto said. 'Then swim *beneath* the waterfall. There's a passage that goes *underwater*, leads to a beautiful grotto.'

'How far is it?' Will asked.

'Far enough to be scary,' Neto said. 'Not so far that you won't make it.'

Harry said, 'Maybe twenty years ago,' and Sue patted his chest affectionately and said, *'Thirty.'*

Claire was already peeling off her clothes to her swimsuit beneath. Letting her leg braces fall away, she jumped in next. Will followed. Eve watched them disappear underwater with a hint of envy; swimming through an underground channel to a hidden cavern sounded amazing, but also beyond her skill set.

At her side, Neto pulled a moist white sphere from a plastic bag. 'This here is quesillo Oaxaca, like string cheese.' It resembled a giant ball of yarn, with thick, interwoven strands. He broke off a piece, held it out to Eve, a peace offering. They locked eyes for a moment.

She took it. 'Thanks.'

Lulu cracked open soursop fruits, which looked like spiky, light green avocados. She picked out the black seeds and gave Eve, Harry, and Sue a taste of the sweet white pulp as Neto screwed miniature bottles of Victoria beer into a soft-sided cooler filled with ice. 'The tiny ones stay colder in the heat. And? You can drink *more of them.*'

Harry picked one up, the yellow label coming loose in his grip, and popped the cap. 'Amen to that.'

Eve lay back on the rock. It was still warm, but charcoal clouds roiled overhead, which she tried not to take as an omen. She pushed up onto her elbows. 'I think I need one of those.'

'There you go, *amiga*!' Neto said, and slapped a cold beer into her palm.

Beyond a brief ridge of dividing jungle, a lazy stream cut through the foliage, a tributary of the tributary that was Sangre del Sol. The splash of the waterfall continued at a calming pitch. Three heads resurfaced in the pool below, Jay giving a whoop of delight.

'Eve!' Will shouted. 'You gotta come see the grotto!'

'I'm good.'

'Come *on*,' Claire said. '*I* swam it, and I'm a gimp.'

'Nah, I'm gonna stay up here.'

'Why?'

Because I don't know that I can make it and would prefer not to drown like an adventuresome dipshit and orphan my seven-year-old.

'The food's too good to leave,' Eve said.

The swimmers hoisted themselves out, and everyone lounged and ate. Eve noticed herself tapping Theresa's ring against the bottle, a *clink-clink-clink* that drew Neto's attention. Their eyes met again, and then Neto went back to hacking coconuts with the machete.

The cracked shells were handed around, and they sipped the sweet water, then squeezed lime and hot sauce onto the pulp and slurped it up. For a moment all was blissful. But as the chatting picked up, Eve found her thoughts drifting again. She pulled off Theresa's ring, studied the crest. Maybe the others were right. Maybe she *was* overreacting. Maybe she should just let go of Theresa Hamilton and grab hold of why she came here to begin with: to drink beer on a stone ledge overlooking an emerald pool.

Eve closed her eyes, inhaled the fresh scent of vegetation, let herself be soothed by the rush of water tumbling across stone. And finally she blew out a deep breath, allowing a calm to descend over her.

That was when Will said, 'Has anyone seen Jay?'

18

Jay stepped out of his wet bathing suit, hopping to yank on one leg of his sweatpants, then the other. After palming dirt off his bare feet, he slipped back into his shoes, forgoing socks, wiped his hands on his T-shirt, and adjusted the bandanna tied over his damp hair.

He'd hiked up past a rocky outcropping for some privacy, and he now unzipped his pants and took a long-overdue leak, tilting back his head and watching the hanging vines sway in the faint breeze. He moved to lean on a branch but spotted movement at the last minute and jerked his hand back. It was a centipede, rippling along at eye level. He watched it distrustfully. Their bites, he'd heard, could be murder.

He zipped up and turned around.

A man – *the* man – stood directly behind him, a sudden mass crowding his space where seconds before there had been nothing.

Jay jolted from the surprise, corkscrewing back onto twisting heels, his arms rising. Before he could utter a sound, the man's hand flew out, fingers bent, dealing a quick, firm blow to Jay's trachea with the jagged ledge of his knuckles.

Jay lurched forward as if to heave, but his throat had seemingly collapsed – he could neither draw air nor force out the faintest whimper. His mouth stretched wide, a muted rictus.

The man considered him. Fringe of beard, puckered flesh, calm dead eyes. He held his hand perfectly flat now, palm tilted upward, thumb folded in, as if he were pointing vaguely with four fingers.

The hand flashed like a snake strike, the tips of those four fingers hitting Jay on the rise directly under the rib cage. He felt a clump of breath – what had been trapped in his lungs – leave him. There was a vacuum in his chest, air all around and yet out of reach. He batted the man away and staggered toward the edge of the outcropping.

Voices rose from below. Jay's mouth wavered, still a bared O, and he felt his lips crack, tiny fissures in the flesh from the strain. Not a noise escaped him, not a sip of air entered.

The foliage grew fuzzy, and he pinballed off a shaggy trunk and went down, breaking his fall with his hands and landing in a push-up position. Through a spray of sugarcane, he made out the others clustered right there below on the flat rock, glancing around and discussing something heatedly. Will's back was to him, and he was pointing away, into the tree line, but Jay couldn't make out what anyone was saying until Harry cupped his hands around his mouth and shouted Jay's name. They couldn't have been more than twenty yards from him. Jay pounded the earth with his palm but there was no way it could be heard over the rush of tumbling water.

If Neto made a half turn or Eve lifted her eyes, either would see him here at the ledge above, see his gnarled hand groping at nothing, trying to part the sugarcane so that more than a sliver of his face would come visible. His remaining arm gave out, and mud suctioned his chest and chin. He heard his name called again and then again, different voices joining the chorus.

He was still figuring out how to scream when two hands clamped over his ankles and dragged him back into the jungle.

19

Eve stood at the edge of the flat stone like a sentinel, her back to the cascade, her eyes picking across the jungle. Movement everywhere – falling leaves, rustling branches, swooping birds. In her ears a tinny ring, like the aftermath of an explosion. She heard the voices behind her faintly, as if underwater, but her own breathing was amplified, thunderous.

'I'm sure he sneaked off to hike up to the waterfall,' Neto was saying.

'I don't know,' Will said. 'We'd just discussed staying close, being careful.'

'Being careful *why*?' Sue asked.

Harry shouted Jay's name again, the sound fading beneath the waterfall's roar.

Neto gave a laugh, but it came out high-pitched, forced. 'He probably went to go – how does he say? – *take the mountain*. We should just wait here and enjoy. There's nothing to worry about.'

Bullshit. We should worry.

Eve seemed to come back to herself as if tumbling into her skin from a great height. A sudden, abrupt serenity claimed her. She turned on her heel to face the others.

'Bullshit,' she said. 'We *should* worry.'

Neto's eyes grew a bit wider at her tone.

'Jay is probably just exploring,' Lulu said.

No. Something's wrong.

'No,' Eve said. 'Something's wrong.'

Harry lowered his cupped hand from his mouth. 'What could be wrong?'

There's a dangerous man in this jungle.

'There's a dangerous man in this jungle.'

Claire and Will were staring at Eve, clearly caught off guard by her sudden assertiveness.

'*What?*' Sue canted her head. Her linen shirt spotted with perspiration. 'Dangerous? Dangerous *how*? Why weren't we told?'

Neto buckled his knees and rolled his head back, appealing to the sky. '*¡Chingada madre!* This is *estúpido.*'

'We need to stay calm and wait for him,' Lulu said.

We're not waiting – this time Eve caught the thought midstream – 'we're searching for him now.'

'A *search*?' Neto coughed out a laugh. 'Hang on. I'm sure Jay will be back any minute. No one's talking about a search.'

Eve said, '*I* am.'

They kept in groups, sweeping the jungle around the waterfall as the thickening clouds dampened the day by degrees. Unable to navigate the steep slopes, Claire waited on the rock. Eve paired with Will, wading through the brush, calling out, trying to wrestle her concern under control. In certain spots the cascade drowned out all sound, but sporadically they could hear the shouts of the others echoing through the treetops like birdcalls.

Forty-five minutes later they reconvened on the stone ledge.

Sitting, Claire rubbed at her ankle where the brace had raised a row of blisters. Sue added a few drops of iodine to her canteen, drank greedily, and passed it to her husband.

Will picked up Jay's Mariners hat where it had been left to dry on the rock. His face looked ashen. He scratched at the top of his head a few times, then hiked up to a vantage point above an outcropping of rock, keeping his back to the group. Eve watched him bow his forehead into his hand.

'How far are we from the lodge?' Sue asked.

Neto bunched his lips. 'Five kilometers or so.'

'We should go back. I want to go back.' She turned sideways into Harry and he patted her shoulder.

'Hey. Hey!' Will scrambled down the slope toward them, his sneakers freeing tumbles of tiny stones. He half fell onto the rock slab and lifted his hand.

In it Jay's blue bandanna.

A line of dark drops near the hem. Dried blood.

Neto's Adam's apple bobbed. Sue made a strangled noise and twisted a finger in her turquoise necklace, hard.

'It was there by that cliff face,' Will said, his voice unsteady. 'I found it by a broken-off ledge of rock that looks like it snapped off about ten feet up. I could see . . . I could see the fresh break on the wall.'

Neto: 'Like he tried to climb to the top of the waterfall and fell.'

'Or like it was *staged* to look that way,' Eve said.

Will's gaze was loose, his eyes drifting across everything and nothing.

'If he hit his head,' Harry said, 'he could be disoriented.'

'Maybe he hiked back to the lodge,' Lulu said, the hopeful note in her voice a touch strained.

Claire blew out a disgusted breath.

'We need to get onto Skype,' Eve said, 'report him missing.'

Neto started to protest, but Will shut him down with a glare. Silently, they headed up to the ATVs.

20

Will's jaw clenched, cords ghosting beneath the skin of his cheeks. 'You're joking, right?'

The tour group stood around the open door of the admin shack in a semicircle, their arrangement funereal. Though it was midday, it felt like dusk, the sun lost behind a shroud of bruise-colored clouds. Harry and Sue had been brought up to speed, Harry taking in the details somberly while Sue twined her fingers in her necklace and made faint noises of despair.

The chair squeaked inside the shack, and then Neto emerged from behind the desk. 'No, I'm not *joking*,' he said, stepping outside, craning to examine the sky. 'It's the storm clouds. They make it impossible to catch a signal.'

The light guttered in the shack, casting the side of his face in sporadic orange.

'How do you know the dish hasn't been tampered with?' Claire asked.

'Let's not get paranoid,' Lulu said.

'Let's not tell me what to do in the first-person plural,' Claire said.

'It's *normal*,' Neto said. 'We *never* get a signal in weather like this.'

'How long can it be?' Sue asked.

'A day. Maybe two.'

'Days,' Will said.

Neto came toward him, patting the air. 'We have an expression here. *"Lo que pasa, es."* It means, "What happens, is."'

Will's lips moved, but his teeth barely parted. 'Well, that's really fucking Mexican, now, isn't it?'

Neto said, 'Take it *easy.*'

'I'll take it easy when we've reported Jay's disappearance.'

'Fine,' Neto. 'How do you propose we report this?'

Claire said, 'We reach a detective –'

'Detective.' Neto snorted. 'There *are* no detectives in Mexico. Not in this entire state.'

Harry's mouth opened in disbelief. 'If someone gets killed, who investigates it?'

'Their family,' Lulu said.

The Americans took a moment with that one.

'Look,' Neto said, 'everyone should wait here. Lulu and I know this jungle *forward and backward*. We can go in the Jeep, make a more thorough search. Jay is probably wandering out there now.'

'What about that man in the jungle?' Sue said.

'You're safe here.' Lulu placed a manicured hand on Sue's sleeve. 'Oaxacans are gentle, honest people.'

'Maybe so,' Claire said. 'But the problem is, *he* ain't Oaxacan.'

Will flicked his thumb against the fingers of the same hand. 'I'm going to that house,' he said. 'In the canyon.'

All heads swiveled to him.

'Wait,' Harry said. 'Wait, wait, wait.' He hadn't shaved, and he wasn't the kind of man that looked good on. Sparse white curls flecked his shiny cheeks.

'He could *have* Jay,' Will said. 'He's a psycho. We saw a picture of him with that local woman, pulling her into the house.' He wheeled on Neto, punching his words angrily. 'And don't give me any bullshit about how he leaves everyone alone. Where'd the guy come from?'

Neto threw his hands wide. 'I do *not know*.' Seeing his exasperated expression, Eve actually believed him. He continued, 'There are all sorts of people –'

Will leaned into him. 'What have you *heard* about him?'

'He makes the *indígenos* nervous. Nothing more. I am not an expert in –'

'How long's he been here?'

'Since before we built our camp,' Neto said. 'He has as much right to these hills as we do.'

'Not if he's hurting people,' Will said. 'If Jay's there . . . I'm *going*.'

'That might not be the brightest idea,' Claire said.

'We were in Little League together,' Will said. 'We taught each other how to ride a bike. How many machetes do we have?' Each sentence sailing out flat as a hammered penny.

Sue said, '*What?*'

Lulu tapped the handle protruding from her pack. 'One left. And we need it. To search.'

'Then I'll take a knife.' Will started for the cantina, the others drawn along as if by gravitational pull.

'You can't just storm around like a crazy person,' Neto said. He reached for Will's arm, but Will yanked away.

He turned, put his finger in Neto's face. 'Actually, I *can*. Didn't you say there's no signal for days? Didn't you say that if someone gets killed, their family investigates? Jay is my family. His mother practically raised me. We know there's a crazy fuck out there, and my best friend is missing, and I am going to go talk to the man, and if you put that hand on me again, I will break it.'

'*Enough,*' Eve said.

The men paused. Everyone took a few breaths, eyes darting from face to face, assessing.

'We've all read *Lord of the Flies*, seen those movies. We're not gonna do that here, now. There's too much at stake.' Eve stepped up on the picnic table and sat deliberately, putting her feet on the bench. 'Let's figure this out smart and steady.'

After a brief pause, Sue and Harry lowered themselves onto the facing bench at the adjoining table. No one else moved.

'So what?' Lulu said. 'You're in charge now?'

'No,' Eve said. 'We don't need "in charge."' She kept her gaze on Will. 'We need to figure out how to find Jay.'

Will swallowed once. Then pulled himself up beside Eve. The others followed suit. They blinked at one another. The bloody kerchief dangled loosely from Will's hands. His jaw shifted back and forth.

'Let's look at this,' Eve said. 'Jay's probably injured. He's either lost out in the jungle somewhere, taken by that man, or –' She caught herself. 'Let's assume it's one of those two. Either way we need more resources. We need to get the authorities involved. Internet and Skype are out. So who's within driving distance?'

'That is wasting time,' Neto said. 'Lulu and I need to be searching for him with the Jeep. We can go in a spiral from the cascade, park to hike the different cliffs and ridges.'

'And while you're doing that, we can be looking at other options.'

Behind them the workers scurried in the kitchen, preparing lunch, pretending not to notice anything amiss.

'The pueblo,' Eve said, prompting Neto.

'Santa Marta Atlixca?' Neto gave a nasty little laugh. 'There is no one there for *this*. They farm coffee and sell *alebrijes* – you know, trinkets? – to tourists half the year. Right now they are busy closing up for the rains.'

'Maybe there's a phone there. We could call –'

'They are under the same sky. At the same elevation. With the same signal interference.'

'So you're telling us,' Claire said, 'that there is no figure of authority within driving distance?'

The silence drew out. A mosquito whined by, and Harry waved it off, a damp crescent marking his shirt under the arm.

Lulu blinked several times, clearly uncomfortable. 'There are *local* authorities.' Neto shot her a glare, but she weathered it, keeping her gaze on Eve. 'They will have channels to pass on the news.'

'An *American* missing? *Here?*' Neto said. 'This *will* be news, Lulu. *Big* news. And if it turns out he twisted his ankle –'

'The guy played two quarters of high-school football with a broken rib,' Will said. 'He didn't twist a fucking *ankle*.'

Eve nodded for Lulu to continue. 'Local authorities?'

'*Indígenos.*' Agitated, she tugged at her mane of blond hair. 'They have different authorities. And different ways to contact the cities for help.'

'How do we reach them?'

'*We* don't. We don't speak their language.'

'Don't speak their language?' Harry said.

'Okay,' Eve said. 'So they speak dialect. Where do we go to find whoever's in charge?'

'We don't even *know* who is in charge,' Neto said. 'We don't deal with our business affairs in *that* direction.' He waved upslope at the looming Sierra Madres. 'We handle our business *this* way.' A gesture down toward the coast and Huatulco.

'*That* way is five hours minimum,' Claire said.

'I want to leave,' Sue said. 'I want to go home. Right now.'

'*Fantástico,*' Neto said.

'Without Jay?' Will zeroed in on the older woman. 'That's it, huh? Just pack up and leave him here?'

'You guys can stay and look,' Sue said. 'But this is . . . this is all too much. We can take the Jeep –'

Claire said, 'The Jeep that Neto and Lulu need to search for Jay?'

'Sure,' Neto said. 'Why not? Have our Jeep.'

Sue looked at Harry for support. 'Then . . . then the van . . .'

'The van is the only thing big enough to get us and our stuff out of here,' Claire said. 'You take that, we're stuck.'

'I don't feel safe here anymore,' Sue said.

'I don't either,' Eve said. 'Believe me, I want to pack up and leave *now*. But I don't want to leave Jay.'

Claire said, 'So these local authorities . . .'

'We don't know who they are,' Harry said. 'We don't speak the language. How do you propose to even *find* them?'

Eve looked past him into the open tent of the kitchen,

where Fortunato diced bell peppers on a cutting board with a folding steak knife. One by one the others turned to follow her gaze.

Fortunato paused and looked up nervously.

'You want find *alcalde*.' Fortunato's cheeks were smooth with youth, no hint of stubble, rouged from the humidity and the sudden attention of the group. In his hands he twirled the folded knife. He kept his dark eyes on the ground before the picnic tables, his forehead gnarled with effort, as if every word were a kidney stone he had to pass. He was speaking in a pidgin blend of Zapotec, English, and Spanish and doing a fair job of it. '*Alcalde* is – how say? – boss? *patrón?* With the duties. But not a real job. It is title. It is volunteer. One year in three, must volunteer. He is can be farmer or shopkeeper.'

Beside Eve, Will had stopped talking and, it seemed, listening. One knee bounced compulsively.

'Who is the *alcalde*?' Eve asked.

Fortunato maintained the same quiet tone. '*No sé.* It change, like I say. *Pero* nearest *alcalde* is in Santo Domingo Tocolochutla. It is one and one half hours' hike. Foot only. Very dense. That way. Up. Top of this mountain. There should be satellite signal to catch for to make report to Policía Federal in Oaxaca City.'

Claire spoke in a tone that seemed to be her version of gentle. 'What do you know about the *hombre malo*?'

Fortunato cleared his throat, looked at his feet, then off into the middle distance. '*Nada.*'

Will rose, plucked the knife out of Fortunato's hands. The teenage boy took a step back, startled.

143

'I sat,' Will said. 'I listened. But given what could be happening to Jay *right now*, I'm not waiting anymore.'

Eve said, 'Will –'

'I don't expect anyone to go with me. You'd only slow me down anyway.'

Neto said, 'It's far.'

'I know my way. Hit the river, follow it down to the zip line.' Will put a sneaker on the bench, tightened the laces. 'If I run it, I can check the house in the same time it'll take someone to get to the *alcalde*.'

'If you get hurt by this guy,' Eve said, 'you're no help to Jay. Or to us.'

'I'm not asking, Eve.' Will tucked the knife into his pocket and jogged off down the bamboo walkway.

They watched until the fronds folded around him, until the sound of his steps faded, until it was as though he had never been there at all. Sue's keening broke the silence. Harry put his arm around her, and she curled into him.

'You'll go,' Neto told Fortunato. 'Find the *alcalde*.'

'With you or Señora Lulu.'

'You're giving orders now? No. I tell you what to do and you do it. At least if you expect to work here again. I can throw a rock and hit ten peons who would *love* to have a job that pays what I pay you.'

Fortunato seemed confused at Neto's anger. 'You need for someone for who they pay *atención*. For to provide the details and make the report to Policía Federal. Last *alcalde*, he had less Spanish than me.'

'Then how is he the –' Harry stopped, made a growling sound. 'Mexico.'

'We are *not* going with you,' Neto said to Fortunato. 'We have to search.'

'Given the importance of the situation,' Harry said, 'you're gonna rely on a kid and a farmer to get it properly conveyed?'

'We are the only ones who know this jungle,' Neto said.

'There is no way Harry and I can make a three-hour round-trip hike through rough terrain,' Sue said. 'Besides, someone should wait here in case Jay wanders back.'

Slowly, Eve became aware that the attention of the group had shifted to her. She looked from face to face and felt something inside her seem to cave in.

Claire came off her perch, each leg landing with a metallic clank. She hoisted the last machete from Lulu's pack and turned to Eve. 'You said you came here to find yourself.' She chopped the machete down, whacking it into the picnic table next to Eve. It stuck in the edge at a gleaming diagonal. 'Well?' Claire gestured at the blade. 'Guess the fuck what.'

21

Fortunato wore sandals and a T-shirt, the sleeves torn down past his ribs to vent air. He and Eve alternated turns with the machete, but he wielded it more effectively, spending the majority of the time in the lead. The clouds intensified, the dense canopy adding another filter of shadow, making it easy to forget that it was still afternoon. Lulu's woven hemp backpack was webbed tightly across Eve's shoulders. In it she carried a canteen, Theresa Hamilton's ring, Jay's passport, and the bloody kerchief. Her paperback of *Moby-Dick* was in there, too; she'd have no time to read, of course, but it served as ballast that kept the items from shifting. She wished she had Theresa Hamilton's camera to deliver with the other evidence, but that had stayed with Jay, and Jay was lost.

Jay was *lost*.

She was still trying to get her head around it. Every time her energy flagged, she thought of him and put a charge into her step.

They picked across trails forged by deer, cattle, and coatimundis, taking switchback routes up the steeper rises. Ignoring the burn in her legs, Eve focused on the ground but kept the white fabric of Fortunato's back in peripheral view. He was patient and considerate, holding aside branches for her, pointing out the best footholds on fallen trees and shifting boulders. The vegetation transformed gradually, more and more tree ferns popping up, spiderwebs glistening against moist, shaggy bark. Trumpet trees cast parasol sprays of fronds around which orange-breasted parakeets darted and chattered.

Winded, Eve leaned against a ten-foot-high prop root of a giant banyan tree. The banyan had encompassed and strangled an ancient mahogany, dropping down stiff aerial roots like witchy hair. A tree consuming another tree until there was nothing left but a hollow space inside – so elegant and macabre. Once those giant roots took hold, they would pull the trunk along, allowing the tree to creep in slow motion across the forest floor.

A bird the size of a hubcap fluttered erratically past Eve's head, her stomach clenching at the realization that *no*, it was a bat. It swooped into the hollowed center of the tree as she stumbled back, one arm flailing.

A firm grip caught her at the wrist, steadying her. Fortunato.

'Vampiros,' he said. *'They feed on cattle sometimes. They roost inside the hollow trees, and their guano, it fertilizes the roots. The relationship, it is – What is the word?'*

'Symbiotic.'

'Yes. This.'

After a few preliminary attempts at English, they'd settled on Spanish as a common ground. They might as well practice; once the federal police were reached, it would likely take both of them to get the information conveyed.

'You are tired?' he asked.

'A bit.'

'Let us sit.' He gestured to where the prop root tapered off to bench height.

Eve moved toward it, pausing as a supersized tarantula lumbered into view along the mossy bark. Using the flat side of the machete, Fortunato brushed it gently to the forest floor. *They are fine. It is the black widows only that are of concern.*

'And the snakes.' Eve gestured to where a bluish-black snake had emerged from the brush. It nosed behind a rock, and the brief visible segment kept coming and coming, as if on a loop.

'No. That is a tilcuate. They are nonvenomous. They eat . . . pests? Rats and mice.'

'Yes. Pests.'

Finally the tail pulled into sight, flicked, and vanished.

Eve took a moment to catch her breath. Leaves trickled constantly from the canopy, pinwheeling down. *'What else is dangerous? Jaguars?'*

'Only if you get between a mother and her young.' He rose from his squat before her. *'Do you want to see something dangerous? Here.'* He indicated a green plant with spiky, dark green leaves covered in white dots. *'See the tiny stinging hairs? The leaves will stick to you, make a burning rash. Then your skin turns purple. Know what it is called?* Mala mujer.' A boyish smile. 'Bad woman.'

It struck her now, removed from the group and the comfy ecolodge and the ATVs, how truly *wild* these mountains were. She pictured Will on his own, navigating through this landscape with all its hidden threats, tromping toward that ramshackle house in the canyon in which an even greater danger waited. An image sailed in – Will last night, leaning back, his hands around her waist, lifting her, guiding her, his grip firm but not too firm. As distant now as a remembered dream. She took a lonely beat to wish him every ounce of luck in finding Jay, then pushed him from her thoughts.

Her focus now had to be on getting from A to B and then home to her son. Anything else was a distraction.

Fortunato had been studying her. *'These mountains, they contain more than danger. They provide for everything.'*

His earnestness was refreshing, and she felt a pull to match it. As unsettling as the ordeal was, it had peeled back the layers, one after another, to the heart of matters.

'The forest is a sponge. Look.' He snapped a frond off the trumpet tree, tilted it to her lips for a few fresh, crisp sips of gathered dew. As opposed to the humble peon role he played at the lodge, he was sure-handed here in his element, a young man rather than a teenager. *'And here.'* He twisted a *piña* from an agave plant and snapped off its spiky top hat. Inside, orange worms squirmed.

Eve took a moment to find the word. *'Protein,'* she said.

'Yes. Though they taste better roasted.' He set down the husk. *'As indios, we know how to live off the entire jungle. To . . . cultivate? Yes, cultivate it from the roots up. The Spaniards, when they arrived, saw only forest, and they cut it down to try to plant crops. They were dying of hunger in a garden.'*

He leaned to the side, peering up through a gap in the leaves. The blood-colored sun had fought its way through a billowy sheet of gray. She stared in awe.

'We must go,' Fortunato said. *'The ring around the sun? It shows there will soon be rain.'*

They kept on, hiking until Eve's sneakers rubbed her heels raw. They came to a plateau where a rickety wooden scaffolding had been erected around a mighty white cedar. Shielding her eyes against falling leaves, Eve looked up to where a bird-watching platform, clumped with moss, encircled the trunk just below the canopy. The view from there must have been spectacular. But moisture from the sodden ground had crept up the ladder, rotting the lower rungs. Just past the tree, the trail split, and Fortunato nodded to the east and said, *'Almost there.'*

Soon enough the trail opened into a dirt path, which veered through a small garden patch where bean vines climbed around stalks of maize. They continued past a pen holding two pigs and a single gaunt cow, arriving finally at a tiny house slanted so severely it was unclear how the walls supported the roof. She hadn't expected anything civilized, certainly, but she had expected more than this.

Eve looked around. 'This *is Santo Domingo Tocolochutla?'*

Fortunato shrugged. *'More or less.'*

They stopped before the porch, chickens zigzagging around their ankles. On the top step, a young boy sat next to a younger girl who was as dark as a tribal African. Siblings? Between them a bottle of cooking oil.

Through a crooked window, Eve made out a stretch of the single big room that constituted the interior. Most of the items inside seemed to be floating: fruit hanging from wall pegs, hammocks dangling from posts, the rafters supporting sacks of grain, rice, sugar.

Fortunato and the boy engaged in a brief exchange that had the tenor of a failed negotiation, and then the boy ran inside.

'What'd he say?' Eve asked.

'I don't know.'

'What do you mean?'

'He speaks only *Zapoteco de la Sierra Sur*. I have Valley Zapotec.'

'How many dialects are there on this mountain?'

'More than I can count. Maybe his father will have the Spanish.'

This was, Eve realized, the *real* Mexico.

The girl swept up the bottle of cooking oil, dabbed some around her ankles and on her neck, then offered the bottle to Fortunato.

Fortunato took the bottle with thanks, applied oil to his own shins, then passed it to Eve, who did the same, catching a whiff of eucalyptus, which must have been added to the liquid. She gleaned that this was a trick the locals used to ward off no-see-ums.

She set down the bottle before the girl and offered a smile. 'Hi.'

The girl blinked at her a few times, then pointed to the forest, then to her eyes. *Watch*. She set her elbows on her knees and refocused her attention on the surrounding trees. A scorpion scuttled through the slats and along the edge of the porch toward the girl. She either didn't notice or didn't care.

'Watch out,' Eve said, dumbly, in English. She gestured, but the girl kept her eyes trained nervously on the forest.

Eve was about to spring forward when the screen door squeaked open and a broad man appeared on the porch. He noted the nearing scorpion, picked it up, pinched off its head, and threw its body to the chickens, who fought over the still-wriggling corpse.

Eve eased out a breath.

'*We don't worry about the big ones,*' the man said, in passable Spanish. '*Only the little scorpions. If they fall off the ceiling into your cooking pot, don't bother calling for the Cruz Roja.*' He gave the forest a long, apprehensive glance. '*They are coming.*'

'*Who are?*' Eve asked.

Rather than answer, he crossed his fingers, kissed them, and touched them to the sacklike hummingbird nests nailed beside the door. Good-luck charms. The girl kept watching the forest, twisting her hands, waiting.

Fortunato cleared his throat. '*Can you tell me who is the alcalde?*'

The boy ran outside with an empty glass, and the man grabbed his shoulder, checked the tree line, then released him. He gave what sounded like a warning to the boy, who jogged into the pen, filled his glass directly from the cow's udder, then trotted back into the house. Only then did the man allow his eyes to flit to Fortunato. Still he did not acknowledge Eve, though whether because she was a woman or a *gringa*, she did not know. He pointed back the way they had come. '*Silverio Aachen Aragón.*'

Fortunato's shoulders descended with a sigh, a rare show of disappointment.

Eve imagined Jay, injured in the woods, stumbling from trunk to trunk. Or captive in that creepy little house. Or dead.

She didn't want to admit it to herself. But there it was. She was risking her life, her son's future, for a man she'd known only three days. Who could already be dead.

'How far away is Señor Aragón?' she asked.

Before the man could answer, the girl stood up abruptly. The man said, 'They are here.'

Eve turned to face the forest's edge. Nothing.

A deer bounded into view, reared skittishly, then darted past the house. Beyond the vines unseen birds spooked. A horrible crackling sound reached a barely audible pitch.

And then grew louder.

Blades of grass rippled, weeds nodded, and then a black wave emerged from the forest, darkening the earth, sweeping toward the pen. It was a living band, three feet wide, fifty feet across. The cow made a snuffling noise and darted across its pen, stamping its feet, and the pigs leapt and curled like bucking broncos, managing to shake what looked like black dots from their hooves.

Eve swallowed dryly. 'Are those . . . ?'

'Sweeper ants,' Fortunato said.

The entire family had materialized on the porch, the boy gripping a kitten and his glass of milk, a weary mother cradling an infant and holding up the front hem of her dress, which bulged with items she'd trapped in the fabric. The front door stood ajar. Inside, every cupboard door was open. They descended the steps and readied for the approaching vanguard. The ants must have numbered in the millions.

'Are they gonna attack?' Eve felt the rise and fall of her chest. Her words had come out breathy.

'No,' Fortunato said. 'As long as you are careful. Bigger animals like us, we can shake them off. Unless you get trapped in a swarm. Then it is not good.'

Eve watched the approaching tide, her heart quickening. Such a methodical approach, the set lines of a marching army.

'*The ants, they are actually very helpful,*' Fortunato said.

'Help*ful?*'

'*They eat everything in their path. Which means they clean out every insect. Gnats, bedbugs, no-see-ums. They come at dusk this time of year. You leave them the house and let them work. There is no other choice.*'

Eve risked a quick glance over her shoulder at the hanging food and supplies, the hammocks. Nothing touching the ground. Beside her the kitten meowed in the boy's arms. She whipped her head back around to face what was coming.

The chickens squawked and fluttered up as if kicked, landing out of harm's way over by the pen. The ants swept closer still, spread out by a few body lengths except where they clumped, piranha-like, to pick apart wayward slugs in seconds. Even dusk couldn't mute the maroon tinge of the shiny black exoskeletons. The living stripe neared the base of the house, and one by one the family members bounded across as if jumping a creek. Eve followed their lead, her heart lurching until she was on safe ground looking back.

They all stood on the far side, safe, watching.

The wave crawled the stairs, the fifty-foot band pulling through the open doorway like a blanket gathering through a napkin ring.

The boy took a swig of milk. The mother spread a bedsheet on the ground, unpacked from her dress bits and pieces of their meal, and the family continued eating dinner. Through the open door, Eve watched darkness scale the walls, a rising flood. The crackling sound floated out, the ants devouring their plunder.

Fortunato had to tap her arm to break her out of her trance. He gestured toward the dark road. *'Many kilometers yet to hike.'*

Her legs ached. Her blisters throbbed. She pictured Jay's face, his big laugh, and steeled herself to keep going.

They said their good-byes and left the family picnicking in what passed for their front yard. Even after the house faded from view, Eve could still hear the crackling, millions of mandibles at work in the darkness behind them.

22

As they arrived back at the corroding bird-watch tower wrapping the white cedar tree, Eve caught a second wind, no doubt invigorated by the adrenaline boost of the sweeper-ant insurgence. This time Fortunato took the west side of the fork, and they labored on, gaining altitude. After a wordless spell, they walked straight through the remnants of a post-and-rail fence and into a cemetery.

The layout appeared to be entirely haphazard, concrete crypts jutting on top of ancient stone tombs, rusting metal crosses shoved at all angles into the earth, corn sprouting from the graves themselves. Ficuses cloaked many of the headstones, squeezing them in skeletal embrace, and Eve did a double take at the just-legible chiseled dates, some of which reached back over four hundred years. Strangely, many of the family names were German, probably inherited from the founders of the scattered ranches and farms the locals called *fincas*.

Cariñitos littered the plots, small tokens of affection that ranged from chocolates to fruit to long-extinguished candles protected by miniature card-house roofs constructed of bark. A rooster flared up like a specter, crowing and flapping violently, chasing them the length of three graves. When Fortunato turned to kick at it, it beat an angry retreat, eyeing them from a distance.

The brief sprint had been costly on Eve's tender blisters. She winced, favoring her right foot.

'*Let me.*' Fortunato crouched and wiggled off her shoe, then her damp sock. One of her heel blisters had burst, leaving a thumbnail of loose, shiny skin. He handed back her shoe and searched the darkening cemetery, mindful of the rooster standing guard. Finally he bent to pluck several green shoots that had taken hold on a boulder. Squeezing their sap onto his thumb, he applied the cool salve to her heel, leaving a thick layer.

Gingerly, she pulled her sock and sneaker back on and stood. The flesh of her heel tingled pleasantly. She bounced a few times, trying out the foot, then nodded.

A branch of spectacular lightning seized the sky overhead, turning night to day. Her mouth literally fell open. Fortunato reached across and gripped her forearm reassuringly. She gave him an uncertain look an instant before the thunder arrived, louder than any natural noise she'd encountered. The air vibrated with the roar; the earth trembled underfoot. The sensation like standing before a speaker at a rock concert.

She'd forgotten to breathe.

Fortunato released her arm. '*You know what we say about lightning?*'

'*That the gods are angry?*'

'*That the Argentineans think it's God taking their picture.*'

She laughed harder than she'd expected, releasing the tightness in her chest.

Raindrops arrived fully formed, filling the air, splattering her hair, instantly soaking her. The water came as a relief, cutting the stifling heat. She wondered where Jay was and if this same rain was falling on him. Or his corpse.

If she hadn't borrowed that Seattle Mariners hat –

If she hadn't had to go to the bathroom just then –

If she hadn't let her curiosity get the better of her –

– then she'd be back at the lodge right now, pouring lavender soap into turtle molds and not huddled in a cemetery in the dark of night, doing her best not to acknowledge just how fucking terrified she was.

As quickly as it had arrived, the rain vanished.

'Let's go,' Eve said, forgetting to use Spanish.

They kept on through sparser forest, requiring less and less of the machete, until at last they broke through onto a stretch of elephant grass, acres wide, the top of the mountain. Taller rises still loomed in the background, but as they waded across the field toward the distant outline of a ranch house, the sudden sense of openness was disorienting. How quickly she'd acclimated to the surround-sound inundation of the jungle. By comparison the purr of wind through the elephant grass was soothing.

They skirted the edge of a muddy wallow the size of an Olympic pool, and Fortunato paused. *'Do not be scared. He will leave us alone if we do not invade his territory.'*

'Who?'

His eyes clicked over a few degrees. She whirled.

About ten yards away, a black bulge in the wallow rotated lethargically, orienting itself toward them. Eve took an unsure step back. And another.

The bulge coasted forward on stunted legs. Twenty feet and change.

She remembered reading somewhere that they never

stop growing, that they can live up to seventy years. Two facts that, when put together, yielded something monstrous.

Another flash lit the scene, Eve giving a soft cry, though the reveal only confirmed the nightmare tableau she'd painted in her mind. Armored scales jutted up along the crocodile's spine, torn from age or battle. The pointy snout ratcheted open, snaggleteeth bared, the creature venting heat through its mouth.

Thunder shook her.

Fortunato's voice stayed steady. *'His name is El Puro –* The Cigar. *Don Silverio's grandfather brought him here from the coast as a baby. He has an easy life picking off stray calves, dogs, chickens. He does not want to eat us.'*

Eve kept one foot pointed toward the house. Ready to sprint. *'Let's not find out.'*

El Puro's obsidian eyes watched them back away from the wallow. Unblinking.

They shoved through the elephant grass toward the house. Two burros watched them approach, staring balefully out from a wobbly structure that was more shed than stable. As Eve and Fortunato passed them, a guttural wheezing emanated from around a thicket of yucca plants. Hoarse, moist, pained exhalations.

The sound of something dying.

Fortunato held up his hand, slowing as they neared, and raised the machete.

A backlit form swung out from behind the brush, pivoting with a raised shotgun to aim at Fortunato's forehead.

Eve's knees sagged, the bottom dropping away, her courage going to pieces, falling like pebbles into the void.

'*What do you want?*' The voice held more panic than menace.

Fortunato dropped the machete, held out his arms. '*Don Silverio. Por favor.*'

The man lowered the shotgun, his shoulders bowing with relief. '*Gracias a Dios.*'

Finally Eve drew a breath.

'*We need to speak with you,*' Fortunato said. '*As the* alcalde. *We have business.*'

The man staggered back a step, seemingly weakened from the shock, then nodded once and beckoned. They stepped around the thicket. A cow lay on her side, her bulging eyeball protruding from the socket, her snout frothed with white cords of saliva. Her frozen legs were shoved stiffly through the flattened grass. She did not toss her head or make any movement at all. Even as each wheeze forced its way up her throat, her ribbed hide barely rose and fell.

A cud of half-chewed flowers lay near her head, clearly excavated from her mouth. They looked like purple irises. Eve crouched, poked a finger at them, casting her mind back to sophomore-year botany. *Delphinium scopulorum*, better known as Rocky Mountain larkspur, wasn't just cardiotoxic; it had neuromuscular blocking effects, shutting down a body limb by limb until paralysis set in. Then death.

'*I thought I cleared it all from the fields,*' Don Silverio said. '*But she ate it with the grass.*' He crouched over the suffering animal, stroked her cheek affectionately. That distended eye stared up at him, helpless. The lips vibrated with each chuff. '*There is nothing to do.*' He rose and gestured for them to give him a moment of privacy.

They nodded solemnly and stepped around the side of the house, waiting in a tangle of pumpkin vines near a chugging generator. Eve tensed, bracing herself.

Gunshot.

Don Silverio appeared a moment later, wiping his mouth. He opened the crooked screen door. 'Welcome,' he said, in near-perfect English.

23

On the battle-scarred farm table lay Theresa Hamilton's class ring and Jay's bloody kerchief, a universe of dark possibilities contained between the two. When Eve mentioned the threatening man with the scarred face, recognition flickered across Don Silverio's features, but he volunteered nothing, listening intently, the leathered skin beneath his left eye twitching as she spelled out the specifics. The rain had made a fervent return, hammering the roof. Wind moaned beneath the eaves.

At the sink, a matriarch – Don Silverio's mother – washed cobalt-rimmed enamel dishes in a farmhouse sink, and a boy a few years younger than Nicolas eavesdropped from the hall, his face half hidden by the doorjamb, one chocolate eye taking in the alien proceedings. No mother was present, but when Doña Bartola snapped her fingers, the boy withdrew quickly, heeding his grandmother with haste.

Eve concluded her account, arriving at the million-dollar question: 'Do you have a phone that can get reception up here?'

Don Silverio bobbed his head deliberately – the man seemed to do everything in slow motion – and excused himself to the other room. Eve blew out a breath, taking stock of the spare, dignified house. An Old World heirloom sideboard. Two framed photographs, yellowed with age and positioned artlessly on a bare, cracked wall, each showing a white ancestor posed formally beside a seated native wife. A humble altar in the corner, votive candles and pictures of saints arrayed on a floor mat. Directly above the shrine with no apparent irony, the rack onto which Don Silverio had nestled his well-maintained shotgun as they'd first entered.

The kitchen, clearly Doña Bartola's domain, occupied a stretch of wall and featured an adobe stove, a tortilla griddle, and a volcanic *metate* slab, worn from use, on which she crushed corn beneath a grinding stone, the sound continuous and grating. The window above the sink looked out to a square of moon-limned blackness, and the warped shelf to the side held packaged pasta, jars of lard, a clump of tomatoes still on the vine.

Don Silverio returned bearing a pottery jug, which proved to house a hand-stitched leather pouch. With great ceremony he unzipped the pouch and removed an antique satellite phone the size of a brick, which, Eve construed, had been handed from *alcalde* to *alcalde* over the years for precisely this purpose. He pushed a button unsurely, frowned at the unit. Rooting in the pouch, he came up with a charger. He plugged in the phone by the sideboard and tried again, waiting, his lips twitching. The entire technological interlude seemed anachronistic.

Eve's hands played nervously with her paperback, now warped from the rain, the pages collectively rippled. On the inside cover, she had jotted key numbers from her phone: her mother in Palm Springs, Rick in Amsterdam, the across-the-street neighbor. Contingency plans in case this troubled situation grew more troubled. And of course she'd call Nicolas, let him know that she was coming home early.

Hear his voice.

Eight o'clock right now at home. He'd have finished his music lesson with the unimprovably named Mr Doolittle. Bath time would have just ended. He'd be curled on the couch in the fall of light from that ugly chandelier they'd never bothered to replace, entranced with Super Mario Kart, wheedling Lanie into letting him play 'just one more game.'

Her eyes moistened.

Don Silverio set down the phone on the sideboard and returned to the table. 'It will not work.'

Her ears heard, but her brain didn't process. 'What?'

'The storm, it is electric. I will try again when it has run its course.'

'Won't that be a long time?' Eve said.

His steady gaze shifted to the window. Lightning illuminated roiling clouds, an endless canopy of gray-purple cotton. 'Perhaps two days.'

'We can't wait that long. Our friend is in danger. He's either injured, or . . . or –' She heard herself winding up and stopped. 'The man with the scarred face – you know him.' Her intonation somewhere between a question and a statement.

The gaze grew less steady now, Don Silverio's eyes giving a telltale tic to the right. 'No.'

'You know who he is.' Eve turned her attention to Fortunato. 'Don't you?'

The grinding of stone against *metate* kept on, steady as a dog working a bone.

Fortunato wet his lips. 'He treat badly the girls *locales* sometime.'

'Well, he's probably responsible for what happened to Jay. And he's out there. So I don't think we want to sit around and wait for a storm to end.'

The grinding sound had stopped. Doña Bartola still faced the wall, her bony shoulder blades tenting the fabric of her blouse. Her hands gripped the inert stone.

A windblown owl perched on the outside sill of the kitchen window, moonlight lending him an otherworldly glow. One wing stuck out, bent.

'*Tecolote,*' she said. '*Trae mala suerte.*'

He brings bad luck.

The cigar-butt head rotated, the wise eyes blinked, and then the owl flailed from the sill and was swept off as if by a current.

Don Silverio had remained motionless. 'You're right,' he said to Eve. And then, to his mother: '*Ama*, load your burro. You will take the trail to the *milpas* tonight. Uncle Quique is waiting.' He raised his voice, but not by much. 'Magdaleno?'

The boy popped out from the hall immediately, removing any doubt that he'd been lurking right around the corner.

'*You will pack now.*'

The boy nodded and scampered off. Doña Bartola dried her hands and drifted back to a different bedroom.

'Why are you sending them away?' Eve said.

Don Silverio returned his attention to Eve, and there was no denying the fear his eyes held. '*La tormenta.*'

The storm.

She looked in his face and knew him to be lying.

'I will take a report to San Bellarmino at first light. It is my duty.'

'How far is that?'

'Fifteen hours by burro. The *presidente municipal* is there. He will call Policía Federal in Oaxaca City.'

'How far is Oaxaca City?'

'Thirteen hours.'

'So it's *closer*? Can't you go directly there?'

'No. Policía Federal have to be asked into an incident by a *presidente municipal*.'

'That makes no sense.'

'It is how things are done.' Don Silverio maintained the same quiet tone. 'When things are done differently, Americans say, "That makes no sense."'

'Fifteen hours,' Eve said. *'Fifteen hours.'* She smoothed her palms against the rough grain of the table. 'Okay,' she said to herself. She wrapped Theresa's ring in the kerchief and handed it to Don Silverio. Then she removed the passport from where she'd tucked it inside *Moby-Dick* and jotted down Jay's name, his date of birth, and the passport number on a pad Don Silverio provided. She stared at the writing. *Jason Rudwick*. Gay Jay. Before all this she hadn't even known his full name.

She handed the pad across, but Don Silverio didn't take it.

'The report,' he said, 'it must be written.'

Eve looked at him, not getting it. Fortunato leaned toward her and said, 'We do not know how to write.'

She nodded and got to work.

*

In the basin of Don Silverio's bathroom, Eve scrubbed ink from her fingertips. She'd written out the report as best she could, employing stiff, official-sounding phrasing, trying not to exaggerate the situation while also conveying alarm and urgency. She hated to think that Jay's life hung in the balance of three scrawled notepaper sheets.

Exiting, she came down the hall, pausing at Magdaleno's room. The boy had thrown a few items into a canvas bag – toothbrush, stuffed animal, pair of tighty-whiteys – then gotten distracted from packing. He sat cross-legged, drawing with crayons.

She surveyed the room, affection warming her chest. The floor, strewn with dirty clothes, stuffed animals, and a few secondhand-looking plastic action figures. A chair on its side, the hollow beneath the prefab desk converted to a mini-fort replete with books, blankets, and carved wooden masks. Drawings taped to the walls, soldiers and monsters and stick figures holding hands. A world apart, and yet how familiar the diorama was.

She thought about all those times she'd shushed Nicolas when he'd crowded her elbow with a new finger painting of Optimus Prime, a macaroni-pasted Buzz Lightyear, a tender spot where his finger *really, really* hurt. His timing impeccably bad, an interruption whenever she picked up a phone or collapsed into a chair. She'd do anything now to be there with him, to have him within reach, self-centered and irritating and disrupting her every third thought. How she'd taken his presence for granted.

Her face grew hot, and she felt wetness on her cheeks.

Wiping her eyes, she sniffed in a breath, and Magdaleno turned at the sound.

'I draw very well.'

'I can see that you do. What are you drawing now?'

'An alien invader.'

'That sounds scary.'

He rose and padded to his blanket fort, tucking himself inside. He picked up a Mr Potato Head, crammed an ear into the mouth hole. *'But I'm brave.'*

'You seem *brave.'* Rain thrashed his window; the hike back would be hell. The sky strobed with brightness, providing a view across the elephant grass to the distant mud wallow and forest beyond. She spotted El Puro's shadowy form and wondered how the boy ever got to sleep with a twenty-foot crocodile in view from his bedroom window. *'Does* he *scare you? El Puro?'*

An undaunted smile. *'No. He is my pet.'*

The grin faded, a microexpression flickering across his face. Fear. As a nurse she'd learned to read similar veiled tells that indicated a patient's willingness to talk, to call out an abuser, to confess an embarrassing bit of medical history.

'Pets can scare us sometimes, too,' she said.

'Not him.' Tucking himself farther beneath the desk, he pulled one of the masks into his lap and played with it. *'The man who came to see him.'*

Her damp clothes felt suddenly clammy against her skin. *'What did the man look like?'*

In answer Magdaleno raised the mask to cover his face. An evil spirit grimaced at her, twisted mouth, peeled-back lips, pointy teeth and horns.

She cleared her throat, which had turned to sandpaper. Crouched to get eye level. She scooped up a well-chewed action figure and a teddy bear. One small, one large. She animated them, making them walk a bit. After a time Magdaleno lowered the mask and watched her curiously.

'This is the man,' she said. 'And this is you.' She offered the toys. 'Do you want to take them, show me what happened?'

Beneath the desk the boy's dark eyes glittered. 'No,' he said, cutting straight through the role play. 'He *didn't* hurt me.'

She took a beat to catch up. 'Who did he hurt?'

Magdaleno shook his head and turned away, curling into his nest of blankets. The motion brought visible a crayon drawing thumb-tacked to the wall behind him.

The picture stopped Eve's breath in her throat.

In the drawing a version of Magdaleno's scary mask had been grafted onto a stick figure in place of a head. The evil form stood with his arms and legs spread jumping-jack wide, taking up much of the page. At his feet the crocodile waited openmouthed, jagged teeth at the ready. The man's hand gripped a much smaller stick-figure woman, stiff as a gingerbread cookie, with yellow scribbled hair.

Falling from her crudely drawn finger was a sparkling blue ring.

24

On aching legs Will had run the entire way from the lodge to the river, and then he worked his way along the frothy bank, finally reaching the zip line. Gathering his nerve now, he leaned out over the raging water, grasping the hand trolley. He stared past his white knuckles at the dense foliage over on the bad man's side of the river, drew in a deep inhale, and leapt. He rocketed along the line, eyes watering, spray flicking up to catch his legs.

He tumbled onto the muddy far bank and found his feet quickly, unwilling to be caught letting his guard lapse. After confirming the folding knife's presence in his pocket, he scrambled down toward the shoal where they'd eaten lunch two days ago. It seemed like two years. Sand sucked at his shoes as he waded across, and then he trotted up the rise through a spray of storm-battered white orchids and found the camping toilet, positioned like a hallowed object on the plateau. He crept to the rotting log at the edge and squinted through the downpour into the canyon.

The house crouched below, nestled into the hillside, the windows dark.

The steak knife, once unfolded, fit the counters of his hand. Firming his grip, he began the hike down the slope.

*

The man leaned forward into the strain, dragging the American's body through the thickening mud. His calves screamed. His bare feet padded as if across lush carpet, feeling the jungle floor. Straps sank into his broad chest, connected to the makeshift sled he pulled. Woven from palm fronds, it curled around the body like a taco shell. One of the American's arms had come unbound a few kilometers back. It trailed behind, fingertips tumbling over rocks, grooving the mud.

The mat distributed weight evenly. Left a negligible signature in the earth. Hard to track. At the cascade he'd secured the body and distanced himself rapidly from the tourists. He knew how to move unseen. How to move bodies unseen.

Each breath a grunt. Humidity doused his throat, his lungs on the inhale. Vines brushed his cheeks, his shoulders. The rain constant.

He had carried many men in his past, dying and dead, some enemies, some brothers. But few this large. At one point he had been trained to sprint up mountains. But it had been years. His muscle he had maintained, but extra meat had gathered at his waist, around his bones. It slowed him. He was sled-dog strong still, but not what he had once been.

With each step a prayerlike murmur repeated in his head: *Almost home. Almost home.*

Behind him a moan rose above the pattering of rain. He paused, turned. The American's hair had fallen across one eye. The eyelids thick with grogginess. He ducked out of the straps, walked back, crouched.

The American coughed out a mouthful of rainwater. 'What are you . . . ? I – I'm not . . . My face is wet . . .'

Weak and disoriented. He gave no resistance, allowing his arm to be gathered to his side and bound again.

After retying the torso straps, the man rested his meaty hand across the American's trachea. Thumb on carotid artery, forefinger on vagus nerve. Gentle pressure. The American's sclera rolled into view. His eyelids fluttered. Then closed.

The man held the compression for five more seconds, then harnessed himself again with the straps and kept on.

Almost home. Almost home.

It occurred to Will as he reached the bottom of the canyon that he did not know how to fight with a blade. The folding steak knife was something he had grabbed for comfort, the way one grabs a baseball bat when awakened by a strange noise in the garage.

If he were honest with himself, he didn't really know how to fight *period*. He was fit, sure, and a gym regular, but designing basketball shoes and taking weekend hikes didn't exactly make him Ultimate Fighting Championship material. The thought of Jay in captivity had charged him, and he'd motored most of the way here on adrenaline and vague notions of heroics, but inching closer to the house now, he had to acknowledge a simple fact.

He was fucking scared.

The concrete box of a house waited, its front windows like the eyeholes of a skull. Runoff streamed down the hillside and poured across the slab roof, waterfalling off the lip. His shoes pressed hoof-prints into the mud, but within seconds the earth closed over his tracks. Through the sheet of water, the windows showed only blackness, and he detected no sign of movement inside. He blinked away raindrops, adjusted his doused shirt where it clung to his shoulders. After circling the house at a distance, he approached, ducking through the cascade and putting his face to the glass. He moved from window to window, the moonlight barely allowing him to discern the furniture and identify the tiny square rooms. Bedroom with closet. Sitting area with couch and chair. Sink with pots and a hot plate. Filthy bathroom.

No sign of life.

Or death.

He exhaled, his breath fogging the window, rainwater sluicing down his shoulders and back. Should he stay here? For what? How long? What if the man with the scarred face had gone off to wait out the storm elsewhere? What if he'd already killed Jay and cut him into pieces in the jungle? What if Jay instead was injured and lost, wandering miles away by the cascade?

If Will entered the house, his muddy footprints would be evident when the man returned. But perhaps there was information inside. Information that could identify who they were up against.

He backed out of the waterfall. Moved to the front door. Reaching through the pouring water, he felt for the knob.

It turned.

As was his habit, the man paused a meter back from the tree line to surveil the canyon from the dense foliage.

There was a light on in his house.

He freed himself from the harness and crouched over

the American on the sled. The big man had regained energy. Fear allowed that. He bucked and flopped in the mud, to no avail. Many straps encircled him and the curled mat. Ankles, thighs, waist, chest, neck, forehead. He would not be able to free himself.

'I can't get – will you help? – these straps off. Why are they . . . ? My shoulder . . . pins and needles.'

The man stripped off his own soaked cotton shirt. Found a stone the size of a child's fist and dropped it in the fabric. Made neat folds, forming a two-inch band.

'What are you doing? Wait. Wait. What are you –'

Straddling the American, he forced the makeshift bit between his teeth, put his weight on either side of the bridle, and shoved, seating the rock hard in the rear of the man's mouth cavity. A faint cracking. Blood dribbled at the corners of the American's lips. He made an animal grunt, shuddering like a speared fish. It was no use. He would learn. Sure enough he fell silent.

The man left the bound body behind, circling his house, remaining several paces back from the tree line. He approached from the east. Leaning against a tree, his plywood target. The machete embedded. He freed it.

Rainwater streamed across the roof, down his arm, off the tip of the steel blade. It blurred his view of the window, but he detected a man's shape inside, on all fours, his torso bare. Wiping mud from the floor with his shirt. As if that would be sufficient to erase his tracks.

Lifting the machete, he split the stream, opening a thin vertical slat to see through. It was the other man. He'd heard his name used last night in the hut. Will.

Will started to look up, so he withdrew the machete.

The cascade turned him invisible outside, in the dark. The fuzzy form inside stayed frozen for a time. The oval of the face looking right at him. Him looking right back. Only one of them could see the other, and seeing was a great advantage right now.

He eased away. Stood to the hinge side of the front door. Waited. There was no risk that the bound American would be heard. Not from this distance. The sound of the storm drowned out all else.

He turned to a statue, Soldier with Sword. Waited.

Did Will *know* or merely *suspect*?

That he would find out. The big man, the spy, would tell him everything, but that would require time and focus.

The front door opened, blocking Will from view. He backed through the stream, shut the door, turning as predicted. Away.

The man stood behind him, so close he could have rested his hand on Will's shoulder without straightening his arm. Will fought his filthy shirt on over his head, tugged it into place. When he pivoted another quarter turn, the man sidled to keep squarely at his back.

He drew back the machete.

Paused.

Better to eliminate Will now? Or would *two* missing Americans cause too many complications?

Perhaps he should allow Will to go back to camp. Report that there was nobody here. The tourists could refocus their efforts elsewhere. Perhaps it could still be salvaged, his place here in these mountains. His home.

Unless Will knew already. Unless he, too, was a spy.

Rain battered them. Washed over his bare torso. Beaded

in the hair of his arms, chest, shoulders. Ran down the arc of upheld steel.

Will started away. Blade raised, the man followed, his steps silent in the soft earth.

His hand tensed around the wooden handle.

He stopped. Watched the American move away. Five paces. Now ten.

He sidestepped and disappeared between two trunks.

When Will shuddered and cast a glance over his shoulder, only trees stared back through the downpour.

25

Gales ruffled the canopy, letting through blasts of rain so dense that at intervals Eve felt underwater. Stumbling downhill, she wiped at her eyes, struggling to see. The drops stung like grit flung against her cheeks.

Fortunato pointed downslope. *'Look!'* he shouted. *'See?'*

Through a jagged veil of trees, she spotted movement. A vinyl banner flapped loosely against a thatched palm roof, the cheery yellow letters undulating into view: DÍAS FELICES ECOLODGE™. The cantina.

A screech of rent wood blasted her eardrums. Fortunato leapt at her, knocking her aside as a bough crashed to the ground, obliterating her last footprints.

She pulled herself up on throbbing legs.

They leaned on each other, half skidding, half falling through the brush to the sturdy bamboo boardwalk. As they reached it, a figure staggered out of the haze toward them and Eve yelped, grabbing Fortunato's sleeve and backing away.

Will.

She hadn't allowed herself to register just how worried she was until she recognized his form, stooped and winded. They embraced, his cheek cold and stiff against hers.

'Jay?' she shouted in his ear.

He shook his head, steering her down the walkway

after Fortunato. As they neared the center of the lodge, Neto stepped out from Harry and Sue's sturdy two-story hut and flagged them down, his mouth moving but the words lost to the storm. They barreled through the door and shut it, the roar dropping by a factor of five. Given the fancier hut's solid adobe walls and actual roof, it was clear why the others had herded in here.

The interior glowed unevenly from a few well-positioned gas lanterns – the generator must have gone out in the storm. Eve's eyes moved hopefully across the uplit faces, but Jay's was not among them. Everyone looked ragged with worry. At their entrance Claire had pulled herself to her feet, clinging to one of the bedposts, her braces resting on the floor at her side. Gripping her stomach, Sue rocked herself autistically, Harry leaning over her, hugging her shoulders. Fortunato crossed to Concepción, who was huddled in the back with three other *indígeno* workers, and embraced her.

'We had to call off the search,' Lulu said. 'Did you find any sign of Jay?'

Will shook his head. 'Or the man. There was nothing in that house. No ID, no papers, no mail. Like the guy doesn't *exist*.'

'We reached the *alcalde*,' Eve said. 'But his satellite phone won't work in the storm. He's taking a report to San Bellarmino in the morning.'

'With fallen trees and trail washouts, that could take *days*.' Neto threw up his hands. 'I told you that going there would accomplish nothing.'

'Not *nothing*.' She pulled the boy's crayon drawing from the soggy paperback, unfolded it, and held it toward Neto.

Neto's mouth wavered beneath the mustache, trying for words. The wind's howls abated, if slightly. The drumming on the roof grew less intense.

Drops from Eve's outheld arm tapped the floor. The drawing fluttered slightly in her grasp, but she kept it there, on display. Lulu looked from the picture to Neto and back to the picture. The stick-figure evil spirit with Theresa Hamilton in his grasp. The eager crocodile. That blue ring, sliding off.

Lulu took two steps toward her husband, her head on aggressive tilt, her tone low and stern. 'Manuel *told* you she got on that plane.'

A choking noise escaped Neto, and it took Eve a moment to realize: He was crying. He gasped and shuddered, his chest seizing. It was like watching a man who had never cried before and didn't know how. His legs collapsed, dropping him neatly into a sitting position at the base of the wall. 'I didn't know. I didn't know this happened to her. I thought . . . thought she got lost and died.' The words came in grunts and sobs. 'She was already gone. I just wanted her gone somewhere *else*. What was the difference? What was the difference?'

'So you *lied*.' Lulu's voice grew quieter, which only underscored its fierceness. 'About Manuel getting her on the plane in Huatulco.'

He nodded, tears streaming. The others, shocked into silence.

'Who packed her clothes?'

'I threw them away. I saw her leaving that night. She was out of her head, crazy, searching horror stories on the Internet –'

'*What* horror stories?' Eve asked. 'The ones you deleted?'

'I don't know. Yes. Killers and violence and death – I didn't *read* them. She was being . . . I thought she was being hysterical. I told her not to go off into the jungle at night. But she wouldn't stop. And she didn't come back. I searched for her all the next day and night.'

'When I took the group overnight to Oaxaca City?' Lulu made a fist in the blond hair at her nape, her knuckles bloodless. 'You said you weren't feeling well –'

'I was sick all day. I *was* sick. In my stomach, my head. But I searched. I found her shoe. I knew she was dead.'

Lulu blinked, beads appearing on her eyelashes. 'You didn't *know*.' The last word packed with fury.

Sue's voice came as a blurry mumble. '. . . think I'm gonna throw up.'

Claire shuffle-walked through the workers, grabbed a trash can from the bathroom.

'The authorities didn't check the flight records?' Harry said. 'No one *confirmed* that Theresa Hamilton didn't get on that plane to Mexico City?'

'Flight records,' Neto repeated. 'This was just Manuel's plane.' He rolled his lips over his teeth and bit them. His head jerked with tiny breaths. 'The government put a *billion* dollars into this region. With a *b*. You think they wanted this to happen here any more than I did? In *this* economic climate? It takes *one* Natalee Holloway –'

'Theresa Hamilton,' Eve said.

Sue's back hunched, and then came the splatter of vomit in the trash can.

'So you covered it up with lies.' Lulu spoke through clenched teeth. 'And now Jay . . .'

Will leaned into the wall, his face pale.

Harry made a solemn gesture at the drawing in Eve's hand. 'We need to get out of here as soon as we can.'

'Before we find Jay?' Will said. 'Uh-uh. No way.'

Eve looked across the room at Fortunato. 'Is leaving an option in this weather?'

Fortunato started to respond, but Neto, from his exhausted slump on the floor, cut him off. 'In a storm like this, we get a *meter of rain* in a day. You can drown just by *breathing.*'

Eve kept her gaze on Fortunato. 'It seems to be slowing.'

Once more Neto spoke first. 'It will quicken again before morning. And the van will not make it across roads this muddy. Look, I'll get the generator back up in the morning and –'

'We could cram into the Jeep,' Harry said.

'And fit no luggage,' Neto said. 'You want to end your vacation like this, leave all your things –'

'*Vacation?*' Lulu said. 'You think they're gonna stay and – *what?* Have *fun?* Make artisanal *pinche* mezcal? Look at you, still trying to protect the lodge. For *what?* To avoid bad word of mouth on the Internet? A woman *died* here. Under *our* care. And Jay, too, now, gone. It's over. Harry is right. We will pack up and leave.'

Neto kept his head bowed, unable to meet Lulu's unwavering stare.

Eve said, 'Fortunato? What do you think?'

Fortunato glanced nervously at the tourists, then at Neto. Without looking up, Neto waved a hand. 'Tell them, Fortunato.'

'Very dangerous for to travel in *tormenta* at night,' Fortunato said.

Sue lifted her sweaty face from the brim of the bucket. 'More dangerous than waiting here? With that *man* out there somewhere?'

'He's one guy,' Claire said. 'And we are twelve strong.'

Battle lines drawn. The rain had quieted to a light tapping on the roof. But sporadic rumbling made clear that the storm was far from over. They endured the semi-quiet uncomfortably, eyes averted.

Harry's hand continued making small circles on his wife's back. Finally he cleared his throat, straightened his spine. 'Okay. I hate to say this – God *knows* I hate to say this – but I'll be the bad guy since no else is willing to.' He half turned to Will. 'In all likelihood' – his nostrils flared – 'Jay is already dead.'

Will said, 'Watch your mouth, old man.'

'You can't say that,' Claire told Harry. 'You don't know that any more than this jackass' – a thumb jerk in Neto's direction – '*knew* that Theresa Hamilton was lost instead of being murdered and fed to a fucking crocodile.'

Harry held up his hands. 'Look, we have to face facts. The odds are –'

'What odds would you take if Sue went missing?' Will said.

'– Jay is *gone*, whether he was injured or got lost on his own or that man took him. Especially now, given this storm. We have done *everything* we can for him –'

Will came off the wall, finger-jabbing at Harry. 'I don't recall *you* doing shit.'

'– and the time has come for us to get down off this mountain.'

'That isn't even a *choice*,' Will said. 'We can't go anywhere. It's pitch-black out there, and we're in the middle of a fucking *tropical monsoon*.'

Harry tightened his grip around Sue's shoulders. 'We're leaving at first light. Storm or no storm.'

Claire wove her arms across her chest, her cheeks rouged with anger. 'Jay or no Jay.'

'That's right.'

Will's focus swung to Eve. 'And you? Where are you in all this?'

Considerations flipped in her mind like quick-dealt cards. No satellite connection and a seven-year-old at home. Loyalty to Jay. The feeling she'd had, minutes ago, of breathing water instead of air. It seemed unthinkable to tell Will, *Sorry, we're leaving your best friend to a maelstrom and a maniac.* Yet as a mother she had responsibilities beyond Jay – beyond even herself.

Her delay lasted only a second or two, but it felt interminable.

'There's nothing to decide until the morning,' she said.

Will shook his head and turned away. She felt awful, deflated, and yet there was nothing else she could think to say.

'Everyone grab the basics from their huts and meet back here,' Harry said. 'We should stay together.'

Lulu coughed out a single note of disgust, seized the crayon drawing from Eve's hand, and threw it at her

183

husband. It fluttered to the floor. She walked out, slamming the door behind her.

Eve paused over the drawing, which had settled a few inches from Neto's feet. 'She deserved better than that.'

Neto pinched his eyes, tears leaking around his fingers and thumb.

She left him there on the floor.

Dark clouds bunched, belching lightning at the horizon. The wind and rain had ceased, though the air still felt wet and heavy, thick with a sense that the worst was yet to come, that the storm had drawn back into itself only to ready for the next charge. Slugs pulsed along the walkway, but for once not an insect buzzed about her.

Eve jogged to her hut and started grabbing items at random – change of clothes, dry sneakers, bag of toiletries. It wasn't until she raised her face to the bathroom mirror that she realized she was crying.

She walked around the pony wall and sat on the bed, then lay back partway on the pillows, her stiff lower back complaining, her feet throbbing. The mattress sagged and creaked. Tears streamed down her temples. She thought of Theresa Hamilton lying in this bed, her journalist brain at work, piecing together a picture that no one else wanted to see. Neto had cleaned out her clothes, deleted her Internet searches, tried to *expunge* her.

What *had* Theresa been looking into with those Internet searches? *Killers and violence and death*, Neto had said.

Eve closed her eyes, put herself with Theresa Hamilton in the chair before the admin-shack computer. Staring at that glowing screen, sandwiched between the credit-card scanner and the battered printer.

Eve's eyes flew open.

Her racing mind fastened on one of the photographs from the digital camera – the shot of Lulu with her arm around Theresa's neck. Based on the time stamp, the picture had been snapped the day after Theresa's sighting of the man dragging the *indígena* into his canyon house. Theresa looked distracted, either by the abuse she'd witnessed or the night expedition to come. Eve recalled the wan smile captured on Theresa's face. The tenseness of her wide jaw. The thin sheaf of papers clutched to her chest.

Printouts. From an Internet search.

She'd gone to Neto, as Eve had, with her concerns, and Neto had disregarded her, tried to dissuade her. But that hadn't stopped Theresa. She'd kept on with her investigation. She'd made her own plan. In the photo she'd held the papers tight to her body so as to conceal the text. She didn't trust anyone to believe her anymore.

Which meant she might have hidden those printouts, maybe in this very hut.

Eve was on her feet, tugging the wardrobe from the wall with a screech. Nothing behind. She searched the toilet tank, beneath the nightstand, in the cracks between the bamboo walls.

Leaning to check behind the door, she paused, a notion scratching at the base of her skull. The rain was still on pause, but thunder rolled through the earth, rattling the floorboards beneath her soles.

With measured steps she walked back to the bed. Parted

the mosquito netting. There on the side of the mattress was that split in the ticking, held together poorly with duct tape. She remembered Neto firming the tape to the fabric with a self-conscious smile when he'd first showed her the room: *Make sure no bugs crawl in there.*

She gripped the curled end of the tape, the back side barely sticky, and peeled it off. Foam crowded the burst seam, innards welling from a cut. She shoved her hand in up to the forearm and groped around the worn batting. Her fingertips struck something – yes, paper.

The thin sheaf she extracted was yellowed and damp. The ink of the first page had bled, rendering it illegible. Her fingernail lifted the corner, and she stripped off the top sheet, revealing an article printed off thedailynews-cairo.com.

Her breath grew louder until it was all she could hear. Thunder registered faintly, something from another world. She blinked once, hard, and refocused.

A sullen man glowered up from the poor-quality news photograph. Massy shoulders. Wispy beard. Burn tissue gnarling jaw and neck.

The heading labeled it an intel shot from an unnamed Egyptian jail in 1998. He looked decades younger in the photo, certainly, his forehead unlined, the bushy beard devoid of gray, and yet his bearing still held an overlord's gravitas.

The caption at last provided a name to go with the face.

Bashir Ahmat al-Gilani.

The Bear of Bajaur.

26

Candlelight licked at the dark corners of the cramped room. A gas lantern remained on the table, dimmed. Bashir leaned forward, letting Theresa Hamilton's camera dangle from a strap. It spun like an American Christmas ornament over the big man's face. Jay Rudwick – he'd given his name – stared up from the floor. His arms bound. His torso as well. Thighs, knees, ankles. And throat. The mat beneath him had been replaced by the piece of plywood Bashir used for target practice. Jay's pinned silhouette overlay the human outline.

'Who sent you to look for me?' Bashir asked.

'No one sent me.' Quick, shallow breaths. The jaw hung awkwardly. Slightly askew. Dried blood lipsticked the corners of his mouth. 'I wasn't *looking* for you.'

'You merely happened to see me. From up there. Looking down.'

'*I* wasn't looking.'

'Who then?'

'I don't know. I don't know who.'

Jay Rudwick had no training in counterinterrogation. This much was clear. He was fragile and untested, like most Americans. Throw a stone and they shatter. This was good on many counts.

Bashir nodded once, a show of forbearance. 'Who else has seen the pictures in this camera?'

'No one.' Jay ran his tongue across his chalky lips. 'Listen –'

'No one else saw my picture in the camera?'

'No. I just – it was found. It's no big deal. No one cares. If you just let me go, nothing will happen. You can let me go.'

'It was found. You did not find it.'

Jay's pupils glimmered in the faint light. Tears pooled like mercury in the crevice of his nose.

'Who found it?'

'I don't . . . No one.'

'No one found it.' Bashir shifted his weight. The floor creaked. 'Someone is gathering information. About me, about Theresa Hamilton. You will tell me everyone in your group who has discussed me.'

Jay closed his eyes, and wet tracks forded his lips.

'Do they know who I am?' Bashir asked.

Jay's chest jerked beneath the strap. Hyperventilating. This too was good.

'N-no. Who are you?'

Bashir set down the camera. Walked into the other room. Returned. His machete now swinging by his knee.

Jay stiffened, the board creaking. 'Listen, please, you can let me go. You *can*. You can just let me go, and nothing will happen.'

'Nothing will happen,' Bashir repeated. 'Yes.'

He lifted the glass chimney from the lantern. Crouched, giving Jay his broad back. He ran the tongue of the flame along the machete's edge. Rising heat prickled the hair poking through the gnarled skin at the edge of his jaw, phantom nerves misfiring.

'What are you doing? What – Why are you – Listen, listen. Just wait, okay? Wait a second?'

Bashir rose, his left knee cracking as it did. He stood over Jay and spoke softly, as always. 'You will die. That much is decided. Either you will answer my questions and die quickly with a stab to the heart. Or you will die days or weeks from now. That will be worse.'

'What? Wait, I – No. *No.* That's not – That can't be possible. I'm from Seattle. I'm a fucking *day trader*, okay?'

Bashir freed one of Jay's arms. Jay did not struggle or resist. His eyes saucers. He gave his arm, limp, over to his captor. Between Jay's arm and ribs, Bashir threaded a strap, cinching it just above the biceps. Tight. Jay stared at the tourniquet. Uncomprehending eyes.

'I brought you here to work on you properly, with respect. There are specific ways we must fight, and we must kill in accordance with the Prophet, may God's prayers and blessings be upon him. This makes us better than you. You are animals.'

Jay tried to pull his head away. Hair scraping along the plywood. Eyes straining. The strap bit into his throat, causing him to cough. 'Wait a minute. You're . . . *what*? You can't be *here*. This is *Mexico*.'

'I, too, am often amazed by the strangeness of life.'

'This makes no sense. You're supposed to be in Fallu-jah, sawing off people's heads and –'

'Al-Zarqawi was a butcher fanatic. We do not slaughter innocents or torture. We do not mutilate corpses.'

A hoarse whisper: '*I'm* an innocent.'

'No.'

'*This* is torture.'

'No.'

It was not torture. It was Allah guiding him, using his arm as a weapon. His hand would become Allah's will. He would feel the warmth of love in his chest as he acted. Every stroke of the hot, sharp sword would be in compliance with the wishes of the Prophet, *salallahu alayhi wasalam*. After, he would feel cured of a sickness.

'Then why . . . why is my arm tied off?'

'I will very cleanly sever your opposite limbs as is prescribed by the Qur'an. Your right arm above your elbow. And then your left leg above the knee.' He paused. Let his words work. 'Unless.'

'What? What? Unless *what*?'

He rose. 'You will excuse me. It is time for my night prayer.'

'No. *No no no*. Hang on. Please? Listen – Please can you . . . ?'

Bashir walked outside. Wet, hot air enfolded him. Clouds gathered. Soon they would open again. A few birds called tentatively, but the jungle had grown quiet. The animals awed into silence by the sky's fury. The sound of dripping filled the canyon. Water draining from every surface.

A bucket sat beneath the corner of the house, filled with runoff from the roof. Here he would make his ablutions. He set down the machete. Dipped his hands in and scrubbed them front and back. Scraped his nails up his wrists. The icy water brought him back to the Hindu Kush, where between missions he performed *wudu* with the freezing melt of mountaintop snow. Cleansing himself for contact with the Qur'an.

The distraction with the American had put him past his usual time for praying *salat*. It was still full dark, and the sun was well past the required eighteen degrees below the horizon, so he was within the valid window to perform the night prayer. Even so, he preferred not to delay the *isha* past the first third of the night. He had made enough compromises here.

These compromises, they were necessary. He was allowed to lie for self-protection. To change his outward guise. To shield. He wore no prayer cap here, no pajama-like *shalwar qameez*. He trimmed his beard. What mattered was that he kept hate in his heart. Nurtured it. Protected the flame so it burned day and night.

Cupping his hand, he brought up a mouthful of water so cold that his teeth throbbed. He scrubbed his finger across the front. Back to the molars. Then shoveled water up his nose. Cleared each nostril with a blow. He washed his face. Forehead to eyes to chin. Again. Again. Making every part clean. Every part pure.

As a young child, he had once taken a shortcut in his ablutions. Spent insufficient time wiping his hair with water. When he'd moved to touch the Qur'an, his mother had called him over to the kitchen. She was cooking stew. She'd asked for his hand, pulled a spoon from the boiling pot, and dropped it into his palm.

The jungle had always been home. His childhood village was two hours east of Sukkur in southern Pakistan, on the wild brink of India. A tribal region, rich with religious recruiting. The madrasas offered free board, clothing, food. He was sent. By the age of twelve, he'd memorized the Qur'an in its entirety. In a Deobandi seminary, he was exposed to the teachings of ibn Othaimeen and ibn Baz, the Saudi scholars who would provide inspiration for the global jihad to come. There was a great excitement in the sixties and seventies, a return to faith. An Islamic revival. During this time Bashir let his fledgling beard grow long and began eating with his thumb and two fingers, as did the Prophet, praise and glory be to him.

His diligence and rigor were noted. As a fifteen-year-old, he was asked to Saudi Arabia. At university in Jidda, in the lecture hall of the theologian Abdullah Azzam, he first met Usama. An economics student, bin Laden struck him as simple-minded and religiously unsophisticated. An amateur. But a rich amateur, whose resources would one day be required. When Azzam was fired in 1979 for issuing a fatwa against the Soviet invasion, Bashir was brought to a different campus in Islamabad. The curriculum there was equally vigorous, yet more practical. Martial arts. Tactics. Strategy. In May the boys were trucked into Afghanistan. They would return in the fall. Their summer school was fighting in the jihad.

It was there that Bashir found his calling.

More precisely in the training camps. Plastics, land mines, TNT, Semtex – he learned to identify explosives by feel, by taste. The puttylike give of C4. The sweet glycerin of dynamite. Training was vigorous. Accidents happened, some more altering to one's appearance than others. Here he learned to sprint up mountains. To carry boulders so large he sank into the earth under the weight of them. To stalk without shoes, silently, shaping his foot to each stone. To crawl through rivers cold enough to turn flesh to rubber. He slept in a sleeping bag stained from carrying corpses out of battle.

Now and then the Saudis drifted through, soft and rich. They dozed late in the mornings, shot guns at the stars at night. But they left money. Money was good. Bashir learned not to trust the Afghans themselves, who were in love with war. Or the Yemenis, who desired to be martyred above all else. But the rest became his brothers, and when they clasped hands and bumped chests and shoulders in greeting, he felt for them a pious devotion.

By his third year, he had grown too valuable to return to campus. The rugged Hindu Kush, with its thick forest and thorny bushes, its mountain haze and fast streams, it felt like home. An incredible labyrinth that stretched across the lines of the map to the Arabian Sea, on to the Indian Ocean, back up to China. A magical veil behind which the mujahedeen drifted. Hid. And attacked. Bashir came to know the smaller ranges as well as he knew the hairs on the back of his hand. Spin Ghar and Tora Bora. Suleman and Toba Kakar. And Bajaur. A staging ground from which Bashir launched raid after raid.

He led countless small operations and three major battles against the Godless Communists. He became a militia commander. He became fully blooded.

He became the Bear of Bajaur.

Not a name he chose. The Soviets called him that. A sign of respect. He would have chosen 'The Lion.' But that would have been vanity. A sin.

He released his thoughts of home. Let them drift away. Bent over the bucket in another jungle in another hemisphere, he continued his ablutions. Scooped water up his forearms. Scrubbed his elbows. The top of his head. Dug his wet fingers in his ears and twisted this way and that. With dripping hands he reached past the band of his loose-fitting cotton pants and spent ample time cleaning there. From inside he could hear the American's voice, pleading to the walls – 'No one saw the camera. I swear. I swear it was just me, and I won't tell anyone anything if you let me go.' Bashir sat to wash his feet, sawing the blade of his hand between each toe and the next. When he rose, he felt pristine and righteous. Picking up the machete, he started back to the house.

By the time the Soviet dogs fled from Afghanistan, jihad ran in his veins. He battled in Kashmir. Fought at Usama's side in Sudan. Joined the civil war in Algeria. For much of the nineties, Bashir was captured and escaped. Jailed and released. The Pakistani police held him for five months. Starved him. Kept him seated in a chair for weeks, dousing him with water every time he drifted off. He gave no names. More precisely, he turned over only the false names he'd been trained to release. He spent two stints in dirty Egyptian jails. Whipped with cables. Shocked with electricity. He survived a year in the inhumane jails of the Northern Alliance, where they bound him like an animal and hung him from his wrists and ankles, dislocating his shoulder again and again. Always he found his way free and back to the holy struggle.

With every conflict it grew clearer that the Americans were interested only in keeping the Islamic world crushed under their heel. Their reach extended into every corner of the Holy Land. There was al-Aqsa in Jerusalem, lost to the Crusader-Zionist alliance. Medina and the sacred house of Allah in Mecca, home of the glorious Ka'ba, occupied by US troops. Ousting apostate Muslim tyrants would not be sufficient to liberate the House of Islam. More drastic action would be required.

A new way took shape. A shift in focus from the enemy within, the near enemy, to the far enemy. Transnational jihad.

The United States was the head of the snake. So the head of the snake they would strike.

The Base: a movement dispersed across nations, hidden and yet present everywhere, like Allah. No center of gravity. The enemy would have nowhere to aim a mortal blow.

Word whipped across the land, a fire finally given oxygen. Usama was a deft self-promoter. Obsessed with international media. Careful to dye his beard before the cameras. He was the face. But Ayman al-Zawahiri, in American terms, was the CEO. The last emir of the Egyptian Islamic Jihad. A qualified surgeon who spoke English and French. Wisdom fell from his lips. The real direction came from him. In one of the great honors of his life, Bashir swore his *baya*, his fealty, to him.

The ideas of al-Zawahiri and the resources of bin Laden opened a new world of possibilities. Back before the United States knew that there was a war, the Base was busy recruiting a new generation of mujahedeen. Battle-hardened warriors who had felt the sting of shrapnel. They remained in Afghanistan in an uneasy alliance with the Taliban. The Taliban were extremists who did not follow the true law of Islam. They were innovators. Too zealous in how they tortured and killed. They overreached shari'a law. Condoned public decapitations and other atrocities. Above all, they were cowards who wished to rule their tiny sandbox and little more.

Something was needed to force their hand.

Nineteen jihadis. Twelve box cutters.

It was sufficient. The Americans waded into the Afghan swamp. Bashir was promoted and became one of al-Zawahiri's operational chiefs. Once again he reigned over the mountainous passes. His name became a thing of lore among American elite forces. The Bear of Bajaur.

But quickly the noose tightened. One by one the Arab nations turned against them. Yemen, Pakistan, Syria – even Iran – drew their nets around operatives. Some permitted drone attacks. Leadership was gutted.

And then the infighting began. Hostility between factions. Commanders clashing with their counterparts. Panicked Taliban delegations piping up. Chiefs from major jihadi groups denounced Usama. Accused him of heresy, of treachery. At times they seemed more like schoolgirls than holy warriors.

In 2007 public outcry forced Usama to apologize. To scold his followers for fanaticism. To urge them to avoid the extremism displayed by the butchers in Iraq. Dirty linen aired for the world to see. Fortunately, the world was not interested in seeing this. The world viewed them as one, gathered behind a single face. Usama's.

One crisp winter day, Ayman al-Zawahiri sent for Bashir. The journey took several days beneath skies luminous with bombs. Bashir arrived at the stark bunker anxious and hungry. He was greeted with a kiss on each cheek by al-Zawahiri. And some dire news. Cracks and rifts had spread through the Base. It was crumbling. Definitive action needed to be taken before it was too late. Pakistan alone provided hope. Bhutto had been assassinated. Attacks on the urban centers were pushing the state machinery to the breaking point.

This success could be duplicated.

Bashir would go to Mexico. He would put the operation into place one porous border away. Wait until the time was right. Then execute.

Now here he was. No guns, no grenades. A man with a machete. He preferred it. The simplicity. The sword of Muhammad. The hand of Allah.

A light patter had started up. Lightning sparked. He strode through the door into his house. Jay's mouth immediately resumed its movement.

'Okay, I *wasn't* the one there. On the cliff. It wasn't me. Wait – I swear. Just wait. I don't know who it was, but it wasn't me. And the camera – no one saw the camera. I found it myself, okay? But I didn't show anyone. Hang on. Please? Just . . . please? I'm telling you –'

Bashir walked into his small bedroom. Shut the door. He could hear Jay beyond, words turning to sobs.

His prayer rug unfurled neatly, facing Mecca. He stood, taking care not to look at his feet. Not during prayer. Folded his arms. Prayed the first two *rak'ah* aloud. His voice drawn out into almost-song.

Jay's pleading penetrated the thin walls. Bashir prayed louder.

He knelt, fixing his eyes only on the spot where his forehead would kiss the ground. He sensed the ghosts of his brothers all around him, praying with him as in the camps. The Chechens with their milky skin and clear blue eyes. Now dead. The Arabs with their schooling and untamable spirits. Dead. Tajiks, Kashmiris, Uzbeks with no education but hands made for weapons. All dead.

He finished the *rak'ah*. Next was the Retreat. He retrieved his Qur'an. Gripped it so tightly that his fingers cramped. He set it before him on a mat of twigs so it would not touch the ground. He sat again, legs crossed. Pulled a sheet of linen over his head, covering both his face and the Qur'an. He could see nothing but the words of Allah.

The sobs from the next room faded. There was only the sound of his own murmurs. He rocked, meditative. Trancelike. The world did not exist aside from him and the holy book. Fifteen minutes passed. Or thirty.

He arose, refreshed. Beside the prayer rug, the machete waited.

He opened the door. Returned to the lantern. Heated the machete's blade on the exposed flame.

Jay tried to raise his head from the plywood. His voice hoarse from weeping. 'Okay,' he said. 'I'll tell you. I'll tell you everything.'

Bashir went to his captive. Crouched over him.

He said, 'We can agree that this is wise.'

27

Curled printouts in hand, Eve stormed down the bamboo walkway, rain tapping her face. Up ahead she saw two figures. In a show of privacy, Neto and Lulu had convened outside the adobe dwelling in which the others were gathered. She shouted at him as he stood with his head bowed, water running down his face. Her words were indistinct but the body language clear. Lulu marched inside, slamming the door hard enough that it wobbled back open. Neto gave the gray sky a doleful look and slid in after her.

Eve approached, paused outside the door, and drew in a wet breath that tasted of leaves. In her mind's eye, she saw the movie-heroine version of herself, standing firm, vowing to search the jungle single-handedly, to save Jay and vanquish the bad guy. The curled papers trembled in her hand, a patchwork dossier on surely the most dangerous man she'd ever encountered face-to-face. Someone like Bashir Ahmat al-Gilani could visit a kind of violence upon them that seemed almost unimaginable. In fact, he'd spent a lifetime mastering the skills to deliver harm with proficiency. As a nurse she was all too familiar with the fragility of life, the cosmic rug-pull, the shadow on the X-ray, but she felt now a sudden, bracing reacquaintance with her own impermanence. She was a speck in the wind, a sidewalk ant in the shadow of a colossal being armed with morbid curiosity and a magnifying glass. Possibilities swarmed her.

She pictured someone else waking Nicolas in the morning, driving him to swim practice. Or him disembarking at the international terminal in Amsterdam, suitcase in hand. Or – *Stop*.

Exhaling, she shoved through the door. The wan faces lifted as one. Will looked up from slotting D batteries into a Maglite flashlight. Sue lay pillow-propped on the bed, her lips pale, gummed at the corners, Harry stroking her forehead.

'What?' Claire said. '*What?*'

Eve tossed the badly printed articles onto the bed.

The others huddled around the mattress, snatching pages from hand to hand, tilting their heads to read. The news settled over them heavily. Sounds of paper crinkling, of throat-stifled exclamations. Lulu threw down one of the pages and stepped back, muffled a cry with her fist.

'You're kidding me,' Claire said. 'You are fucking *kidding me* with this Clash of the Civilizations shit *here*.'

'What if there are more of them?' Sue said. 'An army or . . . or a terrorist training camp?'

'There is no *army*,' Neto said with disgust. 'No *camp*. It is him alone. Me, Lulu, the *indígenos* – I think we would have heard if these hills were crawling with crazy Arabs.'

'Thanks,' Claire said, 'but you no longer have a right to an opinion.'

Harry said, 'If this man is who these articles say, he doesn't want to be – *can't be* – seen by anyone. He wouldn't allow it.'

'He thinks *Jay* saw him,' Lulu said.

A morbid air hung over the mattress, the scattered printouts. Jay's disappearance had raised so many questions. The face glaring up from the Egyptian booking photo provided the answers.

'Who says he hasn't figured out that he's on *our* radar by now?' Sue asked.

'I'm sorry, Will,' Harry said. 'Given what we know now, there's a better-than-strong likelihood that Jay's not alive anymore. And even if he was, *we* couldn't help him.'

Will cast an imploring look at one person after another. He didn't seem to like what he read in their faces. 'We can't leave him,' he said. 'We cannot leave him.'

Harry pointed at the damp papers, that face glowering up from the rippled page. 'This man is number twenty-three on the FBI's most wanted list. He's one of the world's leading experts at mountain warfare. If he decides to come after *us*, we can't do a damn thing to stop him. We've got to get out while we still can.'

Fortunato stepped forward from the group of *indígenos*, his solemn nod directed at Neto and Lulu. 'Go,' he said. 'Before the *tormenta* resume. I will close down *aquí.*'

Neto glared holes through him. Fortunato drew himself up a bit straighter and met Neto's gaze. For the first time here in the lodge, he looked as he had when he was leading Eve through the jungle, a young man confident of his place on the mountain. Neto broke off eye contact first.

'Yes,' Lulu said. 'Okay.'

'That's it?' Will's voice cracked. 'No one?' He looked across at Claire.

'I haven't given up on Jay,' she said. 'Either.' She stood tall, despite the braces.

Eve felt something inside her crumble away.

'How do we decide, then?' Neto asked.

'A vote,' Harry said. 'Who wants to leave now?'

He, Sue, and Lulu lifted their hands. Neto shook his head, kept his arms folded.

Acid flicked at the walls of Eve's stomach. Her chin quivered. Seven years of memories distilled into one: a view from the doorway, Nicolas in pajamas and a cowboy hat playing Legos on the carpet, early-morning light suffusing his still-closed blinds.

Thanks for letting me sleep, Little.

When he looks up, the hat bobbles loosely around his little-boy head, knocking his glasses askew. *Hi, Big. I'm hungry.*

Eve raised her hand, too.

Will and Claire looked at her, shocked.

'What the fuck, Eve?' he said. 'You're just gonna *abandon* Jay?'

'I have a boy,' Eve said. 'At home. I don't care if there's a tempest. I don't care if we have to leave all our stuff behind. I am going to him *now*.' She met Will's stare. 'Understand?'

'Four to three,' Harry said. 'I'm sorry.'

The tension came out of Will as if someone had given slack to the strings holding him up. He sank to the bed, shoulders hunching.

'Passports,' Lulu said. 'The Jeep. Three minutes.'

Neto caught Eve's arm at the door. He spoke quietly,

through clenched teeth. 'You *had* to,' he said. 'Had to keep looking, keep prying. Look what you've done.'

She shook him off roughly and rushed to her hut. Halfway there, she leaned over the bamboo railing and vomited into the lush greenery.

28

The Wrangler coasted more than drove, the tires clinging to the trail, every turn a minor miracle. They were squeezed into the seats, sitting in laps as they had on their way to the rafting trip. That sunshine-bathed journey downriver, with its paddle high fives and seating quibbles, seemed from another life. The air now felt crowded with limbs and faces, breath and body heat, the sultry jungle encasing them like a green-tinted hothouse.

Eve sat in Will's lap, and he wrapped her midsection with his arms, helping prevent her shoulder from knocking the glass with each lurch. His touch, firm and proficient, held none of the warmth she had known it to hold. She didn't blame him.

Sue lay in the cargo hold, curled in the fetal position, murmuring, 'I don't feel so good.'

A few branches kissed the doors. Vines slap-skidded up the windshield, their residue washed away by the quickening rain. Neto drove on. They skipped over a bump and landed, the Jeep rearing, throwing mud but going nowhere.

'Stop!' Will shouted. 'Stop! The back tires are spinning. You're just gonna dig us deeper.'

He shoved at the door, and Eve half fell from his lap into the rain. He was at her side, searching the fringe of the jungle. 'Look for a branch. We need something for the wheels to grab hold of.'

She found one and dragged it over to him. Then they were on their knees in the sludge, wedging it beneath the stuck tire to provide traction, rain splattering their backs.

He worked the branch in and out, ramming it farther beneath the tread. Eve reached over and touched his arm, and he did not recoil.

'I get that you're mad at me,' she said. '*I'm* mad at me.'

'I'm not mad at *you*.' He gave the branch a last violent shove, then paused to wipe his hands on his thighs. 'I'm mad that you're right.'

Heavy drops plunked the trail, kicking up buttercups of mud, setting the ground dancing. They watched the small-scale ballet for a moment, Will blinking against the moisture. 'He's dead.'

She stayed crouched, watching him. A tuning fork of lightning appeared in the visible sky, all at once, as if it had been pressed through the clouds of a single piece. Thunder rattled her rib cage.

Will rose, offered her a dripping hand. She took it and rose.

He knocked on the side of the Jeep. 'Try it now. Slow.'

Neto eased on the gas, and the rear right tire spun over the moist bark of the branch, then finally snagged, the Jeep lurching out of its rut at an angle.

Eve and Will climbed back in, and the jalopy ride resumed. She felt his hands tighten around her waist, felt his forehead press to the spot between her shoulder blades, and she understood his grief and need for contact. She gripped his wrist tightly at her belly. Claire noticed and for once kept her thoughts to herself. For a few minutes, the rocking ride lulled Eve into a false sense of calm.

Then the Jeep crested a rise, bucked like a horse, and slid sideways on a steep downhill. Lulu screamed. Eve's cheek slapped the window, and she reoriented to see a muddy sheet scrolling beneath the two right tires. Ahead and closing fast, a steep bank beyond which frothed the rising river.

The ball of Eve's stomach leapt up, crowding her throat. Time compressed and expanded simultaneously, the Jeep's slide seeming to last forever even as the remaining firm ground whipped beneath the chassis. She put both hands on the glass, trying in vain to push herself up, as though the added inches of buffer would help if they rolled into the river. As the lip neared, the Jeep slowed, slowed, plowing mud until there was none left, until Eve was staring directly down into the furious blast of the water and she knew that it was going to rush up to meet her.

Slowly, she came aware that they had stopped.

The right-side tires were perched at the very brink of the riverbank. Eve remained piled into the door, the window like ice against her brow, foaming white current filling her field of vision. Breaths jerked through her chattering teeth.

Claire kneed open her door, her metal brace hammering the panel, and they unpacked from the safe side of the Jeep. Eve slid across to get out, fighting panic until she felt her shoes sink into earth. Trying to calm her breathing, she took a step and then another just because she could.

Harry helped Sue from the back. 'Why'd you hit the brakes?' he barked at Neto. 'That sent us into a skid. Why'd you –'

He saw.

The narrow bridge ahead now met the road at a severe angle, the front section thrust upward on the right side, several feet higher than the ground. The middle and back of the bridge still held, giving the effect of a spiral that had run out of steam. Had Neto driven forward, the Jeep would've hammered over the raised tilt of the lip, then slid sideways off the bridge and plunged right into the river.

Neto clutched his hair, trudging forward. *'Puta madre.'*

Lightning strobed the canopy, chased immediately with rumbling. They circled up, getting doused.

'Is this the only bridge out of here?' Will shouted.

Lulu gave a jerky nod.

Eve flicked her head to where the road continued on the near side of the river, heading into rougher terrain. Fronds folded in all around, turning it into a tunnel. Past the bend, it might have run ten more feet or ten more miles. 'Can we get down that way?'

'There's a shallow run of river forty kilometers downstream that we can sometimes get across,' Lulu said. 'But not in this. Not now. No way.'

Eve followed Will to the bank, Claire walking at her side, gripping her arm for balance. A boulder the size of a Smart Car had smashed into the closest foundation and somehow wedged itself beneath the remaining length, giving it an inadvertent boost. That's what had knocked the portion of the bridge above it skyward, tilting the front section to an undrivable angle.

They regarded one another in the downpour. Gradually their focus shifted to the dense trunks all around.

Searching for *him*. Vines swayed, battered by the storm. Shadows flailed. Sue gave a faint wail. Claire lost her footing, and Eve grabbed her arm to keep her from going down.

Will moved first, shouting to Neto against the rain, 'Get that Jeep backed off the ledge!'

'What are you going to do?'

Will pointed down. 'If we can shove that boulder out into the current, the foundation'll drop and flatten out the bridge.'

'We can't get across without that foundation,' Neto said.

'The seven others are intact.'

'There is a reason they didn't design the bridge with seven foundations.'

'I'm an engineer –'

'You're a *sneaker* designer.'

'– and I promise you, this'll work. If you all get out of the Jeep to make it lighter and walk across first, I'll gun it across the front part of the bridge. If I go fast enough, it'll hold.'

Neto shook his head, drops of water flying from his black curls.

'What's the alternative?' Will flung a hand toward the boulder. 'He wants us here. That means we need to not be here.'

Lulu stepped in front of her husband. 'Get the Jeep ready,' she said. 'Or I will.'

Neto's hand clenched around the keys. He grimaced. Exhaled. When Lulu started back to the Jeep, he followed her.

Will leapt skillfully down the embankment, and Eve went after him, each footstep turning into a miniature mudslide. The white water had risen, claiming most of the flat ground at the river's edge, but a bar of pebbles thrust above the surface gave them a staging point. Eve reached it, her shoes grinding on the rocks. Almost immediately she was struck from behind, and she stumbled forward, nearly toppling into the current.

'Sorry!' Claire righted herself. 'Sorry.'

'What the hell are you doing down here?'

Claire held up a coiled vine. 'The river's too strong. We need to tie him off.'

'How are we gonna get you back up?'

'I can *crawl*.'

They knotted the vine around Will's waist, and Claire wrapped the other end around her forearm, sat back, and gouged her shoes into the pebbles, the metal braces driving up furrows. The steep rise behind them blocked the others from view, but they heard Neto and Harry shouting directives, the roar of the Jeep engine, the sound of tires spinning and going nowhere. The downpour continued, unrelenting.

Eve followed Will closer to the water, gripping the taut vine, his lifeline. Foam flicked at her legs. He looked back at her, his expression unreadable, then stepped tentatively into the river. Immediately, the torrent almost swept his leg out from under him, but Eve leaned against the vine and he dug in, pausing spread-legged to catch his breath. Cautiously, he waded to the bridge. The foundation had snapped, its upthrust length jam-balanced atop the boulder. He reached the rock, the current pressing his body against it. Fighting himself off the boulder with a vertical push-up, he hand-stepped around to the bank side to get better leverage. Water seethed up his back, pouring around his head. He misstepped, dropping chest-deep, and Eve felt the air leave her lungs.

He bobbed up again quickly, the river dropping to his waist, and gave a nervous smile. Eve coughed out a half laugh. Setting his weight and pressing his cheek to the boulder, he drove into it. The boulder remained, impervious. He stopped, dipped his shoulder like a lineman, and readied for another charge.

Claire screamed.

She was arched against the strain, the cords of her arms pronounced, mud slathering down the slope behind her. Her fists occupied, she flung her head to the right, again and again. It took a moment for Eve to grasp that she was gesturing upriver.

With dread, Eve turned. A rush of white, two feet taller than the surface – a second river riding the first.

Flash flood.

Her only point of reference was the Universal Studios tour she'd taken with Nicolas. The driver had stopped the trolley over a dry gulley, and some unseen hand had loosed a valve upstream. Barreling through the synthetic gorge, the flood had seemed an angry, living thing, gnashing and clawing to get at them. Hidden drains had saved the day, but the special-effects display had awed them in their seats, impressing upon them their absolute helplessness against the fury of nature.

She told her legs to unfreeze, and a moment later they listened. She yanked the vine to get Will's attention and pointed. Will traced the line of her arm to the coming water. His jaw went slack. He lurched for the bank violently. One hand shot up as he misstepped again, his sinking body twisting so he fell back and chest-hit the boulder with a hug. The big rock shifted, settling a few inches in its tentative bed, and Will howled.

He threw his torso away, only to snap into place against the boulder.

His leg was pinned.

29

The surge swept by, Eve leaping back as it washed over the pebble bar and knocked Claire into a sprawl. Using her arms, Claire tore up the muddy bank a few feet, out of the grasping reach of the water. Eve didn't quite get there. The force spun her into a half turn, the cold slapping through her clothes instantly, slamming the breath from her lungs. She set her legs against the current, driving toward the river's edge.

The wall of water smacked into Will, driving him under. He popped up, roaring. Water rose to his chest, his shoulders, shoals of tiny fish pinwheeling in the choppy rise. He sputtered, shouting for Eve.

Keeping to the shallower water near the edge, she scrambled toward the bridge, falling, rising, stumbling. Claire clawed along the bank, staying parallel, both fists gripping the vine to keep pressure on the line.

'My foot —' A mouthful of water gagged Will. He spit, reared his head up for more air.

Thigh-deep, Eve fought her way to him, testing each step. His slip had landed him against the downriver curve of the boulder, barely so, but enough that she'd have to rock the boulder against the weight of the current to free his foot. The physics of this took hold not as a thought but as a prickling beneath her skin.

His head was nearly a foot lower than hers; whatever

crevice had claimed his leg was deeper than she'd hoped. 'Hurry,' he told her, as if this weren't self-evident. *'Hurry.'*

Eve clambered across him, the river adhering her to the bones of his shoulder blades, her body and the water weight grinding him into the stone. But there was no quicker way to get where she needed to be. Though his breaths came in grunts, he didn't protest.

Once clear of his body, she smeared herself along the boulder, rolling into position. The compromised arch of the bridge overhead notched down the already dim glow of the gray sky a few more watts.

Balancing on her toes, straightening her back, she drove into the boulder with everything she had.

Not a millimeter of movement.

She might as well have been pushing a parked bus.

Will tried to shout something, but a swell washed over his face, leaving him sputtering. His head reared up again, his neck flexing. Eve shoved again, screaming into the effort, rock scraping her cheek.

Nothing.

A surge swept over Will's head. His arms rattled against the boulder. His uptilted face reemerged, an oval tilted to the sky, his gaping mouth sucking air.

Straightening her arms, Eve pushed herself up, shot a desperate look at the bank. Not a face in view above, all sound lost beneath the storm and the roar of the unseen Jeep, still trying for traction. Panic gripped her insides.

She turned to Claire. 'I can't move it!'

Face-first, Claire slid down the muddy bank, danger-ously close to the river's edge, grabbing a root that twisted up out of the mud like a human arm. Her legs trailed limply. Water snatched at her hair. The initial surge had been absorbed into the river, the upward creep of the surface now slower and somehow calmer, and yet none of the force had diminished.

'The current's too strong!' Eve shouted. 'It's too strong! There's no way!'

'You *have* to!' Will yelled. 'You –'

Water blanketed his face, a tranquil layering, glassy enough that there was virtually no distortion. His lips stayed barely submerged, his eyes open, his wavering mouth spread wide.

She stared down into his face. A two-inch dip of her head would have pressed the tip of her nose through the looking glass to touch his. She could see the tiny bubbles caught in his eyelashes, along his brow. His upraised arms kept on against the boulder as if detached from the rest of him, fingernails scraping the mossy bulges ineffectively.

He would die here, drowned in the top film of water, his mouth a thumb's width from air.

Eve pulled back, set her shoulder, and drove again, her muscles locked in a single note of strained stillness, calves to neck. She was sobbing.

Claire's voice sliced through the vortex of her thoughts: 'You have to push from the other side! *With* the current!'

A clump of spray leapt to disintegrate across Eve's face. She shook it off roughly, the wet tips of her hair lashing her eyes. 'That'll roll the boulder right over him. It could *kill* him.'

'Maybe it'll just shatter his leg. It's the only thing left. You *have* to.'

'I *can't.*'

Claire clung to the root on the bank, just beyond the awning of the buckled bridge. Though they were less than five feet apart, they had to shout to be heard.

'*Yes*. You're gonna get around the boulder. You're gonna shove with the weight of the river *behind* you.'

The river swelled, then dipped, letting Will's mouth break the surface. It spit and gulped, drawing air greedily with a sound like an inward moan, and then he was buried again.

'I can't crush him beneath this rock!'

'Get up. Get up and do it.'

Eve's tears mixed with the wet of the rain and river, her face awash. 'Why? Why do I have to do this?'

'*Because I can't!*' Claire screamed.

Her face twisted, her mouth crumpling. She was the kind of person whose face became unrecognizable when she cried. She lay sprawled downslope on her stomach, a flipped-over snow angel, her legs slanted uselessly up the bank.

Move.

Eve moved.

She dragged herself around the boulder until the river crawled up her back, splitting at her neck to shoot over either shoulder. The water had ceased being cold, or her body had ceased noticing. The boundaries between flesh and river had blurred; there was pressure and movement and nothing more. She lowered herself until her chin dipped beneath the surface, collapsed her hands above one breast, palms out, and propelled herself against the unforgiving stone.

It didn't budge.

She kept on, roaring, and at last it gave the faintest lift and the current caught, wedging in the crack and levering it further. The boulder reared up, rolling out of Eve's palms, and even above the rush of the torrent she heard a muffled cracking of bone.

As the boulder skip-rolled away, the jagged end of the foundation wavered in midair like the stump of a blown-off limb. The massive rock gained speed as it neared the paired beam and rocketed through in an explosion of splintered wood. The front end of the bridge canted, then shot downriver, stripping the deck from the foundations, pulling it behind like a snake taking to water.

The sudden absence of pushback sent Eve floundering onto her chest, and she paddled upright, searching for Will. A flesh-colored stripe fluttered beneath the surface, and she shot her hand after it and closed on an arm.

She splashed for the vine, came up with it, and yanked Will skyward. He broke the surface with a howl.

Claire towed them toward the bank, Eve dragging Will a few feet free of the river and dropping him heavily into a bed of mud. She collapsed beside him and lay panting, her breaths seemingly timed with his grunts of pain.

Four faces came visible above, peering down at them; the bridge's decimation had finally caught the attention of the others. Neto skidded toward them, shouting, his words sucked away by the wind.

Eve pushed herself onto her elbows and took note of the shard of bone lifted through the skin of Will's ankle.

30

Hideous.

But the rest of Will looked intact.

Eve and others stood around him like reeds rising out of the muddy riverbank, leaning into the incline, summoning strength and averting their eyes from the compound fracture that spelled bad news in any scenario, let alone this one.

Harry spoke first. 'C'mon now.' His creased face had hardened into a weathered resolve. Whereas Sue had seemed to fade into frailty, Harry wore his age now as something rugged and protective, the armor of experience.

Harry and Neto took point on dragging Will up the bank, gripping him under each armpit and towing him backward, his ass plowing through mud. He stayed bent stiffly, letting his legs trail and squeezing his thigh in an effort to hold the injured foot aloft. He nearly blacked out several times, his head lolling forward before a jolt or a bump snapped it upright.

Eve and Lulu each ducked under one of Claire's arms and tackled the slope. Claire was able to drive into the mud with them, and they reached the top, where the others had clustered around Will.

He was bellowing now, unashamed outbursts that drove the others into a low-level frenzy.

'Do something!'

'What do you want me to do, Lulu?'

'– open wound in the *jungle*,' Harry was saying. 'The infection risk if you don't –'

'At least get him out of the rain,' Sue called weakly from her slump in the Jeep, which, Eve noted, had been driven out of its rut by the lip of the bank.

'We've got to get him back to the lodge until this storm blows over,' Claire said.

Neto said, 'Do you have any idea how bumpy that road is?'

'I'm guessing *less* bumpy than the twenty miles downslope to the crossing that's not a crossing,' Claire said. 'Besides, Neto, what's the option? Leave him for dead like you left Theresa Hamilton?'

Rain lashed down. From her position at the periphery, between legs and hips, Eve saw only slices of Will. His hand making a fist in the mud. The small of his back, arched severely. A tremor shuddering the pale skin of his leg, causing that stick of bone to bob.

Eve locked onto that white shard, thrust up through the shin, and felt a great, unexpected settling. This she knew how to do.

She spoke, but no one heard her.

She cleared her throat, shouldered through to the middle, said, louder, 'I'm a nurse.'

The arguing stopped.

'First-aid kit in the Jeep,' she said. 'Bring it.'

Lulu backpedaled a few steps, then turned and ran.

'I need two branches this long,' Eve said. 'We're gonna make a splint, stabilize the ankle.'

'You may not have noticed,' Claire said, 'but his *bone* is sticking out.'

Eve crouched and took Will's foot gently in her hands, cupping his heel. He looked at her, breaths heaving his chest, his lips blue. 'Is this gonna hurt?'

'Yes,' she said, and tugged.

The pulling traction slotted the bone neatly back through the gash. Will's cry reached an inhuman pitch. He writhed in the mud, screaming.

She waited, but his foot kept its whitish hue. Lack of blood supply. Which meant, in all likelihood, a compressed artery.

She said, 'Your foot – pins and needles?'

He nodded.

'You're gonna want to brace yourself,' she said. 'I have to move the bone off your artery.'

His eyes were watering, but he nodded again.

She shifted her grip slightly, manipulating the bone. He kept his lips sealed, muffling his screams against the walls of his mouth. Another tiny adjustment and the skin of his foot pinked up.

Her hands stilled, holding the precise position for the splint. 'Okay,' she said. 'The worst is past.'

The others, Claire included, had taken an inadvertent step back. Without raising her head, Eve said, 'Where are my branches?'

They scrambled.

Lulu stumbled back with the first-aid kit, and Eve said, 'Eight hundred milligrams of ibuprofen. Let's get ahead of the swelling.'

As Lulu pinched Motrin from the white packets, Eve

immobilized the ankle on both sides with stout, snapped-off branch segments that Harry provided. She looked up at Neto. 'Gimme your shirt. Now.'

He stared at her with a mix of wonder and surprise, then tugged off his shirt. Rolling it, she used it as a stirrup, then wrapped the entire splint with an Ace bandage.

'No cold packs?'

Lulu poked in the first-aid kit. 'No.'

'He needs ice and elevation as soon as possible. Let's get him in the Jeep.'

'And go back to the lodge?' Sue said.

Eve nodded to where the bare foundations stuck up out of the river. 'Where else do you propose we go?'

Harry and Neto carried Will to the cargo hold and loaded him in. Eve sat in the rear, twisted over the seat back to hold Will's hand. The bags beneath his eyes were puffy and bloodshot, bulged out from the pressure of trying to hold the pain in.

The engine fired on, shuddering the Jeep, and Will let out a growl of pain through gritted teeth. Neto had the presence of mind to accelerate slowly at first so the wheels wouldn't spin, the vehicle crawling out of the muddy bank toward the road. Once they were moving, he stepped on it, and they fishtailed around, leaving the remnants of the bridge behind.

Claire shot a look back through wet, tangled bangs. 'That boulder didn't get there on its own.'

'Bullshit,' Neto said. 'He couldn't move a boulder that size. He's just a guy. Even if he is a terrorist, how would he do that?'

'How the fuck should I know?' Claire said. 'Am I trained in mountain warfare?'

An impulse pressed Eve to lift her eyes to the rear window and fix on the far side of the river.

His side.

A dark face watched from a bluff above, water dripping from a wispy fringe of beard.

Her throat contracted, choking off her air.

A pulse of lightning lit the thrashing landscape, and it took a moment for her brain to process that it wasn't a face at all, nor a beard, but a clump of moss hanging in a gnarled bough.

The tangled visage returned to shadow, and the Jeep lurched on into the headlight's tracks. Her breath returned, and she felt sensation creep slowly back into her body, not least of all the steady pressure of Will's grip crushing the bones of her fingers, anguish leaving his body, passing to hers.

The trees zoomed past the rain-spotted windows. The storm played games with perspective, making the jungle look perfectly flat, a wallpaper rendering. And then lightning would shock the tableau into 3-D, revealing its boundless depth.

They drove through a long stretch of darkness, the Jeep blazing a fresh trail across ground newly slathered over. Eve kept her hand in Will's, her eyes on the flickering trees. The air felt wet against her skin.

A spot of light winked at her from between the trunks, a stone's throw from the road. It vanished, then returned, stabbing her full in the pupils and proving she hadn't dreamed it.

'Stop the Jeep!' she shouted.

They skidded, plowing up trenches of mud. She knocked the glass with her knuckle, and the others saw it, too.

A flashlight.

It pivoted slightly, catching them directly in its glare.

Staring at them.

Neto opened the door.

Lulu said, 'Don't.'

He stepped out cautiously, keeping the door folded against his body like a shield. 'Hello? Do you need help?'

The beam remained aimed at them, sharp and unremitting.

Then, calmly, it turned away, bobbing back and forth in the invisible hand of its invisible carrier.

Breathless, they watched it vanish and reappear, moving steadily into the jungle until it vanished once more and stayed gone.

The downpour drummed soothingly on the soft top of the Jeep.

'We need to drive away,' Sue said. 'We need to –'

Neto said, 'Shh!'

A muted electronic chime wafted to them, so faint it might have been imagined. The wind shifted, bringing it more fully to their ears.

Tinny music.

At first I was afraid, I was petrified!

Will stiffened in the cargo hold. 'That's . . .'

At first I was afraid, I was petrified!

Eve said, 'Jay's ringtone.'

A swept-back whorl of moldy leaves ringed an oval patch of freshly turned earth the size of a surfboard. They were there in the jungle twenty yards off the road, all of them, regarding the ominous mound. Fighting a scream with every jolt, Will had hopped from trunk to trunk, and Sue had dragged herself along, not wanting to be left alone in the Jeep. It was best, they'd all concurred, that they stay together. Drops filtered through the leaves and fronds, tapping their bowed shoulders.

'Let's make sure,' Will said. 'We have to make sure.'

The ground spoke again: *At first I was afraid, I was petrified!*

A groove ran from the mound toward the heart of the jungle, disappearing through a curtain of vines. A path by which something had been dragged here. As they watched, rain smoothed the mud over, the ground re-forming, removing any trace.

Will wiped his brow, leaving a smudge of dirt.

Eve said, 'Ready?'

They fell to digging, hands and knees, shoveling with their cupped fingers. They worked in silence, Neto, Harry, Lulu, and Eve doing most of the heavy work, but Claire pitching in, too. Pain rendered Will less effective, but he refused to lie down and elevate his foot. Instead he groped at the quick-yielding earth, a band of perspiration gleaming on his forehead. Sue alone sat it out, leaning against a tree, holding the flashlight for them and murmuring feverishly. At one point she bobbled the flashlight, stabbing light onto the seal on her T-shirt: FRIENDS OF THE OMAHA PUBLIC LIBRARY. Eve took note of the shirt. It had been bought back in civilization – won perhaps at a luncheon fund-raiser auction. Perfect for tennis, the grocery store, spinning class. Sue firmed her grip and swung the light back, the T-shirt disappearing, replaced by the unearthed grave.

Headway was difficult, the slop seeming to refill itself, but finally Eve scraped down and hit something firm. She sat up abruptly, the motion causing the others to halt.

They looked at one another, the whites of their eyes flashing. Harry hunched forward once again, his hands working deftly.

An arm was excavated.

Harry pulled it free and when he let go, it remained in place, protruding from the ground stiffly, slathered in mud, the wrist goose-necked. Will pushed himself back and sat, his injured foot kicked wide, his arms dangling before him as if he didn't know what to do with them. Mosquitoes whined, competing with raindrops, and something amphibious croaked at a decibel level and a pitch that seemed wholly unnatural.

They breathed for a time, the arm centered between them like a grotesque centerpiece. Rainwater washed the upthrust hand, mud trickling off in rivulets, unearthing the pale skin.

By some unspoken signal, they started up again, scooping away, flinging sodden handfuls behind them. Different parts of the intact body emerged – a bent knee, the other hand, an ear. Finally Neto stood, taking the two dead hands in his own and tugging to exhume the corpse from the final sheath of mud. His grip slipped, and he tumbled back. He tried again, clutching at the wrists, and the body slid free from the pocket with a sucking sound.

The head rolled, and Jay's face came into view, a spit curl of hair pasted across his forehead. His eyes were closed, the face at peace, carved from marble.

The only sign of violation was a single deep gash at the chest. The slice in the shirt was evident, but the bloody fabric had twisted around so it showed only intact skin beneath. They stared at the body uncomprehendingly, no one moving, no one breaking the silence.

Will sank his face into his lifted hand.

This little movement broke the spell. Claire leaned forward and pried at Jay's jeans. The satellite phone popped free from the moist pocket. She brushed the screen with a thumb.

'Signal?' Eve asked.

Claire shook her head. 'And the battery's run down from searching.'

'Then how was it ringing?' Harry asked.

Claire keyed a few buttons. 'It was a reminder alert. A stock thing, I guess.' She pointed the phone at them, the letters visible on the glowing screen: SET LIMIT ORDERS ON BIDU FOR TOMORROW.

From the depths of his hand, Will nodded.

'Turn the phone off,' Eve said. 'Preserve what's left of the charge.'

Claire's hand pulsed, and her features fell back into darkness.

Eve thought of that flashlight beam, aimed directly at them through the trees. 'He saw us heading here to the body,' she said. 'Now he knows.'

'Knows what?' Sue said.

'That we know what he's done.' Eve stood and sloughed off the sludge from her knees. 'Now he has to kill all of us.'

32

Though the gas lanterns had been twisted to high and positioned and repositioned, their glow still climbed only partway up the walls of Harry and Sue's adobe hut. The ceiling remained black and heavy above the sputtering light of the wicks, the room like the inside of an oven, all of them sitting in their own private hell. Will reclined on the bed, his foot propped on pillows, the others spread around the periphery as if magnetically repulsed. No one had a damn thing to say. Or maybe they stayed apart because every other face was a mirror and the last thing they needed to see right now was their stripped-bare humanness, the flaws and cracks and stark animal needs.

They'd left Jay.

There hadn't been a choice, really. The Jeep had no room as it was, Will and his bandaged leg claiming the entire cargo hold and the rest of them stacked, heads bent against the canvas top. There was nowhere to load a body, let alone an earthy-sticky corpse the size of an NFL linebacker.

They'd arrived back to find the lodge in disarray. Ever-stalwart Fortunato had remained as promised, lashing down the activity center's tents and sheltering the supplies. Ruffian, Neto's favorite of the burros, had run off, spooked by thunder, but Fortunato had secured the remaining few in the stable and tarped off the ATVs. The other *indígeno* workers had left, capitalizing on the break in the storm to make headway toward their family *milpas*, where they'd hole up until the wet season ended. The generator was still down, the power cables running to the huts likely compromised as well. Neto had conferred with Fortunato, concluding that neither could be fixed without daylight and a dry spell that lasted longer than five minutes. The Jeep was safely back in the stable, and Lulu had off-roaded the van from its spot beyond the bamboo walkways to the heart of the camp, parking it beneath the thatched veranda of the cantina within sprint distance – a modern version of circling the wagons. The steak knife and the sole remaining machete rested on the foot of the bed within easy reach, the door was bolted, the windows latched, and they were every one of them within eyeshot, save Sue, who required the bathroom at quickening intervals, her vague malady having resolved in the past hour into Montezuma's revenge. Eve had given her several Imodiums from the first-aid kit, but the meds seemed overmatched by whatever bug had worked its way into Sue's intestines.

It would have been good if they could've opened a window.

Claire stared off into the middle distance, clicking the backlight of her dive watch on and off, on and off, the bluish luminosity mapping onto her chin and one drawn cheek. Eve poked at the blister on her left heel, wishing she had more of the sap Fortunato had squeezed from that plant.

Lulu broke the long-standing silence. 'Check the phone again.'

Claire paused from her watch clicking to power up Jay's sat-phone. The toilet flushed in the other room, and Sue staggered out, leaning on the wall, Harry rising to aid her. He eased them both to the floor, and she lay with her head on his thigh.

Claire thumbed the phone back off. 'Still nothing,' she said.

'There is no point in checking every five minutes,' Neto said. 'Not in this storm. Turning it *on*, turning it *off*, this is just running down the battery.'

'It'd be nice if we could charge the goddamned thing,' Will said.

'I'll have Fortunato fix the generator in the morning –'

'In the morning,' Harry said, 'we'll be gone.'

'Gonna hopscotch across that bridge?' Claire asked. 'Piggyback me and Will? 'Cuz I promise you one thing: I can't swim across a river that fast. And he sure as hell can't either right now.'

Eve looked up. 'We'll get out of here together.'

'You *say* that. And maybe you even think it's true until it comes down to it and the rest of you can ... I don't know, run or swim and get back to safety. And I can't keep up. It's a different conversation then. Trust me.'

'We'll stick together,' Eve said, more firmly.

She looked to the others for confirmation, and Lulu and Fortunato nodded. Lulu's stare found Neto, and he said, 'We will wait here together until the storm passes. The water level will fall, and we will take the Jeep down to the shallow part of the river and drive across. All of us.'

'Between us and that crossing there are *miles* and *miles* of storm-battered road,' Claire said. 'What if it's blocked?'

Lulu said, 'Then we'll unblock it.'

'What if that path by the wrecked bridge is washed out?'

'Then we'll four-wheel it,' Harry said. 'What choice do we have?'

Sue lifted her head. 'When will the storm end so we can go?'

Neto looked at Fortunato and waved a hand, palm up, ceding the stage with acid deference. Fortunato cleared his throat and said, 'Tonight is worst night of rains. Maybe tomorrow. Maybe one day more.'

'Oh, God.' Sue wearily pulled herself up, then shuffled to the bathroom. 'Gotta go again.'

Eve said to Harry, 'You make sure –'

'I know, I know.' Harry raised a water bottle. 'That she stays hydrated.'

'And don't share that bottle.' Eve rose, walked to the end of the bed, and checked the ice pack wrapped around Will's ankle. 'Has it been twenty minutes?'

He set his jaw, spoke through the bars of his teeth. 'Feels like it.'

Claire checked her watch. 'Yes.'

Eve removed the ice, took note of the eggplant hue blooming beneath the skin. 'It's gonna get colorful.'

'I figure by tonight it'll look like a Monet.' Will tapped the pack of antibiotics against his knuckles, an agitated tic, then flipped it onto the nightstand next to the flashlight. 'Sue can have the bed. It's her bed. My ankle hurts the same whether I'm on the floor or on a mattress.'

They'd been over this. Eve ignored him, pinched his toe. 'Feel that?'

'Youch.'

She released. The skin went from pink to white and back to pink. 'Nice capillary refill.'

'Thanks. Nice eyes.' He tried a smile, but it grew shaky, and he looked away and took a deep breath. 'The pins and needles are back,' he said. 'Is that bad?'

'It's not great.'

'On the continuum between "bad" and "not great," where is it?'

'Between "let's see" and "worrisome." Depends how it progresses.' Eve finished winding the bandage around his ankle and returned to her seat on the floor.

Sue reemerged from the bathroom, and Harry helped her down again so she sat propped beside him. Her stretched-out Friends of the Omaha Public Library shirt was grimy with dirt from Jay's grave. She covered her eyes and wept for a time. 'I'm so exhausted. So, so worn out.'

'Drink water,' Eve said.

'I can't. I'm sick of water. It's going right through me anyway.'

'Listen,' Claire said. 'We're past whining here, Sue. Look around. We've all got plenty to bitch about. But our job? Right now? Is to not fucking whine.'

Sue drank her water.

Harry's beard had come in more, a white, tough bristle. He glowered at Claire. 'You watch how you talk to her.'

Sue lowered the bottle, wiped her lips. 'I'm sorry,' she said. 'She's right. I'm just scared.'

'It's okay, honey.' Harry stroked his wife's hand. 'We're *all* scared.'

Sue's eyes were leaking. 'I'm not an exceptional person. I know that. I haven't . . . I haven't done anything special with my life, really. But I want to live as much as if I'd cured cancer or if I was Bill Gates or Condoleezza Rice or . . . or someone who mattered.' She looked peaked, her face crumpled, marionette lines showing at either side of her mouth. 'I just don't want to die here.'

'No one is dying anywhere,' Neto said.

'Except Jay,' Will said.

Moths beat at the windows.

Will worked his lower lip between his teeth. 'You could take everything I worried about before – hell, everything I *cared* about, too – ball it up, and throw it away.' He glared at his foot as if it had betrayed him. 'This is awful. All of it. But at least it's real. At least we're down to the gut-check basics. Us versus nature. Us versus *him*.'

A frog had somehow made its way up to the outside windowsill. Its throat bulged, and it shot its improbable tongue out, suctioning in a white moth. Eve watched with a blend of repulsion and fascination as the tongue launched again and again, picking off the moths.

It would be midnight at home now. She pictured the glow of the night-light across Nicolas's sleep-smooth cheek, one arm hugging the blankie he no longer admitted to needing.

'You're right,' she said. 'I don't care about my mortgage. Or my job. Or how low my checking account is. I care that I'm there when Nicolas wakes up. That I make him breakfast. That's all. Him and being alive. And, I guess, *remembering* that I'm alive when I am. Because, Christ, we can't take it for granted.'

Claire gave a feeble smile. 'But we *do*. And if we get out of here –'

'*When,*' Eve said.

'When we get out of here, we'll all go around with our new perspective and fresh resolutions, stop and smell the roses. But then it'll go back to how it was.'

'No,' Eve said.

'A little at a time.'

'No.'

'We'll convince ourselves that, gosh, our schedule is just wearin' us down,' Claire said. 'But really, we can't live that full *because* it reminds us of being alive. And that reminds us of being not-alive, too, someday. And that's hard to look at.' She flicked dirt off her thigh, gave a low snicker. 'So we look at home-makeover shows and You-Tube videos about sneezing pandas or pigs that befriend fucking kittens. And you can make every promise to yourself here, or to God, but when we're home a month, a year, you'll see. You'll see.' She released her braces at the sides and curled over, bunching her jacket into a pillow. 'I'm gonna get some sleep.'

Eve sat with her back to the wall and Claire's words burning in her gut.

Soon Will's breathing evened out to match Claire's, and then Harry drifted off as well, exhaling with a faint whistle. Sue and Lulu went next. Fortunato kept his eyes fastened on the door, and Neto, too, remained up, tugging repetitively at his black curls.

Waiting there in the room filled with the sough of sleeping bodies, Eve felt the most comprehensive aloneness she could have imagined. On the sill the rain-sleek frog gorged itself on moth after moth. They kept coming, drawn to the faint glimmer of the glass, an unending massacre. The horror of the frog matched the horror mounting inside her. This was the way it was now and the way it had always been, even before, even as she'd dutifully steered her Prius into the employee parking spot each morning, even as she'd pushed her supermarket cart past counters stacked with neatly packaged cuts of meat, even as she'd plugged into her iPod and climbed aboard the StairMaster most afternoons, ascending to nothing. She'd known, of course. But she'd let herself forget, and in that Claire was right. All the layers they'd built, roads and regulations and spotless hospital whites, they were there to aid the forgetting. But the jungle laws had always run beneath it all, a molten stream under the bedrock.

A movement at her side startled her. Neto, squatting, blocking the glow of the nearest lantern. He reached out and gripped her forearm, and she realized that here, under these circumstances, he could do or say anything to her. For some reason her next thought was of Rick and how, despite all his shortcomings and blind spots, he'd not once made her feel physically unsafe.

'When you're a man,' Neto said, his voice restrained so as not to wake the others, 'you worry about taking care of your own.' The faint light flickered in his pupils. 'Lulu and I, we want to start a family of our own. So as a man you think about protecting what is yours. Money. The business. Your reputation. A different set of responsibilities perhaps than a woman has.' His Adam's apple bobbed. He scratched at his cheek with a slender finger. 'But what you said is right. Theresa Hamilton – she *did* deserve better.' He swallowed again, hard. 'I am ashamed of myself.'

Before Eve could react, he padded quietly back to his

spot by the door. She wet her lips, which had gone dry. Neto settled into position and did not look over at her again.

Turning away from the frog on the windowsill, she lay on the floor and put her head down for the first time in thirty hours. She fell asleep to the boom of thunder and the *thwack* of that elastic tongue firing again and again, feeding an unslakable appetite.

33

They had left their brother behind. Exposed in the mud. To rot like a dog. They had no honor. No respect even for their own.

This heightened Bashir's resolve. True, it had been unwise to bury the body in the jungle. But it was prudent to remove it a safe distance from his canyon. In the soft, yielding spot in the jungle floor he had scouted earlier for this purpose. It had seemed far enough away from his house, as far as was convenient tonight, given the storm. But he had been spotted, and so the corpse had as well. He should have disposed of it properly, as he was doing now. There could be no evidence left behind. Not a single bone. The conditions had made him careless earlier tonight, but he knew now that there was no room for carelessness.

Now he was at war.

He ran up the mountain as he had in his days in the camps. Every muscle straining to burst through the skin. No shoes so he could feel the earth. The soles of his bare feet conditioned like leather. Rain washed him. He drove upward through the black of night. Yoked to the palm-frond sled behind him. Straps indenting his chest, his shoulders. Dragging deadweight. Behind, the wrapped corpse knocked against tree trunks, splashed through puddles. The taste of bile singed the back of his tongue.

Another man would have sunk to his knees. Would have wept from the pain. Given up. But Bashir, his will was inexhaustible. It was a thing of legend. He had once navigated the Toba Kakar range with a shattered femur he'd wrapped with horse reins stolen from a stable. His pain was the decree of Allah, praise and glory be to Him.

He passed the rotting bird-watching tower that embraced the mighty white cedar. A barricade of fallen trees blocked the east fork. But that was fine. He was going west.

At the cemetery he paused and took a knee. Panted. Each breath gave a faint rasp. He was not in the condition he had once been. The extra weight cost him. He would overcome his exhaustion, though, as he overcame all matters physical.

Tombstones tilted from the earth around him. He blended in among them. Another herald of the dead. Another thing of stone, worn but undiminished.

From one loose pocket, he pulled a miswak twig precisely one hand span in length, as was prescribed by the Prophet, *salallahu alayhi wasalam*. He picked at his teeth, then chewed it to sweeten his breath. This morning he had cut it fresh from the arak shrub outside his front door. When he'd first flown to Mexico, he had smuggled arak seeds in the cuffs of his pants. A solitary comfort of home that he wanted to carry into his new life.

He had first arrived in the southernmost state of Chiapas with a list of contacts that al-Zawahiri had given him to memorize. The plan had been a grand one. To build a factory of death. An assembly line from which suicide bombers would be launched north into the heartland of

America. These fine young brothers and sisters would be motivated bombers who understood jihad to be an individual duty. They would be trained and expert. A cut above the Waziristan widows the Taliban made sloppy use of. They would be paired up, sent in twos to increase morale and kill radius. They would love death as Americans loved life.

It would be a glorious sight. Hundreds of holy warriors marching into schools, cinemas, shopping malls, turning them into graveyards. Reducing taxpayers to cargo carried out in caskets. These warriors would speak in the only language Americans understood. Messages with no words, written in blood. Messages that scorched the ground beneath their feet. They would stride to Paradise on a path cushioned with burned flesh, irrigated with blood, paved with skulls.

At this image Bashir felt the hand of the Prophet lift him from the fertile cemetery dirt to his feet. He ran with renewed vigor, the weight of the corpse turned to a feather at his back. Allah guided his steps. Bashir basked in His radiance. He felt love in his chest, warming him against the rain, numbing him to the dozen pains of his body. This love was discipline and virtue. It was respect and dedication. It was everything Americans were not. He despised their entitlement. Their arrogance and greed. Their rank hypocrisy. They fattened themselves on oil as they railed against despots they had once installed. They decried the deaths of their own and preached human rights as they tightened their embargos, strangling off food and medical vaccines, killing hundreds of thousands of Muslim children.

Americans turned a blind eye to these atrocities visited

upon innocents oceans away. They drove their SUVs and played their stock market and bellied up to their buffets. At last the massacre would be transferred to their own streets. At last they would reap the seeds of their foolish deeds. As long as they murdered with their bombs and sanctions, their mothers would become childless. Their fathers bled with a thousand cuts. Their economy brought wheezing to its knees. They would have no stomach for seeing such atrocities up close. No resilience. They would crumble as so many crusaders had crumbled under Bashir's proficient hand. The vision was divine.

Except.

As Bashir's time in Chiapas had stretched from days to weeks, he made few inroads. He moved among the former Zapatista territories where radicalization had taken hold. But it was radicalization of a different kind. There were Muslims, but few who understood their duty. Many of the contacts from al-Zawahiri had gone missing or been killed. Some of the leads led nowhere at all, to a house that had been razed or to a mailbox tilting from the dirt of an abandoned lot. Even in success Bashir found mostly ragtag rebels, not professionals. It quickly grew clear: To complete his mission, he would require men and resources from home.

Correspondence from al-Zawahiri was not promising. The Base was disintegrating even more rapidly. Drone missiles rocketed from the skies like lightning. Warriors were lost more quickly than they could be replaced. The new recruits were semiliterate, disenfranchised. Most couldn't even place a land mine, let alone build a sophisticated bomb. The central command, too, had been gutted.

The last seven chiefs of external operations had been captured or killed.

Bashir sent word to Usama, pleading with him to provide leadership. But Usama chose personal safety above all else. Though Bashir waited day after day, no communication came back.

By the end of 2008, it was over. A slow-dawning awareness that settled like a fog. There was no white flag. No formal announcement. No state capital over which to raise a new flag. No army to lay down arms. But it was plain that the Base was no more. The leaders were deep in hiding like Usama himself. The jihadis who remained were little more than roving bands on the run through the rugged border, bounties on their heads, hunted by warlords and crusaders alike.

But the Americans did not notice this victory. They had built a rich propaganda, comforting and familiar in its fearmongering. They had fallen in love with their own story. Politicians warned of jihadis penetrating every border, sneaking onto every airplane. There were magazines to sell. Airtime to be filled. Lucrative contracts to be awarded. Oil to be plundered. Holy lands to occupy.

By then Bashir had moved west to Oaxaca. A jungle that reminded him of his tiny village in the tangled wilds of southern Pakistan. The Mexican government had made a billion-dollar investment in the region. To protect that investment and to keep out the cartels, they had inserted a naval base. The military did its best to keep guns out of the region, and unlike in the rest of Mexico they had a good measure of success at it. It was peaceful and private here, with little crime and scant police presence.

The perfect place to get lost.

And so he had. He simply stepped off the map and disappeared.

Years later on one of his infrequent trips to the *pueblo* for supplies, Bashir had read news of Usama's death. He'd studied grainy photographs of the compound in Abbottabad. All those intimate details laid bare. Tawdry reports of a pornography stash. The Avena syrup Usama kept at his bedside to stimulate sexual appetite. The dye for his beard. Standing there beneath the awning of a banana cart in the market, Bashir had felt a little part of himself wither away.

Worse yet were the stories of the so-called Arab awakening. Largely peaceful, the newspapers claimed. Even the Muslim Brotherhood had laid down their weapons and entered government. Hearts and minds had been lost. The people, they wanted social change. Economic change. Political change. They believed that the jihadis had nothing to offer them. No blueprint for the future. No vision for prosperity. How obscene these beliefs were. What was the future but with Allah? What was prosperity compared to the riches of Paradise?

These nation-states would not remain peaceful. They were built on compromise, corruption, impurity. Extremism would rear its head again, to be sure. Innovators like the Taliban would reemerge. Iran or Syria would keep a tight grip on the reins, perhaps even succeed in demolishing the Zionists and sparking a third world war. But one thing was clear: The Base would not be welcomed into the fray anytime soon.

Whatever the near future held, it would not be Allah's way.

Bashir had returned home from the market that day and burned his coded phone numbers. He had smashed his laptop and satellite phone and cast them into the river. Usama had relied solely on one courier. And look where that had gotten him. So Bashir would rely on nothing and nobody. He would remain here beneath the beautiful boughs. Apart from infidels with their endless distractions. Safe from the tentacles of modern communication. God willing, he would live out his life purely. In submission to the will of Allah and the traditions of the Prophet, peace be upon him. He would have a chance to clear his head. To breathe fresh air. To get out of range.

He believed still. This was a thousand-year war. In the end the word of God would triumph. *Insha'Allah* the crusaders would fold their flag and the banner of Islam would be hoisted above the White House, above Jerusalem. All states would be joined together under the caliphate, under an imam chosen by Allah from the Prophet's purified progeny. The world would submit to Islamic authority. *Shari'a* would be named the high law of the land.

Someday this would be so. But not in Bashir's lifetime.

He was tired. He was resigned. He had found peace in his daily prayers and his quiet obedience. He had found contentment. A spot to live out his final days. He had let go of his role in the jihad, leaving the End of Times Battle for future generations. The Bear of Bajaur had slumbered.

Until they came. Even here. Americans. With their clomping boots and short dresses and alcohol. First the journalist and now the others. Interfering once again, trying to pry their greedy Western fingers into his carved-out nook at the edge of the world.

242

They had awakened the Bear of Bajaur.

Bashir burst through a skein of thin branches onto the plain of elephant grass topping the mountain. The wrapped corpse caught in a bramble, then pulled suddenly free. For a moment Bashir was soaring, the body flying behind him. Then the soggy earth came up under his feet again, and he bulled through the chest-high grass, the resistance growing easier. A single light burned in the ranch house across the plain. The sled whispered behind him.

His feet sank deeper. The mud wallow opened up, a break in the tall grass. And embedded in the sludge, there was his old friend, as still as an upended canoe.

He loosed the straps from his body. Without the burden a sensation rose in him from the soles of his feet. The sensation of floating. Of being made weightless. He took stock. His flesh, rubbed raw at the outer shoulders. His shirt torn. A red line burned across his chest.

He rested a bare foot on the wrapped bundle and shoved. It rolled down the gentle slope and skidded in the sticky brown sheet, the bumps of the heels touching a clear puddle the rain had laid across the mud itself. The vibration registered in the wallow. Bashir tracked the ripple's movement until it bumped against the upended canoe.

The crocodile did not move, but Bashir sensed a flicker of the black eyes.

'Eat,' he said.

El Puro bided his time. He knew there was no rush.

Bashir lifted his gaze to the house. Through the bedroom window, he saw Don Silverio moving hastily from dresser to bed.

Packing.

In a storm.

This was noteworthy.

Bashir left the crocodile and started for the house. Grass parted before him. Flicked at his throat. Tickled the soft flesh beneath his chin.

His stomach roiled. He had not eaten since this morning, and the past eighteen hours had been full of exertion.

He came softly through the garden. Passed a sheltered coop. He looked at the chicken inside, and his stomach leapt.

Since he'd taken Jay Rudwick at the cascade this morning, an electricity had entered his body. Jolted him alive again. Purpose had returned, keen and chill, flowing through his veins. It connected him with where he had come from and the pleasures of the fight ahead. His heart sang with love. He was connected with his brothers dead and those who would come. Desire flared like a sexual charge. He wanted the defeat of the crusaders and heretics and the return of the global Muslim caliphate. But right now?

He wanted a chicken.

He undid the latch. Groped inside. Came up with the legs. The bird flapped and squawked, loosing underfeathers.

He carried it squirming at his side to the front door.

He entered without knocking.

Don Silverio came into the doorway of the bedroom at the end of the hall and froze. As if waiting for someone to take his picture. His mouth was slightly ajar, his lower jaw sawing back and forth.

Fear.

The old man gathered himself. 'Do you need help, *amigo*? Can I offer you something?'

Bashir did not answer. He walked toward the kitchen, leaving footprints of mud on the well-swept tile. A backpack lay against the base of the sink, stuffed and ready. A few sheets of paper rested on the blank wooden table. Votive candles burned in the infidel shrine in the corner.

Don Silverio rushed behind him. He reached for the papers.

Bashir said, 'No.'

A simple word, and it hit the old man like a stone.

With his free hand, Bashir pulled a chair away from the table, set it in the center of the kitchen. He stared at Don Silverio. The chicken bucked and fluttered and then fell limp against Bashir's leg.

The power leaked from Don Silverio's body. He rounded the table and sat.

Bashir walked to the knife block and withdrew a lean, curved boning knife. It was suitable. It would be useful for slaughtering the chicken so the meat would be halal to eat.

He took his bearings. Set the chicken on the floor facing in the direction of the Ka'ba in Mecca. With his right foot, he pinned the claws. With his left, he pulled the wings gently back and held them down. He stroked the chicken's head to soothe it. It was under stress and deserving of mercy and the love of Allah.

He plucked the feathers from the neck so the action of the blade would be swift and unimpeded. He picked up the knife where he had laid it on the tile. Murmured,

'Bismillah, Allahu Akbar,' to bless the fowl. Sliced the neck to the bone, but no further.

In his chair Don Silverio made a soft sound of distress.

Bashir lifted the slack bird and held the head back to let the blood drain. The stream eventually slowed to a trickle and then to drops tapping the tile. This might have taken ten minutes. Or fifteen. Don Silverio lowered his eyes with respect, but never once did Bashir remove his gaze from his face. Though he kept the bird aloft, his arm did not ache. His muscles knew not to complain.

When the drops ceased, he finally turned. Brought the exsanguinated fowl to the counter. With several swift incisions, he freed one breast, then the other. He tossed the pink ovals into a pan. Watched them sizzle. Flipped them. Slid them onto a plate. The entire time he did not turn to watch Don Silverio.

But he listened. He heard nothing except fear coming off the old man.

He rinsed the boning knife beneath the tap and took a fork from the drawer. Sat at the wooden table. His plate beside those papers. Opposite, Don Silverio was pushed back far enough that his entire body was visible. A man sitting in a chair with no table. He looked silly. Reduced. His lips firmed, his mustache bristling. His weather-beaten face looked haggard, old flesh sliding off the bone beneath.

Bashir chewed. He picked up the top page. A feminine hand, voluptuous curves to each letter. He read. He took another bite. Chewed. Read some more.

'I did not do anything.' Don Silverio's words came out bunched together, crowding his mouth. 'This was brought to me. It is not my fault this was brought to me. I am the *alcalde*, and so it was my turn to receive news such as this. I did not choose to. It was my duty to be the *alcalde*. I do not want to make an enemy of a man such as yourself.'

Bashir let the sheet flutter to the table's surface. He sawed another bite of chicken breast. The meat firm, the juice savory. He picked up the next page.

'I will burn that letter,' Don Silverio said. 'Right now. With you here to see me do it.'

Bashir used the sheet of paper to wipe his lips. 'Where is your shotgun?'

Don Silverio's throat jerked once, twice. Fighting the words.

Bashir pointed to the empty rack above the shrine.

Don Silverio said, 'Please.'

Bashir said, 'I will not ask again.'

'I sent it with my mother. She knows nothing. I told her *nothing* in order to protect her.'

'I believe you,' Bashir said. 'This was wise.'

Don Silverio exhaled. His body, slack with relief.

Bashir stood abruptly. The feet of the chair chirped against the floor. The fork was no longer in his hand.

But the boning knife was.

Don Silverio gave a little cry. He rose unsteadily. Dragged the chair before him. Gripped the top slat. His legs wobbly. He pulled the chair farther to the side so it could be swung like a weapon.

Bashir advanced.

The chair rose no more than a few inches off the floor. And stopped there, shaking.

'Please,' Don Silverio said as Bashir closed.

247

Bashir swatted the chair away. It clattered on the tile. Banged the stove.

His grip was sure. The old man arced backward from the points of contact like a hooked fish.

After, Bashir wiped the knife back and forth across his thigh. Don Silverio mattered less than the others. He was not American, and therefore an American fuss would not accompany his disappearance. But still. It would be wise for Bashir to obscure his tracks.

He cleaned the kitchen, handled the remaining matters, then threw the old man over his shoulder. After Jay Rudwick the frail body felt like nothing at all.

He stepped outside. The rain was steady and refreshing. It mixed with his sweat, and he smelled the heat of the day's exertion lifting from his skin. He studied the starless sky. Like a spill of ink. Lightning cracked again, showed the churning clouds. Five seconds to the thunder. The storm moving away.

This would benefit his enemies. There were seven left. He had counted them on the river and at the ruins, and Jay Rudwick had confirmed it. Seven who knew that Bashir was here. Who knew his face. Who could reveal him to the world as Usama had been revealed. Another holy warrior disgraced and diminished. Bashir would be reduced to another set of grainy photographs in a newspaper. Images of his little house, perhaps even his corpse. His personal habits pored over. Undignified details polished to a high glitter. His holy work defiled, spread and dissected like a curiosity.

No.

Between the storm and the bridge, his enemies were

trapped. The range was isolated, the villages cleared out for the wet season. The mountains would be wrecked in the wake of the *tormenta*. The roads a mess. Going up and over the range simply would not be an option. Not for days.

But first light would bring opportunities. Satellite reception might return. They could make their way downslope. The river would be shallower, and there would be chances for crossing.

The warmth drained from the body into his shoulder, his cheek. He hitched it higher and started through the tall elephant grass.

Lightning again. Now six seconds until the rumble. With morning would come a lessening.

But there was still plenty of night left.

He reached the edge of the wallow, squinting into a wet gust of wind. The crocodile had come across now to the near side where the bundle had been. He saw Bashir nearing and spread his mighty jaws. Snaggleteeth pointed this way and that. He showed his pink-white maw, and breath hissed up the meaty tunnel from his gut.

Bashir did not slow. He skirted the edge, drawing within a few yards of the mighty beast. He dipped his shoulder. Don Silverio slid off and landed with a thud behind him.

The mud crackled as the crocodile swung his head to his next meal. Bashir was cultivating in him quite a taste for blood. That was good.

There would be more.

Monday

34

'Mom. Mom? *Mom. Mom? MOM?*

'Mnff.'

'Get up, Mom.'

Nicolas's face looms, twenty-five degrees offset. Those long lashes, that partial squint he wears when he is without glasses. The pillow feels like silk against her cheek. Through a rise of bunched fabric, she notes the time on the nightstand clock – 5:36 A.M. Somewhere through the murk, her brain registers that it is Saturday and that this is an uncivilized hour to be awake on a weekend, not fit for man or beast. She burrows into the warmth of the sheets.

'Come on, Big. Get up. I'm hungry.'

'Mnff.'

'When's breakfast?'

Then: 'I'm starving.'

Then: 'I've been up a *hour* already.'

She rolls onto her back, grinds the heel of her hand into an eye socket. 'You didn't eat anything, did you?'

'Yeah. I ate a gluten pancake.'

Lanie's joke. Less funny at 5:37 A.M. on a Saturday.

'Mom. Mom?'

'Yuh.'

'I want a puppy.'

'A puppy. At 5:37 in the morning.'

'Well, not like *right now*. I don't think the dog stores are open, prob'ly. I want a Labrador maybe, 'cuz they make the cutest puppies. Or a Rhodesian ridgeback like Zach has. He makes this bark like *woof*. Like it's rumbling his whole body. And his face? He gets these wrinkles on his forehead like this?' Nicolas's mouth twists, but no wrinkles appear on *his* forehead. 'Wait – like *this*.' Still no wrinkles. 'On his face? And it's like he's thinking real hard and –'

'We're not getting a puppy, Little.'

'I can take care of him, though. You wouldn't have to do *anything*.'

'Mm-hm.'

Across on the wall, a framed family portrait from a few years ago gazes out. She and Rick with Nicolas tucked between them, a cheery triad against a fake nature backdrop of pine trees and a waterfall. Who had chosen *that*? They looked like suburbanite elves. Sweaters in the Mist. At least once a week, she debated taking it down, but then she wondered what signal that would send to Nicolas, and then she'd wonder what signal she was sending by *not* taking it down, and by the time she got done with all that wondering, she was usually late for work.

'You'd *love* him.' Nicolas: still back on the puppy.

She shoots a breath at the ceiling. Beside her the space Rick used to occupy stretches neatly, the sheets smooth and tucked in. The bed is half made and half unmade, and it strikes her that this would be a delightful metaphor to contemplate were her faculties not muffled by exhaustion.

Two little hands grip her fingers and tug, lifting her

deadweight two inches off the pillow. He lets go, and she collapses back.

'Mom!'

'Just a little longer. I'll let you stay up till midnight. I'll buy you Superman action –'

'*Batman.*'

'– figures. I'll let you skip school for a week.'

'Nuh-uh. You're lying.'

'You're right. Except about the letting-me-sleep part.'

'I'll let you sleep . . .'

She recognizes the not-so-subtle crafty set of his features. 'If *what?*'

'If I can have a puppy.'

She rustles up into a more coherent lump against the headboard. 'Nicolas Richard Hardaway. Don't you make me use your middle name.'

'You just did.'

'There's more where that came from.'

His stick arms fold across his chest, and one foot taps, the bearing of a hustler he's picked up from the playground or the fox in *Pinocchio*. 'Deal or no deal, Big?'

'*Why* do you want a puppy?'

'Because –'

The bedroom wall erupts in a fireball.

Drywall flies in shrapnel chunks. The faux-sylvan portrait shatters outward, shards spinning, the dopey posed grins evaporating into flame. The explosion blows back the sheets, ripping them straight off her body, peeled upward from her toes and flattened, in a carnival effect, against the headboard above her. She reaches for Nicolas,

255

her hand closing around his for a fleeting instant before he is blown away also, propelled into the bathroom, and her mouth is open and she is screaming, but there can be no sound above the awesome rush of the overpressure, the bulge of vivid orange mushrooming across her bedroom to claim her when –

Eve lurched awake on the floor of Harry and Sue's adobe hut, jolting up into a different realm. Nightmare and reality were intertwined, and she knew neither which was which nor which was worse. The adobe walls rattled still with an aftershock, the east-facing window had blown out, and beyond in the lodge a ring of fire burned around one of the activity-center tents. The overhanging branches had been turned to charcoal, and higher limbs crackled, sizzling beneath the rain. Vines waggled, tipped with flame.

Inside the hut everyone bobbed more than moved, lower halves mired in quicksand. Lulu swayed, one cheek feathered with slivers of glass; she'd gotten the worst of the window. Sue curled into the wall, Harry leaning over her protectively. Neto had grabbed the machete, Fortunato the folding knife, but both stood transfixed, staring at the still-closed door. Grabbing the flashlight, Will fell off the bed, landing hard on his good foot and bellowing in pain. Somehow he managed to hop across the hut and throw the door open.

The bitter smell of ash and flame swept in on the wet breeze, laced with something sharper.

Mezcal.

Will said, 'He's here.'

Lulu raised a hand to her cheek, felt the embedded

fragments, and screamed. A web of blood overlay her precise makeup and the edge of her fluffed, champagne-colored hair. The cuts, painful-looking but superficial, were less distressing than the sight of her perfect skin rent; it was obscene and incongruous, like coming upon the cracked head of a porcelain doll. Claire moved toward her, but before she could get there, Lulu careened to the left, a panic sprint that sent her directly into the wall. She smacked into it, bouncing off and toppling over.

Neto seized his wife's arm and hauled her to her feet. Will did his best to wield the Maglite like a baton, but each hop seemed to knock the air out of him, causing him to double over. They moved outside as a group, emerging onto the bamboo walkway. Morning was little more than a premonition to the east, limning the highest leaves with gold. Rain smothered the embers over by the tent. Smoke coated Eve's lungs, and she gagged and coughed, not missing a step. They moved forward toward the central clearing, instinct holding them in a loose circle formation, facing outward. They watched the jungle, and it watched them right back.

'The alcohol,' Neto said. 'He used it to build a bomb.'

'Yeah,' Claire said. 'We got that.'

Sue gave a stifled cry, retreated a few steps from the edge of the stable, and buried her face in Harry's shirt. The sun broke the top of the canopy, casting a sheet of light into the stables as if to highlight the scene within.

The burros had been slaughtered. Fresh blood matted their coats, the limbs and heads twisted a few degrees too far this way and that. The smell was rank – innards and offal. The farthest two were long gone, hack marks mercifully hidden by the way their bodies had collapsed, but the third looked up at them with a bulging black orb of an eye. Its lips peeled away from domino-tile teeth. A notch was missing in its bent-back neck, the machete having taken a doorstop-size bite from the throat, and breath fluttered the ragged skin of the edges. The ribs rose and fell lurchingly, bellows that had sprung a leak, exhaling sonar-deep sounds of pain through the hole. The flies had already begun their work.

Tears fell from Neto's eyelashes as he dropped the machete and crouched over the burro, stroking its nose. It gave a life-voiding gasp, shuddered, and was still.

Neto bowed his head. 'At least Ruffian ran off in the storm,' he said. 'That saved him from being killed.'

'Look over here.' Wobbling on his good foot, Will pointed at the quads, nestled in their stalls. The tires had been slashed.

Harry squatted over a flipped-back tarp, his hands running along the yellow vinyl of the raft as if bunching pantyhose. Eve was unsure what he was doing at first, until he shifted and she saw that he was evaluating the length of the slice gouged through the hull.

'*Dios mío,*' Lulu said. '*Dios mío dios mío dios mío.*'

The burros and the raft were sufficient for Eve to grasp the situation. With slow-dawning dread, she pivoted to face the admin shack, knowing already what she'd see. The satellite dish had been smashed, curved Humpty Dumpty pieces still rocking on the roof. She finished her half turn, shifting her weight to see past the van parked beneath the cantina roof. Her gaze zeroed in on the food-storage cabinets behind the oversize grill. The contents spilled and torched, burned lettuce heads ground into the mud, milk glugging from split cartons, bits of ice floating in moats of melt.

She came full circle, the others clustered loosely around her, having instinctively moved away from the stables into the open. Neto's hands were stained with blood from the burro. But empty. Five feet beyond his sandaled foot, in the place where the machete had been, there was now nothing but a skid in the dirt. Eve's eyes rose to the deep shadows of the stalls, the countless dark patches between the leaves.

'The machete,' she said.

Neto looked at his palms. Over his shoulder at the skid in the dirt. His lips wavered.

'Where is it?' Eve asked.

'Right there. I left it *right there*.'

'Then where is it?' Harry said.

'*He* took it,' Neto said.

'Without us seeing?' Harry said. 'How?'

'Because that's what he *does*,' Eve said. 'The fire was just cover to sabotage –'

A bang sounded behind her – not an explosion but a clap of wood against wood. By the time she whirled to face across the clearing toward Harry and Sue's adobe hut, she caught nothing but the rebounding door and a violent nodding of fronds at the jungle's edge. Fortunato raised the unfolded steak knife and pointed up the bamboo walkway as if the tip of the blade could shoot bullets.

'We need to get inside,' Will said. 'We're too exposed out here.'

'He was just *in* there,' Claire said.

'Shit,' Harry said. 'What did he do? What did he *take*?'

'We'll check it out slowly and carefully,' Will said. 'But we need to get out of the open. And that hut's the only halfway decent cover right now.'

He was right – despite the blown-out windows, Harry and Sue's upscale adobe structure was still the most secure, the only one with actual walls and a roof. They retreated to it cautiously, Fortunato in the front. On the porch he paused to steel himself, then opened the door warily. The rusted hinges gave a haunted-house creak. He leaned inside, leading with the knife, then nodded to them. They nudged their way into the hut. A man's smell lingered inside, the powerful aftertrace of body odor. Wet wind sucked at the window, bringing smoke-tinged air.

Despite the moist heat, Lulu was shuddering violently, her teeth chattering, her arms vibrating so intensely they seemed possessed. In the morning light, Eve caught a better look at the glass slivers crusting her left cheek. Once cleaned up, the mess wouldn't be as bad as it looked; faces tended to bleed impressively. Fifteen minutes with a pair of tweezers could alleviate the physical damage, but Lulu's emotional equilibrium would be tougher to regain. First things first – tweezers and alcohol.

Eve looked at the base of the wall where she'd slept. She kicked aside her jacket, searching. 'The first-aid kit is gone.'

Will leaned with his good knee on the mattress, throwing back the sheets. He pulled the drawer from the nightstand, his skin glistening with sweat. 'My antibiotics,' he said. 'My goddamned antibiotics. I'm *fucked* without them.'

'We're all fucked,' Sue said. Her fierce tone, punctuated with the uncharacteristic curse word, cut Eve to the bone. Sue kept on, growing strident. 'We are trapped here, and he is . . . he is *stalking* us now. He is here, right here, hiding in those trees. We are at his mercy. Why are we here in this hut? We need to leave *now*. We need to get out of this jungle *n* –'

Another explosion rippled the floorboards. They started, Eve leaving her feet in a panicked hop, and Lulu shrieked. Through the open door, a flash of yellow came visible at the lodge's periphery, licking the gray sky. Black smoke followed, pluming up from the protective bamboo wall behind which the generator was housed.

Lulu bolted.

Neto caught her arm, but she ripped free, and Eve felt a wisp of dream memory overlie the moment – her own hand reaching for Nicolas's before the blast shot him out of her grasp.

Neto's voice wrenched high: 'He's waiting out there!'

But Lulu flew through the doorway. She almost tripped leaving the porch, her fist glinting, something clenched in her fingers. Eve scrambled after her, logjamming with Neto in the frame. He knifed through first, stumbling and banging off the bamboo railing. The others rustled behind them.

'*¡Lourdes!*' Neto shouted. '*¡Espere un momento!*'

Sprinting for the cantina, Lulu was yelling, snatches of words whipped back by the wind: '. . . butchered by . . . *not* wait to be . . .'

Eve was on the stairs, Harry bellowing over her shoulder: 'What about us? Hold on!'

Lulu threw open the door of the van and vaulted inside. She shouted through the rolled-down driver's window, 'I'm *not* waiting! You can get in, too, but I'm leaving *right now*!'

Neto ran across the clearing, his gaze darting from the tree line to the stables. 'We'll go together, then. Let's just make sure he's not right here.'

Lulu's fist glinted again. She jammed the keys beneath the steering column.

Eve's vision expanded like a lens to encompass the black smoke rising from the generator across the clearing and the smashed bits of the satellite dish rocking on the roof of the shack, those spots of movement trying to tell her something. It walloped her mid-sprint, an impression of what the next second would bring.

Time slowed to a molasses crawl. She sensed her arm swinging up, her knee lifting to ninety degrees, propelling her forward. The muscles of her throat corded with her scream: '*Wait!*'

Lulu's arm tensed as she turned the key, and the van erupted, blown upward on its hind tires like a bucking horse. Glass ejected from all sides, an expanding disk of coruscating bits, the circumference holding the shape of the vehicle for a fraction of an instant before blurring outward. The flame billowed forward, haloing the driver's seat. Lulu's head swung, her rolling eyes finding Eve's an instant before the blaze cocooned her.

35

The rain-pounded earth sucked at the back of Eve's head. She was staring up at a dense sky overrun with storm clouds. They drifted and swirled, and some part of her brain registered that they were pretty indeed, like one of Nicolas's finger paintings if he'd run through the bright end of the palette and had to resort to purples and grays. She thought – as she'd thought ever since she was a girl – how lovely it would be to skip across the puffy blanket up there, sinking in, getting a cushiony bounce. The ringing was in the air and all around her or – perhaps – only in her ears. She blinked against the falling drops, and they ran down her temples like tears.

She sat up.

Neto, who'd been a few steps ahead of her, lifted his face from the mud. His forehead and cheekbones looked raw, sunburned. He pulled himself to all fours, spit and spit again, clearing from his mouth something invisible. She went to him and helped him up. The others were behind them now, and they stood and watched the thatched veranda of the cantina burn. The rain worked on the flames, muffling them as it had muffled the fire around the detonated mezcal activity center. Holes singed the yellow letters of the Días Felices Ecolodge™ banner, stretching them out of proportion before the tethers pulled free and the whole damn thing curled into itself like a dying insect.

The back half of the van was little more than a smoking hull, though the front looked surprisingly intact. Lulu remained nestled in the scorched upholstery of the driver's seat, clearly dead.

Neto staggered to her. He clutched at the door handle and shrieked, jerking away and shaking his hand. At the back of the cantina, a beam crashed down, smashing a picnic table.

Neto spun to face the others. 'I need to get to her. Help me get to her.'

Fortunato picked up a bucket rolling by like a tumbleweed. He scooped up some puddle water and threw it on the door handle. The hot metal sizzled, then quieted. Neto flung his burned fingers beneath the latch, popping the door. His arms were spread to catch Lulu, but she remained there, propped stiffly. Embers spun down, showering his shoulders.

He tugged at her, and she toppled backward into him. Holding her beneath her still-raised arms, he tottered in reverse, falling onto his rear and shoving away from the fire with his heels.

He sat in the clearing, holding her, panting.

The rain tamped down the burning veranda until the fire was no more.

Neto turned to Eve. 'Her pulse. You have to check her pulse. Give her mouth-to-mouth resuscitation. You helped Will. You can help her.'

The body in his arms was so evidently lifeless that Eve's usual responses in the face of denial seemed inadequate.

She worked saliva into her mouth so she could get out the words: 'She's gone, Neto. Look at her. She's dead.'

Cradling her lovingly, Neto hoisted the body atop a picnic table that the explosion had shot out from beneath the veranda. Lulu sprawled supine, elevated in inadvertent display like a sarcophagus lid, eyes turned to marbles, a ribbon of black drool oozing down one frozen cheek. Given what Eve had witnessed, the body was not as bad as she would have thought. The stomach-churning scent of charred flesh laced the air, but the burns weren't terrible. What had killed her was the pressure from the blast, splintering bones into organs, causing massive internal ruptures.

Neto started compressions on her chest, the body wagging up slightly around the union of his hands. His lips moved continuously as he counted, sweat falling from his face, sprinkling hers. The sight of those drops of perspiration, distinct in the air, made Eve turn her gaze upward. The creamy gray sky sparked with electricity, but for now there was no downpour. She'd almost forgotten what it was like to breathe air with no rain in it. Two vultures crested the mountaintop, drifting in lazy rotation, and it struck her how devoid of life the skies had been since the storm began.

Neto kept pushing, kept counting.

Eve shook her head, the ringing in her ears growing louder before receding to a background whine. She talked loudly to hear herself over the tintinnabulation: 'No one move. No one touch *anything*. He can use all this stuff, anything we touch, against us. This is what he does. We can't act predictably.'

Sue's chest heaved with sobs. 'What's *predictable* in this situation?'

Will wobbled on his one good foot. 'Panic.'

They formed a loose circle in the clearing, talking at one another but keeping their focus turned outward.

'Is he gone?' Sue spun in a frantic full turn. The air wafting from her carried the scent of perfume and decay. 'He has to be gone.'

'Everyone stay close,' Will said. 'As in right fucking here.'

Sue clung to Harry, holding him from behind. 'Why doesn't he just charge us with the machete?'

'Because he doesn't have to,' Eve said.

Claire gave a nod. 'He can cull the herd, one by one. Let's call it like it is: We're all easy targets. Two old folks, one of whom is sick. An *indígeno* kid. Neto's an able-bodied man, but he's . . .' – a glance to him still laboring over Lulu's body – 'well, he's been taken out of the equation for the time being. Eve, a skinny broad who's afraid to swim through an underwater channel.' She flicked her head toward Will. 'And Gimpy over there, competing for my Miss Cripple tiara.' She smirked. 'We're not exactly SEAL Team Six.'

'The longer we stay,' Will said, 'the worse the odds that we'll survive.'

'Next move is the Jeep,' Eve said. 'Next *predictable* move.'

They turned their attention to the stable at the edge of the clearing. Black flies circled the stalls above the remains of the burros. Fortunato stayed back with Neto, but the rest of them eased over as a single unit, holding an amoebic perimeter.

Will used the flashlight to scan the dim stable. The beam crawled over the Jeep, settling on the rear brake light. It had been smashed, the bare plug yanked free of the plastic casing so it dangled over the rear bumper. A few feet away, the gas lid was popped, the cap unscrewed. Clearly the plug had been meant to drop in the tank.

A tap on the brake would send a charge to the socket. A spark and a partially filled gas tank would take care of the rest, as the van had proved. Eve replayed how it had reared up from the back, like a bucking horse. 'Why didn't he leave the wire in this gas tank, too?' she asked.

The pain forced noises from Will every time he moved. He hobbled over, leaning on the stable posts, and pulled the plug toward the open mouth of the tank. It stopped several inches short.

'Not long enough,' he said.

'So the question is,' Harry said, 'what did he do to the Jeep instead?'

'Maybe he didn't have time to do anything else,' Will said.

'Hope springs eternal,' Claire said.

'I'll take a look, make sure it's not rigged some other way.' His speech was uneven, gaining pitch with each breath.

'You gotta keep that foot elevated,' Eve said. 'You're sending too much blood down there.'

Harry stepped forward. 'I'll do it.'

'You don't know . . . what to look for,' Will said.

'I can figure it out.'

'We can't afford for you to be wrong.'

Sue clutched Harry's arm. 'Let him.'

Harry pursed his lips, then nodded, relenting.

Will said, 'Help me onto my back. I'll check out the undercarriage, elevate my foot at the same time. Two birds, one stone.' He tried a grin, but sweat sheened his face and a high color had come up under his cheeks, the pain right there beneath the surface.

Harry and Eve lowered him down.

He paused on his back, squinting up. 'Keep an eye out while I'm under here.' Leading with the flashlight, he wriggled beneath the Jeep. As he squirmed about, they stayed clear of his bandaged ankle, watching him and one another and the jungle all around. Eve sensed movement at the edge of her vision, but when she whipped around, it was just a parakeet taking flight, the vacated frond bobbing in its wake.

Sue's knees buckled, and she sat abruptly in the hay. Harry rested a hand on her head but made no move to help her up, and she seemed content to stay. 'What do we do about Lulu?' she asked.

Claire said, 'There's nothing we *can* do about Lulu.'

They watched the jungle some more. Eve caught her leg bouncing anxiously up and down and, with effort, stilled it.

At last Will shoved himself free of the Jeep. 'I can't see anything out of the ordinary. Pop the hood.'

Eve did as Harry helped Will around to lean against the front, where he poked and pried at the engine. Sue found her feet again but was wobbly on her legs until Harry stepped over to prop her up. The seat of her shorts was smudged with dirt, a few stray pieces of hay stuck to the denim. Eve thought about brushing them off for her, but the gesture seemed hopeless and somehow exhausting.

'Nothing here either,' Will announced.

'Given that we're dealing with the Zen Master of Terror,' Claire said, 'how do you know you'd *notice* a bomb?'

'Don't know that I would.' Will bit his lip. 'Only one way to find out.' He leaned around the open driver's door, dipped the sun visor, and caught the falling keys.

Eve felt her stomach plunge, a roller-coaster drop. 'Really?'

'We wait around here, it's a death sentence anyway. One of us might as well try.'

'Why you?'

'Because of this ankle. I'm the most expendable.' With his good heel, Will pushed himself into the driver's seat. He took a moment with his forehead to the wheel, catching his breath, then straightened up again. A metallic purr as he slotted the key. 'You all probably want to stand back.'

'Will –'

'Come on, Eve. Look at us. Without this Jeep how the hell are we gonna get out of here?'

The others had withdrawn to a safe distance. Sue was again sitting on the ground, too weak to hold herself up. Harry looked gaunt with concern. Claire swung her locked-out legs, concentrating to place each step properly in the deep mud as she put real estate between her and the Jeep.

Eve hesitated at the open window. Will held out his hand, and she took it.

'Okay?' he said.

'Okay.'

He squeezed and let go. She backed away to the others, beyond reach of the blast radius. The top of his head remained barely visible above the headrest, and she fought an urge to shout out and stop him.

'Clear?' he yelled.

'Clear!' Claire shouted back.

Eve saw Will's shoulder's bob as he leaned forward toward the dash. She closed her eyes and braced for a second explosion.

36

A click sounded from the stable as Will turned the key.

Nothing happened.

As in nothing at all.

Eve felt a burn in her chest and blew out the breath she'd been holding. Will had already clambered out, hopped around to the grille, and stuck his head under the hood.

'Damn it,' he said as they approached. 'Son of a *bitch*.'

Eve came up to the Jeep. 'You're angry because you didn't explode?'

'No. I'm angry because he took the positive-terminal lead from the battery. It's only yay big' – Will's thumb and forefinger measured off a two-inch bite of air – 'but without it nothing happens.'

Now that she was looking for it, the missing piece of the connection was clear. Will had pried up the rubber nipple of the battery. Before it a red cable rose to nothing, the nut clamp unfastened.

Will struck the Jeep with the heel of his hand. 'We're not gonna get a cough out of this engine.'

'Is there something else you could use to connect the cable?'

'I don't know. I just – I don't know.' He rested his elbows on the metal ledge, took a few deep breaths, his eyes squeezed shut against the pain. When he opened them again, his gaze was loose. 'I'll see . . . I'll see if there's anything else in here I can use.'

'I'll check the van battery,' Eve said.

'Good luck there,' Claire said from behind.

Eve walked across to where the Chevy Express remained, slant-parked across the cantina floor. The veranda looked semi-stable, if charred, and she took the risk of walking under it to the van. The driver's door was open but gave off no alert chime – not a promising sign. She reached through and popped the hood. Fortunato met her at the front with the refilled bucket, and when he threw water across the metal, it hissed, dancing in ever-shrinking beads. They went another two rounds with the water before she dared tap the hood with her palms. It had cooled sufficiently for her to raise, but still she felt the heat of the explosion preserved deep in the metal.

The engine was useless, the battery melted, the cables turned to charcoal.

She let the hood fall and caught a puff of acidic air in the face.

Across the way, Harry helped Will out from the stable, Claire and Sue trailing, and they all convened in the middle of the clearing.

'Nothing?' Eve asked.

Will said, 'Nothing.'

The trees seemed to bow in over them. Their eyes shifted and their heads twitched, taking in every bobbing branch, each leaf spiraling to the ground.

Neto's counting resurfaced in Eve's awareness; he'd been going this whole time. His sleeves were cuffed, the fabric marked with fingerprints of ash and blood. He timed the compressions, shoving harder and harder on Lulu's chest, her body giving up nothing.

'How long's he been doing that?' Eve asked.

Claire checked her dive watch. 'About twenty minutes now.'

Eve walked over, put her hand on his shoulder. He'd sweated clean through his shirt; it felt as though he'd just climbed out of a pool. 'Lourdes,' he said. 'Lourdes? Lulu. *Lulu*. Lourdes. Lourdes?' He kept on in a hoarse whisper, spittle accompanying each breath.

A muscle in his back shifted back and forth under Eve's palm, heaving beneath the skin like a clenched fist. 'Neto,' she said. 'Come on.'

'Lourdes. Lourdes? *Lourdes*.'

'You need to leave her now.'

'I'm not leaving her. I'm not leaving her.'

'She's gone. The van exploded, and it killed her, and she's dead. She's dead.'

He stopped, and she braced herself in case he swung at her, which had happened to her once before – a bereaved husband in an intensive-care unit. Neto's arm tensed, and she feared he'd pivot around. If he did, there would be little she could do about it. But he just stayed that way, hunched over his dead wife, his muscles knotted. It seemed to Eve that if he unclenched, he would fly apart. He rotated slowly to face her. Big drops of sweat dangled from the tips of his black curls. She could smell the shock and grief on his breath – a bitter, emergency-room smell, all spent pheromones and frayed nerve endings.

With her hand she kept contact with his back, turning him toward the adobe hut and starting him walking.

'Come on,' she said to the others. 'There's nothing we can do out here right now. And it's safer inside.'

Will sagged against Harry, his face wan. The bandage had spotted over his shin, fluids seeping through.

Eve said, 'We need to get that foot up and then get you rebandaged.'

Will said, 'Yes, please.'

With her palm pressed reassuringly to Neto's back, she led them in.

Bashir's thick hands held the blister pack of antibiotics. With the tip of his thumb, he punched through one pill and then another. *Pop. Pop.* Through a gap in the foliage, he watched the survivors file raggedly toward the abode hut. The viewing corridor so narrow that fronds brushed his temples. He was another set of eyes in a vast jungle filled with watchful creatures.

Pop.

He read their body language: defeated. Grunts of anguish carried to him. The shade was cool and pleasing.

Pop.

The door closed behind them. His stare shifted, reading angles and movement, gauging the sun's progress toward this treetop or that branch. He mapped where the shadows would fall, how they would creep along the ground.

Pop.

A shift of the wind brought the smell of burned flesh from the picnic table. A familiar scent. How many sheltered Americans had never seen the insides of another human?

Pop.

His eyes moved from porch to window to dipping sun. Again he assessed the shadows and what they offered him.

The last pill popped free, and he glanced down at the scattering of oblong white pills before his toes. With the ball of his foot, he ground them into the moist earth.

Then he slid from cover.

Fortunato stayed by the closed front door, knife in hand, as they tried to put themselves back together. Sue disappeared into the bathroom numerous times. In between they cleaned Neto up and Harry found him a fresh shirt. Neto sat in the corner, his face glazed and lifeless. It was beyond an expression; it was as if something had shifted physically in the tendons and sinews under his flesh.

Eve tended to Will's ankle. Of course all his movement had aggravated the break. He winced as she checked the edges of the wound.

'We're pretty much screwed, aren't we?' Will asked.

'Pretty much,' Eve said.

'What do you think the odds are that the *alcalde* reached whatever city he was going to by now? And that help is on the way?' His hopeful expression was almost more than Eve could take.

'He was going to report Jay *missing*,' she said. 'It wasn't a murder yet, so that might make it a lower priority. On the other hand, Jay's American, so that'll carry some weight. But the request to the *federales* has to work its way from San Bellarmino to Oaxaca City and then who knows through what else. I put contact info for his family in the report, so if they apply pressure . . .' She shrugged.

'We're fucked,' Claire said.

Eve nodded. 'Yeah.'

She finished with the wound and squeezed Will's toe. 'Pins and needles?' she asked.

Will shook his head. 'It's getting a bit numb.' He read her face. 'That's bad?'

'We need to get you out of here.'

'That's another nonanswer.'

'No,' she said. 'It's not. We need to get you out of here.'

'Oh. Right.' He mustered a smile. 'How you gonna do that?'

'I don't know right now.'

He leaned back on the bed and blew a breath at the ceiling. His hands rose to cover his eyes, a fist gripping the opposite thumb. They rested across the bridge of his nose, tugging on each other, an equilibrium of frustration.

Eve fought the urge to say something comforting, because at the moment there wasn't anything comforting to be said. She left him and headed into the bathroom. As the door pulled open, she started, realizing that someone was already in there.

Claire sat on the lip of the tub, legs splayed before her, rolled outward on the ankles so they looked vaguely froglike.

'You scared the hell out of me,' Eve said.

Claire dragged her legs in, first one, then the other, with a languid dreariness that suggested antipathy toward them. 'Guess we don't have the luxury of privacy. Not anymore.'

'Want me to leave?'

'It's fine.' Still she wouldn't look up. Her hands unclasped, and Eve saw in them Jay's satellite phone.

'Signal?'

Claire shook her head once. Left, right.

She handed Eve the phone. The battery icon was red and blinking.

'No rain, but the clouds,' Claire said. 'Electricity. That's what screws with the signal. That battery's pretty much done.'

Eve thumbed off the phone to preserve what little charge was left and slipped it into her pocket. 'Neto's in shock,' she said. 'And Lulu . . .'

'Lulu?' Claire gave a little snort. 'Lulu has it easy now.'

Sweat darkened her dirty-blond hair at the temples. It hung dead straight, framing her sharp, narrowed features. The expression she kept pointed at the floor was tough and ironic, but that didn't fool Eve for a second. She waited, watching her.

Sure enough Claire's mouth trembled wetly. 'He's still out there.' She pointed through the closed door in the direction of the cantina, then swept her hand to encompass the jungle as a whole. 'Right now. Waiting. I can *sense* him.'

'Yeah,' Eve said. 'Me, too.'

A banging on the door, and then Harry's voice drifted through. 'She needs the bathroom.'

'She's been in here practically the whole time,' Claire said.

'And she needs to be in there again.'

'*Just* . . .' Claire raised her hands toward her ears, made fists. 'Give us a second.'

'Hurry up.' His footsteps retreated.

'God.' Claire shook her head. 'When'd he get so assertive?'

Eve shrugged.

'How's Will doing?' Claire asked.

'His ankle's broken, and we have no pain meds or antibiotics. So about as can be expected.' Eve pointed at the sink. 'Mind if I . . . ?'

Claire shook her head in a manner that suggested that this intrusion was hardly a drop in the bucket of the things she minded.

Eve wet her hands and tried to work the mud out of her hair.

'He's frustrated now,' Claire said. 'Angry. It's sinking in that he'll probably die here because of what his body can no longer do.'

'Claire. Claire? *Claire.*'

Finally she looked up. The women's eyes met in the mirror.

Eve said, 'We're not gonna leave you behind.'

'The only way out now is by foot.'

'By *foot*? There's no getting out by foot. We are miles from civilization. In this terrain? Crossing a single ridge could take half a day.'

'It'll still be a ridge between you and *him*.'

Eve said, 'We're *not* gonna leave you behind.'

Claire gave a skeptical nod and rose. She walked out, pulling the door gently closed after her.

Eve paused a moment, then went back to working the clumps of mud from her hair. Quickly, she realized the pointlessness and gave up. She'd get clean when she was safe.

She leaned on the sink and stared at her reflection. Her face creased and weary and smudged with dirt. *What are you gonna do now?*

Her reflection had little to offer.

She closed her eyes, pictured Lulu laid out on the picnic table just yards away in the clearing. The same pretty face, but inside the parts were all jumbled together, the pilot light snuffed. It didn't take much to cross a body over from one side to the other. And Bashir Ahmat al-Gilani certainly knew all the shortcuts.

An image bobbed up through the darkness – Nicolas. His mussed blond hair, his inquisitive eyes, the slender curve of his neck when he bowed his head to focus on some action figure he'd invested with mythical import-ance. Eve felt herself softening, weakening, sensed an erosion beneath the flesh like the erosion that had robbed Neto's face of vitality. Her thoughts narrowed to a single point: She would stay alive for her son.

She would stay alive for Sunday *Lord of the Rings* mara-thons with microwave popcorn and Nicolas close enough to hide under her arm when the Orcs showed up. She would stay alive for morning swim practices and for bed-time stories that he pretended he had outgrown. She would stay alive for dozens of banal reasons that a man like Bashir Ahmat al-Gilani probably could not grasp, for the innumerable commonplaces that fly by unnoticed until you're languishing on your deathbed or trapped in a jungle hut and you take stock and realize that, added up and mashed together, they form your life – they form *who you are*.

And if she was going to do that, if she was going to

stay alive, it meant she would have to think about nothing except prevailing and outlasting. It meant she would have to think like Bashir Ahmat al-Gilani.

Every item had to be divested of its meaning. Mezcal was a drink, sure, but today it was an explosive. Today a Chevy Express van was a death trap. And the ATV quads with the slashed tires were repositories for limited quantities of gas and oil and –

The quads.

Already she was moving for the door, the others bolting upright as she banged into the main room. 'The ATVs,' she said. 'Have batteries.'

Will pushed himself up on the bed. 'Which means they have positive-terminal leads.'

Eve rewrapped his ankle and helped him up onto his good foot. His arm, slung across her neck, was slick with sweat, and she could sense the pain radiating off him. They gathered at the front door, Neto in the rear, swaying even more than Sue. Harry nodded to Fortunato, who tentatively cracked the door. They regarded the slice of destruction from the safety of the hut. There was the Jeep across the clearing, pulled into the stable. The view opened as Fortunato leaned forward, holding the knife before him like an antique candle holder he needed to light the way.

Everything was as it had been.

'Everyone together,' Will said. 'As in *touching*.'

They held their shape as they moved through the clearing, a tight phalanx, and reached the edge of the stables. Grimacing, Will ventured a few hops beneath the roof and leaned over the outermost mud-flecked quad. He peered at the battery, prying back the rubber cap over the terminal lead. 'Damn it. No, it won't fit. Good idea, though.'

Sue gave a sigh that ended in a sob.

'How about *that* one?' Eve pointed to the last ATV in the row. 'It's an older model.'

He regarded her skeptically, then pulled himself around to it, bending down. The muscles of his back rippled with some hidden effort of the hand, and then he turned, holding a battery lead between his thumb and forefinger like a showcase diamond.

The loose and scattered laughter was humorless, more like vented relief. Neto alone held his focus elsewhere; he was turned one hundred eighty degrees from the others, staring at Lulu elevated on the picnic table, a royal corpse prepped for viewing.

Eve carry-dragged Will over to the still-open hood of the Jeep. He fussed for a moment beneath, then swung himself into the driver's seat. He leaned back, panting at the roof, trying to get the pain under control again. Then he reached for the key. Paused.

He said, 'There could still be a bomb.'

No one stepped away.

'Fingers crossed, then,' he said, and turned the key.

The engine sputtered to life.

The sound – so familiar, so ordinary – was a music of sorts, a roadway melody here among the birdsong and timpani rumble of the clouds. Eve's breath caught, a hiccup of unadulterated joy.

They stepped aside, and Will eased the Jeep out of the stable into the open. He put it into park and opened his door. 'You drive,' he said to Eve. 'I can't hold down the accelerator.'

Sue scrambled into the back first and had herself buckled in before the others could move.

Neto started toward Lulu over on the picnic table. Harry caught him by the arm. 'Where are you going?'

'We have to bring her.'

'We're not bringing her, Neto. When we get out of here, we can send someone back for her body. So you can . . . mourn. But we can't fit her in the Jeep.'

Neto tugged his arm free. 'No. That won't work. We have to bring her with us.'

Sue leaned forward to peer out the open door, sweeping her hair back over an ear with her fingertips. 'She is *not* coming in here with us.'

Fortunato said, 'The roads will be *muy* bad. The river, too.'

'I don't care,' Sue said. 'Let's go.'

'Make no mistake,' Harry said. 'We're going.'

Fortunato's forehead furrowed as he strained for English. 'I mean you need should bring the food. You do not know how much the time down the mountain.'

'He's probably right,' Will said to Eve. 'Who knows how long we'll have to wait at the crossing for the water level to drop, or where the roads'll be washed out, or how long we'll – *you'll* – need to hike if we have to leave the Jeep behind. Could be days. We should salvage any food we can.'

They looked at the food area by the grill. Emptied milk cartons, spilled cereal, heads of lettuce mashed into the mud.

Leaving the Jeep running, she helped Will as they crept across toward the food. The remaining ice was no more than thumbnails floating on the warm ground. Eve looked from the puddle to Will's ankle, and he followed her eyes and shook his head with what seemed grudging respect for a man clever enough to deprive his shattered ankle of ice. He picked up a handful of protein bars from the dirt and assessed a half-stomped banana. Eve crouched before the miniature refrigerator. The door remained slightly ajar. No light shone within.

She reached out a finger, hooked it in the dark crack.

Will said, 'Hang on.'

He hobbled over to her, and they leaned close, a bomb-squad team debating whether to cut the red wire. Behind them they could hear Neto and Harry still arguing about the body, with Sue and Claire chiming in.

Will nodded to Eve, and she inched the door open. He slithered his hand through the gap. His forearm tensed as he seized something. Then he said, 'Holy crap.'

'What?'

'Open the door now. Slowly. *Very* slowly.'

She swung it the rest of the way. Clenched in his hand, a two-liter bottle of Mountain Dew, still tilted as it had been seconds ago leaning against the door. The bottle was partially filled with a milky substance, topped with foam. Dangling inches above the surface was a tea bag, the string secured by the screwed-tight cap. Will's fingers had turned white around the green plastic.

'What is it?' Eve asked.

Will spoke without so much as moving his lips. 'Incendiary bomb.'

'Put it down.'

'I *can't* now.'

Painstakingly, he righted the bottle, the tea bag swinging above the fluid but not touching it.

'Hold the string,' he said. 'And for God's sake don't let it slip.'

She pinned the tea-bag string with a fingernail.

Behind them Neto was yelling. '– not gonna leave her to the *ants and maggots* –'

Will unscrewed the cap, flicked it aside, and held the bottle with both hands. Millimeter by millimeter, Eve guided the tea bag out and free.

They exhaled together.

A sickly sweet scent rose from the open bottle. 'Is that . . . ?'

'Lavender,' Will said. 'Glycerin from the soap-making center.' He sniffed the mouth of the bottle. 'And sulfuric acid. Rust remover.'

Eve glanced at the oxidized patches on the aluminum cladding over the grill. She remembered Fortunato and Concepción scrubbing at them, working away flakes of rust. The scope of al-Gilani's ingenuity overwhelmed her. How many other run-of-the-mill items could be weaponized and turned against them? More than anything else, the repurposed Mountain Dew bottle drove home how thoroughly outmatched they were.

Will tossed the soda bottle aside and took the tea bag from Eve's hand. The top had been slit, and he upended it, granules spilling into his palm.

'I'm guessing this is potassium chlorate,' he said. 'From the pesticide the workers were sprinkling around the camp. The door opens, the bottle tips, the bag drops into the liquid mixture, and we've got one less little Indian in the jungle.'

'Thank God for your engineering degree.'

'It's not a master's in bomb making from Terrorist U,' he said. 'But right now I'll take the B.A. from Puget Sound.'

He reached into the refrigerator and claimed their prize, several knots of quesillo Oaxaca, sealed in intact plastic bags. 'Protein. And it'll keep a day at least.' He armed a bowling-pin array of water bottles off the top ledge into Eve's T-shirt, which she held out from her belly to form a pouch as she'd seen the *indígeno* mother do when the swarm of sweeper ants had arrived. She and Will turned back to the Jeep, which chuffed, exhaust making the air at the tailpipe waver.

'Hi?' Will called out. 'We almost just blew up.'

But the argument had escalated, the others too embroiled to notice. Will leaned heavily on Eve as they started back. Fortunato met them and relieved Eve of some of the bottles. Will tossed the cheese and the protein bars into the cargo hold, then leaned against the side of the Jeep, breathing hard. Fortunato began unloading the rest of the water bottles from Eve's shirt. She saw that he had furnished them with a few other items as well – canteens and flashlights.

'Neto,' Harry was saying. 'It's impossible to get Lulu into the –'

'Don't *tell me* what is possible!' Neto craned up into Harry's face, jacking a finger at his eyes. Harry leaned away, hands raised in a show of passivity. Neto said, 'If it was Sue – *your* wife – would you leave her?'

285

'Funny,' Claire said, 'I seem to remember you being on the *other* side of that argument earlier when it pertained to Jay. You were happy to leave *him*. And that was before we even knew he was dead.'

'You can protest all you want,' Neto said. 'But it is *my* Jeep. Mine and Lulu's. I will let you ride in it, but she is coming with us. Her father and mother deserve to have their daughter's body buried properly. *Lulu* deserves it.'

Something shifted inside Harry. Stubble bristled around the firm line of his mouth. He said, 'Like Theresa Hamilton did?'

Neto shoved him, knocking the older man into the side of the Jeep. Harry staggered a bit from the impact, lowered slightly onto one bent knee, the position underscoring his age and frailty. Flushed in the cheeks, he coughed, then straightened up.

Neto stormed across the clearing to the picnic table. He rested a hand on Lulu's cheek, murmuring something to her, then crouched and slid his arms beneath her neck and the V of her knees. Muscles straining, he pulled her upright.

There was the distinct sound of something hollow falling, a tick, then a tock. A half-filled Mountain Dew bottle rolled out from where it had been lodged beneath Lulu's body.

Eve felt a pulsing at her wrists, her blood lurching. She watched Neto's head dip to track the bottle as it rolled off the edge of the table. Then he lifted his face to look across at them, his brow twisted in an expression of puzzlement.

In slow motion Eve saw the tea bag twirling inside, suspended, liquid whorling up the curved sides all around it.

The bottle struck the bench seat.

The flare was so intense that it seemed to scorch its image onto Eve's retinas. She cringed away, her eyes squeezed shut, the yellow flash preserved on the backs of her lids. An instant later the shock wave lifted her hair. The force was gentle, a caress across her nape.

Then came the fist of the explosion.

37

Neto sat on the ground facing away from them, his legs sticking out lock-kneed before him. Smoke wisped up over his shoulders. The back of his shirt was unscorched. From this angle he looked perfectly intact.

Kicked-up dirt typhooned in the clearing, adding grit to the black fumes. Harry crawled out from behind the Jeep, joggling his head like a dog trying to shake free a collar. Will was doubled over, hacking, his bandaged foot sticking out behind him, bouncing with each cough.

Eve took a cautious step to the side, trying for better perspective. Neto's motionless and formal position suggested peacefulness or prayer. Lulu's body had landed before him in the dirt, and he seemed to meditate over it. Another step brought him further into view.

His front side was hollowed out, a doll held over a flame.

Eve's gorge lurched, shoving at the back of her throat. She waved her way through the smoke toward the Jeep, shouting, '*Let's go, let's go!*'

She jumped in, the still-running engine vibrating the driver's seat reassuringly. Doors opened and shut, and faces bobbed in the rear-view. Will stumbled over and threw himself into the passenger seat, his door flapping open as she screeched in reverse, then slamming shut as she hit the brakes for a three-point. She stomped the gas

288

pedal, the others pitching back in their seats as she peeled out.

Through the windshield the greenery streamed past, Eve bracing herself for the scarred face to appear among the fronds or a dark form to sweep past the hood. He was a ghost – everywhere and nowhere.

She wrenched the wheel, the Wrangler skidding toward the break in the trees leading to the road beyond. She could see it now, a span of mud flickering into sight between the trunks ahead.

Will was yelling. 'Wait a minute! Wait – just wait!'

Eve braked hard, and they heaved forward collectively. '*What?*'

Will was twisted around in his seat. 'Where the hell is Claire?'

'She's here,' Eve said. 'She's in the cargo hold. She *has* to –'

Fortunato looked over the seat back. 'No. She is gone.'

'Gone,' Eve said. '*Gone?* She's on *leg braces*. She can't be gone.'

They pressed their faces frantically to the windows. Smoke billowed and undulated, clearing by degrees to show nothing and more nothing.

– stay alive to see him blow out candles on his birthday cake and to show up for back-to-school night and –

'No,' Eve said. 'No, no, no.'

She rolled down her window, shouted Claire's name. Will followed her lead. She screamed again and again, her throat going hoarse.

'This is insane,' Sue said. 'We have to get out while we can.'

Eve's lungs ached from the smoke and the shouting.

'She's not here,' Harry said. 'She'd hear us.'

'Come on!' Sue shouted. 'We have a chance to save our lives, right now.'

— stay alive for free-comic-book day and post-swim-meet pizza parties and —

Will's gaze was steady on the side of Eve's face. 'Eve.'

She dropped the gearshift into drive again. The dashboard grew blurry. She blinked, and the road ahead came into focus once more.

'We can't,' Will said. 'Eve. We *can't*.'

— be there when he needs shots at the doctor's and for when he has nightmares and wakes me in the middle of the night and —

She stomped the gas pedal. The Wrangler barreled through the break in the trees. Sue leaned back, shot a breath of relief. Fortunato bowed his head. Harry palmed sweat off his forehead. Behind them in the mirror, the lodge receded.

The oval of Will's face remained in her peripheral vision, staring.

Eve was crying.

Another voice spoke in her head, welling up from somewhere deep within: *If you leave her there, to him, you will never forgive yourself.*

They broke free, skidding onto the apron of dirt. The road ahead corkscrewed, weaving and diving down the mountain, vanishing and reemerging. It was potted, puddled, and strewn with fallen branches. But navigable.

She pictured Claire's face in the bathroom. Recalled her own words: *We're not gonna leave you behind.*

Her body made the choice for her; she didn't know

she'd hit the brakes until the locked wheels were pushing up mud and the trees were slowing on either side.

'*Fuck!*' she screamed. She battered the steering wheel. '*Fuck fuck fuck!*'

She was sobbing, the blows stinging her hands, ringing up her arms. She kept on, punching at the wheel until Will reached across and locked down her arms, and then she collapsed forward, weeping.

Finally she shoved her hands along her cheekbones. Everyone sat in stunned silence for a few moments.

Then Eve turned the Jeep around, the tires crackling calmly through the mud.

She expected Sue and Harry to complain, but they seemed too shocked to say anything.

Reversing course, she drove cautiously back through the draped vines, the jungle swallowing them once again. The tires found the ruts the Jeep had made on its way out. They pulled in to the clearing.

Neto's and Lulu's bodies were gone.

One sandal lay by the picnic table. A twisted piece of scorched green plastic remained – a surviving remnant of the Mountain Dew bomb. A dark stain on the ground marked the place where Neto had settled into his final, seated repose.

The rest of the clearing: empty.

Beyond the stable at the trees' periphery, an aqua-blue light, no bigger than a silver dollar, swayed back and forth. A sensor for another bomb?

No.

Dread thudded the walls of Eve's stomach, timed with her heartbeat. She eased the Jeep to a stop and climbed out.

Will said, 'Hang on,' but Eve said, 'No. *Now* he's gone.'

She floated on numb legs past the stable. She reached the jungle's edge.

Fastened around a vine, swinging languidly in the breeze, was Claire's dive watch. Eve reached out, pulled it free. Digital numbers reconfigured rapidly on the backlit screen. The stopwatch was running.

More precisely, counting down.

38

At the edge of the jungle, Eve held Claire's watch, the numbers flying by, counting down, crossing the eight-hour threshold. The rain had started up again, light enough to feel like mist.

The message was clear: eight hours until he killed Claire.

The others gathered around Eve, staring at the watch face. 'Why so much time?' Harry asked.

Will said, 'He wants us there after nightfall.'

'Us?' Sue said. *'Us?'*

'Where?' Harry asked.

'His house in the canyon,' Will said. 'He took her there.'

Harry rubbed his eyes. 'For *what?*'

'For bait, Harry. She's the weakest. The easiest to manage.'

A branch snapped deep in the foliage, and they all started, Sue yelping. They drew back into the clearing and closer together. Fortunato unfolded the steak knife. They stared at the rise of green. The breeze leaked out at them, fragranced with tropical flowers.

Rustling. A footstep crackling into mud. One rock clicked against another. Throaty breathing. At head level the fronds bobbed violently.

And then a protrusion shoved its way into sight. A big

brown muzzle. Broad nostrils, chisel teeth, star of white fur above the nose.

Ruffian. The burro who'd escaped last night, spooked by the thunderstorm.

Sue made a noise that stopped short of a wail. Eve did her best to unknot her shoulders. Will actually laughed.

The burro lumbered out from cover to the stable, where he stood dumbly with his nose pressed up against the outer wall, as if sniffing splinters.

Eve bent, hands on her knees, catching her breath. Will grabbed Fortunato's shoulder to regain his balance. The sky strobed, the lightning weak against the sun's cloud-muffled glow.

Sue sagged onto the hood of the Jeep, doubling over and pressing her forearm weakly to her gut, presumably against the stomach cramps. Her voice was dry, mostly gone. 'If he's taking Claire to his *place*, we need to get down the mountain now. We need to get her help.'

'Look at the time, Sue.' Eve pushed the watch at her face. 'It's five hours to the coast in ideal weather with an intact bridge. How long in these conditions?'

Fortunato was slow to realize she was asking him. 'Road to river crossing *es muy* rough. To go there and then down *los otros* roads to Huatulco after the storm like this? Could be half of one day maybe.'

'Assuming we can . . .' Will's voice faded off. Eve had seen it before in ERs and ICUs, pain snatching the words out of someone's mouth midsentence. Will lowered himself to the ground, wiped at his forehead, continued. 'Assuming we even *get* across the river right away.' He held out his palm, catching rain. 'If that water level stays up, we could get stuck on the bank. Either way Claire's dead before we reach civilization.'

'*He* knows that,' Eve said. 'He knows the timing. He's counting on it. And he's counting on the fact that we know it, too, and that we'll . . . we'll . . .' The thought spiraled off into the void. There were too many variables to grasp at once. She had to keep her thoughts neat and concise, like Rick's, or they'd balloon into panic.

'That's what they do,' Harry said. 'Use our humanity against us.'

'Well, then,' Eve said, 'you and Sue should get off scot-free.'

Harry stepped up on Eve, crowding her, and it struck her for the first time that, though he was older, he was a man with a man's strength. 'You can insult me all you want,' he said. 'But don't insult my wife.'

Will said, 'Back off her, Harry.'

Eve stepped away instead.

Sue took her arm. 'That's not fair, Eve. Listen, you were willing to leave Jay at one point. What's the difference?'

'I figured Jay was probably dead,' Eve said softly. 'And Claire is probably alive.'

'What if she's *not?* What if this is just another trick? To separate us? Because he's *counting* on us wanting to help her.'

Eve bit her lip, watched the seconds scroll past on the watch. 'We can't leave her to him.'

'That's what he's *hoping* we'll say.' Harry blurted the words, a fusion of anger and frustration. 'He's hoping you'll be just dumb enough to make that call.'

'Well,' Will said, 'then he'd be right.'

'I can't believe it,' Sue said. 'I can't believe we're even having this discussion.'

Eve fought for focus. 'Will can't do anything on that leg, but besides him there are *four* of us. Four against one. If we *all* go, we have a chance.'

'I can barely move with these cramps,' Sue cut in. 'I'm in worse shape than Will.'

Eve raised her voice to be heard over Sue. 'We can figure *something* out. Maybe talk to the guy, convince him that –'

'Convince him?' Harry said. '*Convince him?* Are you some kind of idiot?'

'That we'll never tell who he is. Or bribe him or –'

'He doesn't want money, Eve. He is a fucking *terrorist*.'

'*I don't know, Harry! Okay?*' She was crying with anger, with frustration, with terror, and she hated herself for it. 'I don't *know* what the answer is. I just know what the answer *isn't*.'

They gave her a moment to gather herself, or maybe they were just speechless from the outburst. A butterfly fluttered among the vines, and she thought about how two days ago she might have found it beautiful.

Will looked up at Eve. 'There's not gonna be any talking to this man,' he said. 'If you're going there . . .' Again he seemed to lose the thread of his sentence. His eyes were loose, unfocused. He blinked twice, regaining clarity. 'If you're going there, Eve, it's gonna get violent.'

She felt her resolve melting away. Her lips were quaking. She should have just kept on the road toward safety, toward her son, and left all this horror behind. She would've found a way to let go of the guilt, eventually. To not imagine Claire's final hours. To let the thought of her recede into memory, to layer years and decades over it, bury it deep. She looked at the Jeep, waiting and capable. It wasn't too late.

Harry wrapped an arm around Sue's shoulder, curling her into him. 'You all can go back for her,' he said. 'But let me make it clear. We're not. It's as simple as that.'

No one spoke up. A laughing falcon shrieked somewhere deep in the jungle, a predator's cry of triumph.

Fortunato broke the silence. 'I will go.'

Harry's mouth dangled open, the jagged line of his teeth pronounced. His cheeks were stubbled, jaundiced, and a sunburn had left the skin shiny and raw at the folds of his temples. '*Why?* You can just wander off right now to your . . . your village or fields or whatever. You're the only one who could probably get *away* in these mountains.'

Fortunato bobbed his head, stalling to find the right English words. 'Because,' he said, 'Ms Claire is a guest. And I am the only host left.' His features firmed, and again Eve could see in them the grown man he'd become. '*But . . .*'

Her pulse intensified. She felt it flicking in the side of her neck. She sensed his head swing in her direction, his eyes find her face.

'I cannot go alone. I need someone for to look out. Or for to make distraction. And for to help with Claire if I can get to her.'

Now they were all looking at Eve.

She felt her heartbeat rev up further, a terror throb in her chest. She wet her lips, found them cracked and dry. 'Just you and me? To *fight* him? I don't think . . . I don't know that I can.'

'That's exactly right,' Sue said. 'You *can't*, honey. And no one blames you for that. None of us can. It's not our fault if something happens to Claire. Remember that. It's twisted and sick, but it's *not* our fault. It's that *man*'s fault. We have to react like reasonable people. We have to –'

'You have to,' Will said to Eve, 'do the only thing he won't expect.'

Harry turned to him, exasperated. 'Which is?'

Eve couldn't look up but felt Will's gaze on her. He said, 'Not be scared.'

Fright clawed up her throat, black and thick, threatening to choke off her air. She swallowed hard, swallowed it down.

She looked at Fortunato.

She nodded.

39

Muffled noises carried across the front room to Bashir. The cripple. He sat with his back to her, removing a seed-case bur from the dead skin of his heel. The sun had dropped out of view, the jungle cast in burnt orange. A dying light.

She was tougher than he had imagined. Although he should have known. The sturdy ones, like Jay Rudwick, break at the sight of a machete. But the weak and the compromised? They cultivate in themselves ferocity and daring.

Still, with her useless legs, she'd been easily contained.

A groan now, pain and frustration filtered through dense fabric. Then the sound of gagging.

The bur came free from his heel, disintegrating into dust when he rolled it between thumb and finger. The bur – sharp if received head-on, easily powdered if massaged. Every weapon, every strategy, had its advantages. And its flaws.

He rose and moved to the doorway. Let the wind blow through the thin cotton of his shirt. It chilled the perspiration on his ribs. Should he wait here or slip into the jungle and intercept them? What was that American phrase he liked? Ah, yes.

There is more than one way to skin a cat.

*

With a tire iron swinging at her side and a heart full of abject terror, Eve soldiered on. Ahead, Fortunato navigated the trail through the final shades of dusk, leading Ruffian by the reins. They'd brought the burro for Claire so that she wouldn't have to stumble her way back through the jungle at night on her braces. Eve stayed close and tried to steady her breathing. Claire's dive watch clung to her wrist. Though she'd turned off the backlight, she still sensed the numbers counting down. Less than five hours to impact – of one kind or another.

Coos, trills, and chirps issued from all around, the wild-life symphony adding to the texture of the wet, heavy air. She'd doused her ankles, neck, and arms with bug spray, but it might as well have been a condiment for the mosquitoes and no-see-ums. She swatted at her sticky skin constantly to keep from being feasted upon. Progress was uneven. The storm had washed away whole swaths of the path and obliterated other runs with crashed trees or piled-up mounds of debris, forcing Eve and Fortunato to veer around and fight their way through the undergrowth step by step.

Their plan was worryingly straightforward. Rather than drive the Jeep on the winding road to the demolished bridge and hike downstream from there, they'd take the more direct route on foot through the jungle to the zip-line crossing. The last thing they needed was head-lights and engine noise announcing their approach. If they didn't make it back by dawn, Will, Sue, and Harry would take the Jeep and get out. Will had done his best to push back the deadline, but it had been a tooth-and-nail fight just to get Sue and Harry to agree to wait through the night, and they would budge no more.

Eve and Fortunato had left the phone with Will. They had taken no flashlight, figuring the beam could give them away and get them killed. Since Will had jogged to the canyon in an hour and a half, they allotted more than double that to hike in post-storm conditions, timing it so they'd arrive just after full dark. To have any chance at all, they'd need cover of night. That Bashir Ahmat al-Gilani also preferred the dark was not lost on Eve. Once they arrived, they would observe invisibly, ascertain what hideousness al-Gilani had planned for them, generate their own plan or counterattack, and emerge victorious. That left plenty of holes to fill and innumerable contingencies to cover, but if they didn't take it one step at a time, they wouldn't take it at all.

An animal screech carried to them, stilling Eve in her tracks, the tire iron raised defensively by her ear. The burro shuddered, sending off a wave of warm air scented of hay, leather, and dung. The screech echoed back off the cliff walls once and then again. Something out there was angry.

Fortunato paused near a halved boulder. *'Jaguar.'*

'Fighting?'

'No. Happy. A successful kill.'

The air shifted darker yet, the back end of dusk yielding to night. The canopy was like a blanket pulled overhead, drowning out the stars, dousing Fortunato in overlapping shadows. Only the glint of his eyes was perceptible. If not for those floating Cheshire-cat eyes and the stink of the burro, she might have been standing here alone in the darkness. Fortunato's invisibility was reassuring. His feet knew these trails. Somewhere within arm's length of her, his invisible hand gripped a blade. Because of him, perhaps, they stood a chance.

He prodded Ruffian, and they moved forward, wet leaves and moist vines tapping their shoulders, painting their faces with dew. Now that Eve had actually launched into the jungle, dread no longer threatened to choke her. Something in the act of *doing* had reduced it from a razor-edged ball in her throat to something awful yet manageable. Every step left safety farther behind and brought with it mounting anticipation, the effect like balancing on a fulcrum, each foot weighing a different fall. Beneath it all, a dark impulse quickened her blood. At first she mistook it for adrenaline, but as she knifed on through the blackness, she understood it as something different, something akin to exhilaration.

'*Careful,*' Fortunato hissed from around Ruffian, and a moment later a branch whipped back from the beast's hindquarters and smacked her across the chest.

She caught the branch in the darkness, but the momentum shoved her onto her heels. Wobbling, she had a flash memory of Will snapping the branch into Jay on the way to the cascade and knocking him back a half step. Will and Claire had laughed and high-fived with all the humor and energy of a vacation freshly under way. The image like a postcard from another life.

Still holding on, Eve tried to step out from under the tilt, but the branch sagged. She slid to the side, but then a forceful hand gripped her arm painfully and yanked her to her feet.

She tore free, rubbed her biceps. *'What?'*

Fortunato pointed to the spot on the side of the trail where she'd nearly tumbled, and she blinked it into night-vision focus. At first she thought what she was looking at was the other half of the cracked boulder they'd paused beside when they'd heard the jaguar's roar. But then it came clearer – a giant beach ball of papier-mâché wrapped around a fallen branch. She leaned closer yet and saw hundreds of spots of movement scurrying about the surface.

Termites.

White dots and stiff wings. She felt them as a revulsion scurrying beneath her skin.

'When the nest grows too heavy, it brings down the branch,' Fortunato said. *'It would not be good to fall there.'*

'Thank you. Sorry I didn't understand.'

He touched a finger to his ear. *'Listen. Can you hear it?'*

She cocked her head.

A susurration flowed over the rise ahead, barely reaching her ears.

The river.

'Now,' Fortunato said, *'we must turn silent.'*

The next couple hundred yards seemed to take as long as the preceding miles. They didn't speak at all. They communicated by touch and movement, setting down on the same footholds, passing pinned-back branches from hand to hand, guiding the burro with pats and taps.

As they carved upslope, the noise rose by degrees until

it was a roar of water across stone. Soon an openness manifested itself in the gaps in the foliage ahead.

Fortunato tied off Ruffian several strides back from the river, hiding him beneath tree cover, then slipped through the final veil of leaves. A moment later she followed.

Dumbstruck, she stared down at the river, not believing her eyes. It glowed an eerie green, twisting and writhing through the darkness like a snake. On a slight lag, she put it together – the algae coating the riverbed was emitting a bioluminescence. The sight was otherworldly. Alien.

Fortunato had already started down the bank, his movement jarring her out of her reverie. She was sorry it had. For the first instant since she'd left the lodge, her mind had drifted from the dreadful undertaking at hand. In another time she could have stood transfixed for hours, watching the emerald water run.

She clicked the dive watch's backlight and checked the digits. Four hours and twenty minutes left on the countdown. She started after Fortunato, guiding her body carefully. They worked their way along the rocky bank above the seething river's edge. The flash flood had already blasted through, but still the water ran high and furious. It was hard to imagine that it was shallow enough downriver for the Jeep to cross, but that was a problem for the next morning.

If they lived to see it.

It took an eternity to make their way around the first bend and even longer to round the next. They kept on like that, mindful of every breath, every step, every pebble trickling out from underfoot. At one point a spout of water appeared ahead, erupting twenty feet in a perpetual fountain. Drawing close, Eve saw the cause. The swept-away bridge had gathered against a kink in the river, concrete and steel crumpled like paper by the force of the current. Even Fortunato paused before the awesome sight.

The closer they got, the greater the chance of ambush. After all, they were creeping into al-Gilani's trap.

Breathing quietly, they pressed on past the bridge's remains. Numerous times Fortunato halted, hearing something she did not, and she'd freeze in his wake, braced for an assault. A sleeping bird would flutter up from cover, or a snake would uncoil from a nearby rock, and they would exhale and move on.

At last the shiny thread of the zip line split the air before them. The sight of it, linked to Eve's first glimpse of the man in the canyon, brought a wash of sense memories. Her peeping vantage down at the plywood human target. That scarred face, swiveling to meet hers. Her breathless huddle at the base of the rotting log.

They remained still for a very long time, letting their eyes pick apart the darkness, then finally approached. She made a fist around the steel cable. A dividing line between their side of the river and his, between safety and terror, between everything she'd always known and those things she'd yet to learn.

The hand trolley was there waiting, snugged against the tree trunk. It had been flung back across, left for them.

They were expected.

The line stretched across the glowing river, vanishing into the darkness of foliage on the far side.

'*I will go first,*' Fortunato said, and she nodded and did

not argue. He tucked the steak knife into his waistband, grabbed the trolley in both fists, then looked back at her. *'If I land there and he is waiting for me and kills me, flee.'*

It was an effort to find the air to speak, so she nodded again.

Fortunato gripped the trolley so tightly that veins stood out in his arms. He gathered his weight back on his haunches, then hurled himself out over the river. Even above the rush of the current, the noise of his ride was piercing, a man-made zippering of metal on metal. He flew across, dropping to land at the base of the trees on the far side. He whipped in a full circle, knife low at his side, then scurried up what was left of the bank, vanishing into the underbrush.

She waited, river mist tickling her cheeks. She waited some more. Just as her breath began to quicken with panic, she heard a noise.

The metallic drone of the hand trolley rode back to her, empty. As it passed, she caught it by her face.

She held it, breathing even harder now, watching the darkness on the far riverbank. At last Fortunato reappeared and flashed a thumbs-up.

She held the hand trolley, remembering Neto's words about the zip line: *Not for the faint of heart.* And that was back when the water level was lower, calmer. If her grip failed and she went into the white water, there was a good chance she wouldn't get out.

Setting her teeth, she seized the metal bar, took two running steps, and leapt from the bank. The trolley rasped along the line, and she swung awkwardly, her view of

Fortunato on the opposing shore rocking from side to side. She held her legs as high as she could, but foam flared up at her, snatching at her legs and back.

And then she was over and flying at Fortunato, who hissed, '*Let go.*' A moment before she would have rocketed painfully into the underbrush, she released the trolley, dropping onto him and knocking them both into a sprawl. They dusted themselves off and took stock of the surroundings, catching their breath. Then they crept along the bank, staying well above the floodwater that had inundated the sandy shoal where they'd picnicked three days ago.

The trail to the canyon came clear, rising through the rain-battered spray of orchids. Fortunato cut into the underbrush well before it, and she followed him parallel to the trail. They made slow time, but it was worth staying off the main path.

They skirted the clearing with the camping toilet, fighting foliage upslope and then drifting down, emerging at the northern edge of the canyon floor. Trees grew sparser, and they glided between the trunks until the house came into partial view against the cliff wall a few hundred yards away.

The lights were on.

Eve's breath hitched in her chest. She let it out slowly through her nose.

She wanted to check the stopwatch but couldn't risk the light. She guessed that the countdown was somewhere near the three-hour mark. They watched for fifteen minutes and then fifteen more. They became a part of the jungle, part of the stones and the peeling trunks and the beetles moving silently across the moist ground at their feet.

Fortunato broke the stillness, creeping forward, moving like a deer. She kept at his back, her heart pounding so loud she wondered if he could hear it. They came alongside the copse of close-packed trees, those fronds woven together to form a natural carport for the rusted Jeep. Even from this close, the vehicle was barely discernible, the greenery camouflaging it from all sides, blending it into the forest, making it invisible to drone or satellite.

They pushed forward inch by inch until the front of the house was unobscured.

Bashir Ahmat al-Gilani sat in brazen full view in the well-lit front room, his legs crossed, the machete resting across his bowed thighs. To his side, ignored on the floor like a piece of furniture, lay Claire, strapped to the plywood sheet with the human target painted on it. For a moment Eve thought she was already dead. Her eyes looked distended, all whites, her body motionless. A gag indented her cheeks. Her head hung limply to one side. Then Claire pulled her head back weakly, an attempt to flip a lock of hair out of her face. The gesture, so ordinary and small and human, caused emotion to well in Eve.

A falling sensation overtook her, a weight tugging at her bones, putting a vertiginous swoon into her gut. It passed, and she reacquainted herself with the scene, with reality. In his monklike pose, al-Gilani stared out at the window, unmoving, his gaze fixed fifteen degrees off from where Fortunato and Eve crouched. He was totally exposed.

Eve turned her head until her lips rested against Fortunato's ear. *'What's he doing?'*

He pivoted slowly, communicating just as quietly to her. *'He wants us to see him. So we approach. He is not scared. Our one advantage is he does not expect much from us.'*

And our one dis*advantage,* she thought, *is that he's right.*

They were within twenty yards now, close enough that she could see the rise and fall of al-Gilani's chest beneath his gauzy cotton shirt. She remembered the smell of him in the catacombs beneath the ruins. That arm blocking her.

'Let us check the house,' Fortunato whispered.

They moved painstakingly through the darkness, directly across al-Gilani's line of sight. Given the light within, there was no way he could spot them. She stared through the window at his face, and he stared back at her, unseeing. He exuded calmness and supreme confidence. If he became aware of their presence, it seemed he could impale them with a look.

Keeping a wide berth, they finally passed to the far side of the house, leaving al-Gilani behind. Through a window, a back room came into sight. Next to a rickety cot, a mat lay unfurled, and next to that a bound book lay on a mat of twigs.

A Qur'an. And the mat, a prayer rug.

She remembered her Muslim patients over the years, how she'd worked with some of the more devout ones to ensure that they found a good spot in their hospital rooms to pray five times a day. She thought about how important the prayers were, how particularly the times were prescribed, and a notion struck her.

She turned to grab Fortunato. *'He'll pray soon. He has to pray, and we can –'*

He seized her arms violently and said, too loudly, *'Do not move!'*

She froze.

His gaze lowered. He did not move his head, only his eyes in the sockets. With equal caution she looked down.

Across her ankle a floating wire was stretched to the breaking point.

40

The trip wire, two inches above the jungle floor, was rusted, leaving no chance it would catch a glint of moonlight. That was why, in fact, Eve had failed to notice it.

Fortunato said, *'Do not even breathe. Let me see what the wire leads to.'*

She felt her muscles quivering and willed them to stop. Another millimeter could turn her into a mushroom cloud. Her first thought was of Nicolas. She pictured him, his face tilted up to hers, wearing a mildly inquisitive expression as he awaited an answer to a request for a sleepover, more mint chip ice cream, Internet time to determine how many moons Jupiter has. The image rent her, and she forced it out, away.

Right now there were two things: The wire. And not moving.

On all fours Fortunato worked his way toward the house, tracking the filament, keeping it inches from his face. She watched his halting progress, the wire blending with the jungle floor, coming in and out of view. Her attention was split between him and the corner of the house, around which she expected al-Gilani to explode at any second, machete wielded overhead. She was having trouble finding oxygen in the air.

Despite the all-too-real nausea shuddering through her, she couldn't fully catch up to the situation. Was she really here on a dank canyon floor at night, a trip wire stretched to the breaking point across her shin? It seemed impossible that four days ago she'd been grocery shopping in Woodland Hills.

Fortunato finally reached the base of the house, maybe ten yards away. He waved an arm to draw her attention, then pointed. She assumed that there was a hole drilled into the wall through which the wire carried.

He rose quietly and peered through the window into the back room, the one with the prayer rug. Refocusing, she noticed right away.

Rusted cans, clumped like grapes, were bunched at the base of each visible wall. A rudimentary early-warning system – trip the wire, the cans clatter together. Her eyes darted across the metal bouquets, and she realized that each was composed of a distinct type – soda cans, soup cans, hockey-puck-size tuna cans – ensuring a different timbre to the alert depending on which line was triggered. No wonder al-Gilani looked so relaxed in the other room waiting for their approach.

The wire at her ankle must have been stretched just below the tension point that would make the cans jump. She didn't dare ease her leg back for fear that the movement would trigger a clank. Beads of sweat trickled down the sides of her neck, and she fought the urge to lift her hand to brush them away. She waited as Fortunato tiptoed silently back to her.

He gestured for her not to move, then reached down and pinched the wire, holding it in place. She took a deep breath and eased her foot away.

Painstakingly, he inched the wire back to its resting point. They stood a few feet from the wire, watching it distrustfully, as if it might attack if left unsupervised.

'Now,' Fortunato whispered, *'what were you saying?'*

As if on cue, al-Gilani stepped into the back room. His stare swept the window, and for an ice-cold moment Eve was sure he'd spotted them standing there in plain sight. But he moved to the prayer rug and crouched on his knees.

She didn't hear Fortunato exhale but felt his breath change the consistency of the air. They watched al-Gilani there on his knees. His mouth moved rapidly as he prayed. It was mostly silent, but now and again his murmured Arabic was audible through the thin glass of the window.

He repositioned the Qur'an before his knees, then pulled a thin blanket over his head. His ghostly form rocked and swayed, trance-like. All around him the clumps of rusted cans lay dormant. Waiting.

Fortunato said, *'Now. We must go get Claire.'*

Eve followed him around to the front of the house, on high alert for wires. They noticed one and moved over it with exaggerated steps. As they crept to the door, dread pooled in Eve's gut, as pure and black as oil.

The knob was smooth and lockless. Fortunato rested his hand on it. Panic surged up Eve's throat, threatening to choke off her air.

She reached up, clutched Fortunato's shoulder. He paused. She had to fight out the whispered words: *'I can't go in there. I'm sorry. I can't do it.'*

He looked into her eyes. Believed her. *'Then go around*

front. Watch through the window. If you see him rise, kick the trip wire to alert me.'

The knob gave the faintest squeak as he rotated it. The door swung inward, affording them a sliver angle of Claire on the floor. Her head snapped over at the movement, and her wild eyes grew wilder.

Eve held a finger across her lips. Fortunato set a stone to hold the door open, then eased inside, unfolding the steak knife.

Eve moved to the front of the house, mindful of the trip wire. Through the window she watched Fortunato working on the straps binding Claire to the board. But she could also see through the back doorway into al-Gilani's bedroom, where the inhabited sheet bobbed and swayed. Acid licked the walls of her stomach. An urge to scream scrambled up into her throat, and she trapped it there, breathing around it.

Fortunato's arms sawed silently. Claire waited. The ghost meditated. The sheet fluttered with his breath. Now and then the guttural utterance of Arabic drifted to Eve. She realized she was grinding the ball of her foot into the ground with agitation. The sawing and swaying and grinding seemed to go on forever.

Finally Fortunato peeled back the halved straps, setting them delicately on the floor. He stabilized the plywood with a knee so it would not clatter and helped Claire wriggle up to a sitting position, then standing. They crept across the floor, Claire loosening her gag.

Beyond the doorway in the back room, the ghost prayed, oblivious.

Eve met them at the front trip wire, pointing, her finger mashed across her lips. Silence was a necessity. Claire breathed in clumps and gasps, fighting back tears. Eve helped her across the wire.

And then they ran, one on either side of Claire, heading upslope toward the clearing with the fallen trunk, casting glances back over their shoulders to check on the praying form. Soon they were high enough that they lost the angle through the window into the back room.

They scrambled over the rotting log. Beyond, the toilet lay on its side in a spill of waste, washed over by the rains. They flew through the clearing onto the trail to the river, Fortunato now prodding Claire ahead of him to keep her speed up.

Claire shouldered first through the orchids and fell hard, her forearms skidding through the mud. She looked back at what had snared her ankle.

A trip wire.

Eve tracked its course into the brush, threading through eyelets, rising up a tree, running like a telephone line through the canopy back toward the canyon. Toward *him*.

The acid flared to life again in her stomach. The roar of the river matched the roar between her ears. They all stared at one another for a frozen moment.

Fortunato lunged to untangle Claire's foot, fighting the filament off her metal brace. He yanked her to her feet, and they worked their way onto the riverbank and then across the upper rim, luminous green water clawing up at them. The mud slid beneath their shoes. Eve's legs throbbed; she could only imagine what Claire's felt like.

She pictured those cans jumping, al-Gilani flying up from beneath the sheet. His feet, sure and silent, speeding across the canyon floor.

They reached the zip line. Blessedly, the hand trolley remained where they'd left it. Eve all but hoisted Claire onto it. Claire said, 'Wait, I –' but Fortunato hurled her out over the river, hard. She twisted and swung, her arms bent in a half pull-up to try to keep clear of the water. Her legs dangled limply, her feet catching some drag in the swells, but the momentum carried her across.

Eve risked a look toward the orchids. No movement at the main trail. The jungle crouched at their backs, all wavering leaves, concealing countless approach routes. Again she pictured al-Gilani's footsteps flying across the mud.

Claire found her footing on the far side and whipped the hand trolley back across. Fortunato caught it with an expert stab of his fist and put it in Eve's hands. *'You next.'*

It felt craven not to object, but there was no time to argue, so she ran and leapt.

The crossing felt harder this time, or maybe she was just more exhausted. The water seethed underfoot. Her arms ached. She rocked violently on the line, her view going on horror-movie tilt. She could see Claire across on the opposite bank, kneading her hands in the fabric of her shirt, hunched forward.

As Eve winged past the midway point, Claire's face transformed. The muscles bunched beneath her cheeks, and her skin hardened into a shiny hide, a mask of terror. Her gaze had gone wide, focusing past Eve on the far bank. Hanging on with all her strength, Eve couldn't turn to see what was behind her, and this filled her with indescribable panic, the unseen spectacle like a sheet of flame across her back. Claire's hands rose clawlike and tore at her hair.

Eve swayed on the line, rocketing toward her screaming friend, blind to whatever horror was unfolding behind her.

41

Eve released the hand trolley too early, falling five feet onto her back and jarring the breath from her lungs. The pain came on as something removed, filed away for later consideration. She hopped to her feet beside Claire, whirling around, her eyes moving frantically to behold whatever sight awaited.

On the far bank, one hand hooked apelike over the zip line, stood al-Gilani. His bulky chest thundered with breath from the exertion of his run. Mud darkened his bare feet, his shins, his knees. He'd sweated through the thin cotton shirt, a dense mat of chest hair visible beneath. The glowing river uplit his face into that of a specter. He studied them without emotion.

Eve's gaze pulled slowly down to the river itself.

Fortunato lay mostly submerged, pinned by the current against a rock, his torso arched at a severe angle across a broken back. His arms floated, pulled outward by the clear water. His head was twisted fifteen degrees further than possible, his eyes wide and unblinking even as surges lapped over them. Floating flowers and leaves had collected at the hollow of his throat. He reminded Eve of a painting she'd once seen in a textbook, of Ophelia lying dead and beautiful in the brook.

Her lungs finally released, raking in air with a screech. Across, al-Gilani stared at her evenly. He jostled the zip line abruptly, and it gave off an angry metallic twang. The hand trolley shuddered loose. It started to slide back across to him, but Eve grabbed it just before it sailed past her reach out over the water. She held it firm and glowered at him. Calmly, he stared back.

His hand tugged at the zip line now differently, testing it. It was sufficiently long and al-Gilani sufficiently heavy that it seemed implausible he'd be able to haul himself across without the hand trolley. But if he jerry-rigged a belt into a sling later, there was no telling.

Eve grabbed a skull-size rock and hammered at the clamp securing the zip line's loop point around the trunk. Three, four blows bent it out of shape, and with the fifth the cable whipped free with an outer-space warble, slicing past her cheek and onto the dark waters like a cast fishing line. One end stayed tethered to the tree at al-Gilani's side, the main length rippling serpentlike in the surges between them.

The whole time al-Gilani watched her.

Now his eyes lowered to consider the water. Eve stared down as well. The river looked furious; crossing would be hazardous in the dark.

'Fuck you!' Claire yelled. 'Fuck you for taking me and dragging me here and tying me up, you fucking *animal*!'

It was impossible to read al-Gilani's face, but he seemed faintly amused. Eve took Claire by the arm, started tugging her up the bank, but she kept screaming, tears falling from her chin.

'We have to move,' Eve said. Claire wasn't listening, so Eve shook her. 'We *have to* get back to the lodge before dawn. Or they leave without us.'

Claire stopped fighting her and limped along in her wake. At the first bend, Eve looked back to see al-Gilani down at the water's edge, testing the seething river with a toe. Tackling the violent current and the rocks at night promised an injury. She left him behind, considering his options.

They passed the crumpled bridge and the phosphorescent spout. At the next turn, Claire's legs started failing. 'I won't be able to make it back,' she said. 'Not before morning.'

'There's a burro just ahead. You can ride. You need to keep on.'

Claire did.

They reached the spot and broke through into the jungle, the moonlight diffused by the canopy into tiny bits scattered like broken glass across the floor. Eve pushed forward eagerly.

Ruffian was gone.

The branch to which Fortunato had tied him was snapped, twirling from a strip of intact bark.

The night crushed in on Eve.

'No,' Claire said. 'No, no, no.'

Eve tugged the dangling branch, and it came free in her hand. She threw it down. Deep breath. 'He can't have gone far. We have to look.'

Claire sat on the ground. 'I can't. I can barely move.'

'At daybreak we'll be left for dead,' Eve said. 'After what I risked, after what *Fortunato* risked . . .' Her voice cracked. She thought of those floating flowers gathered in the hollow of his throat.

'You don't know what I went through.'

'Right now I don't *care* what you went through,' Eve said. 'Start looking.'

'It's useless,' Claire said. 'I just need to sit here.'

Eve looked down at her. 'If you sit, you die.'

Claire glowered at her. Then she lifted her hand to Eve.

They grasped hands around the wrists, Eve pulling her to her feet. Keeping within eyeshot of each other, they moved between the trunks, searching for broken twigs, trampled bushes, hoof prints, anything.

Claire took a step back and shouldered into a giant prop root to rest. A black mass the size of a beach ball pulsed in the shadow of the root next to her legs, the sight cinching off Eve's breath.

'Don't. Move.'

Claire's calf was nudged up against the black mass. 'Now you *don't* want me to –'

'Don't *move*!'

Eve crept forward a few steps, Claire tracking her focus. The ball clarified as an organic mass, composed of hundreds of thousands of living parts.

Sweeper ants.

A roost of them, gummed together, oversize mandibles interlocked to hold the colony together in defiance of gravity. Mating? Resting? Either way, one step in the wrong direction and Claire would be embedded in the living nest. A few of the ants scattered free from the grouping, scurrying onto her bare leg.

Eve seized Claire's wrist and jerked her forward. At her movement the ball collapsed. It melted into life, spreading like a scoop of ice cream dropped on a griddle. Claire yelped and struck at her ankles. Eve tugged her away from the banyan, both of them swatting at their limbs, shaking off ants, exoskeletons crunching beneath their shoes. The ants grew sparser with every stride the women took. At last they outdistanced the swarm, but still they ran for a while before slowing. Finally Claire stopped and put her hands on her knees, jerking in quick inhalations. Beside her, Eve struggled to catch her breath, too.

She gave a silent prayer of gratitude that she'd noticed the roost, as Fortunato had noticed the termite nest earlier. It occurred to her that maybe, watching him read the jungle these past two days, she'd learned from him without being aware that she had. And she thought about how his maturity had amplified out here beyond the lodge, how she'd seen in his face intimations of a grown man – the grown man that he'd never have a chance to become. As they continued on, she railroaded her mind back to the humid here and now.

The moon streaked in and out of view overhead. They slowed to a limp, coming around a thicket of sugarcane. Eve collided into something huge and warmly soft. She yelled. It torqued its wide head and grunted, spraying her face. She felt not disgust but a flood of relief. Their burro. She rested a hand on Ruffian, calming him and herself.

Claire came up beside her. She tried to sling a leg up and over but failed, so Eve shoved her up. The burro immediately started moving at a fast clip back toward the lodge, picking up the trail and navigating in reverse the detour paths they'd forged on their way here.

Eve clicked the backlight on Claire's watch, checking the time. Four hours till dawn. If they held the course, they'd make it. From atop the burro, Claire looked down curiously at her watch on Eve's wrist. Eve didn't want to give it back, and Claire didn't ask.

The relative safety allowed Eve's body the chance to register its complaints. Insect bites burned on the backs of her arms, her nape, and she dug at them with her nails. The blisters on her heels felt torn open. Her left-side ribs stung with every breath, an effect, she guessed, of the fall from the zip line.

Claire *tick-tocked* in the saddle, her silhouette dark even against the darkness. 'The Jeep,' she said faintly. 'It's waiting for us.'

'Yes. We just need to make it back.'

'Just need to make it back,' she repeated. Her head swung over in Eve's direction, but the empty gaze seemed to move right through her.

From her screams across the river to her collapse on the jungle floor, she no longer seemed to be the same Claire. She seemed diminished. During Eve's freshman year of college, her roommate had been date-raped in the back of a pickup at a beach party. Eve had driven her to the ER and held her hand through the ensuing pokes and prods and interviews. Many of the details were a blur, but to this day Eve remembered perfectly her friend's face during those awful hours. Claire now wore a similar expression of rubbed-raw blankness, that hollow non-glow that takes hold when it is impressed upon you that your body is not yours to control and protect.

'Claire. Claire?'

The head turned again, the eyes fastening on nothing.

'I'm sorry for what I said. That I didn't care what you went through.'

'I killed him,' Claire said flatly.

The burro plodded along, and Eve plodded beside it. 'I'm not sure I understand.'

'I fell, and I – The trip wire when I – My goddamned legs, they – I killed him. Fortunato came to save me, and I . . . and I . . .' The tension drained from Claire's body, her spine buckling, and she slid right off Ruffian as if poured from the saddle. Eve caught her limp form. Claire's legs held no weight. Her arms stayed slung loosely up over Eve's shoulders, her face buried in her neck, and she was sobbing so violently that Eve worried she might choke.

Claire finally found the earth with one heel and stabilized them both, but she stayed pressed to the side of Eve's neck, sobbing for longer than Eve had ever heard anyone sob. At a loss, Eve reached for instinct, and the first one there, waiting and ready, was the maternal urge, burned into the cells themselves. She shushed Claire and swayed, trying to rock her, but staggering a bit under her weight. Claire calmed by degrees until she finally pushed up out of Eve's arms.

'All right,' Claire said, wiping angrily at her face. 'All right.'

She climbed up onto the burro herself this time.

The path stretched before them endlessly, an ever-replenishing corridor of brown and green. They couldn't get to the end; it kept telescoping away from them. Every crest brought another rise, every turn another curve. The pain swelled to a crescendo in Eve's bones and then faded, a survivalist version of runner's high. Ruffian's breathing grew more labored, and Eve understood that the animal had been run too hard for too long.

When the edge of a bamboo walkway appeared, poking out of the side of the trail, Eve feared it was a mirage. But no – they reached it, and the slats did not dissipate; they remained solid underfoot, all but glowing beneath the moonlight.

They had made it.

The lodge came up, the huts and stable nothing more than shadowy blocks. As Claire rolled stiffly off the burro, Eve tied the reins onto the rail before Sue and Harry's adobe hut. Claire reached for Eve, and Eve shouldered under her arm. With excitement they hobbled up to the door, knocked twice.

'Don't worry, it's us,' Eve called through. 'We're back.'

They pushed inside.

Will lay on the bed, alone, gripping the turned-off flashlight, his leg propped up on a pillow. His wan, sweat-shiny face lifted from the mattress. His left eye was bruised, the upper lid hooded.

'I woke up, and Harry was trying to take the keys,' he said. 'I grabbed for them. He hit me with the lamp. They just took the Jeep and drove off.' His laugh sounded like something dying. 'He really loves that bitch.'

42

Eve's arm went loose around Claire's side, and Claire fell away from her, half sitting, half collapsing on the floor. Grimacing, Will reached for the bedpost so he could pull himself up to face them more fully. Eve was incapable of moving, her feet spiked to the planks. The words were still settling in, working their way into meaning.

'Before I drifted off, Sue was getting really bad, really weak.' Will made a helpless gesture at his leg. 'And then . . . I couldn't stop them.' Only now did it register that his voice was hoarse from yelling.

'That fucking dick,' Claire said.

'How . . . how long ago?' Eve had no idea why the time frame mattered, but somehow it did.

'Two, three hours ago.'

They'd been on the riverbank then, laboring along, rushing through the pain to beat sunrise. The Jeep had already been gone.

'How did you do it?' Will asked.

Eve swept the question aside with her hand. Any explanation felt exhausting; the weight of her disappointment had left her barely lucid.

'Well,' Will said. 'Thank God you're both here.' Then: 'Where's Fortunato?'

'Dead in the river.' It surprised Eve how little of the emotion she felt made it into her voice.

Will's Adam's apple bobbed. He worked his lower lip between his teeth. 'And al-Gilani?' A hopeful note ticked up the question at the end.

'Trapped on his side of the river. For now.'

Will gave a nod. He propped his chin on the flashlight, and it occurred to Eve that it had become a sort of security blanket for him. 'We'd better figure something out,' he said. 'And soon.'

Eve looked from him to Claire and felt something inside her snap. 'God*damn it*.' She was spitting out words without thought. 'I can't protect you. Either of you. We don't have numbers anymore. You two are sitting ducks. I *can't* protect you. You're useless here. Worse than useless. You're a *danger*. I can't . . . I can't . . .' She lowered her head, her hair sweeping forward like curtains, blocking her face, blocking the room. She breathed, the blond bangs fluttering. 'Sorry,' she said. 'I'm sorry.'

She reached a hand to the side, and Claire took it. She moved her other hand to Will's good shin. They stayed like that for a time in the darkness, touching.

'Look at the bright side,' Will finally said. 'At least we're spared listening to Sue talk about the Omaha Women's Loyal Order of Water Buffalos for eighteen hours down the mountain.'

'This is dead serious.'

'I know, Eve. But I don't think that water level's gonna drop for them to get the Jeep across. I don't think they can make it.'

'You think you've got better odds here, injured, with us.'

'*Yes.*'

'But I'm the only one, Will. The only one who can walk.

327

The only one left who can do *anything.*' The anger had left Eve's voice; she was pleading, but she didn't know to whom or for what.

'I know.'

He stared at her, the skin beneath his eye twitching slightly, his foot indenting the pillow. Claire made a sound of exasperation that came out like a choked laugh.

Eve took a breath and then another. 'How's the ankle?'

'Displeased. But Harry and Sue left me a few of these to ease the pain.' Will lifted a miniature spirit bottle from a fold in the sheets, the arty label proclaiming DÍAS FELICES ECOLODGE™. 'Food, too. A bunch of protein bars. They threw 'em at me on their way out the door. Oh, yeah, they were real humane.' He took a slug of mezcal.

'Don't drink that.'

'It's fortifying.'

'It's dehydrating. Drink water. We should keep the mezcal in case we need to start a fire. What else do you have?'

'The almost-out-of-juice phone and a hunk of Oaxaca cheese.' He blinked back his distress. 'Good times.'

'You try for a signal?'

'Twice, real quick. Forget it till the cloud cover blows over. I figure when the charge goes, I could use a battery from the flashlight, wire up a basic circuit.'

'Junior-high physics,' Eve said.

He nodded. 'Junior-high physics.'

Eve took the flashlight from him, shone it on the nightstand. It held a sad little collection of survival supplies that Harry and Sue had presumably left there within his reach – a few books of matches, a clean folded undershirt, several canteens and water bottles. Woefully inadequate.

'Drink some water,' she told him.

As he lifted the canteen, blocking his face, she swung the flashlight beam quickly to his foot. In the absence of ice, the swelling had crept to midcalf, the bruising more black now than blue. She touched his toes. They felt cold and hard, the circulation failing. She pinched, hard.

He did not react. At all.

He lowered the canteen and saw her face. Then his eyes dropped to her fingers, only now noticing them squeezing his toes. He said, 'Shit.'

The beam wavered, and she knocked the flashlight near the lens to get it back strong. The batteries just starting to weaken. She pushed away her dread at that and refocused on his leg.

The shin puncture looked clean, the edges neat, but the skin around felt doughy and smelled like rank meat.

'The swelling,' he said. 'It's bad?'

'It'll compress the artery even more, decrease venous return so blood can't get out of the foot. Veins are low-pressure, so they're more susceptible to –' She caught herself. 'Yeah,' she said. 'It's bad.'

'What do we do?'

'See if I can manipulate the bone in there again, get it off the artery. If it stops compressing the artery, the swelling will go down.'

He blanched. 'You sure I can't drink that mezcal?'

'I'm sure.'

'Got a leather belt I can bite down on?' He didn't smile. Eve didn't either.

From the floor Claire said, 'I'm sorry, Will. I'm sorry I got taken.'

'And I'm sorry I wedged myself under a boulder. And Eve's sorry she picked up Theresa Hamilton's camera. We're all sorry. It's not us. It's him. It's just him.' He bared his teeth. 'Now let's get this over with.'

Eve cupped his heel and raised his foot gently off the pillow, and he screamed. From there it got worse. The noises coming from him were barely human. Eve tried and tried again until it was apparent there was nothing to be done. She lowered his foot at last, but Will kept growling with each breath, his fists knotted in the sheets. Then he dropped his head back onto the pillow and stared straight up at the ceiling, seemingly trying not to move any muscle in his body.

'We're just gonna have to wrap it as tightly as possible and get moving,' Eve said.

Claire: 'Get *moving*? Are you kidding?'

'That river's too fast to cross in the dark. But come morning al-Gilani'll figure out a way across. And the first place he'll come is here.'

'So what then?' Will said. 'You want to take to the jungle like Robinson Crusoe?'

'Robinson Crusoe lived on an island,' Eve said.

'If we go,' Will said, 'we'll slow you down. You won't have a prayer with us.'

'You're right,' she said.

'We'll never make it out,' Claire said. 'We'll die out there.'

'I know.'

Will said, 'Then what's your plan, Eve?'

— stay alive to push him on the swings and tie his shoes and pack him lunch on field-trip days —

'First thing?' Eve said. 'We have to hide you two.'

Tuesday

43

Eve couldn't remember ever awaiting dawn with such dread. A spot of gold glowed through the leaves to the east as she led Ruffian off the trail and down an embankment. Claire rode in the front, Will behind her, and bundled on the very back of the animal were the deflated raft and the waterproof dry bag, stuffed with gear. The overloaded burro had begun to drag his hooves, and the sound of his wheezing did not bode well.

Back at the lodge, they'd rationed out some of the cheese, which Eve had devoured voraciously. She hadn't realized how hungry she was until the first bite hit her stomach. The protein bar had disappeared with a few huge swallows, and she'd drunk water until it dribbled from the canteen down her chin. Afterward they'd packed up quickly and headed out in the darkness, hoping to get miles between themselves and the lodge before daybreak.

Guiding the burro down the embankment, Eve hoped she had her geography squared away. Sure enough the slope started to flatten out, ending in the relatively calm tributary to the river that she remembered from their Sunday excursion. Given the storm, the water moved more briskly than before, but the current hardly compared to the Sangre del Sol, and they'd be bailing out well before the point of convergence.

On the open bank, rain spit at them. Aside from a

five-minute torrent they'd sat out beneath a sheltering plant with broad fronds, their early-morning progress had been made beneath a slight dusting shower. After the torrential downpour of the storm, it had taken a while for Eve to notice that it was raining at all.

Claire and Will gingerly climbed off the burro, and Eve slid free the balled-up raft. Will hopped twice on his good leg and swung himself down to sit. Ruffian shuddered and staggered. Eve slipped off his saddle and reins and led him to a puddle so he would drink. After, he dropped on bent front legs and panted, no longer any use. She stroked his nose. 'Good boy. You can rest now.'

She went back to the water's edge, unfolded the raft, and assessed the two-foot slash that al-Gilani's machete had left in the yellow vinyl. Gathering the glossy material around the slice, she wound it up with the leather reins and tied off the split fabric like the end of a balloon. She knotted the strap again and again until her forearms ached. Not exactly airtight, but it was the closest it was going to get.

Will and Claire sat in the mud, watching her work. Ruffian, back up on his hooves, grazed on a spray of elephant grass at the tree line. Eve unfolded the dry bag, removed the foot pump, plugged it into the valve on the side of the raft, and stomped to inflate. At first it seemed to have no effect, and then the yellow vinyl crackled and sighed to life, rising with maddening slowness. For every two measures of air she got in, it seemed that one leaked from the imperfect seal around the gash. Ten minutes in she switched legs, and sometime after that it was engorged enough to bear them.

In addition to the other supplies, the dry bag had been able to fit only two life vests. Eve wrestled them free and tossed them to Will and Claire, then waded out until she was thigh-deep with the raft, holding it in place so they could pull themselves on. Moments later they were floating downstream, leaving the unrestrained burro contentedly lapping from the water's edge. She watched Ruffian until he drifted out of view and felt tears well in her eyes. It felt wrong, her reaction to saying good-bye to the mute beast that had helped them get this far, crying for him as she could not cry for Fortunato and the others.

She sat at the hull near the tied-off gash, squeezing it with both hands to prevent extra leakage. The raft seemed to be retaining air decently. The dry bag sat at her feet, now folded down and snapped closed to make it fully waterproof – the last remnants of civilization, stuffed into a compressed nylon sack.

They were well upriver from the zip line and al-Gilani's canyon, and for a moment Eve felt not entirely unsafe. The sun couldn't break cloud cover, but the morning warmed nonetheless. Turtles rose like halved coconuts from partially submerged rocks. Hummingbirds strobed among wildflowers. At first the beautiful surroundings seemed a mockery, but as the raft floated along, Eve gave herself over to the scents and the lazily passing view. Will kept his bad leg propped up on the tube, his head tilted back to the spot where the sun lightened the clouds.

Huddled into herself, Claire glared at him. 'What are you looking so content about?'

He kept his eyes closed, basking in the faint glow. 'If this is all we have, I want to be thankful.'

'There's a man trying to kill us. Your leg looks like a mosaic. And you're *thankful*?'

'For this?' He glanced at the river, the trees. 'Yes.'

The tributary quickened. Eve tried to gauge their progress but found she couldn't; the hiding place she had in mind could be a mile away or around the next rocky outcropping.

A ripple vibrated under them, and then Eve heard it. Rushing water ahead, a deep subwoofer rumble. She tensed in the raft, rising to a half crouch. They slid past the outcropping, and she saw, down and ahead, a spot where the tributary narrowed into a flume between boulders.

An oar would have been unwieldy to travel with, and besides, she hadn't figured on needing one. Leaning over the edge, she began paddling toward shore furiously with her hands.

'I'll help,' Will said. 'Flip me over.'

Claire turned his hips, and he grunted with pain, and then all three were paddling, their motions growing more frantic as they were sucked into the current, the scenery spinning around them faster and faster.

Will shouted, 'If we go over, get on your back and keep your feet up and in front of you!'

The boulders swept into view, and Eve fought centrifugal force to lean over and snatch the dry bag. She clutched it to her chest, realized too late she'd forsaken the tied-off gash in the tube, and they struck the first boulder, the raft giving out a *thwack* like a dropped jug of milk. Something flew up and caught her across the eyes, and when she grabbed at it, her hand came away with the loose leather reins.

336

They shot the flume on the deflating raft, leaning toward the center to dodge the boulders ripping past on either side. The tubes turned to puddles, and then there was nothing but the drop-stitch floor, riddled with holes for self-bailing, undulating beneath them like a not-so-magic carpet.

They spilled, peeled out in various directions. The sky turned to white foam and then brackish water. The sudden cold knocked the air from Eve's lungs. She clawed back to the surface, one fist locked on the dry bag. Using an arm for a rudder, she swung herself around onto her back as Will had suggested, and elevated her feet until they were bumps gliding above the surface. A backsplash caught her square in the face, forcing its way up her nose and eyelids and down her throat. She gagged. Her view plunged underwater again. The dry bag struck a boulder, buffering her impact, and then she spun away and into a flash of air that she grabbed before going under again. She flipped once, a full rotation, and came up in water that was suddenly, miraculously calm.

Treading, she drew air, looking back up the flume in time to see Claire tumble down the last fall, her hair pasted across her face, hiding her features. She landed near Eve, leading with her hands and knees as if expecting solid ground. Digging in the clear water, Eve hooked Claire's armpit and hauled her up sputtering and gagging.

Eve sidestroked them toward shore.

'Will!' Claire shouted. 'Where's Will?'

They looked back at the boulders and the white ruffled carpet of the flume, but there was nothing flesh-colored, only browns and greens and grays. Eve swung her head to the far shore, where the deflated raft was pasted to a waterlogged tree trunk.

The muffled voice came from behind them: 'Here.'

Will lay on his stomach, having dragged himself up onto the pebbled shore. His face, darkened with stubble, aimed back at them over the knob of his shoulder. His arms stayed flat at his sides, the flippers of a sunning seal. The bandage had come partially unwound, but he seemed more exhausted than in pain.

The grainy bottom finally came underfoot. Claire pushed away, and the women clambered onto shore and lay beside Will. Eve knew he should be screaming right now, that he wasn't only because his leg had gone numb. The good news was actually bad news.

Will shoved himself over onto his back. They panted up at the sky.

'So,' he said. 'That went well.'

Eve laughed first, and then Claire, and they sprawled side by side in the grit, smiling and staring at the churning clouds.

Claire said, 'I see a steak sandwich.'

Will pointed. 'I see a satellite phone with full bars.'

Eve said, 'I see a Red Cross helicopter, coming to save us.'

'Red Cross?' Claire said. 'In Mexico?'

'Hey. It's my fantasy. I can have the Royal Canadian Mounted Police if I want.'

'No one's coming to save us,' Will said.

Eve's grin went cold on her face. She shoved her fingernails into the mud, felt the give of the earth beneath her matted hair. She became aware of another sound

338

above the rush of the flume, coming from behind them. Louder and deeper.

She rolled onto all fours with a groan. Got one foot beneath her, then braced her hands on her knee and shoved herself up.

Through a strip of dividing jungle, a white wall of water was visible – the giant cascade, tumbling into the natural pool. Beneath it the underwater channel led to the grotto, the best hiding place Eve knew of in the jungle.

If they could get there.

44

Treading water in the emerald pool, the dry bag pulling heavily at her shoulders, Eve regarded the majestic rise of the cascade overhead. Will and Claire paddled awkwardly on either side of her, the crashing water blasting mist across their faces. Eve remembered being afraid to brave the underwater passage last time, how she'd been unwilling to take the risk. Today the swim didn't break her top hundred concerns.

She noted Will's grimace. Navigating the twenty yards across the jungle ridge separating the tributary from the cascade must have been enough to break through the numbness at the wound's periphery and introduce a fresh hell to the surrounding nerves.

'Can you make it?' she asked.

'It feels like the entire Inquisition took place in my leg,' he said. 'But yeah. I have to.'

Eve swung to her left. 'Claire?'

'I'm good in the water,' she said. 'It's *you* I'm worried about.'

Eve tugged on the dry bag's straps, tightening them around her shoulders. 'Let's go.'

A deep breath and then she was immersed in a sudden underwater calm. Ahead, the water spun with the force of the waterfall, a glimmering white steamroller drum. Eve breaststroked toward it, diving to get beneath the churning water. Still, it tore at her clothes and the dry bag on her back.

The underwater passage loomed, black and forbidding, and as she swam beneath the rock shelf, claustrophobia seized her. What if the promised grotto was too far? What if her lungs gave out? What if it dead-ended in a cul-de-sac of stone?

The darkness became pervasive, her hands little more than flares of white on the backstroke. The temperature dropped, not by degrees but in a sudden lurch. Her chest burned. Her arms ached as she began to pull with desperation.

At once the water above took on a different shimmer. She kicked up, breaking free, gasping in damp air, the screech of her inhale echoing off the sweating stone walls.

The grotto rose maybe two hundred yards, an egg-shaped chamber. At one side of the oval, the stone had chipped away to unveil a near-perfect circle of sky. Vining plants had squirmed through the hole, reaching down the dark walls like insect legs. The beam of light looked tangible, a white cone ending on a stone ledge that stretched to meet the water.

Eve kicked to the ledge and pulled herself up. She dumped the dry bag, her T-shirt shifting over the fitted tank top beneath, her skin steaming in the wet heat. Her fingers were pruned and pale, the gold band on her right ring finger loose around the knuckle. She watched the water anxiously. A moment later Claire popped up onto the ledge beside her. Together they stared at the dark water, waiting. Nothing but ripples. Eve stood up, stamped her bare feet, searching the murk for Will. She'd just stepped forward to dive in when he surfaced with a splash.

'Help me,' he said, scrabbling to get a handhold on the slippery rock. 'Help me.'

Each woman grabbed an arm and hoisted him up. Groaning with pain, he sprawled on the stone, a few dry sobs racking his chest. 'I had to kick,' he said. 'I tried not to, but my lungs were giving out.'

'Must've hurt like hell,' Claire said.

Will pressed his palms to his eyes. Wisps rose from his face, his arms. He was fevering, his teeth chattering. 'It *redefined* hurt.'

Eve unsnapped the dry bag and laid out the items for them. Cheese, protein bars, canteens, tiny mezcal bottles, matchbooks. The humble mound looked pathetic, dwarfed by the ring of light thrown through the hole above. Rationed, the food might sustain them for three days, four max.

Will's eyes darted about. Distressed, he overturned a canteen, searching beneath it, then grabbed the dry bag and felt inside. 'The flashlight? Where's the flashlight?'

Eve and Claire helped look, though there weren't many places to revisit. He'd kept that flashlight close at hand since Jay's disappearance; from his expression it seemed that the loss of it might be insurmountable.

'We must have dropped it somewhere,' Claire said.

For an awful instant, Eve thought Will might break down. But then he took a deep breath, seating his shoulders lower. 'Light is overrated.' He mustered a grin. 'Who needs light?'

'We *have* light.' Eve swept the food aside, clearing space

in the illuminated ring of the beam. 'Let's pull your leg over here.'

'No one's *pulling* anything anywhere.'

'Bad choice of verb. We'll guide it. Gently. Come on, now.'

Will gripped under his thigh, using both hands to lift the leg, and Eve helped steer it gingerly into the light. She unwrapped the wet bandage. The swelling was even worse, fresh blood leaking from the puncture. A pinch of his toe brought no response.

'How bad?' he asked. Before she could answer, he said, 'I want an answer. I don't want nurse bullshit, and I don't want vagueness. An answer. I want an answer.'

Amplified dripping vibrated the air around them. Way up by the opening, a few bats were clustered on a bulge. Water ran down Eve's back, mixing with her sweat. She looked past his supine body at Claire, and Claire bit her lip.

Eve returned her gaze to Will. 'You'll probably lose the foot.'

They let him cry. Not rending sobs but quiet, desperate sounds that moved off the walls and came back like whispered fears. One of his hands turned to a fist, and he beat at the rock under him once, twice.

After a time he pushed himself up. 'Sorry. I'm sorry.'

Eve's knee throbbed where it pressed against the stone. 'You have nothing to apologize for.'

'That's like a whole other life. I mean – *amputated*?'

'Only if we're lucky,' Claire said, without malice.

They were quiet there on the hard stone, Will flat on his back, Eve and Claire kneeling over him. They did not look at one another. Claire's frank assessment had defined the situation, however imperfectly. Had made what they were up against real.

Eve cleared some of the blood from the puncture, revealing tiny white beans deep in the cut.

They were squirming.

Will noticed her face and then looked down. He jolted back on stiffened arms as if shocked. 'Oh, my God. Maggots – Are those . . . ? You have to get them out of me! You have to –'

'No,' Eve said. 'Let them work. They only eat necrotic tissue. They'll clean out the wound.'

Will swallowed, his head bobbing forward with the effort, as if he were forcing down his revulsion. 'Could they save my leg?'

'They could save your life,' Eve said.

Will tried to smear the moisture from his face. She could see he was doing everything within his power to fight off the panic, to acclimate to the cold, hard facts.

Claire's eyes welled. 'I don't want to die here and not be remembered.'

Something bloomed inside Eve like a swig of booze, hot and caustic and not entirely unpleasant. She said, 'I will get us out of here.'

Claire blinked, and tears fell.

'If he sees you out there, you're dead,' Eve said. 'Wait here until I come back or until I get out and send help.'

'Don't have a lot of days.' Will picked up a protein bar, let it fall to the stone. His skin was ashy and looked fragile, paper-thin. 'You still haven't told us the plan. You going back to the *alcalde*?'

'He could still be gone, waiting out the weather. Plus,

344

it's the wrong way – up the mountain. We need to go down.' She licked her chapped lips. 'We need a vehicle.'

'The Jeep's gone,' Claire said.

Eve said, 'There is one other Jeep in this jungle.'

'Where?' Claire said.

Eve just looked at them.

They stared back, realizing. The dripping continued, louder. One of the bats dropped from its roost and fluttered into place again, its wings rustling against stone.

'*No,*' Will said. 'You're kidding. No, Eve – al-Gilani's Jeep? Are you crazy? You can't go back there.'

'What choice do we have?' Eve said. 'Anyway, it's *already* across the river.'

'He'll kill you. And we'll die here. We'll never be found.'

'It's the last thing he'd expect. No way he'd think I'd be stupid enough to go back there again.'

Claire said, '*Are* you?'

A noise escaped Eve, half laugh, half sob. Claire leaned over and gripped her tight in a hug, almost choking off her air, their cheeks mashed together. Claire's breath was hot against Eve's ear. 'You can,' Claire said. '*You* can.'

Eve pulled back and stood up, feeling the brink of the ledge at her heels. She looked down at Will. His eyes glimmered, but he mustered a smile and said, '*Vaya con Dios.*'

Turning, she faced the rippling black sheet, sucked in a breath, and dove. She hit the water in a clean line, wanting to plunge as deep as possible to spare her exhausted muscles. The underwater channel closed around her, and she stroked hard through darkness, the blind, otherworldly rush like a birth or a death. She kicked through the canal toward the unknown.

Ahead, the gloom turned from black to sea green. The roar of the cascade was muted underwater, so she misgauged its proximity. The downward force caught her by surprise, pounding her to the muddy bottom. She went with the undertow, flattening out as if flying, letting it propel her from beneath the weight of the falling water. With aching lungs she coasted free. Golden rays reached her at last, down here, however faintly. Air seemed very far away. She clawed toward the wavering light overhead, the light of heaven, the light of her son's bedroom in the morning.

She broke the surface.

45

Leaves and branches laid a net of camouflage across Eve's face as she lurked at the jungle's edge, watching the sawed-off zip line flailing in the water. Though she'd knocked the cable free from the near bank, the far end was still fastened to the tree on al-Gilani's side. The length of the line remained in the river, undulating over white-caps and flicking between boulders halfway across. For hours she'd been sitting with a sniper's stillness in the mud, fronds hiding everything but her eyes. The dia-monds of light off the water had turned from yellow to gold, now giving over to the pastels of sunset. The cur-rent had not slowed, but it hadn't quickened either, and the zip line's dance across the surface had resolved into something predictable. Her muscles still had not recov-ered from the day's hike from the cascade, and it seemed likely that the soreness would remain with her until she got out of the jungle or died. At some point soon, it would be one or the other.

Fortunato's body was no longer pinned to the boulder, but now and then Eve would blink and conjure it there with perfect clarity. She figured that it hadn't washed away but that al-Gilani had removed it, covering his tracks. If he had his way, there would be no trace of any of them.

She was the only thing between him and that.

Lulu's woven hemp bag lay on the ground by her knee.

She waited for night to nudge a few shades closer, then reached for it. Inside, a fist-size chunk of quesillo Oaxaca bulged, protected by a Ziploc. Insulated in other plastic bags were Jay's nearly expired satphone and Eve's increasingly ragged copy of *Moby-Dick*, there to bolster the loose-shifting supplies as well as her spirits.

Dusk had thickened to the point where she could no longer read the dive watch clearly without risking use of the backlight; when she'd arrived here in the late afternoon, she had decided that would be the signal that it was time to cross. Right at the tipping point between light and darkness, when it was gloomy enough to provide some cover but when there was still enough ambient light left in the sky to allow her to make out the boulders in the current. The bioluminescence of the water might help her navigate as well, but she wasn't sure how helpful the glow would be once she was submerged in it.

She donned Lulu's woven pack, the contents pulling tight across her back like folded wings. One of the water bottles dug into her scapula, but aside from that she wore the items comfortably. Two fronds waited at her feet. To protect her palms, she wound them tightly around her hands like boxing wraps, squeezing to hold them in place.

Lulu's bag. Jay's satphone. Neto's cheese. The items, a roll call of the dead. A wash of grief moved through her – all that loss, sure, but also the *pointlessness* of it. Jay had died why? So al-Gilani could remain unidentified? Jay hadn't cared who he was or what he had done. Neither had Neto. Nor Lulu.

Eve stepped through the fronds onto the riverbank, moving cautiously, part fugitive, part hunter. After she'd been dug in for so long, the open air and breeze off the water struck her as deliciously fresh. She cut down the slope a good twenty yards upriver from the zip line, crouched a moment to read the water, and then launched herself into the current before she could lose her nerve.

The cold grabbed her, threatening to bring panic, but she stroked forward once, twice, shooting past a jagged upturned tree trunk before she was whisked down a bump in the rapids. Dusk hid the zip line, but she sensed the looming rise of the boulder around which it was looped, the boulder upon which Fortunato had shattered his spine.

She twisted, bringing herself in the best position to grab hold of the line, hands and legs pointing to the far bank, ready to clamp. The metal cord slid sharply through the space between her shoulder and neck, and she fumbled to gather it in. Her palms and knees clenched. One of the frond wrappings tore off immediately, whisked into the freezing unknown, but her other hand held tight, slowing her enough to pendulum through the current so she could brace a leg against a submerged ledge of rock. Water blasted up her arms, power-washing her face, forcing her to turn her head to draw air. But she knew she had it now.

She hand-over-handed the zip line, her thighs burning as she fought to plow her body along the submerged ledge toward shore. The rock vanished underfoot, replaced with the sandblasting action of the immersed shoal. For a moment she flailed, but she managed to haul herself over and into a rise of mud, embedding in the far bank.

She pried herself out and up, rolling over the ridge of

the bank where she lay panting and hacking up water. If al-Gilani appeared from the jungle's edge, she'd be defenseless, yet knowing this – understanding in this moment her utter exhaustion and vulnerability – provided her a break from worrying about it.

He did not appear.

Her breathing settled back to normal, her strength returned, and she managed to stand. She pulled a water bottle from the dripping hemp bag and took a few cautious sips, then rewarded herself with a third of a protein bar and a bite of cheese.

Keeping off the main path, she retraced the route Fortunato had forged through the jungle, making meticulously slow progress, reaching the northern mouth of the canyon floor as they had before. As she inched around low branches, the house came lurchingly into view, squatting darkly at the base of the canyon rise. Every few steps she paused and counted off five minutes, listening, her eyes straining to pick out any movement in the surrounding foliage.

The approach took several hours, but finally she was standing beside the natural carport nestled between trees, the rusting Jeep in reach. She hooked her fingers beneath the handle, bit her lip, and clicked the door open.

She held the frozen pose, staring at the house, ready to bolt. After a time she eased the door open and felt for the ignition hole. No key. Her gaze flicked back through the bug-splattered windshield, checking for movement at the house. Next she dropped the sun visor, but nothing fell out. A sprinkle started up, smearing the glass, distorting her view. Silently, she checked the glove box, beneath the tattered floor mat, panic mounting every second her eyes shifted from the house to search the Jeep's interior. No luck. The key, then, was where she'd feared.

In the house.

She withdrew from the Jeep, leaving the door slightly ajar.

On the balls of her feet, she breezed swiftly through the sparse trunks toward the house, making sure to clear the trip wire. Not yet calm enough to check through the windows, she put her back to the concrete wall and regulated her breath.

For a moment she considered faking footsteps into the jungle, backtracking carefully, then tripping one of the alarm wires to draw al-Gilani away from the house, but it seemed foolish given his expertise. He would know how to read the ground at least as well as Fortunato had. Plus, if he wasn't in the house but in the surrounding hills, she couldn't risk raising a ruckus and losing her shot at getting inside.

Painstakingly, she rolled across her shoulder and peered through the front window. Blocks of shadow checkered the dark room. At first everything looked alive – looked like *him* – but she settled herself enough to shape the dark masses into what they were: a chair looming here, a discarded heap of clothes there. The rain stayed light. Under other circumstances it might have been refreshing, but she barely noticed it anymore. Just as she barely noticed the leeches on her legs or the bugs swirling about her head or the mineral taste of the river lingering in her mouth.

She crept along the side of the house and checked the rear windows. Kitchen, bathroom, bedroom. He was not home. Most likely he was out hunting her.

She had to go in.

Of course she had braced herself for this reality, but facing it now, her very body resisted. She had to issue each command to her limbs, telling her legs to lift and swing, to set down and pull her toward the door. They listened reluctantly.

She arrived.

The lockless knob was smooth against her palm. It turned easily, silently.

Gulping air, she tiptoed inside. The hinges, on tilt, called the door back to the frame, and she eased it silently the rest of the way shut. A wrinkled mat bunched underfoot, drying her shoes. Across the room a fall of moonlight half caught the plywood with its crude human silhouette.

The bedroom first.

As she passed the plywood, it came clearer, pocked with gash marks from the thrown machete and marred with oil-colored stains she knew were not oil. The rain intensified, drumming the roof, starting to spill down the windows, streaking the glass.

The dark doorway to the tiny bedroom waited. She passed through. Each breath a small sip of air.

There was the prayer rug, neatly rolled. The Qur'an rested on its mat of twigs.

She trickled her palm along the objects atop the dresser. Reading glasses, a hairbrush – private things.

But no keys.

She tugged open the top drawer, revealing wads of

clothing. His scent rose from the fabric, musky and strong, the smell of a man living in the wild.

No keys.

The next drawer.

No keys.

The bottom drawer.

Empty.

Panic expanded in her chest, threatening to explode in a scream. She whirled, her wild stare settling on a dark spot on the overturned crate serving as a nightstand.

She raced to the object, snatched it up. Metal, rubber head, jagged teeth. The stamp came visible when she squinted: JEEP. Static clouded her sight, and she realized she'd been holding her breath. Pocketing the key, she spun toward the main room.

That was when she heard the front door open.

46

The instant al-Gilani's first footstep tapped down on the concrete floor inside the house, Eve dropped and rolled neatly beneath the cot-like bed. She was slender enough to slot neatly in, though the bowed metal mesh dipped to within a few inches of her face.

Her only thought had been getting in, finding the key, and rushing out, and yet somehow at the sound of his approach her body had reacted with a plan of its own.

She realized that she was making noises. She mashed a palm over her mouth and put her other hand atop the first, trying to seal all sounds inside. The rain on the roof laid a white-noise wash over the sound of her trapped breaths.

The footsteps grew nearer. A click brought a piercing yellow light to the room, severely slanted by an unseen lampshade. Two muddy boots entered. He stood across the room, facing away, his head severed from view. His shoulders bobbed, and then his shirt peeled back and fell away.

His back was marred with scar tissue, gouges and burns, whip marks and healed-over slashes. So much pain memorialized, carved into the body, an imperfect record of past deeds and torture. It was difficult to imagine the gnarled stretch of flesh as human skin; it seemed more a living parchment.

She pressed her hands harder over her mouth, finger-nails digging into her cheeks. Her nostrils flared, trying to bring in enough air. An image seized her, Sue and Harry navigating the storm-battered roads to Huatulco, clearing the occasional debris and their consciences.

The muddy boots neared. He growled a bit with an exhale, an old man's groan gone feral. And then the boots pivoted and the mesh creaked down abruptly, kissing Eve's forehead. She turned her head quickly so her face wouldn't touch the bowing bottom. The weight of his sitting brought the mesh to whispering contact with her chest, her stomach. Her hands were up as if to shove back, which every instinct in her body was urging her to do. But her head told her otherwise, and somehow she listened.

Thick fingers reached down and flicked at the laces. A stockinged toe shoved off one boot. It landed on its side with a wet thud. The next came off and remained upright, as if awaiting the foot's reentry.

Another groan-growl and the weight above her redis-tributed, mesh rolling south to her stomach, her pelvis, and she waited to be crushed, waited for a telltale yelp to escape through the clamp of her hands.

But it didn't.

The bed rocked, and the light clicked off, and she lay there beneath him, metal mesh barely touching her skin. He murmured something to himself in Arabic, and then all was silent, save the drops on the roof.

She reminded herself to keep breathing.

They lay there, together in the darkness.

The thought of Nicolas asleep in his bed pried into her mind, and she pried it right back out.

After a time she made out a faint rasp from above. And then another. She timed them, these rasps, gauging their regularity.

The rain increased until there were no individual drops, just the angry hum of an insect swarm, overpowered now and again by thunder.

She moved ever so slightly. Her muscles had been clenched for so long that the first tiny gesture, flattening her shoulders to the floor, brought with it an arthritic ache. She wiggled, doing everything she could to keep from scraping against the bowed underside of the bed. Progress was so slow it seemed she was moving with tiny ripples of her flesh, millimeter by millimeter. Her hips slid free first. One arm. A shoulder. Her head lagged, strands of hair hooked on the mesh. She tugged, the follicles popping one at a time.

He grumbled and shifted. Her eyes were closed, but she heard a whisper of flesh against sheet as an arm slid off the bed. A meaty hand tapped her just below the clavicle. She arched onto her heels and shoulders in a silent scream, her hips and lower torso raised from the hard floor. She opened her eyes. The hand, right there beneath her chin, the pinkie nothing more than a chewed-down nub.

He took another ragged breath, the hand lifted, and the mesh creaked again.

She was free.

She pulled herself upright. He lay facing away, squeezing a pillow between his bare arms. His pants remained on – this was just a rest, she figured, before he resumed his search.

She backed away, checking behind her feet before each step to ensure she struck nothing on her way out. She did not risk a breath until she was in the front room. The machete was embedded deep in the plywood. She considered it for an instant, but prying it free would make noise, and the notion of reentering the bedroom with it seemed beyond the scope of anything she was capable of.

To the front door. A silent turn of the knob. Blessedly silent hinges. She stepped across the threshold. Like a benediction, rain doused her face.

She ran in the mud, slipped, came up sticky. The Jeep waited ahead, the driver's door cracked as she'd left it. She was sobbing, but without tears or grief or even fear – it just seemed another way of breathing right now. A flash lit the jungle, and seconds later thunder roared.

She ripped the driver's door open, leapt in, the cracked upholstery powdering beneath her weight. It took some effort to work the key from her wet pocket and fumble it into the ignition. She rolled her lips over her teeth, bit down hard, and turned the key.

Nothing happened.

At first it simply did not register. She turned it again, tapped the gas once, tried a third time. Nothing.

She swallowed a scream of sheer frustration, afraid to make noise even this far from him. Her hands tapped out a quiet panic beat against the wheel, the gold band on her right hand giving off a metallic click. Her sweat-tangled hair had fallen forward in her eyes, and she jerked her head to clear it as she grabbed at the handle to climb out.

Lightning strobed again.

This time she did scream.

Just beyond the hood, al-Gilani stood stooped, rain washing his bare torso. His toes disappeared into the mud. The machete was sheathed across his back. One bulky arm was raised as if to lift a lantern, an item dangling from his hand. Despite the darkness and the slanting rain, she made out what it was.

A positive-terminal lead. From the battery of the Jeep she was sitting in.

He bared his teeth in a kind of smile.

Then he walked calmly to the driver's side. She hit the lock and lunged to smack down the passenger-side latch as well. He was right there at the window, his breath clouding the glass.

She vaulted across to the passenger side, more from panic than strategy. He pressed his forehead to the driver's window, and the soft-top canvas to the side pushed in in the shape of his hand.

Calmly, he walked around the rear of the Jeep. She flung herself back across into the driver's seat. He appeared at the passenger window now, leaning into view, peering at her sideways.

She screamed again.

He seemed to be neither enjoying nor disliking this.

He straightened up. Removed his machete. The soft-top behind the passenger window bent in and then popped, the steel tip poking through. She unlocked the driver's door and tumbled out. He ran around the hood of the car, and she bolted around the rear, keeping him in sight through the windows – a children's game of chase around a kitchen table.

Even beneath the woven fronds providing cover to the Jeep, the earth was wet, slippery. One necessity penetrated the roaring clamor in her head: She had to mind her steps. If she went down, he'd pounce.

They kept at it for a few rotations, reversing direction once, then again, then pausing, staring at each other across the hood. For an instant the terror sucked out of the night air and she saw their dance differently, as something mildly ridiculous. He moved again, and she matched him. When he came around the tailgate the next time, she bolted for the canyon's southern edge. Fueled by panic, her legs seemed to skim across the earth. She could hear his feet slapping mud behind her. Farther away. Farther yet.

Halfway up the slope, she risked a look back. He braced himself with a forearm against a tree trunk, staring up at her, and she understood he was winded. Invigorated, she relaunched into the hill, fighting through brambles and underbrush. The canyon grew denser. She turned but no longer saw him behind.

Passing shoots whipped her cheeks and arms and legs raw. She was unsure how long she ran. Losing sight of the moon, she crested one rise, dipped, crested another. She sensed the canyon diminishing at her back, but she might have been going in circles. At one point she thought she heard the river but couldn't be sure. She reached a peak and stood on a clifflike outcropping, peering down in the rain to trace the line of the pass through to the next valley.

All the way at the bottom, several hundred yards off, he stood, facing away. Somehow he'd gotten ahead of her.

The machete, freed from the sheath, gleamed at his side. His massy shoulders heaved with exertion. Then, as in a dream, he turned.

He looked up at her.

She looked down.

She backed away from the ledge and reversed, running along the ridgeline, descending. She reached the bottom and stared up. A fork of lightning froze him in the very spot where she'd stood minutes before.

The distance between them was sufficient and the terrain rough enough that she was in no immediate danger, but in a way that only made it worse, lending a five-minute buffer to the gruesome fulfillment of her worst fears.

She kept on, retracing her steps, driven back up into the Sierra Madre del Sur. Her mind raced with notions. She should find the river and follow it down to the coast. She should get as far away from his house as possible. She should return to the trails she was familiar with and find someplace to hide.

Don't do what's obvious right now. Do anything *but what he'd expect you to do.*

The rain had stopped.

She reached the brink of his canyon and paused for a few precious seconds. The rain had ceased, but the clouds roiled heavily, tugging at the firmament. Every instinct told her to peel toward the river and familiar ground.

But she ran west, away.

Leaves tore at her face. She got one mountainous bulge between her and the canyon and then another before she knelt in the mud.

Past the tip of her shoe sprouted a spiky plant. Noticing the dark leaves with their tiny stinging tendrils, she breathed a prayer of gratitude that she'd missed stepping in them. What had Fortunato called the plant? *Mala mujer.* Bad woman.

The slightest misstep out here could hurt you.

Despite the humidity her lips felt dry, her throat parched. Two sips of water turned into five. She panted.

It took the better part of ten minutes for her to confirm that her uncontrollable shuddering was not due merely to terror but to the fact that she was cold. Her flesh was hard, taut. Her T-shirt fought her every inch of the way off, clinging to her like a second skin.

Flinging it aside, she caught a rippling reflection of herself in a puddle. The stained, wife-beater undershirt. Her hair, stringy with sweat. Her biceps, firm with exertion.

It struck her that she looked a bit like Theresa Hamilton.

Her teeth chattered, adding a counterpoint to the shivering. Deep in Lulu's bag, beneath the diminishing hunk of cheese, the tiny spirit bottle was wedged, the DÍAS FELICES ECOLODGE™ label worn off. At the base of a sugarcane plant, she found a tuft of dead grass that felt mostly dry. She plucked some, nesting it in the swirl of her T-shirt, and doused it with mezcal. One matchbook had been preserved, perfectly dry, in a Baggie.

She struck a match, held the wavering flame out over the dry grass and alcohol. She was so cold, and the fire would be so warming. But it would also signal her location. Was it worth it?

Her mind raced.

Do anything *but what he'd expect you to do.*

She pictured that rippling reflection of herself, a woman not unlike Theresa Hamilton.

Except Theresa failed. Because she did what he *knew* she would. She let fear make her predictable.

Eve would have to be better.

She dropped the match.

47

If there was one thing he could do, it was endure. His lungs ached. His legs cried out. But still his feet flashed beneath him. All the pain he took from his muscles. Wrapped it in a ball of thorn and thistle. And hurled it to the heavens.

Bashir led with the machete, the sword of the Prophet, may God's prayers and blessings be upon him. He shattered through the jungle. Bulled through the underbrush. Branches snapped off across his chest.

He stumbled over a rise and looked down at his house below, hunched to the base of the canyon. She would head west to the river. This was land that she knew. The rest only faceless jungle.

She was agile. Fleet. Thin. She could out*run* him.

But he would out*last* her.

He rimmed the canyon. The rain had ceased, but sweat ran into his eyes, stinging. He reached the brink of the plateau with the rotting log and the ridiculous camping toilet on its side. No footprints. But she would not have been foolish enough to blaze across open ground. The trail led down through the orchids to the river. She would be there. He would find her scrambling along the bank. Her marks in the mud. Hands, feet. He would finish her. And then it would be down to him against the elderly and the enfeebled.

He started across the plateau, but an impulse seized him. She had proved smart, smarter than this. He stopped. He turned. Faced back across the canyon and his little house.

He waited. The bugs were out. Biting. Unpleasant pinches at his ankles and neck.

It took a few minutes, but at last lightning lowered from the heavens. It provided only a flicker of visibility across the unbroken jungle. But a flicker was enough.

To the west, two ridges over, a plume of black smoke rose from the canopy. Thin enough to be man-made.

The hand of Allah had turned him around. Had urged him to wait. He had obeyed. And now he would have his prize.

On light legs he sprinted through the canyon. Up over the first ridge. He lost vantage descending into the jungle again, but he knew these hills well. Knew where to point his feet to bring him to that plume of smoke. He was glad he had forgone boots. He preferred to feel the earth. To sense the tremor of her steps through the soles of his feet.

As he drew near, he slowed. His approach became silent. He circled the spot once, then spiraled in, cinching the noose. Through a break in the underbrush, he spotted a mound of burned grass as big as a bale of hay. The fire had been so big. Why?

An uneasy feeling began in his stomach and crept outward.

Impatiently, he broke cover. Stepped into the open.

Shoe scuffs where the fire had been stomped out. A few deeper prints – running prints – leaving the clearing.

Pointing north. He followed them into the leaves. Gone. And then there, again.

Curving around. To head east.

Back to the canyon.

To *his* canyon.

He ran.

The lightness that had helped him float over the ridges was gone. He thundered along. Bones knocking together. Chest on fire. Ligaments stretching.

The door to his house was ajar. He stumbled inside. The cabinets open, rifled.

He searched. The bottle of spiked cooking oil he used to protect against bugs was missing. His bananas, too awkward for her to carry, smashed into the filthy concrete. His canteens emptied onto the floor. Two water bottles missing.

Fury rose in him.

He would go into the jungle now and he would seek her and find her. He would dress first – for humility and for protection against the elements. He strode into his bedroom and pulled on his shirt. Instantly, his skin seemed to catch fire. He gave off a pained growl as the fabric scraped across his flesh. In a fit, he tore the shirt off. Ripped it straight off his body from the collar down.

The inside of the cotton, lined with *mala mujer*. The burning leaves stuck there as if Velcroed.

He looked at his arms and chest. Red patches. They would rise further. This would be an inconvenience.

He grabbed another shirt from the drawer. Checked it first. Pulled it on.

Find her. He would find her. She had left the key in the

ignition of the Jeep. He would take the vehicle and circle the canyon. See a trace. Leap out. Run her down. In a short sprint, he would overtake her. Like a lion. Like a bear.

He moved swiftly to the Jeep. Wind fluttered the machete incision he'd made in the soft-top.

He opened the door again. Leaned behind the wheel. Reached for the ignition.

No key.

He felt again. Bent to look. An empty slot.

Breath hissed through his teeth. She had circled back. Destroyed his food. Taken his water. Poisoned his clothes. And now disabled his vehicle.

He pulled himself out. Slammed the door. The noise echoed off the canyon walls. Scratching at his rising welts, he stared up the slope toward the plateau. Suddenly it looked a long way off.

Up until now the tourist party had been manageable. Warm clay in his hands. He had controlled them. Guided them. He had shown them what to think and what to feel, and they had obeyed. But this one was different.

This one *learned*.

48

Eve scouted the boulders and dips downstream from where the loose zip line flailed in the water. Once the river had her, her ability to steer herself would be negligible, but she wanted to know the twists and turns just in case. She returned to where the zip line was tied off around the tree. Shooting glances over her shoulder at the dark jungle, she squatted at the base of the trunk and wrapped her hands in fronds again, tucking in the ends to form makeshift gloves. Not wanting fear to gain a foothold, she didn't allow herself to stop and consider.

Grabbing the cable, she half waded, half rappelled into the river. A few steps in, the current blew her legs out from under her. She clung to the wobbling zip line, trying to hold herself in place, her body skipping across the surface as if she were wakeboarding. As planned, she'd swung out toward the middle of the river in a semicontrolled fashion, but that was as far as the lifeline was going to get her.

Water crashed over her. She fought her head to the surface, gulped in air, trying to mentally piece together the lay of the river from her little scouting expedition. Downstream and well out of sight, the gnarled root of a guanacaste tree protruded from the opposite bank, twisting briefly over the water. If she hooked it, she would live. The bank looked far away. Her hands were weakening, the frond wraps stripping away. If she held on much longer, she'd drown.

She let go.

She shot backward so fast it felt like falling, though her movement was horizontal. Straightening her legs and turning onto her side, she knifed past the first boulder, which whipped by her cheek so close she swore she could feel the cold of the stone. She flipped over, sticking her feet up as Will had cautioned, the glowing water seeming to rush backward at her, into her face, even as she tumbled down two white-water runs.

If she went around the next bend, she'd shatter herself on the boulders, and there it was already, the turn flying at her. She'd rocketed a hundred yards in the seconds since her release. The current sloshed her wide, carrying her around the turn. In a second the gnarled root would zip overhead, her last chance before rock and ruin.

She flipped and pulled hard in a sloppy freestyle, her arms straining in their sockets. Her effort had virtually no effect, but she kept at it, kept at it, kicking violently. Her face was in the water; she couldn't gauge her proximity to the far bank.

The root would be passing at any second. She turned and threw her hands up, hoping to catch the root under her arms so she'd have a prayer of holding on. A bump in the current lofted her upward, and she saw a flash of dark sky before something struck her across the chest so hard that her breath left her in a grunt.

The root.

Slippery with moss and moisture. She clung to it, her mouth fighting for air but finding none. The river ripped at her legs, her hips, and she had to get clear soon or it would tear her away. She didn't have the luxury to wait until she could breathe again.

Hauling herself arm over arm toward shore, she lost her grip but caught herself painfully in the fork of her armpits. She resumed, still with no air coming in, managing to drag her body out of the water. Lying on the bank, she contorted, her head bobbing forward, mouth clutching. Her vision clouded. Would she really die here, like this? Suffocating with air all around?

At last her chest released, and she screeched in a breath and then another, curling fetally, bent hands pressed beneath her chin. When she could, she tested her ribs. The left ones were tender, but from the feel of them she hadn't broken any. In a way she'd been lucky to hit the root so brutally and squarely, her entire torso absorbing and dispersing the shock.

When she was able to sit up, she checked the hemp bag and made sure the items remained inside. She wanted nothing more than to lie back down and dissolve into the bank, but if she didn't get up, Will and Claire would die in that grotto.

She got up.

Swaying, she kept her feet. She had the key to the Jeep in her pocket, so al-Gilani couldn't use it. But she couldn't either. What, then, was the plan? She had to keep close to known terrain. One wrong turn in the jungle and she would get lost, die of exposure. The river was the obvious plan, a drawback but perhaps the only option. She'd follow it to the coast, to the authorities in Huatulco, and she'd send help back for Claire and Will.

Eve would have to get there on foot. With al-Gilani pursuing. And she'd need to figure out food and fresh water along the way. In the best scenario, it would take days.

Claire and Will might not have days.

Downriver, the bank all but disappeared into a wall of rock. Any headway would have to be made through the foliage parallel to the river, which was fine, since al-Gilani would likely search the banks at first light. Clouds muffled the moon; once she cut beneath the canopy, she struggled to see. Mosquitoes swirled around her bare arms, and she shook no-see-ums from her legs. Pausing, she took out al-Gilani's doctored cooking oil and doused her limbs and the back of her neck as she'd learned at Santo Domingo Tocolochutla, the eucalyptus making her skin tingle. The insects stopped at once, a tiny victory that seemed, right now, a triumph.

She reached a wall of thick bushes that forced her farther east, away from the river, and she skidded down a brief slope into a stretch of majestic banyan trees. Mist settled low over the prop roots, cutting visibility. As she edged between them, she became aware of a different energy in the air. She halted. Reaching her nose, a faint animal tang. It was a sharp, acrid smell, one she could taste on the roof of her mouth. Her throat tightened.

Urine. And musk.

A few yards ahead, the fog swirled, then reshaped itself into something living.

A jaguar crept forward, mist rolling off her muscle-sleek shoulders as if she were shedding a robe. Her coat was jet-black, save faint leopard spots glowing along the crown of her head. Her upper lip bunched, whiskers bristling. The fearsome mouth bared. The hiss issuing from the throat was packed with malice.

A mother protecting her young.

In place of fear, Eve felt fascination.

But which way were her cubs? Eve took a cautious half step to the right, and the jaguar tensed, lowering herself for a charge, the hiss now less air and more war cry.

Eve said, 'I understand.'

She lifted her foot, set it down to her left. The jaguar neither charged nor uncoiled.

Eve took another step to the left. Gleaming green eyes tracked her. The wrinkled upper lip lowered a notch, leaving the tips of the fangs exposed.

Another step distanced Eve farther yet. Steadily, she kept moving away. The jaguar straightened herself regally and watched, tail flicking, until enough fog had gathered between them to erase her from view.

Invigorated, Eve crouched and breathed the lush air, reliving how the jaguar's muscles had rippled beneath that jet-black coat. The animal could have torn her to shreds, and yet she'd been allowed to pass unharmed. The mist condensed on the fronds and on her skin, beading, turning her into a part of the jungle itself. She felt blessed.

The detour had forced her farther inland from the river, but, in deference to the jaguar's terrain and an impenetrable run of sugarcane, she took a circuitous route back. Slogging through the thickening underbrush was at first exasperating, then grueling. Her stomach flipped with hunger. The wet sneakers chafed her heels. Her ribs ached from the lifesaving blow dealt by the gnarled root over the river. Exhaustion pulled at her eye-lids. High-stepping through a bramble, her legs simply gave out. She pulled herself to the base of a tree and sat against it.

Given how much energy she was burning, she had to keep fueling her body or it would cease functioning. Her arms felt heavy as she tugged off the hemp backpack and sorted through it. The Ziploc holding the cheese had torn open. Greedily, she ate the last lump, two mouthfuls that only served to stoke her hunger. She had five water bottles left, which was good, but she was down to her last half of a protein bar. She unwrapped it, smelled it, held it to her lips. And then she ate it. She couldn't help herself.

Next she checked the satphone. The Ziploc seal had held, the phone sliding into her hand dry and intact. When she thumbed it on, the signal icon rotated, searching, and the low-battery emblem blinked, two competing electronic drives. After a few seconds of this, she thumbed the phone off, saving the last bit of charge for another hour, another altitude.

Leaning her head against the shaggy bark, she closed her eyes, wavering between sleep and waking.

A crackling sound snapped her head forward. Low at first, but growing louder. She felt the noise as the prickle of tiny feet up her spine, her nape.

'No,' she said. 'Uh-uh.'

She pulled the hemp bag onto her back. Somewhere in the darkness ahead, birds erupted from ground roosts. The underbrush started shaking, as if hit by a small-scale earthquake. She didn't know how she got her legs beneath her, but she was standing.

The black wave emerged from the foliage, creeping across the jungle floor.

Sweeper ants.

She couldn't outrun them, not now. They poured forward. A lizard shot from a log before her but was instantly ensnared. It stiffened, lurching, then disappeared beneath the black, crawling mass. When the sea parted, only a jumble of bones remained.

The living stripe flowed toward her. She remembered how the *indígenos* had calmly lunge-stepped over the ants up at Santo Domingo Tocolochutla, but this wave was broader, beyond Eve's jumping ability, even if she were rested and nourished.

They swept toward her feet. She leapt up the trunk, hugging it, holding herself up though the bark cut into her cheek and the tender insides of her arms. Terrified, she peered down over the bulge of her shoulder. The ants pooled around the trunk, the mass seeming to sniff upward.

Then the collective brain spoke and the ants surged up the tree.

The wide ribbon of black pulled toward the trunk as if sucked into a vacuum hose. Her sneakers were maybe three feet off the ground. The distance was breached instantly. She drew her legs up under her and shoved off.

A brief, weightless moment of flight. The ground beneath crawling, alive. She'd picked the spot where the black flecks had thinned. Hitting the ground on her side, she rolled over her shoulder and up, leaping to clear the squirming carpet.

Gasping, she slapped at her legs, her sides, batted at her

hair. A pinch bit into her neck, one at her inner thigh. She danced and whirled, knocking the ants off. On her forearm one insect head remained floating, knocked free of the body, the mandibles still sunk into flesh. She pinched it free like a tick.

The ants slid back down the trunk, rejoining the wider band of their colony. They swept on, away from her. She watched until the grass stopped shaking, until no more birds spooked. The crackling, she knew, had faded from the air, but she still heard it, still felt it across her skin.

Adrenaline kept her upright. She had to find food. She couldn't remain this weak out here and hope to survive. Shoving through the foliage, keeping the river sounds on her right, she hiked for ten minutes, then ten more, looking for she knew not what.

She arrived at a gorge and halted abruptly. Down below in the darkness, nestled into a spray of trees, was a blocky shadow with straight, man-made lines. A clear trail of broken plants and tire tracks described its course into the gorge.

She blinked a few times, realizing what it was, then hiked down.

The Wrangler's grille was crumpled around a tree trunk, the windshield pebbled across the seams of the upthrust hood. Black forms sagged the branches overhead. One hop-fluttered to a lower perch, and she caught a glimpse of the distinctive blood-red head, ducked on a vulture neck.

Using handholds, she lowered herself to the crash site. Behind the wheel Harry's body remained seat-belted in, his face and arms covered with hundreds of red spots.

Ant bites.

He was twisted sideways, an arm hooked over the seat back.

Beside him Sue was tilted to the passenger window, the skin of her lips broken into white dehydrated squares, her wan face spotted with welts. In the end the two must have proved too large or unpalatable for the ants to manage, but the swarm had certainly given it the college try.

Eve stared at Sue. She felt neither horror nor disgust nor sadness. She felt nothing at all.

When she opened the back door, she saw what Harry had been reaching for in his last moments of life. A carry-on bag. She nudged his stiff hand aside, unzipped it. There on top of some folded clothes rested a two pack of EpiPens. Just out of reach.

The smell inside was nearly unbearable. Eve dumped the bag, and then the two others, but found no food. There were several partially full water bottles on the floor mats and a protein bar, thrown there presumably by the crash. When she reached for the protein bar, the intact wrapper collapsed into nothing – the ants had slipped inside and heisted the bar itself. That explained why she'd found no cheese or fruit. The swarm had stripped the Jeep of all edibles, leaving everything else more or less as it was. She couldn't risk catching Sue's stomach bug, so she did not take the water.

She backed out of the rear seat and stood regarding the mess inside, then circled to the front where the hood was tented up. Reaching through the gap, she wriggled the positive-terminal lead free from the battery. It was scorched from the collision, one end snapped off. Disappointed, she cast it aside.

One of the turkey vultures swooped down to land on the hood with a great scraping of claws. Peering through the shattered windshield, it shifted its weight from leg to leg.

Eve looked from Harry and Sue to the bird.

She left it to its business.

Threading between gorges, she searched the foliage more closely. She found an orange tree, but the green orbs were still inedible. Some distance farther, she noticed hard spiky balls dangling from branches and recognized them as the soursop fruit Neto had served by the cascade. She cracked open a hard shell and slurped at the white pulp like a monkey, spitting out the black seeds. It tasted unripe, a ways from the sweetness she remembered. By the third one, her stomach began to ache, and she knew she'd have to move on to something else or she'd pay for it. She continued her search.

Ahead, she came upon a patch of agave plants. Stopping, she stared at one of the smaller *piñas* that had sprouted less pronounced spikes. She tore it free from the earth.

With effort she snapped the spikes off to reveal the barrel of the core beneath. There, squirming like maggots, were the little orange worms. She felt her gorge lift, press at the back of her throat.

Eat.

She ate.

After, lying beside the grove, she tried the satphone once again for a signal, to no avail. The clouds had made the sky impenetrable, so for now it was just her and the covered stars. She sent a quiet good-night thought to her boy, latitudes away.

She used the paperback, still wrapped in its Baggie, for a pillow. A memory hit her of Will smiling at her across the picnic table: Moby-Dick *is your Moby-Dick*.

As she closed her eyes, the paperback pressed against her cheek, and her last waking thought was that she'd probably die without reading it.

Wednesday

49

When Eve wound her way back to the riverbank in the frail, straw-colored light of early morning, she stood for a moment above the rushing water, crushed at how little progress she'd made. The gnarled guanacaste root that had walloped her across the chest last night protruded above the river only a few hundred yards up. All her wanderings in darkness had taken her in a loop. Whatever invigoration she'd felt from last night's nourishment and the few hours' sleep now drained away.

If she was going to undertake the days-long hike to the coast, she would require a lot more food, and the river was the best place to find it. Despite the intermittent rain that had persisted since the fierce downpours, the water level had dropped slightly. Minnows and trout churned in the clear swells, and, below, she made out a few wobbly shadows that she thought might be crayfish. After last night's painful crossing, she knew she wouldn't allow even her hunger to drive her back into the rapid current, but she stood there looking at all that food, there for the taking. As if to mock her, a shiny green kingfisher dove artfully again and again, coming up each time with a bigger beakful.

She focused her attention on the near bank. Any sandbars that might have existed were either washed out or submerged, so there'd be no digging for shrimp. A few slider turtles sunned on rocks. She'd read somewhere that their meat, though tough, was edible, but smashing the shells would be loud and work-intensive.

Fighting her way south along the steep bank, she looked for boulders at the river's edge. Beneath an overhang of vines, she finally found what she was looking for. Numerous hand-size brown crabs rested on the stone, ripe for plucking.

She grabbed one, but it twisted in her hand and, freaked out, she dropped it. A stupid girlish impulse, one she could no longer afford. It took some stalking, but she came up on another and snagged it. It squirmed and pinched, and she dropped it as well, but on dry land. She pinned it with her sneaker while she grasped for a rock, and then she lifted her foot and smashed the shell. Sitting, she picked out the cold white meat and ate it.

As she rose to search out another crab, she found herself staring at al-Gilani across the river. He stood perfectly still, his hands at his sides, as if he had known all along where she'd been. Perhaps he had.

Again she felt that sensation of slow-unfolding terror, the familiar, bone-deep dread of a recurring nightmare. Here again. Staring from bank to bank, a torrent of well-placed water her only protection from this man who wanted her dead.

The river here was wide and the current vicious. There was no threat right now, or even five minutes from now, but it would be the two of them in the jungle for days and nights, and the next time she slept or slowed, his hands could very well close around her neck.

The machete was slung across his shoulders. Welts rose

along his arms, likely from the *mala mujer* with which she'd lined his shirt, and she felt a stab of vindication, even pride. He regarded her without malice or rage, but simply as an object he'd like to possess. It was her first full daytime view of him, and she noticed black mole-like freckles across his cheeks and the bridge of his nose that she hadn't before.

She thought about shouting something at him, but the rush of the water would have drowned her out.

She started south, picking along the bank.

He mirrored her.

She halted.

He halted.

So it was going to be like this, then, for days and miles? It seemed inconceivable she could progress out of the mountain range to the coast under the pressure of his constant presence. But she supposed that was the point.

On his side the bank was wider and unobstructed, giving him an easier go of it. A few times she had to detour through the jungle to get around a bad patch, but when she came back, he was right across from her point of reentry. Now and again he'd veer off briefly and pop back into view, having held pace even when he was out of sight. She tried dropping behind the jungle's edge and backtracking, but sure enough she reemerged to find him there waiting across the water.

'Leave me alone!' she screamed.

He regarded her, barely even blinking, his calm countenance only underscoring her foolishness at not preserving her energy. Well, then, enough of that. She imagined Claire beside her, mocking her hysteria: *Great job, Eve. Wanna hurl a high heel at him, too?*

383

Eve knew better. She had to keep her head down. There was nothing left to do but prevail and outlast.

She put her energy toward making progress, and he stalked her along the opposite bank. Every few seconds she looked over, gauging his location, quelling her fear. They kept on like that for the better part of an hour, and then, all at once, she looked across and he was gone.

She whirled, instinctively checking behind her, as stupid as that was. Then she ran up the slope and searched among the foliage, panicked. There was movement all around, bobbing fronds, flicking vines, her eyes fastening on everything and nothing. He could be standing right beside her, lost in a car-wash rage of movement. But of course there was no sign of him here; he hadn't teleported across the river. As she'd learned last night, crossing required great effort and risk. There was no way he'd slipped across in the short interval she'd taken her eyes off him.

So, then, no choice but to keep going. Darting glances all around, she crept back to the riverbank and stumbled her way around an outcropping.

The sight downriver set her scalp tingling.

A tree, fallen in the *tormenta*, had lodged lengthwise in a narrow stretch of water below, buffering the current. Behind the log al-Gilani's broad shoulders and head bucked into view at intervals as he forded the river like a beast, paddling hard, holding his face aloft. He had a ways to go, but it was clear he would make it.

She slipped back behind tree cover and ran, at first in a blind terror and finally slowing to find a pace she could hold. He was older and heavier and would not catch her unless she twisted an ankle or made a tactical mistake. As she settled into a jog, she realized she was running the wrong way, up into the mostly deserted mountains, and it struck her that that was precisely what al-Gilani had intended her to do. Her thoughts blurred.

Will and Claire in that dank grotto, blinking up at the circle of sky, perhaps the last they'd ever see.

Nicolas waking up – or, more likely, waking up Lanie instead of her.

Food and time running out and her running the wrong way, toward nothing. She came to what was left of a road, its muddy breadth smeared to one side and heaped with flood-tattered fronds. Still, it made for easier going. Though she was far from the river and truly lost, the hills and trees here resolved into something familiar. She'd seen this before. Below, partway down the slope, a cargo truck lay smashed against a tree, its cracked trailer now empty. Yes, she'd seen this truck before, villagers pilfering grain from the back, but she was too exhausted to place *where* she'd seen it. A brief ways later, the road ended in a cascade of blown-over hillside, and she angled off and in, scaring up a cormorant that scared her right back. It spread its wide, oil-black wings and soared away, leaving her leaning back in a half limbo, hand spread over her fast-beating heart.

She continued. It dawned on her where she was an instant before she pushed through a wall of green and confronted the vast jungle chamber housing the ruins of El Templo de las Serpientes. The *tormenta* had littered leaves and whole branches across the courtyard and the pyramidal rises. Storm water puddled on the ancient stone. Coral snakes, with their bright reds and yellows, sprawled over the steps like worms in the wake of a rain.

If she wanted to rest, she should seek the highest point so she'd have a vantage on the surrounding terrain. She took a few steps toward the sloping staircase of the temple, wincing as the insides of her soaked sneakers wore at her blisters. Remembering Fortunato's trick in the cemetery, she paused and surveyed the nearby rocks and stone. Sure enough a few green shoots clung to the lowest step. She tore them up and brought them with her on her ascent. The corals proved lethargic and easy to dodge. From beneath one wide limb, she heard a rattle, but the steps were sufficiently broad that she could steer clear.

She reached the top, her head mere feet from the canopy. The sun broke through cloud cover, falling in patches on her face, the warmth hypnotizing. Surveying the grounds like a high priestess, she sat and pried off her waterlogged shoes. Her socks peeled back wetly.

The blisters were horrendous, seeping together around her heels to form half rings of raw flesh. She squeezed sap from the shoots and applied it liberally, then sat, airing out the skin. She scanned the vining roof for boa constrictors but found none. Considering her height here, she gave the satphone another try, and joy surged through her when a single reception bar flickered into view.

She tapped o for the international operator. Her thumb coasted back to the SEND button, which gave a reassuring click.

And just as quickly the reception bar was gone.

All icons, all images, all lights. The battery finally dead. She stared at the metal-and-plastic rectangle for a long while. Then she returned it to her bag. After so much time, she couldn't bring herself to part with it.

She looked out at the commanding view. The breeze up here was pleasant. In this moment she was alive and resting and not in terrible pain. Somewhere in the world, her son was pouring cereal or watching morning cartoons. Rick and Anika might be lunching in an Amsterdammy café, sipping espresso and munching syrup waffles. Claire was making fun of Will or Will was mocking her as they passed the hours in the hidden grotto, pretending not to wait, pretending that everything would be okay, that Eve would come back with the Jeep, the *federales*, the US Marine Corps.

This time Eve sensed it before it even happened. Her gaze shifted to a particular patch of fronds at the edge of the chamber. A blade hacked them aside, and al-Gilani stepped into view.

It struck her that she now shared some heightened connection with her pursuer. They could *anticipate* each other in the wild.

She sat still, her spine erect. He scanned the ruins, not yet seeing her. He strolled across to the sunken courtyard, the machete glinting as he reseated it in its sheath. Watching him beetle his way around down there, she felt not scared but superior. It would be only a matter of time before his gaze lifted and found her.

He paused in the courtyard with his back to her. The clouds shifted overhead, sunlight falling through a break in the canopy and striking the brilliant crushed-oyster patch at the base of the temple. The reflection shot a beam across the courtyard toward the catacomb tunnel, but al-Gilani intercepted it, a heavenly light framing his broad back.

He turned to look over his shoulder. Directly up at her.

She began pulling on her socks.

Keeping in the clear shaft of light, he crossed slowly toward the temple, toward her.

She had her socks on now, and one shoe, and was working on the other.

Approaching the temple, he ran his hand over the polished stone surface of the tablelike jaguar carving on which the Aztecs had once placed still-beating hearts. He bent to put his head down in the sacrificial bowl, craning to look up at her at the same time. He showed his teeth.

A smile.

Then he trudged out of sight around the base of the temple.

Eve stood, surveying the sides of the pyramid, seeing no movement beyond the lazing snakes. Vigilant, she made quarter turns, peering down.

His head reared into view on the north side, bouncing as he jogged up. She started down the south side, minding the down-and-out *talud-tablero* steps, not checking behind her. She'd come to trust her estimates of his pace. She reached the bottom, near the jaguar carving.

He came into view atop the temple and paused with his hands on his knees, breathing hard. Pulling himself upright, he started down.

Again she felt that uptick of terror at the slow-motion chase. What should have resolved itself in a burst of adrenaline and a rapid, violent clash had instead been stretched long like taffy, soaked in anticipation, each hideous possibility given time to breathe.

She jogged down into the sunken courtyard and started across to the rubbled structure. When she reached the mouth of the catacomb, he was well back, still laboring down the last of the temple stairs. She ran inside. In the darkness her foot struck a snake, but she heard no rattle. The air felt dense with dust, which she imagined as particles rising from the skeletons on the stacked, inset ledges. She went maybe fifteen feet into the darkness and slid into a lower berth, feeling bits crumble beneath her hip. Something crawled up her arm, but she did not move. She lay in perfect silence, breathing death, and felt no need to cover her mouth.

The light shifted at the front of the tunnel. She heard breathing, sensed movement. His bare feet made only the faintest vibrations as they set down. A reptilian hissing echoed off the stone, and then there came a sweeping sound and a wet smack, and then the hissing ceased.

From her low, floating perch, she saw segments of his legs ease into view – midcalf to thigh. They breezed within a foot of her cheek. Paused. A thick hand descended, scratched at a meaty calf. His chin dipping into view. His breaths audible. She rolled her lips over her teeth, bit down. At last he moved again, progressing from view, his steps crunching softly away.

She leaned out and watched his diminishing form as it ran toward the square of light at the end of the passage. As soon as it vanished, she rolled out from the ledge and sprinted in the opposite direction.

Daylight struck her face, making her blink. She stumbled up the disintegrating steps out of the courtyard, jogged on screaming feet, and crashed into the jungle. Chopping with her arms, she breached the underbrush for a few hundred yards, and then at once the resistance ceased and there was nothing before her and she was tumbling into the open, onto a road. She pulled herself upright.

She'd come out on the far side of the blockage from the collapsed hill. The storm-battered road stretched ahead, the way mostly clear. Her legs wobbled beneath her. She wanted to stop, to lie down and sob, but instead she willed them to carry her.

Her jog felt like a half stagger. The hemp bag chafed her shoulders. Despite the cloud buffer, heat beat down mercilessly from above.

She reached the top of a rise and turned.

Sure enough a tiny dot pursued her, maybe a mile back.

She took a knee and immediately knew that it was a mistake. Her muscles locked up and wanted to stay put. She was down. She was down on the ground, and she couldn't rise. Exhaustion overwhelmed her. How much easier just to stop.

Getting up felt like snapping herself out of rigor mortis. It took a few steps for her muscles to unknot, but still she walked for a time beneath the weight of a dull, steady ache. When at last she came off the back slope of the rise, the road simply ended, a casualty of the storm. Where it used to carve along a ridge, it now crumbled away, falling into a sheer, wooded slope.

She started down, her thigh muscles nearly unable to hold her upright. If she didn't change direction, she'd never shake him. A fold came up, and she hugged a stone lip, moving around and beginning a descent into the adjacent gorge. Beyond, it seemed there would be many valleys, branching off, and she might lose him, but perhaps also her way.

Trying to slow her descent into the gorge, she pushed off tree trunks and sawed through plants. Five feet from the bottom, her ankle hooked a vine.

A spray of olive leaves rushed at her. They broke the fall but not the following tumble, and she rolled toward flat ground, the rocky bottom rushing up at her face, and then there was blackness.

50

Bashir followed the broken twigs, the scuffs in the earth, and he came to the top of a gorge and looked down to where a feminine form lay at the bottom, twisted and still.

He allowed himself a rare smile.

Then started down.

51

A tugging on her hand.

'I want French toast.'

More tugging.

'Get up. Mom, get up. I'm hungry. And? And?'

'I know,' she grumbles. 'You want a sleepover at Zachary's.'

'No.'

'Batman action figure?'

'A *puppy*.'

'A puppy day, is it?'

'Uh-huh.'

A glance at the clock. 'Five fifty-three?'

'It's light out.'

So it was going to be one of those mornings. She rolls over. Her white sheets seem unreasonably bright.

'Get *up*!' he says. 'I'm serious.' His voice cracks.

She turns over, notes the tears in his eyes, and wriggles up onto her pillow. 'What's going on, Little?'

'Nothing.'

'Nothing?'

'Nothing.'

'Fingers out of your mouth.'

He complies.

'Why do you want a dog?' she asks.

'Look, I just do.'

'That's not an acceptable answer.'

He blinks at her. 'I don't have any brothers or sisters.'

'So you want a playmate?'

'Yes.' But his eyes dart away.

'What *else*?' she asks.

'I just . . . What if something happens to you?'

'Nothing's gonna –'

He raises his voice to talk over her. 'Or if you leave like Dad left, there'll be no one around, okay? And a dog *would* be. He'd be mine, and he wouldn't . . . he wouldn't leave me. Not ever.'

The words move through her like electricity. She touches his impossibly smooth cheek. 'Honey, I will never leave you.'

'What if you get in a car accident? Or cancer. Like Zach's aunt? She got it in her utopian tubes.'

Utopian tubes?

But his face remains so earnest, so vulnerable, that she cannot smile or correct him.

'What *then*?' he asks.

'I won't.'

'But you can't say that. You can't *promise* that.'

Responses crowd her brain, a parental cue to hold her tongue, to take a beat. She makes a point of not lying to him. If she tells him she'll look in on him after he falls asleep, no matter how tired she is, she drags herself down the hall and peeks into his room, just to have a clear conscience when he double-checks the next morning at breakfast. Where babies come from, why the lady at the gas station has a lower-back tattoo – all fair game. The birds-and-bees discussion had progressed only as far as 'in the mom's belly' before Nicolas lost interest, but she'd been prepared to go all the way. Rick gives more soothing answers, especially now on the phone, long-distance. Every time he takes a shortcut with veracity for the sake of comfort or convenience, she feels a pang.

And yet now she looks into her son's watery blue eyes and she decides to lie. She cannot overcome her instinct to reassure him in this moment. 'I *can* promise you,' she says. 'I'll be here until you're all grown up and old enough to take care of yourself.'

His face actually lightens, like it says in children's books. She can see the concern lifting, and then he is just seven and hungry.

'Anything else?' she asks.

'Yeah.' His small hands close over her fingers again and tug. 'Get up.'

The memory vanished in a blaze of brightness. Clouds and trees peered down at her with minimal interest. Her head throbbed, and her ankle pulsed with pain.

Nicolas was gone. Bath time was gone, and holding his hand during the scary scenes of movies was gone, and so was the rest of him, the remaining parts – graduation caps and nuptials and a first house and –

Get up. Mom, get up.

She forced herself up onto her elbows, tried to lift her three-ton head. The view above was a haze of leaves and bark.

And a point of focused movement, growing larger.

She squeezed her eyes shut. Opened them.

There he was, al-Gilani, moving down the slope toward her in controlled hops. Twenty yards away. Now fifteen.

She shot up. The ache in her ankle nearly dropped her back to the earth, but she bit down and went, limp-running up the slope, lit with panic. Branches crashed behind her, closer, closer, and then finally farther as she – miraculously – opened up some distance between them.

At last she risked a glance over her shoulder. He was back there, tangled in a web of vines, hacking away. Her slenderness was to her advantage here, allowing her to slip through gaps in the vegetation. While she had the advantage over distance, he could beat her readily in a wind sprint and would have here if not for the denseness of the flora.

As she ran, she gauged her ankle. Not broken, then. But a respectable sprain. For now she could push through the pain, but as the swelling rose, it would slow her.

Up and ahead she spotted another road, a real asphalt road, and her sense of direction, of *location*, pulled into sudden clarity. The ruins behind and west. Which meant there, ahead, should be the village.

The hillside turned from a hike to a climb, and she used roots as handholds, finally hoisting herself up onto the baking road. She rose and looked back, but al-Gilani had vanished from sight.

Up ahead, looming like a mirage, were the brightly colored buildings of Santa Marta Atlixca.

– a person a vehicle a weapon –

Eve staggered into the public square. 'Hello? *Hello?* Is anyone here?'

The windows, boarded up with plywood. The kiosk knocked over. Two of the school's windows were shattered in, and a section of roof had collapsed, brown water drip-drip-dripping.

In disbelief she turned a slow rotation in the center of the abandoned village. Not a single sign of life. Ahead, the battered walls of the church rose. She limped toward them. The dented church bells that used to hang from makeshift scaffolding outside were simply gone. Washed up in their place, an old rusted truck with fronds sprouting beneath the hood.

She stepped through the torn-wide doorway into the building's semi-embrace. The soft pastel walls had been blasted by the *tormenta*. More of the roof was missing, the meticulous gilded ceiling eroded to the skeletal rib arches, all that artistry gone to ruin. Swamp water filled the apse, and dark olive green slugs spotted the shattered pews.

Nothing here either.

She ran back toward the *zócalo*, shooting a desperate look down the road. No sign of al-Gilani yet. Had she been here two minutes or ten?

A whacking sound, irregular and loud, echoed from the space where the open-air market used to be. Eve went light-headed with relief. Overriding the pain in her ankle, she ran toward the sound. It had to be someone and – *yes* – there was a wizened woman at the edge of the forest and – *yes* – she turned, and Eve saw her face, another human face, the brown skin baked dry, like jerky. A rustic hovel stood behind her with the door ajar, and she held a machete and a length of firewood. She'd paused from the act of chopping.

Her deep-set eyes watched Eve approach, her face expressionless, unreadable, older than time itself.

'American?' the woman said, and for a moment, Eve thought she might be hallucinating.

Eve clutched at her, confirming that she was flesh and bone. 'Oh, thank God. You understand English.'

The woman nodded.

'I'm being pursued by a man who is trying to kill me. He's already killed others in my party. Do you understand?'

Another nod. '*Sí.*'

'Do you have a vehicle – a *truck*. Something that can get me out of here?'

'*Sí.*'

Eve allowed in a ray of hope. 'I need to go. Can I take your truck?'

'*Sí.*'

She realized that she was still clutching at the old woman's blouse, speaking rapidly into her face. 'Are there others around? Other villagers?'

'*Sí.*'

'Thank God. Thank *God*. Do you know the cascade? With the underwater channel and the grotto? My friends, they are hidden there. Something might happen to me. I might not make it. Will you send your friends? To rescue them?'

'*Sí.*'

'Okay, I have to go. He'll be here any second. Where are the keys? Where's the truck?'

The old woman nodded once again. '*Sí.*'

Eve felt the held breath burning in her chest. She clutched it there in her lungs, holding on to it even as all hope drained from her body, tugging at her insides as it went, bleeding down her legs, pouring from the bottoms of her feet, mooring her to the earth.

Her fingers released the old woman's shirt. The air leaked through Eve's teeth.

A rustle of leaves at her back. She smelled him before she saw him, the body odor pronounced in the humid, breezeless air.

Thick arms wrapped her from behind, pinning her hands to her sides. She stared at the woman's still-expressionless face.

'*Please,*' she said.

The voice came from beside her ear, the breath rustling her hair. '*Mujer loca.*'

The old woman nodded a final time. '*Sí,*' she said.

The arms dragged Eve backward into the jungle, the grip too tight for her to scream.

52

He pressed her through the foliage with the tip of the machete at her kidney. Eve felt the point at intervals, but never did he let it puncture the skin. When she slowed, he prodded her forward with an arm. At turns in the route and when panic overtook her, he steered her roughly, but not so roughly that it was ineffective or detrimental to progress. If she struggled, a callused hand encircled her neck or her biceps, the latent power in his grip evident, a vise that had been cinched just enough to hold an egg unbroken. His experience, when it came to death marches, was evident. In short, he *operated* her.

'Where are we going?'

'Back to my home,' he said in faintly accented English. 'I prefer that we have privacy.'

The word wrenched the air from her lungs.

When she'd recovered, she asked, 'How do you plan on getting across the river again?'

'We will cross by the fallen log. It is calm enough there.'

'That's *miles* away.'

He said, 'You seem to be equal to the task.'

She could not see him clearly behind her, but she'd caught glimpses and knew that he walked with a hitch that indicated a sore left leg, perhaps a groin pull. One of his bare feet bled, cracked at the outer heel. With every step she contemplated breaking free, but she knew that despite his minor injuries he had superior closing speed. Unless she started with a good lead, he'd run her down.

The Bear of Bajaur.

She was afraid to ask, but she couldn't stop herself either. 'Why do you need privacy? Why don't you just do whatever you're gonna do with me here and get it over with?'

'There is a proper way to interrogate. There are acceptable procedures. I cannot perform them here.'

'So that's what you're planning on doing. Interrogating me?'

'Yes.'

'Like you interrogated Jay?'

'Yes.'

She walked in silence for a time, doing her best to baby her ankle. 'What do you want to know from me?'

'I found the old man and woman in the Jeep. But where are the others?'

'What others?'

'The cripple. And the young man with the fractured leg. They are here, still, in these hills.'

'No,' Eve said. 'There was another burro, and they rode him out of here.'

'This,' al-Gilani said, 'is why we are going back to my home. So I can take my time with you.'

She decided not to ask any more questions.

They reached a rise of bramble, and he held her to the side and chopped a gap with the machete. She slipped through, thorns scraping her arms, and they continued as before.

'You don't beg like the others,' he said. 'You don't plead.'

'I've learned the value of my words. I'm not going to waste them on you.'

He hooked the hemp backpack, pulling her to a stop as if tugging reins. More yanking ensued as he loosened the top and drew free yet another of her water bottles. He went through her supply as he saw fit. These were the new rules. She was a pack mule and he her owner. He chugged, then started to put the half-full bottle back.

'Can I have some?'

'No.'

She turned to face him, and he permitted it. 'If I get dehydrated, I'm no good to you. It'll slow us both down.'

He regarded her, the bottle at his chest. It was odd to be facing him this close, to make out the strands of his wispy beard, the raised moles around his eyes, the whorls of marred flesh at his chin. The welts along his arms had risen, oozing yellow fluids. It gave her satisfaction to know that they covered his torso beneath his shirt as well. A fresh slice glimmered in his cheek, probably from where a passing sprig had cut him during his pursuit.

He tilted the bottle to her. 'A sip.'

The plastic felt odd against her lips, and she realized they were swollen, sunburned. She drank greedily until he tore the bottle from her lips, spilling down her chin.

'You don't listen with respect.'

'You haven't earned my respect.'

'*Earned.*' Amusement hitched his chest. 'You are purely American.'

'Thank you.'

He turned her and gave her shoulder a little prod.

'Wait,' she said. 'Why do you do what you do? It's a dumb question, I'm sure, but I want to know.'

He scratched at his arms and then his chest, his eyes distant and glazed with remembrance, grief, or rage. It seemed he was not going to respond, but then he cleared his throat softly. 'Palestine, Kashmir, Chechnya, Tajikistan, Burma, Assam, the Philippines, Sri Lanka, Afghanistan, Ogaden, Somalia, Eritrea, Bosnia, Iraq, Lebanon, Algeria. It is all a single chapter in the same book. And our leaders. Not leaders – whores lying back, spreading their legs for the Zionists and their American dogs. We have suffered under the yoke of it long enough.' He cocked his head, leaned closer, and she could smell his surprisingly sweet breath. 'You know nothing of this, do you?'

'Some,' she said.

'Some.' His lip curled. '*Some*. This is why we bring bloodshed to your door. On 9/11 America tasted for a single day what the Islamic people have been swallowing every hour for centuries.' He jabbed a finger into her ribs, bringing a shocking amount of pain. 'You are soft. You cannot bear a life of terror with the Sword of Damocles dangling overhead.'

'That's why you're here, then? To plan an attack? A nuclear bomb?'

He surprised her by laughing. 'A nuclear bomb? Your propaganda does not account for the complications.'

'Such as?'

'Building a nuclear bomb is difficult. And expensive.'

'So you're planning on what?'

He seized her arm and squeezed, reacquainting her

with the true power contained in his fist. 'I just want to be left alone.' He spoke calmly as ever, but there was shocking rage behind each word.

'So what do I have to do with it? Or Jay? You're just killing people at random –'

'As do you.'

'No,' she said. '*I* don't.'

'Do you vote?'

'Yes.'

'And you pay taxes?'

'Yes.'

'Then you are not exonerated from responsibility. Your vote elects the government that pushes the buttons. You pay the taxes that purchase the planes that bomb our children. You fund the armies that occupy our homes. The American people are at war with us. You speak of *earned*? We have *earned* the right to shed your blood.'

'Nobody earns that,' she said. 'And it's not a right. Under any circumstance. For any reason. You can *do* it. *We* can do it. But let's not pretend it's just.'

He finished the water, cast the bottle aside, and scratched at his welts. 'What do you know of what is *just*? You disappear into your lives like cattle. Our eyes stay open. We are close to death. Which means we are close to life. You are weak and cowardly. Not worthy enemies.'

Eve felt her jaw firm. 'How's your rash?'

He looked down at his weeping arms, then up, surprised. A smile split his beard. 'Let us walk.'

She continued for hours, favoring her ankle, falling into a kind of trance to keep the pain at bay. Aside from the pressure of the machete tip and the occasional grunted directive from behind, she might have been alone. The sky leaked through the canopy in snowflake patterns. They circumvented the lodge, cutting onto the trail to the river that she recognized all too well. Her apprehension mounted as they neared.

He said, 'Wait.'

He plucked a guava from a tree, threw it at her, and gestured to a halved boulder. She realized they'd reached the spot where she and Fortunato had heard the jaguar's cry in the night. Here, when the branch had snapped back into her, Fortunato had caught her in the darkness, saving her from a fall into the termite nest. Hours later he was dead in the river.

When she sat, her muscles instantly clenched, her lower back stiffening so badly that she wondered if she'd be able to rise again. Chewing a guava of his own, al-Gilani rooted in the hemp bag she still wore, coming up with another bottle of water.

He sat on the other half of the cracked boulder, across the trail but still within leaping distance. His eyes did not leave her, even when he tilted the bottle back to drink.

'That's why you killed Theresa Hamilton?' Eve said. 'She was gonna disrupt your plans?'

'My plans?'

'To attack America. Unleash a dirty bomb. Bring down another plane. Whatever.'

'That is behind me now. I told you.'

Parched, she stared at the bottle in his fist. The clear water sparkled. 'You want to be left alone to do terrible things to people.'

'Only when they interfere with me.'

'Do the *indígenas* interfere with you?'

'Which ones?'

'The ones you *rape?*'

He rotated the bottle in his hand, swirling the water. 'This also you do not understand.'

'Did raping her help drive American troops from your lands? Did it avenge the innocent children killed by our bombs? Let's call it what it is. You lost your way. This isn't some higher calling. Killing Theresa Hamilton. Killing Jay. Killing me. You want to protect yourself. That's all. It's a selfish motive dressed in a bullshit justification.'

He rose, stepped across the trail, and backhanded her off the stone. The force of the blow knocked her lower jaw sideways to the hinges. The ligaments of her neck burned as if torn. The guava bounced off into the brush, knocking into the fallen termite nest. She stayed down on her knees and arms, her forehead resting on the union of her wrists, drooling a little and waiting for her eyesight to return to normal.

Then she pulled herself up, sat again on the boulder, and looked at him through the tendrils of hair stuck down across her eyes. He took another bite of guava, washed it down with a healthy gulp. A trio of butterflies danced past them and up the trail.

'I realized a truth about Americans,' he said. 'What they do, they do to themselves.' He screwed the cap back on the water bottle. 'We were ready for a thousand-year war. Poised to deplete. Terrorize. Exhaust. But we did not need to. We brought down the Towers. This is true. We gained a foothold in the American imagination. But you did the rest. Your fear, stoked to a bright white flame, consumed you. You fell captive to your propaganda. Spent trillions on war. Billions on new government agencies and private companies. Bled yourselves to the point of bankruptcy. We didn't need any suicide bombers.' His shoulders lifted an inch and settled again, a show of loss or perhaps amusement. 'That is where Usama was wrong. We didn't *need* to go to war with you. You defeat yourselves.'

He extended his arm across the trail, offering her the next bite of his guava. He circled his hand impatiently. She opened her mouth tenderly, testing the jaw. Then she shook her head.

He scratched his chest and then his shoulder. Some of the welts had cracked open, leaking a clear, viscous fluid. 'You are stubborn. I will have my work cut out for me.'

A small, tender memory caught her off guard. She and Nicolas had been eating French toast, and he'd reached over, put his hand on hers, and smiled up at her. So much of parenting – so much of *life* – was composed of tiny moments like that, gestures all too easily overlooked. She was crying – silently, yes, but she could feel the tears, so she turned her head, knowing that al-Gilani would misinterpret this and not wanting to give him the satisfaction. There to the side of the trail, ensconced around the branch it had weighed down and snapped off, was the giant papier-mâché ball of the termite nest. Letting her tears evaporate, she watched the white dots scurrying anxiously around, enflamed by the guava's presence.

'What are they gonna say happened to us all?' she asked. 'What will our story be?'

'You got lost in the storm. You were washed away. No bodies were ever found. Except the man and woman in the Jeep. They can remain. But the rest of you vanished.'

That he was using the past tense was not lost on her.

'Now stand.'

Her lower back raged as she threw her weight forward onto her legs. Her ankle threatened to buckle. She tottered unevenly. He, too, looked stiff, twisting his torso from side to side in order to limber up.

The machete rose, the flat edge tapping her shoulder, as if knighting her. She turned in the direction indicated. The point found her kidney, prodding her forward.

She started down the trail. There was the familiar branch that had nearly knocked her over two nights ago. She approached, took it in both hands, and pushed into it, bending it nearly to its breaking point.

Then she dropped her weight and let it whipsaw back over her head.

She saw al-Gilani rear up, the branch catching him right across the bridge of the nose. His arms flared wide, and he toppled sideways, losing his balance. Falling backward off the trail, he crashed into the termite nest. It collapsed as he sank into it. He bellowed and flailed, white spots swarming up his arms.

Tearing herself from the sight, she hurtled into the jungle.

53

Already Eve could hear him behind her. Roars of pain and fury. The machete whistling through the air, razing foliage. She had not accounted for how his anger would fuel him. Despite her head start, he was making up ground quickly.

She broke into a glade beneath towering trees and spun, panicked. Ahead, massive prop roots, ten feet tall, radiated from the base of a giant banyan tree. They tapered to the ground as they unfurled. She stumbled across the glade and pulled herself over the snake tail of the nearest root, hoping to hide behind it. Her hands burned, scraped by the bark. One root in front of her, one at her back; it was like being in a trench. Ducking her head, she looked around frantically. In the enormous trunk, between the juncture of the roots sandwiching her, rose a slender black hole, a tiny doorway into the tree itself. Wide enough for her to squeeze through?

Behind her, footfall quickened, al-Gilani crashing through the brush.

She darted toward the aperture. The hollow tree exhaled a rich, earthy aroma. Spiderwebs clung to the bark around the opening, glistening with dew. There was no time to be afraid.

One leg in first. Ducking, she bladed her torso, exhaled,

and popped through just as she heard al-Gilani charge into the glade.

The stench inside was suffocating. Her sneakers sank into the mud and kept sinking to the laces. It wasn't mud.

It was guano.

She stiffened. Her ears strained. Above, she heard a faint rustling, the noise reverberating around the tube of the trunk and coming at her from all sides. Her trembling hand found Claire's dive watch, still strapped to her wrist. She knew that al-Gilani was just outside, and she wanted to stop herself, but she couldn't.

She clicked on the backlight. The aqua-blue glow reached only a few feet above Eve's head, but its outer reach was sufficient to illuminate thousands of sequin glints stretching up and up, coating the inside of the tree.

Eyes.

She did not have to worry about screaming; she could find no air.

Warmth emanated from the excrement below. She heard al-Gilani lumbering heavily toward her, his fist tapping the prop root at intervals – *knock, knock* – and then his shadow fell across the opening. It wobbled back and forth as he neared the trunk, the raps growing less frequent but louder.

Knock. Knock.

With painstaking slowness Eve crouched into a ball, her knees pressed to her chin. She lowered her face. And covered the back of her neck.

He was right outside now, leaning in, close enough that she could have reached out and flicked his face.

Knock!

As his fist struck the trunk beside the aperture, Eve felt the air around her suck back as if the banyan core were inhaling.

And then the tree exploded downward. A fire-hose stream blasted across her hair. Countless bodies skimmed over her head, rocketing out the hole. Leathery tips brushed her cheeks, battered her shoulders.

She sensed al-Gilani fly back and away from the opening, though she did not dare to lift her head. She kept her chin tucked, drawing air from the tiny space between her mouth and her chest. It kept on, the torrent of bats, for longer than seemed imaginable – one solid minute and then another and another.

The deluge lightened by degrees until she could make out the distinct sound of individual bats. Mustering courage, she lifted her head. No sign of al-Gilani in the narrow view afforded her between the walls of the prop roots.

She slid out, gasping for fresh air, wiping at her matted locks. Summoning courage, she crept past the shelter of the tall roots, taking it step by step, letting her back slide along the bark. But when she at last stood free, he was not in sight.

She rotated her sore ankle once and then again. Searching the vegetation, she found a plant with slender, tough leaves, and she plucked two and used them to wrap her foot outside the sock. She tied her laces as hard as she could, rose, and began to hike. The brace loosened quickly, but it was better than nothing.

The trail was off-limits. The river itself was off-limits. No matter where she went, he would be searching for her, tracking her, but she'd have a better chance to slip past if she avoided any obvious routes.

She'd head south toward Huatulco, using the sun as a gauge – the same plan as before but now inland from the river. She was more confident in her ability to forage for food, so the main concerns, aside from the homicidal terrorist pursuing her, were whether her body would give out and whether she'd reach anyone before Claire and Will starved to death. When she'd left them, they were due to run out of food in three or four days, and twenty-four hours had already passed with Eve no farther down the mountain range. She had to make up time. Assuming she didn't get lost – a big assumption – how long would it take her to reach civilization on an injured foot? Four days? Five? All she needed was to get down to where the roads were open. One passing truck. A car. A ranch house with a phone.

A Hail Mary, do-or-really-die plan. Not an hour could be wasted. She had to keep her legs moving. She had to fuel herself and sleep little. She had to remember Claire and Will in the hidden grotto and Nicolas drawing pictures of the outer reaches of the universe.

– alive for Sunday burrito night and zipping up his jacket and buying him shoes that fit and –

The sun was directly overhead, relentless. She reapplied spiked cooking oil to ward off the bugs and checked her water supply. Given al-Gilani's guzzling, she was down to two and a half bottles. At some point today, she'd run out, and then she'd have to risk drinking from fronds or a stream and exposing herself to the same bacteria that had knocked Sue out of whack. She'd worry about that then.

Ridges and valleys rolled underfoot as she fell into a

rhythm, shocked at the pace she was able to maintain. She remembered the girl she was in high school, the soccer player who always got up no matter how many times she was slide-tackled. She had found her again, found herself. One sip of water for every hill she crested – that was the deal she struck with herself.

She came upon the remains of a house, washed down a hillside and left scattered postapocalyptically when the water had evaporated. A toilet, a bed frame, a doll. She gave the strewn items a wide berth. She passed a stream that stank of sulfur, a boa constrictor sunning on a rotten log, a lizard with its head inexplicably smashed. She moved past spiders spinning beautiful golden webs and across trails of leaf-cutter ants conveying their hauls, green bites of vegetation rising up from their backs like tiny dorsal fins. Her ankle worsened. The clouds, still fat and puffy, had lightened to a snow-white gauze, diffusing the sun. She estimated where the glow had been fifteen minutes ago and adjusted her heading.

The jungle thickened until she needed to hold her arms before her as if shielding herself from boxing jabs. Thoughts of rest lulled her. She pictured herself sitting down, unwrapping her ankle, chugging water. She broke through a curtain of vines, and her teeth clenched down hard enough to make her sore jaw throb.

She stood, swaying, poleaxed. Staring.

At first the bamboo walkways and huts did not seem to be what they were. Another ecolodge perhaps, in another zone of the jungle. After all, there were no bodies, there was no scorched van in the cantina.

But the rank smell wafted from the stables, cutting through her denial. An orb of black flies swayed above blood-mottled fur of the slaughtered burros.

She was back at Días Felices Ecolodge™.

After exhausting herself and her resources, burning another half day that she – and Claire and Will – could not spare, she had merely come full circle to the spot where it had begun. Back not only to the danger zone but to one of the places al-Gilani would most likely come to pick up her trail.

Disbelief gave way to despair. She staggered through the splintered picnic tables into the clearing. He must have returned at some point and rolled the van into a gorge somewhere. Always covering his tracks, always one step ahead. By the time anyone came looking – *if* anyone came looking – even the burros would be picked clean, the machete slashes chewed away by millions of insect mandibles.

This was not a redeemable mistake. She could not recover the half day nor the energy she had spent during it. The coast was out of reach. Between her and civilization, al-Gilani waited. Will and Claire would die. There was not enough sand in the hourglass now, and what remained would keep falling until they were layered under, until they disappeared. Lanie would receive the phone call, and then Rick would be informed. He'd fly home. He was a flawed but good man, and he would do right by Nicolas. It would be hard, but they would figure it out.

She was on her knees now, keening, clawing at the dirt, bathed in the abattoir stench of the stable. She saw herself keeled there, shattered, broken. She clutched at the shards of herself, clutched until she bled, until she shuddered with grief and dread and the primal terror of aloneness, until she coughed and gagged out a cable of snot-thickened drool. Then she balled up all the abject desperation and consigned it to the little box in her chest where her Inner Voice once hid.

Get up, Mom. Get up.

I am, baby. I will.

She lifted her head. Through the tangle of her bangs, she caught a glint on the dirt just past the steps of the adobe hut.

Will's flashlight.

She turned her gaze to the sky. The clouds were pulling thin, letting through holes of blue. She pictured that single bar of reception she'd gotten atop the temple ruins just before the phone went dead. She thought about Will's plan for when the battery went out. Junior-high physics.

She looked back across at the flashlight. She crawled to it. Her thumb indented the rubber button, and it threw a faint beam.

She unscrewed the bottom, and a heavy D cell slid out into her palm. She smashed the flashlight lens and unseated the housing behind the pinprick bulb, twisting it to yank out the wires. Using her teeth, she stripped the ends.

She found her feet, started limping for Harry and Sue's adobe hut. In the bathroom trash can, she found crumpled medical tape she'd used to secure the bandage around Will's ankle. Painstakingly, she straightened it. It still held enough stick to seat the battery to Jay's satphone. She positioned the wires to connect the poles to the metal contacts inside the phone's compartment.

Juggling the wires with her fingers, she closed her eyes, took a deep breath, and pressed the ON button.

The phone turned on.

The battery charge was red but not yet blinking. She waited while the reception icon spun and spun. It found nothing. She powered the phone down. It had locked onto a signal at a higher altitude, atop the temple. She needed to go upslope, then, instead of down. Toward the heart of the Sierra Madre del Sur.

Into the jungle instead of out of it.

54

Fallen trees formed what looked like a World War I barricade at the fork in the trail. The way east, to Santo Domingo Tocolochutla, was blocked. But she wasn't heading there.

She leaned back on her heels, taking in the rise of the mighty white cedar. The wooden scaffolding that formed the bird-watching platform looked in even soggier shape than she remembered, the storm having taken its toll. She rested a hand on a saturated ladder rung, and it crumbled away.

Not promising.

She took out the satphone and tried for a signal again, just in case she might be spared the climb. At every knoll or clearing on the way up, she'd stopped and tested the phone. The first D cell had stopped giving juice halfway here, and she'd fought a momentary panic when the next two batteries from the flashlight had held no charge. But the last one had come through, producing the red battery icon on the screen, and she'd checked the connection more sparingly the rest of the way.

As she fiddled with the wire connections, she sidestepped until she found a patch of warmth where the sky let through the canopy. The phone lit up, the connection icon rotating infuriatingly. It caught, holding a single bar, and her heart leapt. The bar disappeared, came back, flickered, then vanished for good.

Back to the ladder, then.

Returning to the tree, she reached for a high rung and tested it. The moss-covered wood sagged a bit but held, and she hoisted herself up onto the ladder, quickly redistributing her weight across other rungs. Some wobbled under her grip, others broke free. Her bad ankle proved almost useless on the vertical, holding little weight. Progress was halting, but she arrived at the open, spiderwebbed hatch cut into the floor of the platform and then hauled herself through the glistening threads and onto the soft wood.

Beetles scurried through dead leaves. One rail dripped with ants, though they stayed oddly confined. The view rode the canopy underbelly out in all directions; it was like floating just beneath the ocean surface, confined and yet also vast beyond comprehension. Azure backdropped the green above in colored-glass fragments. To the west the overgrown trail blazed uphill toward the *alcalde*'s. Eve swept herself a spot, sat with her swollen ankle kicked wide, and checked the phone.

One and a half bars.

She bit her lip, holding back optimism.

Her thumb pushed down on o and held it. A run of faint static and then a distant ring. The sound of civilization, of order, of safety. The next ring muted partway through but came back.

A voice said, 'Hello, international operator.'

Eve's mouth moved a few times, making no sound. Her jaw ached at the corner from the blow.

'Hello?'

'Hi, hello, hi, you can hear me, can you hear me?'

'Yes.'

'You can hear me. You can . . . My name is Eve Hard-away. I'm . . . I was staying at the Días Felices Ecolodge in the Oaxacan Sierra, north of Huatulco. Can you hear me?'

'Ma'am, yes, I –'

'And there's a man here, trying to kill me. His name is Bashir Ahmat al-Gilani. He's number twenty-three on the FBI's most wanted list, but he's here, here in Mexico. He killed the rest of my party, except for two others. They're hiding in a grotto through an underwater passage in a cas-cade, a well-known cascade if you ask someone. You have to ask where Días Felices Ecolodge is and send help here for me and for them.'

' 'am   not sure I   don't   '

'Wait. No. No, please. Hello?'

'   location   manager on   '

Eve shifted the phone to check the screen, the solitary bar ghosting in and out of existence. 'No. You're still here. You're still –'

Her hand slipped, and one wire pulled free of the connection. She bent over the phone, sweat dripping from her forehead onto her hands as they worked furiously on the wires. Connected again. The call lost. One bar. Battery light blinking.

'Goddamn it, no no no no *no*.'

She shouldered to the railing, staring at the screen, one fist squeezing her hair in the back so tight it strained at the roots. A flash of movement caught her attention down below, just to the side of where she held the phone.

With dread she shifted her gaze off the platform in time to see al-Gilani melt from the jungle's edge.

55

Treed.

She was treed, stuck and helpless. He circled the base of the trunk, staring up. His cotton shirt was raked open on one side, his flesh covered with lumps and welts. Angry maroon dots – termite bites? – spotted his face, neck, and arms. His gait was slightly crooked, that left leg seemingly more sore, and yet he still moved with a briskness that spoke to unspent reserves of strength. That gave him an advantage. Not to mention the fact that he was down there.

And she was up here.

She set down the phone and stood, wanting to face him on her feet. As he wound around the tree, she shadowed him above.

'I reached an operator,' she called down. 'They're sending help. Right away. They know your name. You should get out of here.'

With the machete sheathed neatly across his back, he came around to the ladder and set his hand on various rungs, as if playing a musical instrument. He found a combination and pulled himself up. The ladder strained.

She ran a tight circle around the platform, looking for a branch within reach that could hold her weight. But there was nothing, the cedar commanding the clearing's full space, the other trees holding a respectful distance.

She returned to the open hatch and looked down. He

was halfway up. She braced herself, waiting, her foot pulled back to drive down into his face. He paused and peered up.

A standoff.

He climbed back down, hopping to skip the rotted rungs at the bottom. Moving a brief distance from the trunk, he sat, keeping her in view. From his pocket he removed a guava. He took a lusty bite. Chewing, he watched her.

For the first time, the full force of defeat shuddered through her. She sagged to the platform, hands snared on the railing. She would die up here. The best she could hope for would be to perish on her own terms without letting him get her. That would be acceptable. Eve Hardaway, a skeleton in a cage floating in the Oaxacan canopy. How diminished her hopes had become.

His legs were crossed and his stare constant, pinning her. An impulse seized her – to jump and lead the fall with her head. She peered down, gauging the distance, actually considering this.

The phone rang.

The sound was positively futuristic here among the whispering leaves and birdsong. Below, al-Gilani's head tilted in puzzlement.

The operator. Calling back.

Eve lunged and scooped up the phone. 'Hello? Hello, can you hear me?'

'Mom?'

Her mouth hung ajar. Had she *conjured* his voice? The chain to the impossible slowly lifted into visibility. She'd given Lanie the number of Jay's phone back when –

'Mom? *Mom?*

421

'Yes, Little. It's me.'

'Where've you been? You haven't called in, like, for*ever*.'

She eased over and put her back to the railing, needing all the support she could get. 'Hang on, honey, I –'

'Can I sleep at Zach's tonight? I redid the book report and even finished my last summer project, and it's really, really good. Lanie said so. It's called "Where I'm From," and all the kids hafta say all the stuff –'

'Listen, Little, I need to –'

'– read it to you? Please, Mom? Please? Hang on. Lemme get it.'

'Nicolas, *wait*, I –'

A click as the phone was set down.

Her throat threatened to close, all the emotion collecting there in her windpipe. She shifted to keep al-Gilani in sight.

Nicolas was back. Paper rustled, and then: '"Where I'm From," by Nicolas Hardaway.'

'Honey, put Lanie on. I need to –'

His voice cut out, and she looked at the screen, the bar holding firm, though clearly the transmission from her end was unsteady. The tiny outlined battery blinked in red, the last of the charge.

Nicolas wasn't hearing her, at least not clearly. She fought an urge to scream at him to shut up, to put Lanie on the phone. But then it settled over her, the realization that whatever help could come would come too late. That there was no time left. That if she were lucky, she might have one last thing she'd get to tell her son. Would it be the name of the man who was going to kill her? Or that she loved him?

Nicolas's raspy voice continued as he read, '"I'm from the sound of my dive hitting the water. I'm from "Pick up your toys" and "Get your fingers outta your mouth" and barbecue in the backyard. I'm from finding out I can wiggle my ears."' The connection skipped out again but came back quickly. '"– from *Go, Dog. Go!*, sweat, chocolate, the smell of lemonade, and sour juicy apples."'

Her fist was pressed to her lips, mashing her teeth, tears fording the knuckles.

'"I am from nurses and lawyers. I'm from short hair, 'cuz my mom hates to comb it when it gets too long. I'm from "Try it once" and "You'll do better next time." I'm from French toast and Batman comics. I am from a dad who loves me from far away and a mom who loves me up close."'

I can *promise you.*

'Mom?'

I'll be here until you're all grown up and old enough to take care of yourself.

'Mom? Did you like it?'

'Yeah, Little. I liked it a lot.'

'Can I sleep over at Zach's? I'll be super careful about food, I promise. Can I please?'

She couldn't unlock her throat, so she nodded, dumbly, and swiped at her cheeks. She put the receiver to her shoulder, took a deep breath, swung it back to her mouth. 'Okay, baby.'

'What? Really? *Really?*'

'Just don't be . . . don't be scared if I'm not there.'

'I won't be. Don't worry, Big. I'll be okay.'

She sensed the connection go, sensed the dead air at

her mouth and in her ear. The phone trembled as she pulled it away. The screen dark, the battery gone.

She curled the phone to her chest and clutched it there. She sat and breathed and watched the quality of light in the sky change from yellow to gold. Soon enough it would go to orange, and then it would turn dark. Woodcreepers walked down the tree trunks, pecking up bugs. A swirl of glasswing butterflies floated upward as if being raptured, their transparent wings shimmering turquoise. They moved past her face, through a gap in the canopy, and bled into the sky.

She did not want to die thirsty, so she dug in her bag for the last water bottle and drank it halfway down. She wanted to finish it – why not? – but couldn't bring herself to face the finality that that would represent.

Light leached from the air. Below, al-Gilani positioned himself and began his evening prayers. The Arabic words drawn out like a song. She remembered this prayer from one of her patients. What was it called, the one right after sunset? *Maghrib*. A beautiful name. And such beautiful words, on the lips of a hideous man. A curious blasphemy.

She nodded off, snapping awake to find al-Gilani crouched on the ground, ready to sprint for the ladder. He had learned and was not about to lose himself in prayer again.

He returned to praying.

Her blinks grew longer.

Until finally her eyes stayed shut.

56

Prayer trickled from Bashir's lips. His forehead kissed the ground. His torso lifted, and he halted.

Her form now slumped on its side. Her hand dangling out past the platform's ledge.

He kept on with the low chants, not wanting a break in cadence to awaken her. But he remained erect, watching.

Her head lolled, her grip loosening on the phone. It slipped from her hand, tumbled through the air, and landed on a mat of leaves before him.

He rose. He faded out his prayer gradually, soothingly, as if turning down the knob on a radio. The rungs rose crookedly up. He had chosen his holds already.

He moved quickly. The wood too moist to creak.

From above, not a sound.

He reached the hatch. Hesitated. Hunched his shoulders against the bottom of the platform. Then stuck his head through.

She was sleeping. Her leg right there within reach.

He pulled his arms up. Set his palms silently down on the wood.

She whipped over onto her back, drew back one leg, and drove her heel into his face. His cheek gave way. Fissured somewhere beneath the skin.

The blow rotated him nearly a hundred eighty degrees. One foot slipped off the rung. His hands scrabbled for purchase across the mossy wood. He almost went down. Plummeted to his death. But his elbows stuck.

Blinded with pain, he hauled himself through. Her foot pistoned at him again, glancing off his shoulder. He rolled around the narrow circular platform. Behind the vast trunk. Away from her.

She flashed through the hatch. Too quickly. He lunged back. Grabbed for her. His arm down the hole, his fingers grasping her shirt. His fist clenched. She jerked back on the ladder, and he thought he had her well enough to haul her up or fling her to death or ruin. But when she spun around on the rungs, she led with an elbow that clipped his cheek. He heard his own wet grunt as if from afar. His head thundered between the temples. The fabric fled out of reach.

He peered down the hatch. Blood rushed to his face, jumbling his vision. She dropped in a freefall for several feet. Then somehow caught again. She scrambled down. A rung broke near the bottom, and she fell onto her back. But she got up quickly. She found a stone and began hammering at the lower rungs. Breaking them. Leaping and swinging.

He forced himself to roll over and start down.

The smashing sounds continued. Static hazed his sight. A burning claimed his right eyeball. He pushed away the pain and lowered himself.

He heard the banging noise stop. He heard the stone strike the soft earth. And then her footsteps, running away. Taking the west fork. Upslope.

He paused, clinging to the side of the tree, fifteen feet up. Surveyed the condition of the rungs beneath him.

Two more solid bars, but beyond that it did not look promising.

He lowered himself. And again.

His weight bowed the rung.

It snapped.

He tried to turn in midair, but the ground struck him before he could, wrenching his leg. His knee twisted painfully, and his sore groin muscle simply tore, pain lancing up through his lower belly.

He lay on his back. Staring up at the leaves and stars. Bellowing.

His cries more rage than pain.

He let it come on. Fury. Washing away the agony.

More rage than pain.

More rage than pain.

He rose and started after her.

57

When Eve staggered into the dark cemetery, the rooster flared up and cawed at her. Unintimidated, she made for it, and it believed her and fluttered to safety. The footing was uneven, all chunks of marble and ivy bulges, headstones tilting this way and that. A mile or so ahead was the *alcalde*'s house, her final chance at a satellite phone or a shotgun or another soul to help. It would be, at last, the end of the road one way or another.

She moved among the plots. Most of the little *cariñitos* left at the graves had been washed away, but a white candle stub remained in the mud, a heart carved in its side.

It moved her.

She plucked it up and set it down on the nearest tomb. The name was worn off, only a few grooves remaining from the letters. It was Everyman's tomb and Anyman's tomb and maybe even her own.

She knelt and pulled her old wedding band from her right hand. This was not something she had planned or even considered; it was something she was watching herself do. Pushing the ring into the wet earth, she thought of Rick and Anika, and she wished them well. She was not the praying type, but the sight of the forlorn heart-marked candle there, a tiny stroke of white in the darkness, found resonance in her own heart, and she felt something beyond words and beyond even her own love for her son.

For the first time, she understood that it would be okay no matter what happened when the sun rose over the Oaxacan foothills and Los Angeles, and she covered the ring with dirt, rose again, and strode hard on her failing ankle until she breached the forest edge, emerging onto the dark, vast plain of elephant grass.

A light glowed from Don Silverio's house.

She moved toward it, toward the man, toward the shotgun on the rack above the shrine, toward the antique brick of a satellite phone inside the hand-stitched leather pouch inside the pottery jug. The mud wallow stretched to her right, El Puro slumbering at the far edge, lost in crocodile dreams.

The shed came up quickly, a burro nose poking over the Dutch door, bringing with it a blast of optimism. Don Silverio had returned. He had reached the *presidente municipal* in San Bellarmino who would have contacted the *federales* in Oaxaca City who by now would have –

She pushed through the screen door into the kitchen. 'Don Silverio!'

The name froze in her throat.

The farm table pushed askew. One chair lay on its side by the stove. Propped against the counter was a backpack, stuffed to the hilt, still packed. The corner shrine had been stomped, the votive candles and picture frames shattered. The gun rack above it, empty. The pottery jug lay shattered on the chipped tile floor, the leather pouch off to one side like a discarded sock. The satphone was spread in pieces, taken apart, the motherboard ground into shards. At her feet a few smudges of brown marked the tile, swirled where the blood had been toweled up.

Without knowing it, she had drifted forward into the room. She stood centered, regarding the wreckage of her last, best hope. Her reflection in the broad kitchen window looked depleted, beaten.

— stay alive to check his temperature when he's fevering and for Space Mountain at Disneyland and —

The burro, then. Maybe the burro.

She took a step back toward the door. Another. Her hand reached over, clicked off the light, and her reflection vanished.

The view through the window opened up — to the elephant grass and al-Gilani surging through it, coming for her, the sight of him having replaced her reflection almost perfectly. His steps were ragged, but his progress preternatural, the chest-high grass parting for him as before a plow. He passed the shed with the burro, closing in.

She had no internal reaction, only a numb throbbing of spent nerve endings.

She slipped backward through the screen door, the night air enfolding her, freezing the panic sweat on her arms. Every other step sent a pulse of pain from her ankle up into her leg. She hobbled around the far side of the house a second before she heard al-Gilani bang through the screen door to search inside. The shed with the burro was too close and visible, so she struck out for the forest edge past the far end of the mud wallow.

The elephant grass here grew boggier, sodden with storm water. She heard the screen door bang again and looked back and saw al-Gilani standing there, staring out. His head rotated toward her, then stopped. He started coming. The ground sucked at her feet. She tumbled, and her knees sank as well. Getting up was like prying herself from quicksand.

She lunged again and tumbled to the edge of the wallow, the long-suffering hemp bag falling free, spilling its contents. She tried to rise again but could not. Her cheek kissed the edge of the wallow. The grass felt soft beneath her legs. Hidden cicadas shrilled, and she wondered if their call would be the last sound she'd hear. A ways back she could hear al-Gilani's sucking footsteps as he began his pothole approach through the soggy ground.

Get up. Mom, get up.

I can't, Little. Not anymore.

It felt so blissful to lie here, not to give up but to know she'd spent every last ounce and now it was finally out of her hands.

C'mon, Big.

She spoke to the grass and the leaves and the mud and her son: 'I'm sorry, Little.'

The earth vibrated beneath her cheek from al-Gilani's uneven approach. A few pretty purple flowers, like irises, pushed up on reed-like stems, presiding over her death. She watched them sway in the breeze.

The footsteps neared.

58

Eve lay as she'd fallen, on her stomach, her arms at her sides. She heard the grass rustle behind her and then al-Gilani panting. He circled her. Crouched before her so she could see him. His face was an unholy mess of welts and bites. His cheek bulged cartoonishly where she'd kicked him, smearing his lips and eyes into something inhuman.

'Now,' he said, 'it will be bad for you.'

She lowered her eyes, defeated.

He regarded the fallen backpack, the strewn items. 'I saw the raft washed up in the river. I know now that you floated the others to hide them. I will search the banks, the inlets, the natural pools. After I kill you, I will search. I will find them.'

With a medieval motion, he reached over his shoulder and slid the machete from its sheath on his back. He touched her face with the tip, then tapped her elbow. 'Your arm, here. Then your leg.'

Still in a squat, he sidled forward into position, then paused. She could feel the heat of his breath across her cheek, her neck. She was too tired to brace herself. The last water bottle lay in the mud by her face. He reached for it, unscrewed the cap, and held it a moment before his chin, catching his breath.

She watched and waited. There was nothing else she could do.

He took several deep gulps. Wiped his lips. Took a few more.

She exhaled, rippling the blades of grass by her mouth.

Then he took another crouch-step forward and flipped her over onto her back. She lay, arms flung wide, a tangle of sweat-dark hair across one eye.

His hands were at his buckle, and then he pulled his belt free. 'I will make a tourniquet to . . .' His voice wobbled oddly, the vowels drawing out. He reached for her arm and tried to weave the belt around it, but the leather band slipped through his fingers, his grasp suddenly weak.

He looked at his hand, puzzled, then at her.

Eve summoned what energy she could and started pushing herself backward, her heels and elbows shoving into the mud. He collapsed onto his knees, just missing her shoes.

'The neuromuscular blocking comes first,' she said. 'That's what you're feeling right now. The cardiotoxic effects follow. They will kill you. You're already dead. Right now.'

He blinked twice, heavily, then swung his head to the side, taking in the water bottle lying in the mud. It had landed on a tilt, catching moonlight, which brought into clear relief the purple flowers floating inside.

'*Delphinium scopulorum*,' she said. 'Glaucous Rocky Mountain larkspur.'

The same flowers that had sent Don Silverio's cow into excruciating paralysis.

433

When Bashir turned back to her, his eyes were burning, his upper lip textured into a sneer. The machete was at his side, the tip trailing through the grass.

He brought his torso forward in a half topple, half lunge, falling over her even as she tried to scoot away.

His weight crushed down on her, forcing her breath out in a bark. She felt the damp press of his flesh, the stench of his body. She fought to slide out from under him, her palms shoving at his face, the bone of his broken cheek clicking beneath the skin.

He swung his arm at her, and his hand landed on her shoulder but could not clench. She knocked it away, kept pushing back, back.

The machete was still gripped in his other fist, and she watched it rise. It wavered by his ear, then plunged forward, whistled past her ribs, just missing, and embedded itself in the mud. His fist turned white around the handle as he dug the blade deeper into the earth, dragging himself farther onto her. Veins bulged in his biceps. But his muscles were locking down, his movements turned glacial.

His mouth strained in a pained grimace, his face close to hers, breathing raggedly against her neck. She kept shoving at him, the heels of her hands finding his shoulders, forcing him off.

Finally she kicked herself out from under him, sliding free. He rolled to his side, wheezing.

She pulled herself to her knees, looking down at him.

He made a choking noise. His hand slid out from under him, depositing him flat in the mud. He tried to say something, but the words came out garbled. His other hand rose an inch or two, the fingers straining. She watched until the hand settled back onto the ground.

Then she squatted over him and patted his pockets. He made noises. She felt something hard in the right pant pocket and pulled it out.

The positive-terminal lead for his Jeep.

She slipped it into her pocket, next to the key. His eyes bulged up at her, wrenched to the side to keep her in view. He could no longer turn his head. Soon enough he'd be unable to draw breath.

She rose, swaying on her feet. Her upright. Him lying helpless, still.

'Lower your eyes,' she said.

She put her foot on him and shoved. He rolled down the brief slope into the wallow itself. A ripple moved across the watery surface, and then El Puro lifted his mighty head.

With a flick of his primordial tail, he propelled himself through the sludge. Bubbles rose in the mud near al-Gilani's mouth, quickening. The tail thrashed once more, and the crocodile glided up and stopped, his snout inches from al-Gilani's face. Breath from El Puro's nostrils fluttered al-Gilani's hair. They stared at each other.

Eve turned and started back for the shed housing the burro. She listened for the snap of jaws but heard nothing.

She did not look back.

Thursday

59

By the time Eve reached the zip line undulating in the water, morning had broken. For several stretches she'd either fallen asleep or lost consciousness on the back of the burro, and yet somehow they had arrived. Her hemp backpack pulled at her shoulders, filled with food and water from Don Silverio's house, all of which she'd water-proofed in plastic bags. The Sangre del Sol had slowed significantly, and in the light of day she had little problem swimming to grab the line.

The sandy shoal had reappeared, and she hiked across and over the main trail into the canyon, moving brazenly in the open. Her momentary fearlessness vanished, how-ever, at the sight of the squat house. As she passed, she gave it a wide berth, as if it might suck her back through the front door. She kept her eyes on it all the way until she reached the Jeep.

After she'd fitted the missing piece back onto the bat-tery and connected the cable, she climbed in and turned the key. The engine coughed and sputtered through two false starts, nearly freefalling her into despair, but it caught on the third try. She nosed the Jeep onto a trail at the southern end of the canyon, and a ways down it let onto a path that turned into a dirt road that, miles later, turned into cracked asphalt.

On the descent from Don Silverio's, she'd debated

long and hard about taking the big detour to Will and Claire, but she doubted she could make the underwater swim given the condition she was in and doubted more her ability to be helpful even if she did. They'd have food and water for at least another two days, and so she'd elected to get out and send help back.

The landscape looked like the wake of a bombing, trees knocked over, cladding and fronds heaped on the asphalt. For hours she weaved around and through the obstacles, heading down out of the mountain range. The vegetation shifted gradually, turning subtropical. Royal palms and coconut trees, cacti and papayas, banana groves and tamarind trees with peanut-shaped pods. When she saw a pelican winging overhead, she figured the coast was within reach.

A washout came up abruptly, and she had no choice but to veer off-road. Squeezing between tree trunks and banging over plants, she blew out one tire and then another. She managed on the rims and tattered rubber for a surprisingly long time, aiming more aggressively downslope until she skidded sideways into a lagoon. She braced the gas pedal to the floor, but the Jeep was going nowhere, the tires spinning wetly, the engine's rev drowning out all sound. The vehicle sank slowly, not in a particular hurry. Water claimed her feet and shins, rising to her knees as she rolled down the window and pulled herself free.

She waded along the milky terracotta bank, ducking mangroves and dodging turtles. Green iguanas bobbed on broad leaves, and flycatchers zipped through the air like hallucinations. Her tank top was soaked through, and the air started to grow fuzz, so she paused and drank water from a canteen and forced herself to eat a banana, though she felt like vomiting. She reached the far side of the lagoon and slipped, falling into the warm, soothing mud. She'd read that lagoons digested and purified nature's waste, and she lay for a moment, decomposing along with it. When she'd gathered strength, she rose, a thing of mud and muscle, born anew.

The way down was evident, but as she hit thickets and tangles, she felt fear creep back into her chest. She was weaker on foot than she'd thought, her ankle blown out, her muscles strained to a point well past exhaustion. The flora jerked by in streaks and lurches, and she blacked out for a time and came to still walking. When she looked down, she saw blood leaking through her sneaker.

She sipped more water but did not sit, because she knew now for a fact that if she went down, she wouldn't get back up. A row of palm trees ahead beckoned, aligned neatly like a fence, presaging the presence of man. As she started up the hill for them, they swung back and forth more severely than she was moving her head. She did her best to keep them in her sights.

An ocean breeze struck her when she arrived. She could taste the salt, see the curve of one of Huatulco's famed nine bays below. Seagulls circled, distant specks. Peeking over a rise was the naval compound with its concrete-block buildings, its white stucco walls and clay-tile roofs. Tantalizingly close. And yet she could still fall down here and die of exposure, one ridge away.

She charted the gentlest descending slope, which was not the most direct. The sun pressed on her shoulders.

She trampled through a patch of weeds and was standing on a major four-lane thoroughfare. A sign nailed to a tree trunk told her it was Highway 200, which ran from San Diego to Guatemala, and yet, right now, there was not a car in sight.

She trudged toward the bend a half mile away. This distance seemed the hardest of all. The turn wavered with asphalt heat, and when she came around it, the sight beyond wavered as well. A military checkpoint built of white sandbags and a thatch roof, dusky green-gray trucks, soldiers with soft camouflage caps and no-fucking-around anti-narco automatic firearms. She squinted, trying to get them to stop wavering, and she didn't realize that they were not off in the distance but right before her.

'Ma'am? Ma'am? Are you all right?'

'Yeah,' she said, 'I am,' and the road rushed up and hit her in the face.

60

Eve came to with IV lines in both arms and her mouth moving: '– underwater passage to a grotto beneath the cascade.' The naval doctors calmed her and treated her while also taking her ravings seriously, which she knew from experience was no small medical feat. Word reached the US consulate in Oaxaca City, and then things moved lightning fast. Helicopters were dispatched. The *secretario de gobernación* gave personal assurances.

Eve asked someone to reach Lanie at home and Rick in Amsterdam, and both were to be given instructions not to discuss this with Nicolas. That she would do in person. She had *lived* to do that in person.

The staff treated her for severe dehydration, second-degree sunburn, a sprained ankle, a cracked rib, and more contusions and blisters than seemed physically possible. The handsome salt-and-pepper doctor had called her a marvel of science, and she had liked that plenty.

Now she lay in her bed, itching to use the phone as soon as the doctor cleared her to talk. A young nurse came in to change the dressings on her sunburn, and Eve paused and laid a hand on her slender brown arm. 'Thank you.' Her voice still husky with dehydration.

'It's my pleasure,' the nurse said in beautifully accented English as she peeled away the gauze.

Eve admired her pressed green scrubs and latex gloves and said, 'I need to do this again.'

The nurse looked at her, puzzled. Then she said, 'May I wheel you over to the window?'

'Why?'

'There is something I would like you to see.'

She got Eve into the chair and pushed her across the room. Eve stared out at the empty parking lot below. A few minutes later, a helicopter appeared over the ridge, a big red medical cross on the side announcing it as CRUZ ROJA.

Eve leaned forward. 'Is that . . . ?'

'It is.'

The chopper landed, and Claire climbed out and into a wheelchair that was guided to meet her. She asked something, and one of the paramedics pointed to Eve's window. Claire looked up, then folded her arms across her stomach and bent over a little, crying with what looked like relief. Will remained inside the helicopter, strapped to a gurney. Claire wheeled herself back and shouted something to him, and he lifted his head and looked up at Eve.

She saw that he saw her. He was struggling to hold back emotion.

'Is he coming in?' Eve asked.

'No,' the nurse said. 'He must go to Oaxaca City for a more serious procedure.'

The paramedic said something and reached for the helicopter door, but Will spoke back to him. Again he looked up at Eve.

He waved to her.

She waved back.

The door closed. The helo pulled up and away, and Eve watched until it was a dot against the Sierra Madre del Sur.

'The woman will be treated,' the nurse said. 'And then you can see her.'

'Can I use the phone now? The doctor said I have to wait, but I have a son, and I haven't –'

The nurse said, 'I believe that can be arranged,' and gently took the handles of the wheelchair.

Eve floated down the halls, arriving at a VIP room with a phone waiting on the nightstand. Everything about it – the air-conditioning, the green-tinged cantera tile, the basket of fruit waiting from the consul – struck such a contrast with her past five days that it felt as though she'd been wheeled into another dimension. A basket sitting out in the open. Filled with food. There to eat if she wanted. She fought an instinct to pocket a ripe orange.

'There is a call waiting for you,' the nurse said. 'Someone on hold. I will allow you your privacy.' She withdrew, leaving behind the fragrance of jasmine perfume and a lingering air of goodwill.

Eve rolled herself over to the phone and punched the blinking red button. 'Hello?'

'Eve? Evie?'

'Rick? Hi.'

'I've been holding for forty-five minutes. I was getting worried. They told me, and . . . and . . . I guess I just wanted to hear you. Know you're okay.'

'Thank you. I'm fine now. I really am.'

A stern feminine voice said something in the background, and Eve heard Rick's hand muffle the receiver. He came back on. 'Sorry. She's rushing me out to dinner. She's been waiting, but I didn't want to go until I got you. She's . . . *energetic*.'

'Well,' Eve said, 'good luck with that.'

'I was wondering if you want me to come out for a few weeks. Take care of you. And Nicolas. I mean, after what you've been through.'

She thought she detected a hopeful note in his voice, but it might have been her imagination. 'Thanks,' she said. 'But I'm okay now.'

From the delay she could tell that was not the answer he'd expected.

After they signed off, she worked up her courage and dialed the number she'd been waiting to dial.

'Jesus H,' Lanie said in a hushed voice. 'Really, Mizz H? I mean, *really*?'

'Yeah, Lanie.'

'Hang on. I'll grab him.'

Hammering footsteps. 'Mom? Mom!'

'Hi, Little.'

'Hi, Big. I was okay, Mommy. I was *okay*.'

'What do you mean, honey?'

'The sleepover. I slept over at Zach's, and I was fine. I did good.'

'I bet you did.'

'Lanie said you're coming home. Really, Big? Your vacation is really over?'

She covered the receiver and laughed a little. Cried a little, too. Then she put the phone back to her face. 'Yeah, Little,' she said. 'It's over.'

61

Eve had never flown first-class, but the Mexican government and the consul had arranged for her to coast home on a cushion of luxury, and she wasn't about to argue. The 737 banked gracefully and rose above the twinkling lights of Mexico City. The flight attendant came by shortly and offered champagne, and Eve took a chilled glass and settled back. She played with her seat controls – legs up, legs down, lumbar support, headrest squeeze – until the woman beside her shot her a dour glare.

Back at the hospital, Eve had seen Claire, of course, and talked to Will, who had called from his ICU bed. He'd lost the leg just below the knee. Preserving the joint was a huge win, which boded well for future ambulation. He and Eve had exchanged numbers, but she didn't know what the future held for them. While what had happened in the jungle had bound them irrevocably, it could also hold them apart. The shared memories were sharp, and they'd cut easily.

But sharp edges didn't frighten her as much as they used to.

Jay's family had been reached, as well as the relatives of the others. Lulu. Neto. Fortunato. Harry. Sue. Don Silverio. And at long last a visit had been paid to the survivors of Theresa Hamilton – an older sister and two parents, who could now begin the painful process of laying her memory to rest. The wake of destruction al-Gilani had left was breathtaking. And the heat of the media spotlight, fixed on the quiet Oaxacan hospital, nearly strong enough to melt the staff's sanity. Terrorism experts and talking heads filled every TV screen, book offers and news-show invitations flooded the mail room, journalists showed up with their quaint pads and zoom lenses. One enterprising paparazzo had gone so far as to feign injury to infiltrate the ward. It acquainted Eve with how little fun it would be to be famous, and she made a vow to steer far and wide of the fallout, to hold the tiny human moments of what she'd encountered in confidence to herself.

She turned now to the dark window and caught an intimation of a visage there – wispy beard, mottled neck, intense brown eyes. Terror thrummed through her, a low note like jungle thunder, but she didn't jerk away.

She stared back.

The face was already gone, replaced by her own reflection. She tried to settle her heart rate, her mind racing. In a way she'd carried him out of the jungle with her. He'd be there in windows and mirrors for some time, maybe forever. But she had brought something else out of the jungle, too – a different sense of how expansive and varied the world was, and how expansive and varied she'd have to be herself to partake of it.

She settled back and let the cool air from the fan blow across her cheeks. Then she reached down into her new carry-on and pulled out a battered plastic bag. She opened it and let the heavy volume slide out into her hand. She angled the chair back, putting her footrest up and shooting her neighbor a pointed smile, and opened to the first chapter.

Call me Ishmael.

Acknowledgments

My research for this novel took me from Mexico City to the wilds of Oaxaca. Immense thanks are in order to:

– Guillermo Rode Escandón, a gentleman and a scholar, unafraid to get his spectacles wet on a Class IV white-water-rafting run (or his whistle wet on some mezcal served with a pinch of sal de gusano in La Condesa).

– Álvaro Ricárdez Scherenberg, who showed me around the spectacular Monte Albán ruins in Oaxaca City, offering invaluable archaeological and historical perspective.

– Alberto España Chávez, the finest private tour guide in Huatulco and the only one I couldn't run ragged, who showed not only stamina but insight into so many aspects of Oaxacan culture, wildlife, and history. Beto, I still regret missing the giant snake, *amigo*.

– Dr Andrew Glassman, a generous host whose help and planning were mission essential. Andy went to great lengths to share his love of Huatulco, going so far as to bribe the pilot of our prop plane to alter course upon our approach, granting me the best view of the glorious nine bays. Andy's wife, Pilar Frausto de Glassman, not only graciously lent him to me for the trip but gave me the hometown view.

I must also thank Dr Bret Nelson, M.D., and Dr Melissa Hurwitz, M.D., for their aid in dealing with the various injuries inflicted upon our long-suffering cast.

My tireless editor, Keith Kahla, was predictably terrific. I'd also like to thank my publisher, Sally Richardson, as well as Matthew Baldacci, Hannah Braaten, Jeff Capshew, Cassandra Galante, Paul Hochman, Christine Jaeger, Martin Quinn, and the rest of my team at St Martin's Press. Matthew Shear, you and your grin are missed.

Rowland White of Michael Joseph/Penguin Group UK has been all keen insight and great fun. I should also like to acknowledge Katya Shipster and the other members of that fine, historic house.

I do have the benefit of peerless representation in Lisa Erbach Vance of the Aaron Priest Agency, Caspian Dennis of the Abner Stein Agency, and a crackerjack legal team in Stephen F. Breimer and Marc H. Glick.

I relied on Philip Eisner, April Watson, and Maureen Sugden for editorial assistance, and Dana Kaye for publicity and a whole lot more.

No picture is complete without Rose and Natalie raucously underfoot and Simba languidly underdesk.